RESURGENCE

C. J. CHERRYH

RESURGENCE

A *Foreigner* Novel

DAW BOOKS, INC.

DONALD A. WOLLHEIM, FOUNDER

1745 Broadway, New York, NY 10019

ELIZABETH R. WOLLHEIM
SHEILA E. GILBERT
PUBLISHERS
www.dawbooks.com

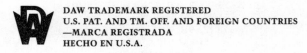

In Memoriam, Lynn.

Table of Contents

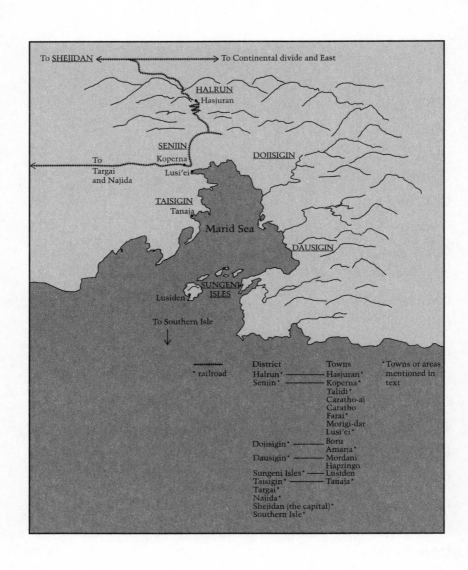

To SHEJIDAN ⟵ ⟶ To Continental divide and East

HALRUN
Hasjuran

SENJIN
Koperna
Lusi'ei

DOJISIGIN

To
Targai
and Najida

TAISIGIN
Tanaja

Marid Sea

DAUSIGIN

SUNGENI
ISLES

Lusiden

To Southern Isle
↓

	District	Towns	*Towns or areas
⸺ railroad	Halrun* ⸺	Hasjuran*	mentioned in
	Senjin* ⸺	Koperna*	text
		Talidi*	
		Caratho-ai	
		Caratho	
		Farai*	
		Morigi-dar	
		Lusi'ei*	
	Dojisigin* ⸺	Boru	
		Amarja*	
	Dausigin* ⸺	Mordani	
		Hapringo	
	Sungeni Isles* ⸺	Lusiden	
	Taisigin* ⸺	Tanaja*	
	Targai*		
	Najida*		
	Shejidan (the capital)*		
	Southern Isle*		

1

The wind was fair for the passage as *Brighter Days* knifed through the light chop of Najidama Bay, with the afternoon sun astern and the distinct edge of land ahead and to starboard. Najida village lay along that coast, and they passed fishing boats with due respect and proper clearance. The fishermen knew *Brighter Days*, knew who was aboard, and waved as they passed.

Bren Cameron waved back when he saw them, happy to be home again. He was looking forward to a quiet evening at his estate with his brother Toby, who owned *Brighter Days*, and Barb Letterman, Toby's love and companion.

Here, in the isolated peace of the ocean, Bren's bodyguard, his aishid, Banichi and Jago, Tano and Algini, were able to stand down too, however briefly. Atevi, they were, as the fishermen were, as all the inhabitants of the approaching mainland were—tall and black and golden-eyed. Bren himself was the one exception to the exclusion of humans from the continent: resident on the mainland, and not only human, but Lord of Najida, Lord of the Heavens, paidhi to the aiji of all the aishidi'tat.

He was on his way home from a ground-breaking trip to the human-held island of Mospheira, across the straits.

He'd been back to the island of his birth many times in his official capacity as paidhi-aiji, but he had never put himself in the public eye on those trips. He had certainly never gone in full atevi court splendor and he certainly had never arrived with his atevi bodyguard surrounding him.

Now Mospheira had seen him differently, and the reaction of the Mospheirans had been, well—varied.

Since the War of the Landing had set aside Mospheira for a human enclave, atevi had not officially set foot on the island of Mospheira. By the treaty that ended that bloody conflict, all the vast mainland remained atevi territory, with only one human, the paidhi, allowed to cross the strait to communicate with atevi authority, and to do that only in writing, with great caution and with university approval and review. The belief was that a fundamental incompatibility of language, culture, and biology had created a miscommunication that had brought down war on humans, and the island had lived in fear it could happen again, from some future flashpoint.

One might also note that humans had dropped down from the heavens uninvited, with nothing but data for resources, and their survival at all had been dependent on atevi charity and forbearance. They had been welcomed at first. But when war had broken out and gone against them, humans, vastly outnumbered, had offered information—technology . . . in exchange for a place to live apart.

The original paidhi, a human crossing the strait, had been the appointed mediator in that exchange—and carefully monitored exchanges had been the duty of the paidhiin for two hundred years.

The rules had changed, dramatically, in the years since Bren had taken office. The current aiji had *spoken aloud* to the paidhi. And against all precedent, Bren had *answered* him, conversed with him, gone on a trip with him—without consulting Mospheiran experts.

The University had not been pleased.

Tabini, the aiji in Shejidan, was very pleased.

Theirs had become an unprecedented cooperation. And fortunately so. In Bren's first year in office, the long-lost human colony ship, two hundred years absent, arrived at the mothballed orbiting station in desperate need of help, and found that atevi were the only ones with the manufacturing capacity to build a space program from scratch, while Mospheiran humans held the only key to communicating with them.

The ship needed the station operating again—it needed people, it needed resources, and Tabini-aiji had seen an opportunity. Consequently, space age tech flooded down onto a world barely beginning to fly, and the flood was predominantly on the atevi side of the water. For better or worse, the ship's return had intersected the partnership of an aiji hungry for human tech and a paidhi who had broken all the rules. The once-mothballed space station had come alive, shifted to low earth orbit, and became a home to a carefully-equal number of humans *and* atevi, a situation settled by a new treaty, with two stationmasters and a set of bulkheads to restrict social contact.

Everything had been headed in an astonishingly good direction, until the ship admitted its own dire secret and organized a rescue mission for its *other* stranded colony.

Two years later, the ship had returned with refugees of a human settlement far less fortunate than the one on Mospheira. Five thousand refugees, the only survivors, completely overburdened the station, and brought the world into brief and frightening contact with an alien species.

They managed to survive that. But the station was in internal meltdown. The refugees had to be sent down to Mospheira in the small loads the space program could manage, while supplies had to go up. And Mospheira was far from ready to cope with outsiders.

Atevi were not willing to lose the station's integrity while Mospheira debated. They wanted the matter settled. They also had interest in three of those refugee children who, through circumstances, had become irrevocably attached to the aiji's son and heir.

By atevi law, they could not live on the mainland. They had

to live on Mospheira. They were also, by virtue of being children, less alarming to the Mospheirans, who had had historic
reasons to distrust the new arrivals.

That—had been Bren Cameron's job. Reassure Mospheira
about the aliens, who had left the scene peacefully; and reassure
them about the refugees from Reunion.

That was the reason he had just been on Mospheira—and
why, for the first time, by the aiji's direct order, Mospheirans
had had to receive the paidhi-aiji not as an employee of their
own State Department, with no real authority on Mospheira—
but as spokesman for the atevi government, in all the cuff-lace
and brocade of the atevi court, *with* his atevi bodyguards, in
their black leather and silver, and *with* their weapons plainly
in evidence on all occasions.

It was done. The children were down safely and installed in
a secure residence on University premises.

And the island now began to understand: the paidhi-aiji was
no longer under Mospheiran authority. The office was now
being used by atevi in its historic way, what Mospheirans might
call an ambassador or a diplomat, but one instructed to represent both sides of the situation with equal energy.

He had done that. He would do it when he reached Tabini's
office. And Mospheirans as a whole, while dazzled by the lace
and brocade, might not realize how profound a shift that was,
but he knew. It was irrevocable. He was human, but he was no
longer Mospheiran. He spoke as Tabini to the human Presidenta. He spoke as the Presidenta—to Tabini-aiji.

Was everybody now ready to take a step beyond a two-
hundred-year standoff? Were humans and atevi ready to start
interacting, one on one?

It was working in the heavens, in the orbiting station. Tech-
nicians understood each other better than governments did.

And could it be done on the island—with a human government?

In a period of peace—it had begun to happen. He had found,

to his uneasy surprise, a quiet group of human students dedicated to the most esoteric of atevi artforms, the machimi plays—young Mospheirans striving, as he had on his own and to the frustration of his professors, to *understand* the atevi, not simply maintain a truce.

It would scare hell out of some people. The University was not amused. But now they had official status—tutors to the three children and their parents.

The next immediate challenge to Mospheiran attitudes was to accept five thousand long-lost cousins, biological humans who were, in some ways, more alien to them now than the atevi. Mospheirans had to find a way to welcome them, and the refugees had to accept that, flat horizon and inner ear objections not withstanding; they had no choice.

God, what a handful of days had done.

And for the first time since the space station, he could relax—homeward bound for good and all, *homeward bound*, to the mainland, on Toby Cameron's boat—a rare chance to see his brother, and a leisurely transition to the mainland after days of stress and worry and an armed assault.

With the atevi navy riding at the mouth of Najidama Bay, providing surveillance, Banichi and his team were down to black tees and easy manner, isolate from every threat but weather. Elderly Narani and young Jeladi, household staff, were entirely off-duty and enjoying the sun.

And Bren could go ship-board casual, in a turtleneck and Mospheiran-style trousers and deck slippers—Toby's. He could do nothing more challenging than lean on the rail and watch the water, with Banichi a looming dark assurance beside him. An Assassin. His bodyguard were all Assassins' Guild, the four people nearer and dearer these days even than Toby.

One could not say *friends*. That was a human thing, and they were not. Their feelings were passionate, but they were not *love*. He was their principal, their center, their loyalty. The atevi word for their emotional connection to him was man'chi, and there was no exact equivalent in human terms, but man'chi went upward through their own hierarchy to him, and entailed his deep responsibility downward to them. Four was an infelicitous number in atevi reckoning. Five was a unity. And he was their fifth, their fortunate fifth, center of their world.

He was the first paidhi to have an aishid, the first human in two hundred years to deal with man'chi first hand, and he'd rapidly discovered that human and atevi emotions ran comfortingly parallel until they didn't. But learning to sense stress and accommodate each other—they'd arrived at a very real, very warm state of affairs in which he felt more than protected—he felt—well, *attached.* Deeply so. It was the best he could do. But they seemed happy.

And now his aishid had seen humanity en masse, both on the station, and on Mospheira. They had seen an assassination attempt. His aishid would have suggested hunting down the key problems, going straight for the individuals in nice suits who gave the orders.

As it was, human security had handled it, and though they had deep reservations about the limited response to an attack, they took his word that their job was done.

And once they'd boarded Toby's boat and put open water between them and Mospheira, he could feel all the tension ebb, and the outrage—well, not lessen, but go inactive, as no longer theirs to deal with. And it was time to take his foreign presence off the island and let Shawn—President Shawn Tyers, his old friend and one-time defender in the State Department—take it from there.

It had been a long, dangerous, and exhausting trip. Full kit. Court dress. And backup equipment for his bodyguard, should things have gone seriously sideways. The massive crates that sat lashed to the deck of *Brighter Days* contained mostly clothes, and some things the Assassins' Guild did not talk about.

Coming in, now, the declining sun astern casting *Brighter*

Days' sail in gold and making the spray sparkle—they could spend the night at his Najida estate, all of them, Barb and Toby as guests. They could afford one evening celebrating.

But he was due in the capital. The next morning he had been assured the aiji's personal train—which would easily take on the packing crates and their equipment—would be waiting for him. He'd have another decently-paced trip back to the capital, which would give him time to finish his written report to Tabini. He would sit in the Red Car with his closest associates, readjust his mind wholly to atevi speech and atevi thinking, and sip atevi tea while doing it.

Job well done.

The shoreline grew, and Bren used the binoculars affixed at the bow to watch Najida come into view. Before he could get them focused, Toby came up from below, a single sheet of folded paper in his hand.

"From Shawn," Toby said and handed Bren the paper. "Just came in."

That was a moment of anxiety. He shoved the binoculars into their rail-fixed case and took the note.

Hope the crossing was smooth. Released last night. Doing fine. Had dinner with the kids and their parents. Seemed happy with everything, especially their tutors.

Shawn was out of the hospital, and the kids meant the kids newly landed.

That was good news, all of it. For security reasons, and with the general upset about the shooting, he had headed for the dock straight from the airport, the crates and all having been boarded when he left the Presidential residency. He'd had little chance to talk to the three youngsters privately, although a small packet of letters had managed to change hands.

Don't worry about the kids, Shawn's letter said. *Cards and flowers are inundating my office and their residence, along with toys, in their case, cookies and candy which security won't let through, and offers of beach vacations, which are a little premature. You can relax in a job well done . . . at least on this side. Give the aiji my respects and my thanks for sending you. We'll be in touch, I'm sure.*

No need to tell Toby. Toby had received the communication. Toby had taken up the binoculars himself, scanning the shoreline, while Barb managed the helm.

The high cliff at the end of the bay was in view, lit by sunlight.

"It looks as if *Jaishan* isn't in," Toby remarked.

"Out on a run," Bren said. *Jaishan* was Bren's own yacht. He had put *Jaishan* at the village's disposal for hauling construction materials and such to the dock over in Kajiminda Bay, where the Edi people were building a new and modern tribal center—the Edi were not much for roads, being fisherfolk, and having little to do with outsiders. *Jaishan* was essential for their moving supplies.

"Makes it easy to come in," Toby said, regarding their approach to dock. It was not an extensive dock, more a floating platform with stairs up to the larger platform ashore.

"Are the cranes up?" Bren asked.

"Looks as if. Yes."

The dock had a removable crane at the dock and another atop the cliff that the household could use to set cargo on and off. So Najida was ready for them, and they would have the cumbersome crates off the deck and shifted up to the road in short order. They would call the house, and the house staff would make sure the truck was up there.

"One sees no reason to take the crates inside," Bren said in Ragi, as Banichi joined them. "They can sit on the truck all night. At least the large one. We shall have an early start in the morning."

"The crates should be safe on the driveway," Banichi conceded, but with a frown that said they would not be left unguarded out there. There was no likelihood at all of thievery in the district—but considering the Guild equipment the smaller crate contained, yes, somebody from the house staff would be sitting out there all night with a communications link.

"We shall call the house once we pass the rocks." They had communicated with the mainland very little during their passage—security being always a concern despite the navy ship watching them at a distance. What word they had passed had been to and from that navy ship, which was now well behind them, though still watching, doubtless aware of every fishing boat. The navy trusted nothing—but the local Edi fishermen would be faster than the navy to question one not their own— and this deep in the southern side of Najidama Bay, they were deep in Edi tribal waters. Najida's was a private dock, on this side of the bay, an extended private shoreline that merged gradually with that of Najida village. Beyond the rocky point, they were definitely in safe territory.

The household had been advised to expect them sometime today or tomorrow, and with at least an hour's warning, Cook would have ample time to expand dinner plans—grill a few more fish and stir up more sauce. Bren looked forward to it. He knew the others did—despite Tano's new-found fondness for Mospheiran street food.

"And you *will* stay the night and go off with a good breakfast, won't you, Toby?"

"Delighted," Toby said. Toby and Barb had enjoyed none of the luxury of the Presidential palace for the last while, no fancy cuisine and none of the stress, either. They'd lain offshore, near the atevi navy ship, and fished and read and watched the water during Bren's stay in one of Mospheira's Presidential residences. They were due at least one first-class supper they hadn't cooked themselves, and they would have a typically hearty atevi country breakfast before they set out again.

So as they came within convenient short-range, Tano made the call and hailed the estate in Ragi, listened via the headset, frowning, then looked about with an expression that did not bode well for the evening's plans.

"Nandi," he said. Not Bren-ji. Nandi. Formally: my lord. With a slightly dismayed expression. "The *dowager* is visiting."

"Alone?" In the sense of—not with her great-grandson, who might well have wanted to meet them.

Tano asked the question, and signed yes, alone.

Business, then. Serious business. *Alone* would still mean her chief of bodyguards, Cenedi, probably Cenedi's second in command Nawari, and an attendance of others he could name. But *alone,* meaning something was up.

Bren looked at Toby and at Barb, who was managing the wheel. Their command of Ragi was sketchy and limited in topic. Dowager, they certainly heard.

"No question," Toby said, "we're not intruding. You get up to the house soon as we dock. Barb and I can talk to staff sufficient to communicate: we saw the crates go on: we'll get the crates off."

"Thanks," Bren said, as his mind raced. There were a thousand possibilities. A crisis in the family, a threat to the household, or the dowager's sincere displeasure with something that was going on—it was far from certain, and there *had* been upheaval in the family situation in the short time he'd been gone, on the details of which he had yet to be informed.

But the dowager's unheralded visit was not a situation in which he wanted Barb and Toby as bystanders.

"I'm sorry," he said. "I am sincerely sorry. I don't know what it is. Small, I hope. Very small. But escape while you can. I'm sorry about supper."

"Another time," Toby said. And: "You may want your shore clothes, Bren-ji."

"God, yes." The thought of walking into the dowager's sight in a turtleneck tee and casuals—no. He had what he had worn onto the boat hanging in reasonable condition down in his cabin. Tano was still with him. Narani and Jeladi, who were substituting for his two valets, were below, doing a little tidying up, and might be packing the few things he had used on the voyage. "Tano-ji, the clothes I wore aboard . . ."

"Yes," Tano said, and went off to advise those two; and bet on it, Algini and Banichi and Jago, gathered at the bow, were also aware there was a problem: they were looking this direction, and they read him like a book.

"Excuse me," Bren said to Toby and Barb, and went a little forward, in the ambient rush of water and the working of the sail, to pass the situation to Algini and Banichi and Jago.

"The dowager is at Najida," was all he needed say. Expressions went both sober and bemused. "One has *no* idea," he said, to the unasked questions. There was no need speculating. They all knew the same set of facts. The dowager would *not* come out here to congratulate him on retrieving the three children, avoiding assassination, and forcing on Mospheira the prospect of five thousand refugees who had never felt a planet under their feet.

No. The dowager's agendas were quite apart from that. Several things were at issue on the mainland, she was accustomed to having her way, Tatiseigi had been involved in a major incident, so had Cajeiri, and she wanted to talk to him before he got to the capital.

That was abundantly clear.

"You go," Toby said, when they had made dock, and while Najida staff were hurrying to make fast the mooring and prepare to operate the freight lift. The small crane mounted on the dock could move cargo on and off, and into range of another, with a truck parked high up on the road. The system affected only the dockside, did not scar the ancient pathway the estate used, or impinge on its view.

And right now it meant not having to unpack the crate: it could go up to the house intact, sit unmolested in the driveway, then be off to the train station tomorrow morning. They would travel comfortably in the air-conditioned bus.

More comfortably than Bren was at the moment. Narani and Jeladi had him kitted out in the court dress he had worn at the shuttle landing: brocade coat, lace collar and cuffs, proper trousers and boots, and—his bodyguard's orders—a contrasting brocade vest. Bulletproof. It was *not* his expectation that the dowager posed a hazard, but she attracted those who did, and if there was a problem—it made sense.

"Take on a full tank," Bren said to Toby. "Never hesitate at that."

"I still owe you a bilge pump."

"Brother, the aishidi'tat owes you far, far more than a bilge pump." He was under atevi witness now, not that he would shock his staff or his bodyguard if he hugged Toby and Barb—they had all just come from the land where such gestures routinely happened—but Najida staff was lining the dock and the walk above, anxious to see him and to catch whatever gossip there was.

"Take care of yourself," Barb said quietly.

Bren gave a little bow, automatic on *this* side of the strait, with all the feeling he couldn't put into a handshake or a hug. A gesture these two, after all these years, completely understood. "You take care. Both of you take care. Barb, don't let him do crazy things."

"Same goes, brother," Toby said. "Go. Respects to the dowager, thanks to Ramaso for the stay here. Everybody understands everybody. We'll take care of this, refuel, and be on our way up to the North Shore, maybe give a shout to my kids, do supper, and check on some old friends."

"Thank you," Bren said, two simple words which encompassed days and days of reasons, and leaving Toby to oversee the offloading, he turned and followed Banichi and Jago down the gangway to the dock, with Tano and Algini, carrying bags the Guild would not let out of personal possession, following them. Narani and Jeladi would stay aboard just long enough to oversee the offloading.

They made their way along the dock, up to the landing, and struck out on the winding, evergreen-edged path that led up and up the hill to a sprawling native-stone house that had grown by stages, part of it dug into the hill, part of it, the newest, rising a story above it, and the whole fronted by a portico the size of the original main hall, and a garage that could contain the estate bus.

Nobody with a bodyguard moved unanticipated by staff or an allied bodyguard. They no sooner rounded the corner of the house and came under the portico than the front doors opened wide and his estate manager Ramaso came out, with a number of the household staff, servants to take charge of what luggage they were allowed to manage—of that there was very little, the rest being in that huge crate—and to welcome them inside.

Ramaso took Bren's coat in the stone-and-wood foyer, and an assistant provided a lighter, more comfortable substitute—he did maintain a wardrobe here, and so did his aishid, things more suitable for the country if they had been staying, but his aishid kept control of their traveling gear, and their own baggage, and staff ebbed backward, affording access to the sitting room and the hall and the several suites beyond.

"Is the dowager expecting me, Rama-ji?" Bren asked.

"In the sitting room, nandi," Ramaso answered. "She has ordered tea."

That she would. "Banichi. Jago," Bren said. "Ceremonial attendance. Rani-ji, I entrust everything else to you."

"Nandi," Narani said—no doubt at all things would be handled, baggage would be loaded, everything readied for a departure at whatever time they could get the train in the morning.

Early morning, by Bren's preference. He had looked forward to a dinner, a quiet rest in his own bed here, a morning departure that let him rest, think, and edit his report on the way to the capital.

If things were ideal.

By the dowager's presence, possibly they were not that.

"How long has she been here?" he asked Ramaso, and Ramaso, totally devoid of expression, cautiously exact: "Two days, nandi."

Dear God. Waiting for him from fairly well the time he'd headed out from Mospheira. And they hadn't raced across the strait at all speed. They'd taken a little time to unwind on the way.

There was no Guild standing watch outside the sitting room. That was fairly uncommon for the dowager's sense of state. Tano and Algini were off seeing to house business, since he had not detained them; he'd held Banichi and Jago to come in with him, because two experienced witnesses able to recall the conversation in detail were both customary in such visits—and because a second and third opinion could be a damned good idea where the dowager was concerned. He let Banichi give a rap on their own sitting room door, and then open it, and he was not surprised to see the dowager's own senior Guild, Cenedi and Nawari, standing attendance inside.

The dowager had taken one of the smaller chairs. She had a cup of tea in hand and two of her own servants providing the service from his buffet.

"You are *late*, paidhi." Ilisidi was of diminutive stature for an ateva, no taller than Bren was, but there was nothing *small* about her.

"One had no idea you were here, aiji-ma. Or we would have hurried, certainly." He walked over to his chair, gave a little bow and sat down, while Banichi and Jago took their posts at the opposite side of the room from Cenedi and Nawari, Guild black edging their meeting, the dowager in ruby-sparked black formality, himself in somewhat abused court finery. He took an offered cup of tea, took a sip as she did. One *never* talked serious business or unpleasant business without tea for an opener, and her expression betrayed no great annoyance in the matter.

"Did you have a good crossing?"

"Indeed, aiji-ma. The weather favored us."

"And the Presidenta?"

"He sent a message en route, to the effect he was back in his office. His physician expects a full recovery."

Ilisidi nodded, and took a sip of tea. "And the children?"

"They and their parents are in good hands, well-protected, well-housed, and their tutors have been introduced to them. They are happy. They will wish me to wish you well. As does my brother-of-the-same-mother and his companion."

Ilisidi nodded again, and did *not* say *invite them up the hill*. Well enough. It was actually a relief.

"And the persons responsible for the assault on the Presidenta?"

"The Presidenta has discovered the person's connections. He has informed the public at large, aiji-ma, and opinion has shifted from unease at the children's arrival, considering that they presage the arrival of other Reunioners—to outrage at the attack and support for the children. They have been inundated by toys and offers of good will."

"Have you communicated with my great-grandson?"

His business—disposed of in a few succinct and polite questions. And straight on to *hers*.

"No, aiji-ma. I have sent word to the mainland only through the Guild."

"My grandson has doubled his son's bodyguard. Cenedi assures me they are good people."

"I am similarly assured, aiji-ma. I had heard."

"And my great-grandaughter will likewise be due a personal bodyguard—as Lord Tatiseigi's heir."

"One has heard about the appointment." Seimiro might be a babe in arms, but her appointment shook the landscape. The most powerful Padi Valley lord, long without the prospect of an heir, *gained* one with blood-ties to Ilisidi and Tabini-aiji *and* through her mother, blood ties to the formerly disaffected neighbor, Ajuri. In the same handful of days, Ajuri, lordless and disgraced, had also gained a lord, at least a candidate for the lordship, a man with ties to Seimiro's mother. It was a political earthquake, and it had struck while he was entirely otherwise occupied.

Click went the teacup down onto the side table. Any pretense of chitchat was at an end. Bren set his cup down and waited for Ilisidi's *reason* for her long and inconvenient trip.

"You may know that my great-grandson has raked up a cousin, a grown cousin, to take Ajuri. And that Damiri-daja is approving of this person. A rail worker of entitled parentage but with no training for the post. Nomari, alleged to trace his ancestry to Nichono. My grandson has requested an investigation of him."

"One has heard some of it, aiji-ma."

"Well, well, and how much else have you heard?"

"The bare minimum as of two days ago, aiji-ma, and not much else. Security has been an issue."

"You intend to take the Red Train tomorrow morning. You have called it."

"That has been my intention, aiji-ma, but not if you wish otherwise."

"*Our wishes* were not consulted in much of this, paidhi. And in fact, unless you wish to take passage by air or ride the regular freight to Cobo, you and we shall wait a day. The train will not be here in the morning. The *aiji-consort* has engaged the Red Train for her descent upon Tirnamardi. She has likewise taken your bus. Which is under repair, we understand. *We* had to arrive here by *market truck*, as we shall go when we do go, in current plans."

He knew from his aishid that Tabini had called the reinforced bus up from Najida for secure transport, but that it should be in repairs and not yet returned . . . there was evidently more to learn about the situation in Tirnamardi.

"The bus is far less my concern than your displeasure, aiji-ma. Honestly. What happened?"

"Oh, many things happened, paidhi, not least of which was risk to Lord Tatiseigi's life. An attack while my great-grandson was on the premises. The mecheiti being loosed on the grounds resulted in injury to Lord Tatiseigi and to the Taibeni girl in my great-grandson's aishid, And following that, the *unlicensed* assassination of that malicious woman who was in charge of Ajuri, who undoubtedly ordered that attack."

Geidaro, she meant. Cajeiri's great-aunt.

"There *was* indeed a proper Filing of Intent against her," the dowager said. "Lord Tatiseigi Filed, a motion in which we would cheerfully have participated, but the persons who actually took her down were *not* acting under Guild orders, and are not licensed, and have not been found. *That* is under investigation. The aiji-consort and Lord Tatiseigi are returning to Shejidan on the Red Train late today, in company with this mysterious cousin, after which they may condescend to route the Red Train to Najida for your convenience. They will also be, one understands, loading your bus onto the rail for return to this estate, though in what state of repair one dares not presume. But in the way of things, they will be cycling the Red Train the long way round to avoid its passage through Senjin, and of a consequence, it will *not* be here tomorrow morning. We *refuse* to take it tomorrow afternoon. We *abhor* a night trip through the midlands. So we shall stay here, and we trust we may enjoy your company, since you are similarly stranded."

His staff . . . had worked a miracle, entertaining the obviously displeased dowager for two entire days before he could get here. She actually seemed in relatively good spirits about the proposed delay. "One is honored to wait in your company, aiji-ma. But I greatly regret the inconvenience."

She waved a hand. "The delay offers convenience of another kind, since I have things to say, and concerns to mention. More to the point, I would rather *not* arrive until the dust of the doings in the north has settled and until some of the facts make their way to me." From the capital, that was to say. Cajeiri and his mother Damiri were returning to the Bujavid, along with Lord Tatiseigi. And, evidently, this person Nomari, now claimant to the lordship of Ajuri. The aiji's apartment in the Bujavid would be in chaos. There would be baggage to move, the lifts would be busy; and the dowager's residence, and his own, and Lord Tatiseigi's, were on that same floor of the Bujavid as Tabini's.

Dust to settle, indeed. Not the least of which would be questions swirling about the Ajuri candidate himself. Tabini had some misgivings about this person, his activities over recent years, and connections in questionable places. Tabini had asked the dowager to investigate, quietly, but the dowager never liked to be the background presence in a situation, oh, no. As Bren put the pieces together, the attack had come during Cajeiri's much-publicized solo trip to visit his uncle. Ilisidi must have headed immediately to Shejidan from her Malguri estate, intending to bring her bodyguards in at Tirnamardi, only to discover, upon arrival in the capital, that that situation had been taken completely out of her hands—along with the train she would have used. *Not* a state of affairs she would accept or even acknowledge—hence her immediate withdrawal to Najida to await *his* return and prepare her own reentry into the Bujavid. She was fundamentally incapable of sitting in her Bujavid apartment looking impotent, and, worse, awaiting the triumphant return of the woman who'd suddenly stolen control in the Midlands from her after so many years of conflict—a contest in which, until now, Ilisidi had *always* emerged on top.

Dig into this Nomari's background, oh, undoubtedly she was doing that. He had had his own information: Nomari had some sort of connections down in the Marid, a troublesome area lately part of the dowager's own plans. One assumed Tabini-aiji had told her that, and that it had been a surprise. The dowager did not like political surprises. And she particularly did not like them keeping close company to her great-grandson.

She'd come here, he suspected, probably by air and a very uncomfortable ride in the market truck, not for any substantive reason other than to get *out* of Shejidan, to get information that did *not* flow through the Bujavid, and to return with *him*—after the dust settled. He would, as Ilisidi well knew, take advisement from her and pass messages that she might be too wrought to deliver or receive. When Ilisidi came back to the capital and took up residence in her Bujavid apartment, she would demand her grandson's full attention—and Lord Tatiseigi's. One was not even sure her precious great-grandson would be immune from her displeasure this time

"And you, paidhi?" Ilisidi's voice implied too long a silence. "Having influence over some of the principals in the matter, you *must* be directly interested."

"Indeed, aiji-ma, I am. For security reasons, my communication with your grandson has been limited to the most basic information. I hope you will help me to fill in some of the details, while we await transportation."

"We shall share what we have, which is to say, far too little, and we shall hope for timely updates from my grandson when we do get to Shejidan.—Is your brother and his associate to join us tonight?"

"Not unless you wish it, aiji-ma. They felt there might be business of a sensitive nature. They are offloading the baggage to the truck and will be on their way within an hour or so."

"Well, well. Their discretion is commendable. Persons of good sense and breeding. Cenedi!"

Cenedi, seniormost of all the associated bodyguards, moved forward a step. "Aiji-ma."

"Ask Ramaso to send down a case of good wine to the boat, with my personal gratitude for services rendered. We shall absorb all material costs for their refueling and provisioning."

"Yes." Cenedi left, informal as the meeting was.

"They will be honored," Bren said. It *was* a generous gesture on the dowager's part, though *Brighter Days* never paid a charge at Najida, on his own order. As for the wine, Ramaso would send the best they had, and Toby understood enough Ragi to be told from whom—and to take it for a clue his brother was not, at least, under a cloud of the dowager's disapproval.

Good, Bren thought. A good parting, minds eased. Ramaso

would assure them something to the effect that the dowager was here to take the air and inform him on some details not appropriate to say by phone.

If it were only that uncomplicated regarding the Damiri situation.

Ilisidi was in reasonably good humor right now because nobody was countering her, but Ilisidi, Tabini-aiji's grandmother as well as former aiji in her own right, had a difficult relationship with Damiri, the aiji-consort, Tabini-aiji's wife and the mother of Tabini-aiji's son and heir. In theory, Damiri should be an extremely influential woman. In reality, she'd never found a way to escape Ilisidi's shadow. The birth of Cajeiri had been Damiri's first real opportunity to establish her place within the balance of this household of powerful personalities, but Cajeiri had been, for security reasons, sent away to Ilisidi's care when very young. As a consequence, Ilisidi had established a far, far stronger influence over the boy than Damiri had. The lost years could not be redone, and Ilisidi would not surrender her attachment, nor give Damiri any advantage in the tug-of-war.

The sudden vacancy at the top of Ajuri clan had given Damiri another opening, hence her direct involvement in the matter of an Ajuri heir. Damiri was Ajuri—and she could have claimed that lordship for herself, giving her more than a consort's status in the court, a vantage of power and dignity she very much wanted, especially in the long battle with Ilisidi; but Ajuri had a habit of assassinating its lords, one after the other, and Tabini would *never* confirm her in that post. Cajeiri was likewise in that bloodline, but Cajeiri was Tabini's heir, and that set him absolutely out of contention.

Now another branch of Ajuri's lordly family had surfaced, this cousin—to challenge Geidaro, a great-aunt, who had been running Ajuri. That was one reason for the dowager's concern. There was another and unknown player in the events—a player who claimed some consequence thanks to his childhood connection to Damiri, who had looked to Damiri for validation and endorsement.

And Damiri, it appeared, had been quick to take advantage of opportunity, taking herself and her infant daughter to Tirnamardi where, for the first time, she and her children could interact with Lord Tatiseigi—her maternal uncle—without Ilisidi's presence.

Out of that meeting . . . had come an heir to Tirnamardi. An infant child. *Damiri's* infant child. Seimiro was Taibini's biological offspring, as Cajeiri was Tabini's, but this child, by the marriage terms, was under *Damiri's* authority, and inherited *her* connections, including her link to Tatiseigi's clan. Tatiseigi, it seemed, had made that so-significant decision to appoint an heir . . . without consulting Ilisidi.

Small wonder the dowager was displeased, and not simply because Damiri had gotten a leg up on her. Ilisidi had nurtured and built the aishidi'tat over her entire adult life. Stability within the Midlands had been under threat from Ajuri's machinations for over a generation. Two clans were currently lordless and had this recent attempt on Tatiseigi's life been successful, had he died before declaring an heir, yet a third would have joined the chaos.

Nomari's bid for the Ajuri lordship had become a matter of immediacy, when the place-holder in that lordship, Geidaro, herself had died. Assassinated. Illegally. That in itself only meant Ajuri was running true to form. None of the recent lords had died by legitimate hands and none had died of natural causes. Now its acting authority had gone down to an unlicensed attacker, and Cajeiri and Damiri *and* the new baby, Seimiro, had all three been staying with Damiri's uncle, Lord Tatiseigi, right next to the Ajuri border, when this murder had taken place.

Just after Nomari had made his bid for Ajuri. And Nomari had been safely ensconced in Tirnamardi, and was now being supported by the most powerful lord in the Midlands.

Small wonder, indeed. Ilisidi, who had been consulted for every major decision childless Tatiseigi had made for decades, had reason to question his simultaneous—and unilateral—endorsement of the unknown Nomari and this sudden declaration of an heir.

In addition to possible involvement in that illegal assassination, there was another side to Nomari that had caused Tabini-aiji to message Bren directly while he was on Mospheira—information that this new candidate had ties in the Marid, directly linking him to Machigi of the Taisigin, Ilisidi's most questionable ally. He was reluctant to mention that message, under present circumstances, but he might need to.

Tabini had said he had asked Ilisidi to investigate—specifically—this person's ties to a region that had produced assassination after assassination on its own.

Nomari was now, by Ilisidi's report, apparently on his way to Shejidan—with Tabini's wife and children and strongest ally—to ask Tabini for a major lordship.

And Tabini himself had questions.

"So they are en route to Shejidan?" he asked.

"They will be. The Red Train is on its way to Sidonin to pick them up. And there is a sizeable Guild presence around them, and over in Ajiden."

That was the Ajuri lord's estate—the scene of Geidaro's murder. One could imagine the Guild was all over that house.

"And this cousin is traveling with them," Bren said.

"He is."

It had to be said. "I had a message, aiji-ma," Bren said. "I think that I was informed as you were, and I am concerned. One understands this Nomari has some connections in the Marid."

Arch of an eyebrow. Ilisidi certainly had an idea by whom he had been informed.

"He has been living and working as Transportation Guild," Ilisidi said. "A rail worker. He claims his family was killed some years ago, by order of Shishogi, and as best we know:

that *is* true. *This* person, Nomari, survived. He currently leads a band of other survivors, about whom we know far less, who also seem to have been fugitives from Shishogi's actions. But whether this group was infiltrated before Shishogi's death, we do not yet know."

That was a valid assessment. Shishogi, yet another Ajuri, and source of most of the region's unrest, had been Officer of Assignments within the Assassins' Guild. He had also been founder of a splinter group of the Assassins, the Shadow Guild, and he was recently dead with a good deal of blood on his hands. A little old man in an untidy little office in the headquarters of the oldest and most powerful of guilds, he had moved agents like chess pieces, and played power games that had, though briefly, unseated Tabini-aiji himself and put a puppet in his place.

In Shishogi's bloodstained career before and after that period people called the Troubles, he had taken down lord after lord in Ajuri and done murder where it served his purpose, which *seemed* aimed at breaking ties with humans on Mospheira, undoing the accommodations with humans, and turning back the clock to a world before humans in spite of a shared space station and a starship in orbit overhead, impractical though that idea might have been.

Because of Shishogi's actions, Ajuri clan was now in economic ruin, and the allied Kadagidi clan was stripped of its authority and set under Guild management, possibly to be disbanded and broken into smaller clans.

There was a great deal the Shadow Guild had done in the Midlands that had yet to be set right.

And it still held a small foothold down south, in the Marid, a seafaring region loosely connected to the aishidi'tat, but refusing the Guild system and sometimes, clan by clan, being at outright war with the aishidi'tat. Or its own Marid neighbors.

Ilisidi had made inroads into that situation, allying with the Taisigin Marid—where this Nomari also had ties.

And now the man was traveling with people Bren deeply cared about, while he had Damiri supporting his claim on a lordship which had nearly overthrown the government.

Ilisidi, who could set off a family firestorm if she intruded on Damiri's business, clearly was worried—on several accounts.

Now *he* was.

2

Uncle's stable was not that far from the back door, and it was a relatively slight risk to go out, with so many watchers all around the premises. Cajeiri stuffed his pockets with treats from the kitchen . . . a small act of banditry . . . and slipped out in company with his younger set of bodyguards—the older set being busy in the house, getting last minute updates from the Guild investigation over at Ajiden. It was evening. The bus was in the drive, ready to leave for the train station.

And Cajeiri was supposed to be headed for it.

The mecheiti came immediately on guard as he approached the pens. Heads turned on tall necks, amber eyes all on movement the other side of the rails. A quick glance affirmed the gate was properly shut and the latch handle was down and secure—the herd had learned it could shove the gate open, and he did not think he would ever again fail to check that point of safety.

His own mecheita, Jeichido, had already recognized him, and had begun moving through the herd with purpose. She was young, but she was insistent—too strong, Uncle said, to leave in this herd, destined to contend with the herd leaders. She needed her own herd soon, or somebody was going to get hurt.

"Jei-ji," he called her. He was dressed for travel, clothes that moved easily and that were forgiving of a little dirt, so he was able to climb up onto the rail and hold out his hand with a pilfered tidbit. Jeichido shoved interested herdmates aside to claim the treat from *her* rider. Her tusks, long as a man's hand, but peace-capped, flashed brazen in a last bit of sunlight. Dark nostrils worked as her head turned this way and that, one amber eye and the other trying to spot the expected treat at close range—and trying to figure, he was quite sure, whether there was a halter involved.

Not that she would be reluctant to go out of the pen and burn off that energy, and he so wished he could have one last good ride, but there was no time, and no way. Since the trouble, the most that he had done with Jeichido had been limited to treats delivered from the pen rails, and talking to her, to let her remember his voice associated with the treats. Today was the same, with even less time to spend, and no prospect of tomorrow.

He had had days of being sensible and responsible, days and days of being pent up inside, and waiting, waiting, waiting, while bloody politics sorted itself out over in Ajiden. He had been so sensible his mother had actually approved of him. He had been so sensible the senior bodyguards his Father had assigned had scarcely even asked where he was going in the downstairs. They were busy talking back and forth to the Guild setup over in Ajuri clan's manor house, and mostly spending time in the security station. They had trusted his junior bodyguard to tell them if he was far out of line, and in this last forlorn stretch of the rules, his junior bodyguard was with him all the way.

Great-aunt Geidaro was dead over in Ajuri territory, in Ajiden. The Guild had moved investigators in to search the clan offices from top to bottom, and there was no telling how long that would take, his bodyguard said, because Ajiden sprawled in three directions and had five stories, counting three basements.

And what would they search? Every piece of paper, every book, every record, every note in the desks and anything hidden in the back of the bookcases, so it was going to take the rest of the summer and into fall to be sure. The Guild was, however, determined. Cousin Nomari had gone over there for less than an hour, just to show his presence to the clan and the subclans, and tell them formally that he was indeed asking to be appointed as lord of Ajuri, but the Guild had guarded him every step of the way, because Shishogi, who had run Ajuri through the lives of various lords, had been up to no good for so very long nobody in Ajuri could trust anybody.

Nomari was going to the train station with them, now, hoping to meet Father in Shejidan and to convince Father and the legislature to approve his claim. There probably would be an argument about it. There was always an argument where the legislature was concerned. Ajuri was conservative. The lord of Ajuri was always a conservative vote. The liberals would want to change that, and Father was a liberal most of the time.

But with Mother and Great-uncle Tatiseigi backing Nomari, and if they could get Great-grandmother to back him, too, it was fairly likely Nomari *would* be the next lord of Ajuri, and Cajeiri truly hoped he just stayed alive longer than the others had.

He was too young to have a voice in the matter, being only fortunate nine—though he was sure Father would ask his opinion of Nomari, and he did have one, first that Nomari seemed a good sort of person, and second that Nomari was indebted to Uncle Tatiseigi—another important point—and third and certainly true, that whatever he did, he was bound to be better than Aunt Geidaro. Nomari would have less idea than *he* did how to run a clan, because it was a lot of business and accounts and sometimes sorting out people at odds with each other, but Nomari was clever and he did listen to what Uncle told him, and tried to get advice from reliable people. That was better than one could ever say of Grandfather *or* Aunt Geidaro.

Jeichido took the treats one by one, whuffing and swinging her head at herd-mates who thought they might crowd in, until there were no more treats to be had. Jeichido, unbelieving, took to nudging the rail with her tusks, which, even peace-capped, were apt to damage the wood.

"Stop that," he chided her, and shoved her soft nose back, following with a chin-scratch. He had *not* brought a quirt, which was really not the thing to forget with mecheiti, but it was a short visit, and he needed to get back inside. He hopped down backward from the rail and Jeichido grunted at him, which was a good thing in their relationship. She was starting to talk to him, probably complaining he was stupid for being out of treats. And his hand was wet with mecheita spit and shed fur, which he wiped on the fence post, not his clothes.

His aishid was right behind him—his Guild-senior, Antaro, had her arm out of its sling today, but it was still tender and he did not want to bump into her backing up. Her brother Jegari was taking care to open doors and watch out for her. So did the number two team of his aishid, Veijico and Lucasi, who were older, stronger, and at the moment, properly paying more attention to their surroundings than to the mecheiti. They had brought their rifles out, just in case, and they were watching the orchard—occasional lodging-place of trouble—and the stables, less likely because of the herd, who would alert instantly to a foreign scent.

Uncle's house, Tirnamardi, sat on a grassy hilltop, with towering ancient hedges round about it all, an expanse that was grand to ride. It sat with the road to the Atageini townships outside its front gate—and Ajuri land over that horizon of prairie land beyond, tall grass and scrub, a hunting range in common with Ajuri clan in the west and Taiben to the south. Beyond the stable, past the orchard and the tall hedge to the east, there was a much closer boundary, one Uncle shared with Kadagidi clan—two manor houses which sat uncommonly close, almost back to back with each other, with only Uncle's ancient hedge between.

Kadagidi clan administration was being run by the Guild at the moment. The Kadagidi manor, Asien'dalun, perched on its own hill almost within sight if one stood at the hedges, was still repairing a hole nand' Bren and Jase-aiji had blown in it, and the former lord was in the cold and mountainous south, working in a mill and learning how to run looms, which Uncle said, might teach him something he could actually do that might be of more use to the world, since he had not been much of a lord.

The prospects for peace in the world were better this year than at any time Cajeiri could remember. There was peace in the heavens. His associates from up there had just landed, first down of all their people finding a home on Mospheira, and Father had approved of the arrangement, declared them under his personal protection. Just as important, he had approved their visiting the continent from time to time.

Here on Earth, the Shadow Guild that had caused so many problems for so long was slowly being hunted out of existence, and might be gone from the north altogether. Uncle had made peace with Taiben—that feud had gone on, active and not, for two centuries. Cajeiri's own little sister Seimiro would inherit Atageini clan from Uncle someday, so *that* succession was settled, which nobody had thought would happen, and if Nomari did win approval, Uncle might have a good neighbor to the west, which he never had had, not from the days when Grandmother died and Grandfather had caught the blame. Now it would all be better in that direction, too. There was still the question who had killed Aunt Geidaro, but at least she was gone, and he was not sorry for her. He had seen enough of the world to believe that truly bad people would never learn to behave.

One thing *was* certain: that although things were headed in a good direction, the area around Tirnamardi, Asien'dalun, and Ajiden was not yet safe. Father wanted them back in the capital, and under protection.

Peace in the heavens, peace on the earth . . . but in his father's household, he feared another kind of warfare was brewing.

By what he knew, Great-grandmother had come back from her province, all the way from the East, because she was worried about him, and worried about Uncle, who was Great-grandmother's closest associate and strongest ally.

But by the time she arrived in Shejidan, *Mother* had already taken the Red Train and headed here, herself Ajuri, and bent on settling matters with Ajuri in a way Great-grandmother could not.

He had no idea what Great-grandmother had thought or felt when she had heard Mother had decreed the future of the region all on her own, without ever even consulting Great-grandmother, and not really consulting Father, so far as he knew. He truly, truly did not look forward to hearing what Great-grandmother and Mother might say to each other when they next sat at the same dining table.

But he would have to. The latest news was that Great-grandmother had gone out to the coast to meet nand' Bren on his return from Mospheira, and she was very likely upset and wanting to get nand' Bren on *her* side, before they both returned to Shejidan.

He wished Great-grandmother had been here to see how well Mother had handled things. She might not be so upset. But if she had been here, Mother never would have had the chance. It was a side of his mother he had never seen. A very good side. But nobody got past Great-grandmother when she was in the room.

A noise disturbed the quiet, an engine. Out on the front drive, the bus was starting up.

"Jeri-ji," Antaro said. "We should go."

"Yes." Cajeiri gave his hands a final dusting, with a regretful look at Jeichido. Jeichido gave a loud whuff, indeterminate what she thought. But tomorrow there would be no treats. No treats for a good while, except now and again from the grooms. When they wanted something.

He so wanted time to spoil her properly.

But with the bus running, that meant time had run out. He heard the market truck start up, too, and that meant hurry, because people would be getting on the bus.

A piercing screech carried over the noise of the engines out in front of the house, making him think perhaps spoiling Jeichido too much was *not* such a good plan.

Not far away, out on the drive, a very, very spoiled parid'ja was very, very unhappy. Boji and his huge filigree cage would be on the truck. So must his servants ride the truck, in the open air, taking care of the rascal. They put a tarp around the cage to shield Boji from the wind, but Boji hated it, hated not being able to see, hated the racket assaulting his ears from the unseen world.

And poor Eisi and Liedi had to ride with him and try to keep him from panic.

The house door opened as he came toward it, and there was his senior aishid, gray-haired Rieni, Haniri, Janachi, and Onami, come to fetch him, with no nonsense about it. Mother would be coming down to the front doors, with Seimiro, and Uncle. And Nomari. And security dictated they would board quickly.

"We can go around by the side," he said as Rieni and the rest joined them. Around the house by the garden path was all open ground, and that route was far less trouble than negotiating the inside hall and the up and down of the formal steps.

The stable precinct gate in the curtain arbor was repaired since the night that had injured both Great-uncle and Antaro. It was all new wood, that the staff had not gotten around to staining, waiting for dry weather. The surrounding overgrowth of flowering vines had suffered a bit, but it would regrow by the time he saw it again, the same as ever. The tents were off the front lawn, and the lawn would grow again. Some of Nomari's people had taken the regular train yesterday, to get to the capital and support his bid for the lordship. And several were coming with Nomari on the train.

So was a double unit of Guild, to be sure Nomari stayed alive. Besides those eight, Mother had a double guard, and so did he and so did Lord Tatiseigi—that was thirty-two persons, not even counting the servant staff. The Guild presence was an absolute wall of black uniforms, so they were certainly protected—heavy weapons were in evidence as well as sidearms. Along with all that, Antaro and Jegari's parents and kin would be waiting to join them out on the road—Taibeni clan riders, an honor to them, but likewise a fast-moving protection in case anybody had notions to repeat the assault on nand' Bren's bus.

"Well," Mother said as he joined her at the foot of the grand front steps. "You *are* here."

"Yes," he said. The nurse was by Mother's side, holding Seimiro, a little bundle in a green and white blanket—Atageini colors, that blanket, for the new heir of the house. And all that overwhelming Guild presence closed about them, so many that some had to ride the market truck and some, it seemed now, were going in Uncle's grand open-topped automobile, a noisy lot of engines and a smell of fuel that Cajeiri found exciting—but Seimiro fretted and waved a small black fist at the disturbance.

It was a very big bus that waited for them. It had been shiny red and black. Now it was dented and scarred and with some of its armored panels replaced, as yet unpainted—very sad to see. But the engine was as strong as ever.

Nomari's senior guards boarded first of all, and then Cajeiri's, and Mother's and Uncle's, with Seimiro and the nurse, and no other servants. They all would have to come to Shejidan on the regular train—the truck would be back for them.

His setting out from Shejidan to come here had been quiet by comparison, even with the news services involved. There were no reporters here now, but he was amid a whole crowd of people, on their way to a little wooden station in the forest, and *somehow* they were going to load that huge bus onto the train, too. He hoped they would let him watch that process, but he doubted he would get to see. The Red Car had no real windows, only the look of windows, and the Guild would be in a hurry to get them safely loaded and moving, so lingering outside the train to watch was out of the question.

He boarded the bus with Antaro and Jegari, Lucasi and Veijico, and he settled in the seat they appointed for him. Everything went quickly, considering so many people involved, but Guild moved like that, interested in getting them from point of safety to point of safety with as little delay and exposure as possible. The doors shut with a thump, the bus almost immediately began to roll, and they were on their way.

He was sad to leave Tirnamardi, and sad to leave Jeichido.

He was sad, too, that he had been here while the shuttle was landing, and that right now, and for a while to come, his three associates, the only people his own age he had ever known, would be down on Earth, but not able to visit him. He had wanted so much to be there to meet them—which was just impossible. And politics said they had to land on Mospheira, and live there, and it would be a while before they could even talk to each other.

At least nand' Bren had been able to be there to meet them, though there had apparently been some unpleasantness. His aishid said it all seemed to have been settled for now—but was there anything in all the world that just made everybody *happy*?

At least they *were* down, and safe, and eventually they *would* come to visit, and in the meantime they could send messages and perhaps even phone. They were down, nand' Bren was back . . . and for the first time he ever remembered, *Mother* was happy with him, so there was a lot for *him* to be happy about. He hoped, though he doubted it, that Mother would *stay* happy with him. *Unhappily*, he reminded Mother of Great-grandmother in most everything he said and did . . .

But since Mother had come here to make peace with Uncle, and since Mother had out-raced Great-grandmother to get here, and since he had *not* done something Mother would disapprove of since she had been here—

He was in Mother's good graces for the first time since *he* had been the baby in nurse's arms. It proved he *could* do it.

At least until Great-grandmother got back to Sheijidan.

Brighter Days left the dock toward a setting sun, a curl of water behind her as she moved under engines, and Bren wished them well.

He had come down to bid Toby and Barb a safe voyage, and

to tell them that it was internal atevi politics that was at issue, politics swirling about the prospective appointment of an Ajuri lord, and that *that* was what had the dowager concerned and wanting to talk to him before he got to the capital. It was nothing that threatened him, or relations with Mospheira.

That relieved them of worry—atevi problems were not their problems, and they had, besides, the handsome gift from the dowager to prove she was in no wise displeased.

Beyond that, the great wardrobe crate and the equipment crate had gotten safely onto the truck up on the bluff that overlooked the dock on the east, and the truck had come down again to park in the drive by the time Bren and his aishid had climbed back up the evergreen-bordered path to reach the portico. There was no need to delve into that case short of its destination in the Bujavid, in the capital. For tomorrow, he had an easy, comfortable wardrobe here at Najida that, thank God, did not come with a bulletproof vest. He had not worn the thing down to the dock—although there had been a little argument over his *going* down to the dock after shedding it in favor of a plainer, more suitable coat for outdoors.

He had won that round with his aishid. "I shall not stay. I promise," he had said, and added: "I have learned to duck, nadiin-ji."

Jago snorted.

But he *had* been quick about the visit, and lost no time getting back into the house.

"Dinner, nandi," Ramaso stood by to tell him as he came in, and staff was there with the formal court coat again for dinner. "The dowager has already moved to the dining room."

A definite signal to hurry. He shrugged the coat on and let a servant quickly tidy his queue, while Banichi and Jago shed their heavier armament to Tano's and Algini's care in the interests of speed. It was a brief detour to wash, then on to the new wing, and up a little set of steps to the grand new dining hall.

A huge window gave a high view of the sunset harbor, a vista framed in stained glass that shed splashes of color onto the paneled walls and into the table crystal.

Ilisidi had claimed the head of the long table, and a place was set to her honored immediate right, a warm gesture. It was potentially a seating of two, infelicitous in the numerology which ran through the Ragi language and through atevi hearts, with a basis in practicality. Two was an intimacy conducive to improper topics at dinner. Two could fall to arguing, and in the old days, cutlery could easily become involved.

Which was why, in this dinner for two, Ramaso, as major d' and estate manager, set himself at a slight remove, midway down the table—assuring that conversation was limited to the delight of the new windows and the niceness of the weather. The stained glass windows with the clear center panels were the dowager's extravagant gift, one that Bren himself had never had a chance to see in full splendor.

They discussed the view. The artist. The labor of building the new wing, a topic Ramaso knew top to bottom. They strayed to the progress of the Edi building their new center on the neighboring Kajiminda peninsula, and Ramaso mentioned exchanges Najida had had with the Kajiminda estate. Lord Geigi, whose domain was Kajiminda, had served for years as atevi-side master of the space station, and showed no sign of retiring. He had given up the lordship of Maschi clan to take that post, retaining only Kajiminda estate, his precious orchards, and his extensive collection of porcelains, pieces of which were *still* being tracked down, each with a story worth hearing.

Ilisidi did have news on Geigi's nephew Baiji, responsible for the illegal sale of those porcelains and other misdeeds. He was alive and well in the remote East, and apparently performing the one function he *could* contribute to Maschi clan—since his Calrunaidi wife was pregnant and the offspring was contractually destined to be Maschi. Geigi had no heir, nor was likely to produce one, but Baiji, after all his misdeeds, might at least have assured a continuance of the lordly line.

And, Ilisidi was quick to point out, Baiji would not rear that child, and would not pass on his opinions or his manners. The contract marriage would end with the birth, the woman, a daughter of the respectable Calrunaidi clan, and distantly related to Ilisidi herself, would take the baby and move into Kajiminda estate. Baiji could rust away in relative harmlessness in the remote East—though watched: definitely watched.

Inheritance and lordships slid perilously close to a topic they should *not* discuss, active and argumentative business being barred from the dining hall. So they moved on to discuss Ilisidi's harbor project in the East, which was making progress. They discussed the local weather, the stormy spring, the fishing—the schools were running late this year, but they were arriving.

The sunset faded in the windows. Candlelight became the ambient, before the colors had quite left the glass. When an accident involving the garage had set the house to constructing a new wing, and when the windows were proposed, Bren had asked himself whether this space should be a new sitting room—the one near the front doors was fairly small, its furnishings showing a little wear—but it was the nature of dinners to happen at sunset, and for brandy afterward to happen in the sitting room after sundown. So there was no benefit to the great windows except to be here when the sun was setting. He was glad, he expressed the thought, to have made that choice, and he was more than appreciative of Ilisidi's gift.

"An extravagance appropriate to this happy place," was her observation. Her own mediaeval holding was all stone and timber, usually chill, with a few rough-paneled rooms made cozy by the many fireplaces. "We have admired such windows in other houses. We are delighted to see them in this most fortunate of situations."

"You are always welcome to this place," Bren said, "whether or not I am here."

"It is a fine hall. But alas, the show is past."

"Shall we then go down to brandy, aiji-ma?"

"We shall," Ilisidi said, and reached for her cane, which Cenedi—their aishidi were both present, about the periphery of the room—was instant to provide. He pulled her chair back. Banichi was similarly quick to assist, at Bren's back, and Algini and Tano assisted Ramaso, who bowed to each of them and excused himself, his numerical usefulness at an end.

They went down the short stairs, each attended by the appropriate aishid, down two halls to the vicinity of the main doors—not that they needed protection in the heart of Najida; but that Guild was always about them, always witness, always ready to provide information, or to discuss, later, what wanted discussion.

And with Ilisidi, indeed, it would be a comfort not to rely solely on his own memory, his human understanding of the discussion; as she, likewise, might want a second opinion on the paidhi-aiji's responses. In discussion over brandy, most any topic was valid, and she would expect frankness—Ilisidi, in converse with her allies, insisted on it.

Discussion, like the brandy, did have a morning after, and it was no time to be muddle-headed. They settled in first with tea, that cup to calm the mind. Servants served. But they took only a few sips before the dowager set her cup down, and he did.

Then the brandy came round, and that deserved a sip before conversation, everything in due course, in a calm and quiet place.

"So," Ilisidi said, "you know, paidhi, that my great-grandson has been given a double aishid. That he was sent to visit Tatiseigi, after all that noise about appointing a new lord for Ajuri."

"One witnessed the trip, aiji-ma. Mospheira received the news feed. And one was informed about the doubled guard. One was entirely surprised to see him traveling alone."

"He is growing up," Ilisidi said, "and his first aishid is very young, and scanted their training, being pulled directly into duty. One has no quarrel with the appointment of a second unit.

We were at least consulted in that." A sip of brandy. "We were not consulted, however, in other matters. And he is *not* now traveling alone."

There was a sting in that.

"Nor was I consulted, aiji-ma, though I believe Banichi was consulted before we left. I am informed of the troublesome association, this cousin. It is the sequence of events that I have missed."

"Regarding the vacancy in Ajuri, Lord Tatiseigi made a white nomination," Ilisidi said, "on which we had had conversation and agreement. You understand the term—a nomination intended to fail, and to give the question time to cool down in the legislature while it wended its way through channels. A procedural delay. Tatiseigi went to his estate to ignore the inevitable chatter and to be out of convenient reach for phone calls and social invitations—as *we* went to Malguri, *not* to be seen as embroiling the East in midlands politics. It seemed wise at the time, to let the midlands take care of the midlands. And my grandson insists *he* had no inkling that there would be a problem. He sent my great-grandson to Tatiseigi for a holiday, and to end any speculation that there had been any rancor in his veto of Tatiseigi's nomination."

Sip of brandy. Bren waited. And Ilisidi reprised:

"We did *not*, however, foresee that an Ajuri-clan rail worker with a sizeable following would come looking to have Tatiseigi nominate *him* to the lordship. We did not know at the time that Geidaro, detestable woman, would be so *stupid* as to show up in Tirnamardi and demand Tatiseigi do this or that at her bidding, with *my great-grandson in residence.* She was clearly there to find out what she could, and arrogant enough to think Tatiseigi would give way to an implied threat. Her advisors might not have told her Cajeiri was there, but common sense should have told her, when she arrived and found him there, that she had entered upon dangerous ground, and should leave, if she had had half good sense."

Cajeiri's great-aunt had not been welcome in Tirnamardi on her best day.

"Tatiseigi knew one thing," Ilisidi said, "that his approving this Ajuri claimant would agitate her beyond good sense, and whether or not he meant to follow through with a nomination, he ejected that woman and extended hospitality to this claimant. *We* heard. *We* were alarmed. Tatiseigi does have a temper, and she had pushed him past limits. We immediately made arrangements to intervene—but the aiji-consort, who has never made a political move since her marriage, *ordered* the Red Train, gathered up my infant great-granddaughter—yes, we do claim her—and took that innocent babe to the heart of an impending three-clan war. Oh, *yes*, Taiben was in it. And very likely a remnant of Shishogi's operations was immediately involved on the Ajuri side. Mecheiti were loosed, Tatiseigi and one of my great-grandson's aishid were injured, property was damaged, lives were threatened, and *your bus*, which the aiji-consort had likewise set at her disposal, was damaged. Tatiseigi Filed Intent on Geidaro, and the Guild accepted the Filing, considering the risk she had presented to my great-grandson, and within hours, Geidaro was dead, but she was *not* killed under that Filing."

Disturbing news, amid general disaster. "She surely did not lack enemies within Ajuri itself who *might* be passionate enough to do it."

"This was not an act of passion, but of precision and stealth. Someone entered her office in Ajiden and did the deed quite professionally before Guild assigned to the matter had arrived. The perpetrators then set fire to the house, possibly to cover their escape, more likely with the intent to destroy records. House staff controlled the fire before any major damage was done. Theories vary between an Ajuri with a grudge, and Shadow Guild fearing what names she might release, and we support the latter theory. The Guild is now in control of Ajiden and is making a top to bottom search of the premises. This proposed legitimate lord, Nomari, is out of Nichono's line."

"Out of the Kadagidi," Bren said quietly and with his own misgivings.

Ilisidi's left brow lifted. "Your knowledge is accurate. There *is* a Kadagidi strain in that branch of Ajuri clan. And that particular Kadagidi line is related to the Dojisigin Marid—therefore distantly related up the ladder and down again, to Murini."

Murini the usurper, who had murdered Tabini's servants and bodyguard and driven Tabini and Damiri into hiding in hedge-rows for a time. They were rid of Murini and his regime. But the politics, including the Shadow Guild, despite the fall of Ajuri, was not dead *enough*.

"Shishogi may well have killed the parents and brother of this young claimant," Ilisidi said. "I have no difficulty believing that. Shishogi had a great deal to do with deaths inside Ajuri, and he was picking and choosing the lords he would support. Nichono's heirs did die, and not of natural causes. What remains to ask is *why* they became Shishogi's target."

Whether the parents and brother were playing a hand of their own—or were refusing to do Shishogi's bidding—was indeed a question—considering the survivor of the family had gained access to Tatiseigi's house and to Cajeiri and Damiri, *and* had blood ties both to the Kadagidi in the midlands, and, down south in the Marid, to the Dojisigi, who had backed Murini's coup. It *was* worrisome.

"This Nomari may detest the Shadow Guild with great passion," Ilisidi said, "but his aims in his own claim on Ajuri are not clear, nor has he thus far offered any proof of his identity that I am willing to accept. Yet. Followers, yes, he has them. But who knows on what proof? And if he *is* who he claims to be, there *is* that connection to the Marid, of which we are both advised. This person is, at this moment, nestled very close to my great-grandson and great-granddaughter, and to Tatiseigi. The aiji-consort says he does know particular things that might prove his identity, memories from childhood. *We* are more re-served in this matter, especially where it regards handing over a province. We do not rush to extend courtesies to this person.— And did I mention that Damiri has given *Seimiro* to Lord Tatiseigi? Figuratively speaking, of course. The next lord of the Atageini will be brought up and instructed by Damiri daughter of Komaji, and *she alone* has made this decision."

God, *that* was a blunt description. Komaji, lord of Ajuri, Damiri's father, had been banned from court after a press to have unsupervised access to Cajeiri had roused Tabini's mistrust—not least because Komaji had kidnapped Damiri herself shortly after her birth, and kept her from her Atageini relatives, including Tatiseigi, for years. One could never say Komaji himself had had any such designs on Cajeiri, but Tabini had suddenly bidden Komaji leave Shejidan, go back to Ajuri, and stay there.

Then Komaji himself had been assassinated, like every other lord of Ajuri—Komaji had allegedly been trying to reach Tatiseigi at the time, possibly to tell things the Shadow Guild had not wanted told, possibly to try to mend relations with Tabini. But no one knew that for certain.

It was a tangled, tangled family. The Kadagidi, the clan bordering Tatiseigi's holdings on the *other* side of the map, to the east, had supported Murini, had supported Shishogi, and there had been contract marriages and offspring back and forth involving all three clans, Ajuri, Atageini, and Kadagidi. Kadagidi was now likewise in Guild hands, the clan itself under Guild management and possibly facing forced division. Tabini had yet to propose it to the legislature, but it remained a possibility.

Now Ajuri, the clan primarily at fault, might be pulling itself back from the brink.

And finally, after all the murders and schemes—Ajuri was to be closely allied to Tatisiegi's Atageini clan, over which Cajeiri's infant *sister* was someday to be lord.

Could he have gone over to Mospheira to mitigate the political shocks after events in the heavens and *not* expected similar upheaval on the mainland? But—*God*, they had been busy!

His absence alone could have triggered certain moves—if he

flattered himself. But, too, events on Mospheira among humans *also* upset some atevi interests, and while his making the aiji's voice heard over on that side of the water was a stabilizing move in general, it could agitate certain interests on both sides of the water. The refugees Mospheira was taking in had never in their lives stood on a planet—human, yes, but not Mospheiran, with no common history, no cultural context except a long ago quarrel between their ancestors. Tabini-aiji had agreed to break with all precedent and let humans land on the mainland, granted the arrivals were quickly shipped across the strait—humans landing on atevi soil was controversial. Tabini had also agreed to let the station clear passenger space on the shuttles by parachuting heavy cargo onto atevi hunting lands—*more* shipping to Mospheira, which was already at an all-time high—and more contact of individuals involved.

Separation of humans and atevi was mandated by the Treaty of the Landing.

That fundamental principle was coming apart in places, and three human children had been in the atevi court to witness Cajeiri's investiture as Tabini's heir, a situation which was not going to please the Conservatives.

So was it a surprise that, while he was across the strait trying to assure that *human* affairs did not veer out of control after the recent scare aloft, there had been a political power struggle on this side of the strait—not because of his presence or lack thereof, but because diametrically opposed groups, human and atevi, were set off by the same trigger?

"Traditionally," Ilisidi said, "the lords and representatives of the midlands clans have been mainstays of the Conservative caucus. Ajuri's betrayal of the Atageini fractured that structure—possibly in *collusion* with the Kadagidi, possibly aiming to move against them—this, when Damiri was born. I stepped in at that time, lest we lose Atageini. I made alliance with the Atageini. Lord Tatiseigi's concerns for tradition, the wild lands, and the continued prominence of the midlands all accorded with my opinions and my own purposes. I am Eastern. I view western politics more objectively. The cohesion of the aishidi'tat *needs* midlands conservatism to *balance* my grandson's passion for human technology. Tatiseigi had wanted the Ajuri alliance very badly—hence Damiri's existence. But *she* has swung back and forth between Ajuri and Atageini man'chi so often I would not, for your ears only, paidhi, call her stable, even now. She has *never* reckoned the effects of her flitting to this side or the other. Lifelong, she has viewed herself as a pawn, at best a secondary player. She is *correct* not to seek a lordship. And will *she* now train a successor to Lord Tatiseigi?"

Blunt and exact. Bren sat warming his moderate serving of brandy, mostly untouched. "Aiji-ma, I am valueless if I do not answer such a question with a perhaps impertinent third question."

"Ask it."

"Do you think it wise to take *another* child from Damiri-daja? And would not nand' Cajeiri experience some distress at it?"

"That is *two* questions, paidhi."

"I think, aiji-ma, perhaps because I am not ateva, that it is actually one."

Ilisidi was not accustomed to be questioned at all. Even by Tabini-aiji, who might swear at her and shout, but stop her? Not easily. But she had posed him a question. He had to believe it *was* a question.

Ilisidi heaved a sigh. "It is an infelicitous duality of questions, with only *one* solution, which is to hope Cajeiri will shape his sister, as I have, to a great extent, shaped him."

"That you have, aiji-ma. As you brought up his father, who will also shape this child. And I see hope in this solution. Lord Tatiseigi *with* an heir is much stronger. His rivals will have to rethink their moves. They cannot now hope for a battle over *his* succession. And can you think your great-grandson will *not* influence his sister? Or that your grandson will not?"

"So." Ilisidi moved her fingers and the servant poured more

brandy for both sides. "You do see our situation, paidhi. We are poised on the edge of major changes. A solution for the midlands is desirable, but let us not be blind as to the nature of the participants. Ajuri has been a primary source of trouble for centuries, and it has deeply scarred its own children by murder and betrayal. I strongly opposed my grandson's marriage to Damiri. I never trusted Komaji alive or dead, nor has Tatiseigi, considering the very strong possibility that Komaji murdered Damiri's mother, or at very least delivered her to those who did. I was not surprised to learn Shishogi's character, and I have known Geidaro far too well and too long to believe anything she might say. Her death is the bright flower in this arrangement. I do not know what sort of blossom this Nomari may become, once he breaks free and is confirmed, if he is confirmed. And I fear too great a haste in that process and too much pressure from people who are not looking closely at the details. Most of my fellow Conservatives are beside themselves with anticipation that the Ajuri vacancy will be filled, so that they will have one more vote on their side. They will be positively slavering after the Kadagidi replacement, now, and we should *not* have haste driving that one, either. This Nomari has flung himself at Tatiseigi— justifiable, given the Ajuri lordship had been put in play by the Conservatives' drive to fill that seat. And that he may have sought safety during the Troubles in a region that, its other actions aside, *resisted* the Shadow Guild, is not in itself a stupid move. But let us not hasten to commit ourselves *or* approve."

He parsed that for what it was worth—Ajuri's long history of intrigue, murder, and its creation of the Shadow Guild had all worked for years to support the radical end of the conservative spectrum, an unsavory minority within the Conservatives which had repeatedly thrown up roadblocks to Tabini's dealings with Mospheira, and particularly to the space program. The prospective appointment of someone of Nichono's tangled line to the lordship of Ajuri sent a long, troublesome thread of connection next door, to the Kadagidi, the clan on Tatiseigi's *other*

border. Kadagidi and Ajuri had recently conspired to take down
the aijinate. Some of the Shadow Guild to this day held out in
the south, in the northern Marid, where distrust of the north
and opposition to Tabini had long simmered along in local politics. Some individual agents might still exist in the north as
well: Shishogi had spent decades moving his players about the
map like chesspieces, to lie dormant until useful, and such
might remain a problem almost anywhere. Nomari's prior connection to the Marid did raise questions. Vital questions. But—

"One so hoped to have buried the Shadow Guild," he said. "I
take your warning, aiji-ma. I shall trust very carefully. And I
am relatively sure I shall be asked."

"We rely on it," Ilisidi said, and took a large sip of brandy.
"Now—"

She was about to say something, doubtless important. But
Guild stirred from their ordinary quiet at the edge of the conversation. Cenedi and Banichi both moved, each to his charge.

"Bren-ji," Banichi said in the faintest of whispers. *"Lord
Machigi* is approaching Najida. He is asking a hearing."

It was pitch dark outside. And Machigi—Lord of the Taisigin
Marid, longtime enemy of the district, wanted a conference with
him, who might or might not have been on the premises yet?

Or was it a conference with the aiji-dowager, who was not
supposed to be here in the first place?

The lift of Ilisidi's brow as Cenedi delivered the same news,
the glance in Bren's direction—seemed a question.

"I have not invited him, aiji-ma. I have kept my own schedule as quiet as possible."

"If he is asking a meeting with *me,*" Ilisidi said, "it is beyond
irregular, and we shall have a close look at Bujavid security, if
they have let slip our movements. We took off for the East, at
some inconvenience, before turning for the west coast. But we
shall see, shall we not, what motivates this disturbance?"

Considering the situation in the north, there *was* reason for
Machigi to approach *him,* even not knowing the dowager

was here. He had negotiated with Machigi in the Marid. He had set up Machigi's contact with the dowager.

But did Machigi now have cause to come here? Machigi was an old enemy of the west coast . . . indeed, a potential enemy to the whole aishidi'tat, if the agreement with the dowager broke down.

The Guild guarding Ilisidi was going on high alert, that was certain. Likely the information was already escalating to Guild headquarters in Shejidan, and wherever else that network felt it should go.

To Tabini himself, likely: Tabini's own after-dinner brandy was about to be interrupted.

It was quite possibly Ilisidi whom Machigi had come to see. She had been here two days, and there might have been spies positioned at a distance, to watch for signs of activity at the house. Quiet espionage on staff was how the lords of this and that managed to believe in each other's honesty. But infiltrate a mostly-Edi staff, ethnic and ancient enemies of the Marid?

That was far less likely.

Bren caught Banichi's eye, and exchanged a glance, nothing blithe about it.

But there was that estate truck, and that massive crate that sat out in the drive. Sign enough, if someone were watching. He had not been quiet enough in his arrival.

3

The train moved—finally—and Cajeiri settled into the table group he much preferred, with his younger aishid. It was well into the night, too late for tea. Mother and Uncle were sharing a glass of wine back at the rear of the Red Car. He and his aishid and all the rest shared fruit juice—none of the Guild of whatever age would touch alcohol on duty, and they were definitely on duty. Cousin Nomari coming to the capital to meet Father was going to upset some people.

The Red Train was usually only one passenger car and one baggage car, but they had brought out two passenger cars, what with Mother's staff and Mother's guard and Uncle's staff and Uncle's bodyguard, and Cajeiri's own bodyguard—Eisi and Liedi were, as usual, not riding with them. *They* were in the baggage car keeping Boji calm and content with a supply of eggs, and he was beginning to be embarrassed about that situation. His servants, grown men of some dignity, should not have to ride in a baggage car.

The other passenger car was for Nomari and *his* bodyguard, along with several Guild officials who would be asking Nomari a lot of questions during the trip. There were also a couple of Uncle's household staff who were doing temporary duty with Nomari—and who might become permanent, so that they would be in a position to observe things . . . Uncle would certainly want to know what Nomari was doing, especially at first.

Then there was the flatcar with nand' Bren's bus.

It was the bus that had held them up. They could have been on the way hours ago if he had not strongly insisted to Uncle and to Mother that they *had* to get nand' Bren's bus back to him, that it was a debt of honor—and to his surprise, Mother had actually backed him on it. The damage to the bus had not stopped them using it to get to the train station, but when they had started to load it, there was some part underneath projecting and preventing them getting up the ramp, so they had had to send the baggage truck all the way back to Tirnamardi to get tools to cut something away—then, in the confusion, and to Great-uncle's displeasure and embarrassment, not the *right* tools, so there had been one *more* trip to and from Tirnamardi.

They had sat, and sat, and the Taibeni riders had gotten down from their mecheiti, made camp and had supper in the woods that surrounded the little train station. All of them who were going on the train had had their own supper aboard: the train had arrived with it.

Antaro's and Jegari's parents, and three cousins, too, were part of the Taibeni escort, so Lucasi and Veijico had been invited out to the fireside to be introduced all around and to share what the riders had. One was sure they were having a much nicer time. But his older aishid stayed with him, and assured him they were perfectly happy to have supper inside.

It was not that bad. After all the rush and worry of recent days, it had actually been *nice* to have time to sit and relax and hear nothing but quiet conversation—except Cajeiri worried that nand' Bren was supposed to arrive soon, and the bus, *his* bus, would be late.

And nand' Bren relied on that bus for his own safety.

"We shall get to the capital by dawn, all the same," Uncle had said, as the evening freight from the much larger township station thumped along past them, the second train to pass them, doubtless with passengers amazed and intrigued to see the Red Train sitting on the siding. Its noise disappeared into the distance, coastward bound with a load of passengers, baggage, mail, and freight. Cajeiri wondered what sort of freight, tried to think what those at one end of the rail would be sending that those at the other end would need, but not knowing the specifics of that train's route, he could only guess. Nomari would know both the routing and the types of goods. Nomari, because he was Transportation Guild, knew a great number of interesting things, things Cajeiri had never even thought about, before spending time with this newly-found cousin. He grew curious about things he had never even wondered about.

And still they sat, now in the dark, while outside the bus finally roared to life and sounded as if it were moving—positioning itself, perhaps, finally to be loaded up onto the flatcar. *How* they were going to get that huge bus onto the car was truly a question, and Cajeiri would gladly have gone out to see, but Mother and Uncle would not permit him sightseeing in the woods in the dark, as Mother put it. So he just listened, and after a good lot of banging and thumping, ratcheting of chain and motor-noise, his younger aishid came aboard and shut the door again.

"It has loaded, nandiin," Antaro reported. "They are securing it with more chains. And the escort is putting out the fire."

A fire. In the woods. He was alarmed. Sidonin was a precious forest that reached deep into Taiben. But his aishid settled back at the table, assuring him it was a little fire, only small brush near the track, and the Taibeni would be very sure it was out and cold before they left.

Then his aishid, who had watched the whole process, began telling how it was done, while the Red Train began to build up steam, preparing to move.

At the very last, Uncle's Guild came aboard, announcing the bus secured, and assuring them all that the fire was definitively out and the bus was securely on the flatcar.

Uncle's Guild-senior tugged a cord to signal the engine, and finally, finally, they began to roll.

"There are days," Uncle said, "when nothing seems to go smoothly."

4

An approach in the dark, this late, and at such inconvenience, *did* send Guild out quietly to query those *with* Machigi as to the makeup of the company and the intentions.

Word slipped also down to Najida village—Bren ordered it, because the Edi folk had good reason for uneasiness in any visit from the Marid, and he had no desire to have them learn about it after the fact. His message to the Grandmother of the Edi, was simple: *We have received a request from Machigi-nandi to speak with us. Indications are that this approach is respectful and will not intrude on village land, nor will it be long in duration. I am present. I shall assure this meeting is appropriate and proper, and that Edi rights are respected throughout.*

The fact that every servant at Najida was Edi offered the Grandmother more assurance than that. If Machigi for some reason had wanted to conduct a conversation not overheard by the Edi folk, Najida estate was not the place to hold it.

The Guild unit that had gone out to meet the visitors reported their visitor was on the road headed up to Najida, about half an hour out, and that the party involved one market truck and a load of fishing nets.

The market truck was not utterly unusual. Roads on the mainland were few, trucks capable of navigating the bush served many uses, including moving people about, but the fishing nets were a question. The cargo had provided an answer, perhaps, should anyone wonder at a strange truck on the Great

Coastal Road—but fishing was not the reason the lord of the Taisigin Marid was driving at night in a district he had promised by formal treaty to leave alone.

"The man has always done the unpredicted," Ilisidi said in the long wait. They had changed to tea, and strong tea, since brandy, as the dowager said, was better at promoting honesty than it was at promoting good sense.

Ramaso and others of the staff hurried about arranging the possibility of an overnight stay—word was from Banichi and Cenedi that it was *only* Machigi and his aishid, themselves only recently recognized by the Guild as entitled to access a limited number of Guild codes and communications, and that after considerable negotiation.

Tonight that access was a great convenience. The servants provided one chair, one cup, and a correct arrangement of the buffet centerpiece for kabiu, a felicitous and comfortable design.

The front door opened. There was a quiet stir in the hall, a brisk tread of several men entering, and as Ramaso opened the sitting room door—there indeed was Machigi and his aishid.

Bren rose. Ilisidi stayed seated. Ilisidi nodded, Bren and Machigi bowed. Two of Machigi's aishid distributed themselves along the far wall, two to remain outside, northern-style protocol.

"Welcome," Bren said.

"Nandi." Machigi, a middling-young man with cold eyes and a scar that raked his chin and jaw, gave a curt bow to him, another to Ilisidi.

"Do sit," Ilisidi said, "presuming you have come for discussion, Lord Machigi."

"I have, nand' dowager." A second bow, and he subsided into the indicated chair. "I understood that you were here and nand' Bren was not." Machigi gave him his lordly title, which some did not. "Forgive the hour. I came through our hunting lands and I shall go back the same way."

"If it is urgent," Ilisidi said, "get to it, nandi."

"The opportunity is urgent. The need is considerable. If I am known to be absent from Tanaja and meeting with you, there might be moves against me. However, I could not let the chance go, nand' dowager, and I am pleased to have nand' Bren's presence. This is an unexpected benefit. Regarding my railroad . . ."

Machigi's *railroad*. Bren hoped his face did not betray bewilderment. There *was* currently no such thing. The historically problematic railroad link between the central aishidi'tat and the Marid had been a small footnote in the dowager's prior negotiations with Machigi, a very small footnote, as he well knew, having mediated the agreement. Certainly a rail link of some sort, connecting Machigi's capital to the main line, was a next step, once the proposed sea route between the Marid and the East began to bring in goods that needed to move on to the west, though there was the short-term possibility of sending them northward by ship, the long route around the coast and up to Cobo. Right now the rail line coming south from Shejidan took a sharp westward bend up at Koperna, capital of the Senjin Marid, north of Machigi's territory, and headed toward Najida on the coast, where it took a northward turn north to Cobo District and then turned east, back to Shejidan, or on to places east and north.

As for any future rail coming out of Machigi's district, it was problematic where to send it. The most direct link for any such theoretical construction would go up to Koperna, in the Senjin Marid, where rail served both inland Koperna, and the port at Lusi'ei, but Senjin was allied to the Dojisigin Marid, both having a very dark history with Machigi's Taisigin Marid and its association.

In what regard, Bren asked himself, could a desire to have a rail connection have become so urgent as to bring Machigi on an exceedingly rough and lengthy wilderness drive to seek an unannounced meeting with Ilisidi at this hour? Certainly it was nothing he wanted publicized.

"Does it bid fair to break out in war," Ilisidi asked, "or do we have time for tea, nandi?"

"Tea, yes, nand' dowager," Machigi said, which put immediate clarification out of the question and gave a mind ample time to process the uneasy possibilities behind this sudden visit.

Marid folk were not Ragi—in fact, they were a remnant of an ancient and foreign culture, one diluted by two thousand years of migration, warfare, and mixing with the southern clans of the mega-continent. The Maridi clans cherished their legendary past, maintained their separate ways, rejected the northern guilds, and disparaged the etiquette and culture of the north, though they were signatory to the aishidi'tat and counted as member clans.

Unfortunately, whatever they had been, poverty and scarcity had been the condition of the Marid. They fished. They traded. They spent most of their energies battling the southern storms and each other, what time they were not trying to take the west coast from the Maschi of the southern plain.

Then they had met the Ragi of the newly organizing aishidi'tat, and it had been war at first encounter—a war which they lost, hence their inclusion in the aishidi'tat, and their nominal governance by the north, which rarely bothered with them.

It was a long, long and uneasy history Machigi's people had with the Ragi-led north, and if ever there was an ateva prone to rush headlong and bluntly to the point, and to use whatever means necessary to achieve his ends, it was Machigi—Lord of the Taisigin Marid and chief lord of the Association of the Southern Marid, the aishihai'mar.

But he met his match in the Lord of Malguri, the aiji-dowager. Ilisidi herself was not Ragi: she was Eastern, yet another culture, another district in many ways like the Marid, wed to the sea and the mountains, and somewhat disinclined to obey midlands customs. Ilisidi, however, had learned the intricacies of the Ragi-dominated aishidi'tat, had *ruled* it twice as regent, successor to both husband and son. Machigi had found his match and found reason to sign a trade agreement with her. It was notable in their interaction—and one was certain that the dowager noticed—Machigi never said aiji-ma, always using the honorific of proper degree, but not giving it the -ma syllable of personal connection. This was a man who acknowledged no equals in his region, a man who gave up his position only gradually, demanding this, agreeing to that, only for due consideration, piece by stubborn piece.

Tea suspended discussion. It did not suspend the forceful presence of the man—a very young man to sway what he did. A decade younger than Tabini, and he was working to turn the Marid into a power that could hold its own against the political and economic force that was the Western Association. From the time his father was assassinated, Machigi had had as his stated aim the unification of the entire south, including the all-important shipping townships of Separti and Talida clear over on the west coast, with all the vast territory in between. Once, he had even threatened, possibly to garner the people's support, raids into Edi territory over the piracy issue—the *Edi's* piracy, not his, an issue that had, thankfully, found a more peaceful resolution. Ilisidi had won, in the north, the admission of the Edi to the aishidi'tat and gotten them to forswear interference with shipping.

Though Machigi had sworn away his ambitions on the southwest coast in return for an alliance with Ilisidi's East, his father had drawn into his circle all the southern Marid—the Taisigin, which he ruled; and the Sungeni of the Isles and the southeastern coast, the Dausigin. After his father was murdered, Machigi had held off the Senjin and the Dojisigin, his northern neighbors, during the brief interlude of Murini's takeover of the aishidi'tat. The Senjin and the Dojisigin had supported Murini, who had Dojjsigin blood; and when Tabini returned to power, the Dojisigin had become the primary haven for the remnants of the Shadow Guild . . . among various troublesome elements.

But the northern Marid had made a serious mistake in

assassinating Machigi's father. Machigi hated them. He had stood them off, he had claimed the man'chi of all three southern clans, and following Tabini's return to power, and the containment of the northern Marid, Machigi had found in Ilisidi an ally. He agreed to the aishidi'tat—on a limited basis—and was slowly accepting the northern guild system, choosing, however, which of the guilds he *would* accept, insisting, among other things, on his own security.

In all of that Machigi and Ilisidi, lord of the East, had a great deal in common. The dowager herself, with her own style of independence within the aishidi'tat, had pried him away from his coastal ambitions by offering him access to her East by sea, if he could reach it. Those were stormy seas, a route deemed commercially impossible—and she'd offered him satellites, accurate weather forecasts, and the resources of the orbiting station—help that Machigi had accepted with more than a hint of Tabini's own enthusiasm for human technology.

Build great new seafaring ships, supported by designs from the recently opened human archive? Space-based weather forecasting? Machigi's rivals called that southern sea route a grand daydream. Nothing, in their estimation, could overcome the southern latitude storms. So, also in their estimation, Machigi's deal with the aiji-dowager must be a cover for some other ambition closer to home.

Now, one had to wonder: were they right? Was he going to go for something his enemies could assuredly see as a threat? A rail line that would give him a direct, land-based connection to the aishidi'tat?

The west coastal districts of the aishidi'tat, those same Separti and Talida districts he'd sought to control, districts whose livelihood depended on the transport of goods between the Marid and the aishidi'tat—by sea—were going to fight that competition. If Machigi was hellbent on pushing rail *ahead* of his southern sea route, they were going to come out of their lethargy and know he was an imminent threat.

Rail *first?* God, yes, he needed to think about this one.

But the southwest, Ashidama Bay, with its stubborn antagonism to the Edi, its feuds with Kajiminda, its resistence to the railroad and its several feuding trade houses—that Ilisidi had tried for decades to bring to the conference table?

He saw the gleam in Ilisidi's eyes. *She* didn't need time to consider. *She* had it figured in an instant, top to bottom, what this railroad might do.

One cup of tea, and half of another, before they could politely *discuss* business. The dowager set her cup down, definitively. They all followed suit.

"So," Ilisidi said, "the paidhi-aiji and I have been delayed here. And you found this out. We are intrigued."

"One has sources."

"And we are *still* intrigued."

A moment of silence. "I have agents at the airport. I knew you had landed on the coast, with respect, nand' dowager, and from there it was a reasonable guess the aim was Najida, and a consultation with the paidhi-aiji. Mine was a considerable trip, by market roads and hunting tracks. One *hoped* you would remain to meet the paidhi-aiji. The Red Train had not yet made the trip."

"Ah," Ilisidi said, as if satisfied. The words *Transportation Guild* had not *quite* figured in the explanation. "And would you have pursued us all the way to the capital with this idea of yours? You have been very reluctant to venture there—but this venue can be no more comfortable. I do not recall you willing to exit your own lands."

"I rely on our agreement."

"And now wish to alter it. Why this urgency?"

"Because time has become critical, nand' dowager. One by no means wished to surprise you with our project. But we are beginning—we have, in fact, already begun to review old records—previous surveying for a rail connection."

There was half a breath of dead silence, Machigi waiting in vain for Ilisidi to break back in.

"May one ask *why* this has become so urgent?" Bren asked, the most polite and least explosive question he could think of on the fly. *Ilisidi* was perturbed by the security issue. Ilisidi was fully aware Machigi had dodged her question.

"Because," Machigi said—fairly cheerfully, for Machigi—"Lord Bregani has had a falling-out with that damnable child in Ajuran. Bregani is in a bad position. He fears the consequences of his misstep. One hopes to take advantage of his situation."

Child. Tiajo, he meant. Daughter of the Dojisigi lord and de facto ruler of the clan. *Not* the most stable of individuals on a good day.

"Falling-out." Ilisidi lifted a brow. "And a fear of his old allies. We are *always* interested in gossip."

"Bregani has a problem," Machigi said. "He would very much like someone else—anyone else—in charge of the Dojisigi, which is only logical. But he made a rash move and now it is exposed. Bregani had had enough of Tiajo even before the coup attempt in Shejidan—there has been mistrust, how not? And Tiajo, since she became lord of Dojisigin, has been setting her own people in place in Senjin and extending finance to certain people in that district, corrupting and terrorizing. The housecleaning in the Assassins' Guild in Shejidan has not put sensible fear in the girl. In fact, since that time, she seems to have acquired additional assets."

"Names," Ilisidi said.

"Pureni, Asama."

"Interesting," Cenedi said, from behind the dowager. They were not names Bren knew, but he was willing to lay bets if Cenedi recognized them, Banichi did.

"So," Machigi said. "The child has a vicious temper. Bregani evidently concluded Tiajo had been weakened by the dissolution of the Shadow Guild—which indeed she is, considerably. But not weakened enough. His latest attempt on her life not only failed, but she reciprocated and nearly succeeded. She still has resources at her disposal, who will not always move at her command—but if they see profit in it, and if it is at least convenient, they will act. She delights in being feared, she reacts to provocations in extreme anger, and Bregani is now afoul of her concentrated temper. So: I have sent a message to Bregani. I have advised him that were I to build a railroad—which was always part of my planning in conjunction with my agreement with you, nand' dowager—I have several choices for a route between Tanaja and the existing system. The shortest and most economical link would be his capital at Koperna, where the north-south rail comes down from the mountain pass and turns toward Najida. Alternatively, I could negotiate with Lord Haidiri of the Maschi to extend rail from Tanaja to Targai, thus crossing far more of our hunting lands than I would like, but it would have the advantage of avoiding Senjin's volatility. And should Haidiri refuse, I still might have the option to join it to Najida, still disturbing our hunting range and duplicating a great deal of railway to no good advantage, and certainly none to Senjin, who would profit by the warehousing of goods and by other fees. The advantage of an agreement with me at this time must be clear, even to him."

"What is your point of contact with him?" Ilisidi asked bluntly. "Have you persons in his court?"

"I have engaged the Farai to speak to him."

God, the Farai. A clan which had had *far* too many daughters, and had fingers in far too many districts and properties for anyone's comfort. During Murini's short term as aiji, the Farai of Morigi-dar had tried to claim both Najida *and* Bren's Bujavid apartment, as former holders of both properties. They had stubbornly lodged *in* Bren's apartment during the usurper's administration, then tried to hold on to it on the grounds that they had risked their lives assisting Tabini's return, a completely fictitious heroism, but it had still taken a great deal to pry them out. The fact that they were incurring Tabini's displeasure had not daunted them: they had been willing to fight it in court, until it became clear the aiji-dowager was involved. Ilisidi had the reputation of involving the Guild.

"Your mother was Farai," Ilisidi observed.

"She was," Machigi said. "So is Bregani's wife."

"Do you retain that much influence with that clan?"

A dark amusement touched Machigi's face. "Certainly more so than with Bregani. But that might change, given Bregani's falling-out with Tiajo. He needs an ally. If the lord of Koperna wishes to be reasonable, it would be not only a shorter route for northbound goods, but a means to sever Senjin from the Doji-sigin Marid, an additional situation of benefit."

"Possibly one of hazard."

"It does not daunt me."

"And a great provocation to the west coast."

"Only one thing stops Separti from building its own rail north."

Jorida, Machigi meant. The private island empire of Hurshina Shipping, the owner of which had fought tooth and nail against a rail extension south from Najida.

God. *One thing* was not a minor opposition. Hurshina ruled Ashidama Bay and everything that moved down there. Not as a clan lord, but with an economic stranglehold. There were three sizeable cities down there, and Hurshina had agreements with all of them. No rail. No alternative to Hurshina's shipping company . . . that lasted long.

Ilisidi nodded slowly. "To build rail up even to Koperna would take steel currently assigned to your shipyard project."

"It would."

"And how long would it delay your shipbuilding, while *we* continue to build a port to receive such ships, and Lord Geigi in the heavens interrupts his vital work to consider weather prediction? *Our* building, nandi, is on schedule."

"Which is why I am here to discuss the matter, truly to

discuss it as an immediate matter, nand' dowager. I have survey work that will certainly do until we come into Koperna itself. *You* have a supply of steel. We might leave the shipbuilders at work and bargain for *more* steel."

The man certainly had nerve. That had never been in doubt.

Ilisidi's mouth actually smiled. The eyes did not, quite. "Lay out your expectations, nandi, do. You are here at some effort and you have some valid observations. We have leisure."

"First," Machigi said, "the harbor facility would also contain the rail terminal and requisite machinery . . . cranes for the docks, and whatever else trains require. Means to turn the engines about. Means to service the equipment. Means to load and offload, and to move goods between ship and rail car. If, nand' dowager, you would ship steel by rail, my ships could pick it up at Adaran, in Cobo."

"Conveying it right past Ashidama Bay."

"As we do with all our shipments, nand' dowager. *Unless* we can arrange to pick it up at Koperna. If we gained Lord Bregani's agreement, we could lay track from both ends."

"And how would this steel be bought?"

No flinching. "With a peaceful resolution in the western Marid and complete isolation of the Dojisigi and their governing fool. Senjin may mistrust our motives, but because the Dojisigi certainly will oppose it, we stand a chance of dividing them, and linking Senjin's financial interest to you, nand' dowager, in a very direct way."

Dangerous, Bren thought. Dangerous and very clever. Dangerous ever to have dealt with this clever man. Dangerous to have so much of future policy dependent on him. And Machigi had only indirectly alluded to intelligence sources, and given only a cloudy excuse for the timing of his visit.

The dowager likewise was dangerous, dangerous in her power, but with well-known frustration in her agenda for the southwest coast, a region which still sat ideologically apart from Najida and Kajiminda, two lordless townships under the iron political control of one wealthy—and ruthless—shipping company.

One of the long-held political positions of the southwest coast, where Separti and Talida were located, was adamant opposition to a rail connection from there up to Najida. Why? The southern townships relied on ocean shipping up to Adaran in Cobo District, where the oldest part of the rail system went directly to Shejidan and points north. Adaran would not suffer in either event—increased rail traffic, or maintenance of the status quo of the seaport. Which *family* in Adaran stood to benefit, however, was another matter.

"Adaran," Bren said, "is about to become involved in the landing of goods and the transport of humans from the spaceport. This proposal would add another potentially troublesome element to that situation. Forgive me, aiji-ma, nandi, but it will raise questions. Najida is hardly more than a shed and a watering and sanding tower. Every time improvement to the Najida station comes into question, Separti flares up in opposition. I have paid for a warehouse out of my own pocket."

Machigi frowned at him. "Najida, one understands, is not that interested in expanding its rail station."

"It most definitely is not. The Edi value their isolation here. I am honor-bound to raise that objection. And Hurshina is no ally of the Edi. His household from the beginning has been their enemy."

"Removal of Najida from consideration in no wise troubles us."

"Were we to approve Targai as an alternate connection point," Ilisidi said, "the Maschi will come into the controversy, and we have particularly promised Lord Geigi not to start a war with his neighbors."

"Then a link to Koperna," Machigi said, "is the most sensible idea. And it should not trouble the Maschi *or* the Edi folk or that bastard on Jorida Isle. We will not send large cargoes northward in the next few years. But we will *receive* supplies from the north with far less trouble than shipping around the coast, and *that*, nand' dowager, will hasten the ship-building and save both time and money."

"Granted I send you twice the steel," Ilisidi said. "Virtually free."

"Granted that, yes, nand' dowager."

"Also granted that Senjin will desert the Dojisigi and agree with you, nandi. It is an interesting idea."

So many incidents had begun with that word *interesting*. It did not mean the dowager would cooperate, or that she would not turn and do something obstructive. She was gathering information. She might be Eastern bred and born, but she had twice ruled the aishidi'tat, and twice been frustrated in bringing the entire southwest and its quarreling companies firmly in hand. Bringing the tribal peoples into the aishidi'tat, knitting up a weakness in the aishidi'tat as old as human presence in the world—that had been a major triumph.

Separating Machigi and his association from the political stew that was the Marid, getting him to trade his ambitions to take the west coast for an agreement that gave him the prospect of a sea route to the East—that had been an even greater one.

Now came Machigi with just a little delay in the trade agreement on which Ilisidi had committed so much prestige, asking just a little delay and a blind eye—oh, well, and double the steel—while Machigi made a move on the chessboard that not only involved the old, old issue of the west coast, but rattled the stack of china that was Senjin's momentarily peaceful abstinence from political agitation.

Yes, receiving shipments directly from the capital down this new rail connection could speed things—and bring direct access from the capital to the middle of the Marid for the first time in history. The mountains had insulated the north somewhat from the continual ferment in the south—but not entirely successfully. The Taisigin Marid had brewed trouble very well *without* a rail line for two hundred years.

And at no point—absolutely at no point—had either Machigi or Ilisidi mentioned the small fact that one of Machigi's spies active against Senjin had just declared himself a candidate for a lordship in the north? A spy who just happened to be a cousin to Tabini-aiji's wife and the mother of the heir?

Was that *nowhere* in Machigi's sudden rush to discuss a potential earthquake in his agreement with Ilisidi?

Did he imagine she had no idea?

Or did he want this begun before she did know?

God, Bren thought. *Will* she?

Ilisidi cocked her head and smiled that dreadful smile of hers, the one that went with the wrong sort of tea. "Convince us an approach to Senjin is a good idea," she said.

Machigi's expression was no less worrisome. "Nand' dowager," he began.

"We are willing to hear details," Ilisidi interrupted him, two words in. "But should we back this move, we have expectations of achieving a *more structured* relationship between the Taisigin Marid and the capital."

There was a moment of silence.

"Such a relationship at this moment," Machigi countered, "would not aid my calling on Senjin to break with the Dojisigi."

"Would allowing Senjin to associate closely with you, nandi, truly encourage a *future* tightening of our own association? Or the contrary?"

Again the moment of consideration. "I rule as aiji in the south, but it is a small aijinate, respectful of the north and of the East. I do not encourage the lords of the south to make independent associations with you, nand' dowager, because the more and less of your favor, ample as it is, might create competition and intrigue among them, to which they are, by nature, all too apt. I by no means question your ability to hold them, but doubt your interest in doing so, while I have the utmost reason to give their politics my full attention. I take the same view regarding the northern Marid. I am the best guarantee of peace. I can deal with Senjin, I firmly believe, and I shall cede to you, as I have done, influence over the western coast, utterly relinquishing my ambitions in that sphere, though I shall undertake to assist if called upon."

Ilisidi's smile persisted. "Indeed."

Machigi, no fool, smiled back gently. "One would never doubt your ability, should you have to. But why would you? I have the better part of the Marid in hand. I offer not fragments, but an association, a survey map which has not, for the most part, changed, and *time* is critical. Will the Marid as a whole form a tighter association with the aishidi'tat? Only after we have become one voice. Right now, our interests are diverse even from each other—and you, being what you are, considering what the East is, I think you understand that."

God, *that* was blunt. True, however: Ilisidi's region was indeed its own challenge; and if anyone understood the pressures on Machigi—she had *beaten* her opposition. She had seized control over a fractious East, made a compact with the aishidi'tat and secured that, and her compact with Machigi, the sea trade, the port she was building—those were her lock on the East.

But she served back equal bluntness. "Know that, should you betray my interests, nandi, I shall not be approachable for amendment."

"I have staked my life and the welfare of the Southern Association on what some call impossible, nand' dowager. I have confidence in the paidhi. I have confidence that his representations of your position are true. I have confidence in *you*, that you *can* understand my situation. Your thinking does not go down habitual northern paths—nor do you mistake compliance for sincerity. Do I hold ambitions that would challenge Shejidan? *Absolutely* none, and you know it. I have enough to do in the south. Do I hold myself and my association of *value* to Shejidan? I do. We will never bow to Shejidan because it is Shejidan.

We will work with Shejidan because we see it brings benefit to the people in the northern regions, and governs where it governs with a fair and even hand. Being what we are, we know how difficult a balance this is. I ask, nand' dowager, that you give *me* latitude—and supply—to unite the Marid. We have come on a moment and a situation in which something can be done to the advantage of all of us *except* the Dojisigi, and after the numerous attempts the Dojisigin have made to remove me, I am *glad* to return the attention. With Senjin in hand, with prosperity flowing to all the Marid but the Dojisigin—the Dojisigi may solve their own problem."

Ilisidi listened gravely, frowning. Then the ghost of a wicked amusement quirked one brow.

"So," she said. "We shall see how that falls. We should be sorry should you suffer a reverse, nandi, or fail in your representations to us. Losing you would inconvenience us. Is it necessary that you build a railroad immediately, or will various rumors, and a site declared in Tanaja, suffice to stir things up for now?"

Machigi broke into a brief and real smile. "True, nand' dowager. A shipment of steel would aid the illusion. More to follow would aid the reality, because what I promise, I am ultimately constrained to deliver."

"More may be arranged—should Senjin be as fluid as you think. Gain them, and that rail link may happen very quickly, nandi. Create problems, and you may find it takes forever."

"We hear that there will be landings in the north. And humans arriving at the spaceport. We remind the aijinate that we also have a broad hunting range—and an expanse of calm sea, where petal sails would trouble no one—*should* politics in the north prove a problem."

"A generous offer. However—we believe we have that matter solved."

"This new lord of Ajuri."

"Rumor *does* fly fast."

"Indeed," Machigi said. "Will Kadagidi be next to have a new lord?"

"You are remarkably current—except in your connection of Kadagidi's vacancy with this one. That may wait a while. Are there other matters to discuss?" A pause. "No? Then brandy."

The servant made the rounds. The dowager signaled a more generous serving, a risk, Bren thought. The meeting had not been contentious, for which one could be extremely grateful, but oh, God, the omissions in it. Bren kept his own consumption on a slower schedule than Machigi's.

"Will you stay the night, nand' Machigi?" Bren asked. "You would be sincerely welcome."

"Thank you, nandi, for the gracious offer—but I am reportedly on a hunting trip in my own range. So I had best get back to it tonight, and sleep at the camp to make it true—before I gently let slip to my intimate advisors the news that we may all have met, and that there may be a change of program, by your good grace, nand' dowager." Machigi took a generous sip, a trusting sip, counting it was an unknown servant in charge of the brandy.

"Surely you will take a bottle or two with you," Bren said, "for the comfort of your staff, once you reach your camp."

"That, gratefully, yes. As my guard will have offloaded a supply of net and cordage in your driveway—to better relations with Najida. I trust you to distribute it, nand' paidhi, by your sense of fairness, to the good of the district."

"That I will do, indeed, with thanks, and I shall name you as the donor." *That* was a fine gesture. There had been conflict between the Edi and the Marid—though mostly Edi wreckers had preyed on west coast shipping, no concern at all to Machigi. Putting nets and cordage into the hands of the netmakers would not hurt their business, and, in the Edi way of sharing, they would see that the most deserving cases were helped first.

The brandy flowed and so did outright gossip. Machigi had a likely accurate account of the lord of the Dojisigi, who had had an enemy slip her grasp and turn up in the Senjin Marid with a load of family treasures and far more details about certain agreements and her personal behaviors than the tyrant liked made public. *That* hinted that Machigi did indeed have sources in Senjin. And gossip did please the dowager, particularly as it involved Tiajo.

Machigi left with half a case of brandy—and the understanding that he *would* be free to practice a little chicanery with the dowager's blessing, given an actual shipment of steel from the East.

But his silence on the matter of the Ajuri heir—lingered after him, and the dowager had entered a thoughtful mood.

"Do you still rely on him, aiji-ma?" Bren asked. "I would think he has multiple things in mind—but the main proposal seems sound."

"He has not betrayed a former agent," Ilisidi said. "Or ruined his chances of holding Ajuri. One may be virtue. The other may be . . . well, we shall see. And his darting at this project and that is troublesome. But then, outright paralysis is a problem among other Marid lords. Everybody has taken positions centuries old and nothing moves. We can tolerate Machigi's sliding about, granted he does not find an association more to his advantage and forget to tell us *that* matter."

"He is not likely to find a better position, aiji-ma. One does not believe his thinking is short-term. And there is no one in the Marid that could intimidate him."

"No," Ilisidi said, "not that one. He will have his way until someone stops him, and his bodyguard is adequate, we understand. The lord of Senjin would do well to deal with him *and* the aishidi'tat. Centuries of ties bind Senjin to the Dojisigi—but if Machigi can change that, it would be worth a delay and a load of steel. I may ship him formed rails and ties, to be *sure* his intent is a railroad, and watch *that* reaction."

5

The working of the engine had changed, become the slow and labored chuff that meant they were climbing now, inside the Bujavid tunnel. It was dark, the lights inside the Red Car dimmed to let them sleep, and Cajeiri had found himself a comfortable place against the cushioned wall. He stirred, aware he had slept the whole ride through, hours and hours, slept even through the switching point, a jolt which usually did wake him.

He was not the only one. Antaro was still asleep, and so was Lucasi, and Onami, who received a rough nudge from his partner, Janachi. Mother was awake, but nurse, herself asleep, was holding Seimiro, despite a perfectly fine nest improvised for her on the bench seat at the rear. Uncle Tatiseigi was just stirring.

The train wound its way up the passage, slowly, slowly. He rose carefully and went back to Mother, with a little bow.

"Nomari," Mother said, just loudly enough for him to hear, "will go under Guild escort to the guest apartments. We shall leave him to his escort and go straight up, ourselves. Your father is waking to receive us, but we should go as quietly and quickly as possible. It is halfway to dawn, and most of the Bujavid will be asleep, do we agree?"

"Yes, honored Mother. Absolutely." In his mind was the problem of Boji and that huge rattling cage—with Boji himself, who simply would not hush. But he could not help it. Boji could not sit out on the loading dock for an hour—he would be frantic;

and Eisi and Liedi certainly deserved to rest in comfortable beds into as much of the morning as they pleased. Everyone did.

He went back to his seat and propped his head on his hands.

A turn or two more and the train braked. Impossible to look out and know where they were, but Cajeiri could put it together in his head. They were on track number one, facing the back wall of the station, and they would disembark to the left in that great echoing space. They would walk quickly to the lifts, himself and Mother and Uncle Tatiseigi and their considerable escort. Nomari and the several people with him would go with Nomari's own newly-appointed bodyguard, taking a different lift, if he was going to the first level, where the official guest apartments were. It was important to move quickly, not delay the lift, and to be organized.

One of his bodyguard, Rieni, Guild-senior of that unit, went forward, opened the door and jumped out. The steps would have to come down. Rieni would surely see to that, and there would be Transportation Guild roused out to assist the late-arriving train, as well. The rest of his senior ashid exited first, and then Cajeiri realized—dismaying thought—*he* was not to give precedence to Mother or Great-uncle. They had boarded in a disordered way, since the train had been delayed, but he suddenly thought—they were doing it differently here, in the basement of the Bujavid, and there was nobody in all the aishidi'tat who would take precedence over him except Father, and except Great-grandmother, who had twice *been* aiji. Mother was, among the other changes she had worked in coming out to Tirnamardi, observing protocols.

Mother giving place to him—that had started at Uncle's, in little instances, and now it happened here—it forever would.

That was just a little unsettling.

He left the train, stepping down onto the gray concrete siding, and ordinarily he would have made it a jump—because he always had, from the time the step had been too high for him, until now. He just—stepped down, even if it was a high step, and let his senior aishid join his junior one, as Mother's body-guard moved up, and then Uncle's. Nomari came out of the next car with his appointed staff and his bodyguards, and was with them as they went to the lifts.

Mother and Uncle and he and all their bodyguards could not all fit in a single car, but Guild solved that in their own prece-dence: it was his elder aishid and Mother's that went up with them to the floor they shared with Uncle and with Great-grandmother. Uncle would follow, but Nomari would take an-other lift altogether, and get out on the first floor, in the place people stayed when Father called them personally to the capital, supposing their clan had no Bujavid residence. It was a sort of an honor, to be housed there, instead of down the hill in the hotels.

He and Mother exited on the third floor, their floor, which they shared with Uncle and Great-grandmother and nand' Bren. Nand' Bren was reported in Najida, but even if he was there, he could not travel yet, because *they* had the train *and* the bus. Mani was definitely stranded, having gone to the coast when she could not go to Tirnamardi. He *knew* he would hear about that.

Mother said not a word. They walked the corridor in silence toward home. The doors opened as they arrived, flung wide, and despite the hour, Father met them in the foyer, even before the major d' and his aides could take their traveling coats.

"Back and safe," Father said, with a very happy nod. "Well done."

That was good to hear. That was very good to hear. It might be the first time Father had been that happy with both of them at once. "The bus will be on its way to the coast, then," Father said. "One trusts the problem was minor."

"So they said," Mother answered him. "There is surely no reason for the paidhi to hurry at this juncture."

"No reason except Grandmother," Father said dryly, "who has gone there to meet him."

"She will be angry," Mother said, with more concern than Mother usually showed for that situation.

"She is frustrated. She is determined," Father said. "She is not used to being outmaneuvered. But we shall smooth it over. She will see the advantage in what was done."

Certain things never could be smoothed over, Cajeiri thought. Grandmother and Mother had quarreled forever. Grandmother had not come to Tirnamardi when they were in trouble because Mother was there. Two courts could not show up on Uncle's doorstep at once, and it really *was* two courts. His own little court presence was part of Great-grandmother's most times, but right then, Mother's was attached.

And if Great-grandmother *had* shown up, there would have been problems, and he *never* could have worked out a peaceful agreement with Mother.

But he was thoroughly sorry that nand' Bren was having to deal with mani's outrage.

Father was paying attention to Seimiro now—Seimiro had no idea: she was sound asleep, but Father did look at her, in nurse Beha's arms. "Lord-to-be," Father said, pleased by that, too. "Well done in that, too, Miri."

One wondered what Great-grandmother would say when she heard that his sister was to have Tirnamardi. Things like that were hard to know, because one never knew all of Great-grandmother's reasons.

He *wished* he could just run down to the train station right now and get back on the train and be with it when it picked up Great-grandmother and nand' Bren tomorrow. He would be able to explain it all in a way mani would understand, and nand' Bren would keep everything quiet.

But that was out of the question. He simply stood there and quietly surrendered his traveling coat to staff, as Mother did, and as their bodyguards dispersed to the inner corridor that led sideways off the foyer.

Mother had staff to meet her when she went back to her apartment.

His staff was still downstairs trying to get Boji upstairs.

That was a problem for everybody. Boji was always a problem.

But that *Great-grandmother* was off intercepting nand' Bren—that was more than a problem. When Great-grandmother was *not* in the middle of things, she was making her own plans, and planning things in other directions, and *her* plans would almost certainly involve nand' Bren, and working herself up to some action or other.

Which only meant Great-grandmother was going to come here and have words with Father *and* Great-uncle Tatiseigi.

6

Breakfast was quiet . . . quiet and laced with the dowager's displeasure, since the train was reported *not* to be waiting at Najida station, supplied and ready for them. It would arrive at noon, they were informed, perhaps a little after, and that meant their own arrival would *still* be late at night, and well after dinner, a schedule which the dowager detested.

"Well, well," Ilisidi said, stabbing an egg, "we shall simply have to make do."

One did not believe the dowager was *entirely* upset at Machigi's proposal last night, and in the back of his mind, deeply buried, was a suspicion that Machigi's visit might not even have been a total surprise to the dowager.

But she had given Machigi every opportunity to mention the small fact that he was acquainted with this Ajuri claimant.

And Machigi had not.

"She is thinking," he said to his aishid, back in his suite, as they sat taking post-breakfast tea and mulling over events in the midlands and here on the southwest coast. "She is in such a stage of thought as may make our trip to the capital a very quiet ride."

Ilisidi had indicated previously she would *not* take a late departure, that she had rather take another day here and go tomorrow morning. She seemed, since Machigi's visit, to have changed her mind.

"One waited for Lord Machigi to say something last night,"

Jago said, "and if he did understand her hint, he avoided the topic."

"Lord Machigi certainly provides a very interesting life for his bodyguards," Tano said.

"Self-trained bodyguards," Algini remarked, propping his feet on a footstool. His aishid and his staff had stood through breakfast. Now they relaxed. Narani and Jeladi sat with them, having worked as hard as any of them during the trip, and now having nothing at all to do but wait for the train to arrive. Banichi and Tano were likewise disposed in large, soft chairs that fit atevi stature. They had all endured too-small furniture and cobbled-together mattresses in Port Jackson. On board *Brighter Days*, Mospheiran-built, they had cheerfully slept on deck, fortunately under cloudless skies for the crossing. Now they had begun to relax—and would have relaxed altogether in the comforts of Najida—except for the dowager's presence, with Cenedi, Nawari, and the rest of *her* security and staff, who of course had volumes of information to offload onto Banichi and his associates. There was information aplenty—except on the matter of the visit last night, in which there seemed to be a dearth of information. It was entirely possible the visit had *not* been invited or forecast. It was equally possible Ilisidi had asked for it, and that a certain part of the performance was to get certain information delivered matter of factly to the Assassins' Guild—by way of Banichi and Algini, who had given no indication what *they* would say.

"We can say there was more good news than bad in Cenedi's initial report to us," Banichi said, "Though the dowager is justly concerned about disturbance in the north. They see the naming of the aiji's daughter as Tatiseigi's heir as an entanglement for the aiji's household in midlands politics, but a move that will strengthen Tatiseigi considerably. His rivals can no longer plan so immediately for his replacement."

"In fact," Algini said with some amusement, "they may beseech the gods-more-favorable for Tatiseigi's health and very long life. Having the aiji-consort as regent in Atageini would certainly make a good many people anxious."

"One day Seimiro will have that post," Tano said, "and one day her brother will be aiji in Shejidan, with, apparently, an allied lord in Ajuri—a constellation which the aishidi'tat has *not* seen before. The pressure to name someone to Kadagidi will only mount, now, and certain people may wish to see some lord not so closely tied to this new constellation."

"If Tabini-aji *were* to break up Kadagidi," Algini said, "in the current situation, it would mean there will be no meaningful counterweight at all to Ajuri-Atageini power in the midlands. So that solution would meet opposition."

Bren's own thought had been running down those channels equally, but also—"I think Machigi does see it," he said. "A change in the midlands—and suddenly Machigi wants to change his own relationship with the northern Marid and make an ally and trading partner of Senjin, who is historically the enemy of his district. One does not think this is unrelated."

"There is a man on Jorida Isle," Banichi said, "who both detests Machigi—and does not favor the rail going anywhere it does not now go."

"Hurshina," Bren said. That was no hard guess. Hurshina was not himself a legislator, but he owned a few of them in the lower house.

The richest man in Ashidama Bay—not a lord, but ruling like one. Shipping, fishing—it all was related, all part of Hurshina's jealously defended economic empire. Hurshina had made his objections a problem when *Najida* had passed into a human's hands. Hurshina had been a lifelong problem where the Edi folk were concerned, no matter what the issue. Hurshina would have hated the Edi even if the Edi had never wrecked a Jorida ship—but unfortunately the Edi had indeed made part of their otherwise difficult living off the treacherous rocks on Najida Point, as ships out of Ashidama Bay, largely under Hurshina's colors, moved goods from the southwest up to the port and railhead at Adaran. It had been a long battle of wits, weather, and will, and the fact that the Edi had sworn off wrecking and joined the aishidi'tat as law-abiding citizens had not changed the old antagonism.

Hurshina had likewise incited the townships around Ashidama Bay to an outright state of economic war with the Marid over their shipping passing near Ashidama Bay, harassment and interdiction from the bay, which he assumed would force the Marid to use his ships to move goods. Senjin could ship by rail, but the Taisigin and points south could not.

It had not worked. The Marid, all the Marid ports, with ships capable of the stormy southern coast, still sent ships to and from Adaran. They just put riflemen aboard.

Hurshina had been fairly quiet about Machigi's dealings with the dowager, and Ilisidi's proposed sea link to the Marid. Nobody believed it could be done, and everybody believed it was all politics and smokescreen aimed at the Dojisigin, now in deep disfavor in the north.

Machigi's railroad would increase stock in that suspicion, no question, but the north had not settled its own problems yet.

Where it would ultimately lead—was another matter. There was Kadagidi still lordless.

But say that Machigi, whose own desire for power had included Ashidama Bay not so long ago, was talking to the dowager about a rail link from his capital to the Senjin capital, and might actually persuade Lord Bregani into an agreement—

If that rail line materialized, *that* changed the picture. Hurshina might well conclude that the sea link was a pretense, that the far East was actually going for a rail link with (in Hurshina's mind) the greatest threat in the south, and creating a trade route that would bypass Ashidama Bay altogether, ironically, since Hurshina himself had led the opposition to a rail link from Najida down to his territory. He did not want the Marid shipping goods past him on the water—but he assuredly did not want the townships bypassing his ships and getting goods up to Cobo District by rail.

"Hurshina in the west, Tiajo across the Marid Sea," Algini said, "both have grounds to oppose Machigi's rail link. And both naturally oppose the dowager's trade agreement, on the grounds it helps only Machigi. There is bound to be trouble."

"Does the Guild have specifics as to moves they may make? Can we get information out of Hurshina's establishment?"

"Less than the Guild would wish," Banichi said. "But you, Bren-ji, *you* have a unique asset that may serve in the Marid, and they may be of use—if they are still alive."

"Momichi and Homura," Bren had not thought of those names in a while. They were a Guild unit—or half of one. They were Dojisigi, but trained in the Shejidani Guild, and assigned by Shishogi to serve in their own clan—and when Murini's regime had gone down to defeat, the Shadow Guild had taken their two junior partners as hostages, against their performance as Assassins sent north, assigned to take out Lord Tatiseigi.

It had not worked. They had been caught, could legitimately have been killed on the spot, but they had cast themselves on Lord Tatiseigi's mercy—and Bren's own—a shift of man'chi, in his aishid's uneasy estimation. Bren had accepted it—having no inner sense to tell him, having no desire to see two men killed, either. He had always been uneasy about it. It was like being blind, absolutely bereft of a sense that everyone else could use. Asked what to do with them, he had sent them back south to try to rescue their two partners. But he had had no news from them since.

"I have no sense of this. I truly do not, nadiin-ji. Nor ever have had. Can you contact them?"

"There are ways," Banichi said. "There are signals we can send. They will come to us. We will not go to them. That is the kind of arrangement we have."

"They have never found their partners," Bren surmised.

"No," Banichi said flatly, and Algini:

"They have stayed alive, however—remarkable in itself, where they have been."

"You know where they are," Bren said.

"They have been various places in the Marid," Banichi said. "Headquarters may know more."

"If they are *willing*," Bren said. "That is a condition."

"There is no question of willingness," Banichi said. "Their restraint given a chance to act is less certain. They are a hiltless blade, at the moment. No hand has wanted to pick them up. Not even Machigi."

Algini moved his foot from the chair, sheathed his boot knife. "We will not have you stand close to this team, Bren-ji—we could never be easy in that. They *say* their man'chi is to you, and this may be true—but they were willing to turn, twice."

"Giving them a usefulness," Tano said, "might save them."

Save them. There were emotions a human could understand and emotions a human could somewhat imagine feeling, but the man'chi within a team, between partners within a team . . . that was not one of them. Banichi and Jago had a loss in their past. Tano and Algini had come together in other circumstances, but what lay behind them—there had been doors in that, too, that he felt he should never open, lacking the capacity to understand what was in those dark places. Man'chi, the cohesiveness, the nature of an atevi relationship, was not in his wiring. Love was. Pride was. Instinct to protect was. But he didn't connect those things the same way, didn't have the same triggers and cross-connections.

These two . . . their partners held hostage by their own leadership to force them into an assignment they would not have taken—they'd aborted it, forsworn their man'chi to everything they *had* served and handed it to him, the object of the Shadow Guild's intense opposition. And that move might have killed their partners. They had to be in emotional turmoil. His aishid said the pair was chancy, and giving orders where they were concerned—was just not safe.

"Do what is right to do with them," he said, all the while knowing their judgment of the situation would not risk his safety or that of his allies. "I wish them well, nadiin-ji, but I will *not* endanger you, nor people near me, and I trust you to deal with it. I have no true sense of the pressures on them. Understand me in that."

Banichi nodded solemnly and cast a glance at Algini, whose nod was more a downward glance, that subtle an exchange. Things would happen. Something would result. They would use their judgment.

They talked for a while. Najida was as safe as shipboard for them to sit and discuss sensitive matters—as little chance of eavesdroppers or malice afoot as anywhere on earth, with absolute discretion and good sense on the part of Ramaso's staff, or there would be Ramaso to deal with. Najida staff had once smuggled significant pieces of his Bujavid apartment furniture and two very large, heavy rugs out of the Bujavid and kept them in hiding, with the whole Bujavid in enemy hands. He never forgot that loyalty, that extravagant, defiant gesture. *And* they had not lost anyone doing it.

He trusted Ilisidi, as well . . . not saying she would not lie to him outright, not saying she would not put him in harm's way if needful. How close she had come to killing him herself once upon a time, he was not sure, but she had certainly run the risk of it without a qualm—for the good of herself and her grandson, as she saw it. Her circle of interests was both extremely broad— the whole aishidi'tat, which she had twice ruled; her allies; her household; her province—and extremely narrow in focus: her precious projects, one of which had walked in on them tonight and offered her—

—offered her Dojisigi. And a quiet Marid.

Offered her, remotely possible, Hurshina, or at least a good excuse to make him unhappy.

Her grandson Tabini had the ultimate power of decision. She was in favor of that. Her grandson did not obstruct her projects—one of which had been settlement of the tribal peoples, the Edi and the Gan. She had done that. Settling the uneasy politics of the whole west coast, the activities of which abutted, yes, humans? That remained elusive. From the time when she had ruled the aishidi'tat as regent for her grandson, she had perceived the west coast and its unsettled situation, not the Marid, as the problem that could rise up to undo the aishidi'tat. Humans had created the problem. Humans centuries back had dropped onto the world unasked, lost a war—and the aishidi'tat, to settle the peace, had displaced the tribal peoples from Mospheira, the only territory the aishidi'tat could effectively isolate—and given it to humans on the condition that they stay there. Period. Forever.

Hence his job as paidhi-aiji, which had *used* to be as Mospheira's representative to the aiji's court. Now he was Tabini's own diplomat, not only to the humans, but to other atevi as well, negotiating what Tabini wanted others to do—and the dowager had appropriated him on no few occasions.

He had the feeling that the dowager's intentions were still concentrated on this coast—which was not Ragi, ethnically, which was differently organized from the Ragi clans of the north, and a region which had been a concern to her in both her terms as aiji-regent. It was old business, unfinished business, the problem she had never been able to settle: this region—this coast—with tribal peoples who had been displaced by the human settlement, themselves settled on confiscated land in a region politicked-over for generations by people like Hurshina and, from a considerable distance, Machigi. To this day—the whole southwest quarter of the continent remained a part of the aishidi'tat, but deeply involved in its own politics, its feud with the Tribal Peoples, its tendency to raise up moneyed interests while letting poverty take whole areas of the townships. The population was a mix of broken clans, small remnants of sub-clans generally represented by the Maschi, whose reach extended from the Senjin border to Kajiminda Bay; but mostly conducting a completely fragmented, lordless politics in a model actually closer to Mospheiran society. It was an area where, once, a fractious group of humans *had* held influence, until defeated, at heavy cost. Now wealth and patronage spoke louder than historic clan connections, an uneasy mix of human-like economic structure and atevi institutions, and Hurshina of Jorida ran two great townships and numerous coastal villages with no legal standing to do so.

To their east, with a hunting range claimed right up to the Great Coastal Road, was the Marid, not closely tied to the central government in Shejidan—and not all speaking Ragi, for that matter. An older civilization on the Southern Island, as the Ragi atevi called it—had gone down in ruins, a result of the Great Wave and the subsequent breakdown of civilization there. That lost civilization was Machigi's heritage—refugees from a thousand years ago, and still fighting among themselves. No clan in the Marid had been able to gain power over all the others. Ever.

Machigi's forebears had tried to expand their backdoor territory clear to the west coast—territory that would give them control of the entire southwest coast and all of Ashidama Bay. But their plans had all gone down in local quarrels, infighting among the Marid districts—until Machigi had begun to talk about it again, and gained the loyalty of both the Dausigin and the Sungenin Marid.

That new threat had actually had been fortunate for the north, because Machigi had stood off the Dojisigin and Senjin at a time when Murini's conspiracy, with connections to the Dojisigi, had overthrown Tabini and put the aishidi'tat into the hands of the Shadow Guild. Machigi's allies in the Dausigi and the Sungeni areas had seen that situation as threatening, and they had stood with him—making him a power in the southern Marid that could stand off Dojisigin authority.

At that point *Machigi* had, with Shejidan back under *Tabini's* rule, gotten a message from Ilisidi: resign your ambitions for Ashidama Bay and we can make a deal.

One Bren Cameron had carried that particular message, one of the scarier trips he'd made, in a career that had found him on the wrong end of gunfire more times than he could count. That offer had been one of the dowager's more outrageous moves. But one that worked.

Ilisidi was unique among atevi. She had constitutionally distrusted humans—but she had decided to trust *him*. She had been and was still a bastion of mediaeval ways and attitudes: her holdings at Malguri, in the far East, scarcely had electric light. But she had supported atevi involvement on the human space station, involved *herself* and her precious great-grandson on a voyage to settle a human problem lightyears distant, had involved herself again when an alien power came calling, and, just as recklessly as she had dealt with one Bren Cameron, she had broken through an alien language barrier and *talked* to beings that well might have ended atevi and humans.

Dealing with other atevi, in the Marid? That had been no stretch of *her* imagination. Machigi was not all that foreign.

Remarkable woman. Change kept happening. And Ilisidi kept running before the wind, using technology and people with ruthless practicality—but with a fierce sense of *her* people, *her* way and *her* *assets*.

So now . . . Machigi suddenly produced an ambition to have a railroad link to the main system, which was going to annoy hell out of Senjin and the Dojisigin *and* upset the west coast into the bargain?

Oh, yes, she had listened.

Yes, there were advantages—God, there were. If Senjin could be weaned from the Dojisigin *everyone* would be better off . . . except for the Dojisigin. And the potential reaction from the Southwest Coast . . .

Currently, the use of the rail's great loop was highly cargo dependent. When the Red Train finally reached them tomorrow, it *might* have taken the shorter route, coming down the steep grade from the mountains, a route which ran from the capital of the aishidi'tat to the capital of the Senjin Marid, where it would take a westward turn through Maschi clan holdings and over to Najida, But that would be a very unusual routing for the aiji's personal train—which was as security-sensitive as a train could be. No. It would almost certainly take the substantially longer route, going north out of Shejidan before angling west, using the transcontinental rail until it took the southern spur to the Najida-Adaran line. Najida station—by no means a rail yard—still had a turning-wye that let it reverse, making it an easy matter for the Red Train to go back the way it had come— its usual pattern.

Likewise, heavy cargo out of the Marid did not return north up the steep grades and switchbacks: it used the much longer route, to Najida and north, conducting freight traffic from Doji-sigin and Senjin, to trade for things the Marid did not produce.

So now Machigi wanted to build a rail link northward to the Senjin capital to join that trade, a link to carry trade goods to Shejidan and receive northern goods in the south.

It had been part of the plan—as Machigi's trade with the East by sea began to find its way in—a link not to Senjin, but over-land to Najida.

They had planned on time. The Tribal People, the Edi, of Najida and Kajiminda were determined to preserve their rural peace. If Machigi's plan went through, they could not turn Na-jida into a major station.

And there was yet another factor to be considered. Ilisidi had her own plans, already in progress—plans that included im-provement of the transcontinental rail that linked her province to the aishidi'tat, and the building of warehouses in Hasjuran, on the transmontane line, to the excitement of one Lord Topari, who sat atop the southern pass. It had seemed an economic move: furs and leather out of Hasjuran were competition for her own district, but taken another way, they were supply. A minor project—Hasjuran. A warehouse or two. It had mills. Tanneries. A processing plant. The mountain air produced a unique dried meat product.

The tiny three-clan district of Hasjuran, highest pass except the continental divide, had the last station before the steep descent to Senjin.

Her encouragement, her economic favor and social advancement of rough-edged Lord Topari of Hasjuran—which had seemed typical of one of the dowager's constant little projects—was unifying the fur industry all of it?

Now came Machigi, with a proposal to reverse the order of ship-building and rail, advancing a scheme to pry Senjin away from alliance with the Dojisigin Marid, and into alliance with the Taisigin Marid, Machigi's district, on Senjin's southern border.

Senjin might have felt the activity in Hasjuran as ominous, hanging almost literally over his head.

Dojisigi, east of Senjin and across the Marid Sea, might likewise feel a cold breeze off the heights.

Neither would like Machigi's trade agreement with the dowager, but most of the aishidi'tat felt it would never come to fruition, that the seas were too rough, the storms too unpredictable, and that the sea trade would only be a gesture, a clever ploy to get the Shejidani guilds admitted into Machigi's district, something which might prove far more important to the north.

Now—Machigi, in a clandestine visit, indicated Senjin was vulnerable.

He had had amazingly few cares coming into dock, where he had assumed everything would come down to a pleasant evening with Toby and Barb and people he trusted implicitly, before a return to the capital and resumption of business, which *might* be a shade tense given Tatiseigi's doings in the north—but nothing that couldn't be handled at leisure.

Now—he had cares enough to keep him up late at night, just

thinking, thinking, thinking—in which matter he was sure Il-isidi was well ahead of him, benevolent in her intentions toward him and his, generally, but, *God!* there were so many points of risk here.

Tall stacks of china, the atevi proverb had it. Very tall stacks were at issue, centuries in the making.

7

The Red Train was—Cajeiri had wanted to be notified—now out of the city and on its way to Najida, and the late family dinner, including Father, was done with a minimum of fuss. Everybody was exhausted—hard to say why, since most of the day had been sitting and waiting, but Cajeiri wanted nothing so much as to stop moving and not answer questions any longer. Boji had had his cage-rattling tantrum in the outer hall and on arrival in the suite, but even he had quickly settled, curled into a furry ball on a perch, likewise weary from the trip. Eisi and Liedi had more right than any of them to plead exhaustion, having ridden in baggage with Boji, but they still insisted on unpacking and dealing with wardrobe, their real and essential duty, as if to say—remember, young gentleman? *This* is what we signed on to do.

Cajeiri, in the bedroom of his own suite, having shed both coat and vest, on the edge of taking off his boots and preparing for bed, collapsed into his soft bedroom chair and stared, wondering how they were all going to manage.

He had had four bodyguards when he started his trip. Now he had eight, in the same little suite of rooms. His four longest serving were only a little older than he was—that was Antaro and Jegari, Veijico and Lucasi, two sets of brothers and sisters. His father had added the gray-haired seniors on the trip: Rieni and Haniri, Janachi and Onami, who were far more than high-ranking veterans. They were Guild *instructors*, respected, and—for which he was very grateful—possessed of a good sense of humor, along with a willingness to adapt and teach, and flexibility enough to let him escape with his younger aishid, just occasionally.

His younger aishid had offered the seniors their beds, in two rooms attached to Cajeiri's bedroom, the proper place for a lord's seniormost security to sleep. But Rieni and his unit had declined the courtesy, saying they had already solved that problem, and would take quarters right against the bedroom wall, in the rooms that belonged to the servants' passage, moving Eisi and Liedi and Father's general staff in sequence down a couple of doors. The servants' hall offered, Rieni said dryly, all-hours access to the kitchen, and gave them the ability to come and go without waking the household, and no, they were too high-ranking to worry about appearances and prerogatives. They would manage quite comfortably, given a few needful items.

It was generously done. His senior bodyguard technically outranked everybody but the very highest clearances, even Father's bodyguard. They had seniority just short of the Assassins' Guild Council.

And they had a perfect right to have asked for far more than a place in a common hall with domestic staff, but Onami said slyly that they would be furnishing those rooms with a very wide permission, and taking a third room as a backstairs security post—his personal security, apart from the security post Father's guard maintained. They wanted television, armchairs, a small refrigerator and a microwave. Guild Headquarters would supply the rest. And they wanted to section off the area they needed, create a new doorway, wall off the upward stairs and maybe keep the downward stairs and take some storage space below . . . it would entail a lot of construction.

It scared him a little, these new arrangements that had arrived and started rearranging his household. His expanded aishid would henceforth protect *him* as separate from Father, or Mother, or his sister, who were not, emphatically *not*, in his mind, disposable—but he understood he *was* their primary, their principal charge, and that was the way it had to be. He was fortunate nine, and he had seen far too many assassination attempts—one during this last trip—not to mention Aunt Geidaro being murdered while she was on the phone.

And curiously enough, he had actually felt more nervous about the new bodyguard Father had added to protect him than he had been about the people who might want to attack him, though he knew in his good sense that that was a stupid way to feel. And certainly he had been glad to have them at Tirnamardi. There was nothing they were doing that put him in *more* danger. It only pointed up that there *was* more danger, there would be and would always be, and that people had died, and could die.

Aunt Geidaro was gone now. He so hoped cousin Nomari could stay alive.

Someday, Atageini was going to belong to his sister. And someday he would be aiji. Someday. Someday. Someday. He did not want that to happen for a long, long time.

But—and that was what upset his stomach—it could happen any given day.

That was what all this security meant. The world was always changing. But suddenly, throughout the world and above it, a lot of changes were happening at once. Humans had been forbidden on the mainland for hundreds of years, except for the paidhiin, and in a very short time, for the first time since the War of the Landing, thousands of human strangers were going to land on atevi soil, even if they were being shipped right away over to Mospheira.

And goods were going to fall down from the space station on the petal sails, as they had done with people aboard, hundreds of years ago. The new petal sails, carrying only cargo, would land in a hunting range shared by the North Coastal association and Ajuri. Some of those goods were atevi goods. Others would be put on ships and sent to Port Jackson.

That had never happened before.

And he had three human associates now living in a sort of manor house in Port Jackson. So close—compared to their being on the space station—but still so very far from him, in a city that looked nothing like an atevi township. He wanted to call them. He so wanted to hear their voices. There would come a time he *could* call them. That was the *good* part of the changes.

But everybody said that they were settling in and should not be distracted yet. Their parents were with them, well, Gene's was, and Artur's were, but Irene's mother was still up on the station, in a good deal of trouble, and with Irene not speaking to her. He wished he could do something about *that*, but he had no idea how, or whether it ever could be fixed, or even if it should be fixed. Irene's mother . . . was a puzzle to him.

"You look worried, Jeri-ji," Jegari asked, dropping down to one knee by his chair. "Is there a problem?"

"Nothing that was not there yesterday," he said.

Antaro was nearby. Lucasi and Veijico came over to hear what Jegari asked.

"So what *is* the trouble?" Antaro asked.

"I think Eisi and Liedi should have a holiday. They really should. But they cannot." He cast a glance at the large filigree cage, at the black ball of fur hunched on one of the perches. "Boji is only waiting to wake up in a bad mood tomorrow, and upset the whole household. One feels stupid even to be talking about Boji, but *he* is a problem." He drew a deep breath, and sighed. "I have decided I have to find a place for him, and I have spoken to Onami on the matter. Eisi and Liedi have been very patient with me. But Boji is a problem for everybody. And I cannot go on imposing on my servants. They came to do far more for us than feed Boji eggs."

"Are you determined to let him go?" Jegari asked.

"I have to. I believe I have to, for his sake as well as the household's."

"I think Eisi and Liedi will actually miss the little creature," Antaro said. "So will we. He has saved us more than once, a very effective alarm in the night—excepting the times he simply wants his breakfast at an indecent hour. But if you truly are determined . . ."

"His manners will not improve." Things had been flung, and broken, and stolen, not to mention a scratch on the dining table his staff took special pains to cover. It was historic furniture, all of it, and now the table had Boji's signature, as long as his own hand. "And he is cramped in that cage. I owe it also to Eisi and Liedi. And to him."

"Shall we consult with Onami, then?"

"That, yes. Finding him a place will solve one problem."

"What is the other, nandi?"

He hesitated to say. He hesitated a long moment, not wanting to cause trouble, not wanting to sow discontent, as Great-grandmother would say. But coming home—realizing that the changes wrought on his trip were coming through the door with them—that *everything* was changed . . .

"One is disturbed, Gari-ji, not even to have been *warned* I was getting another aishid. I was upset at first. And I was truly glad they were with us in the trouble at Tirnamardi. But here we are, home, and we have no room, and things are having to change. You were not warned, either, were you?"

"We were not. But they are the best we could hope for. And there was bound to be a second team. The heir has to have two."

"I *cannot* break my promise that you should be first."

"Jeri-ji," Antaro said, "they are *by far* senior. The promise is to us, and we can forgive it."

"But I cannot put them in your place. I will not. And I do not know how to sort it out politely." .

"They did not displace us from our rooms. They are trying very hard not to disturb the order of things."

"But they displaced Eisi and Liedi further down the hall. Into a *storeroom.*"

"That is tonight," Lucasi said. "But the whole hall is going to be for them and your staff. That is the word from your father's people. They will be installing security doors and clearing space."

"If we were a proper household, Eisi and Liedi would have rooms nearest my door."

"More important that the seniors be nearest," Veijico said.

"And the new team is the best we could get," Cajeiri said. "I know. I know that. But—I do not want us to change, nadiin-ji. I cannot send the seniors away. I agree I should not. We need them, but—"

"We do absolutely need them," Jegari said. "For *our* training and your safety. We want to be *good*. They can make us be."

"But I cannot have them displacing you or upsetting everything in the household. They are tremendously skilled. We are all safer for their being there. But how do we manage at home—with them? They are just—older."

"Which is their usefulness," Antaro said. "We have talked about this, all four of us. And we are *young*, Jeri-ji. We have been young together, and we have learned together, but the older we get, knowing our responsibility, the more we worry about our protecting you, because we have *not* been through the Guild courses. We are *not* as well-trained as we could be. We have learned things from Cenedi and Banichi that we would never have learned in courses, and we have codes we are not supposed to have . . . that we must admit to the seniors, and trust they know why we have them. But we do *not*, sometimes, know the simple things we should have learned . . . procedures, the working of certain equipment that we shall need. Veijico and Lucasi have at least had some higher courses. They were actually put into the field. While we . . ."

"You all do very well," Cajeiri said. "Banichi says so. Cenedi says so."

"But, Jeri-ji, we dread, we greatly dread, the day we make a mistake that could let harm reach you. Yes, we are a little set back by their arrival. We dread being fools in front of them. How could we not? But . . . they are *instructors*, and we are *all* benefitting. They have pointed out things we need to know. *Should* know. They have the ability to reach sources in the Guild we did not even know we had available . . . and they will open doors at the highest levels, even for your *father's* aishid, that is how much they help. We are not unhappy in this arrival. Everybody in the household can benefit from their presence,"

"And there is a political point," Jegari added quietly. "They are not Taibeni. *Nobody* can object to them."

Father's mother had been Taibeni. Father had insisted on Taibeni for his own guard, after the betrayal of the unit the Assassins' Guild had given him. The Guild had objected to such heavy reliance on Father's maternal clan, and so had the west coast. Great-grandmother had lent senior Eastern Guild for Father's guard, but politics in general was not quite happy with that, either, nor quite happy with Antaro and Jegari, also Taibeni, as *his* senior bodyguards. Veijico and Lucasi were highlanders, at least *not* Taibeni, but not known quantities, either.

His new aishid, however, being central Guild to the hilt, with ties to the Council—that would make the Guild Council so much happier and it would make the legislature a lot happier, too. He understood that. He might be only fortunate nine, but he well knew how households were woven together by staff with all sorts of ties. Everybody was connected to somebody who was connected to somebody else, and Council connections meant an instant audience for high-level problems—without going through the lower halls of office. Even *Father* had had difficulties, when he had taken a lower-level bodyguard and fought Guild Administration and Guild rules.

But there had been other reasons for that opposition, too, as it was a very good thing Father had taken the action he had. Guild Administration had changed, in the same action that had broken the Shadow Guild.

"The seniors say, too," Jegari said, "that they hope to be here at least a few years and continue to teach us."

"You are senior," Cajeiri said. "I said you were, and they cannot change that."

"It will only confuse the household, Jeri-ji. They are willing to take orders through us, but they *are* seniormost, and outsiders will call them that—we are perfectly willing to have them take that name for their tenure here, and receive communications, without confusing your father's staff, or the Messengers' Guild. Someday they will retire and we will truly be senior, and because you have to have a double guard, we will be taking on a younger aishid ourselves. Meanwhile *you* will be safer, and we will become better protection than we would otherwise have been."

"Your junior aishid plans to keep you *alive*," Veijico said. "And these four will help us when Banichi and Cenedi are *not* with us. Eisi and Liedi are not unhappy in this change, either. Probably they are not happy to ride in the baggage car with a screaming parid'ja, but they are very happy in being your staff. Should they spend their whole lives doing what they do now? No. But now your father will be sending you out alone. Your travels may increase. Your household is growing, and you also have your associates, who may visit, perhaps at Najida, perhaps without nand' Bren and his aishid in residence. So yes, we shall adjust. Nothing essential will change. We do not mind being called junior. To them, we are."

"I shall call you younger. Not junior."

"That will do," Antaro said. "And moving Boji out will ease the work Eisi and Liedi do, so that will help them, too. Staff is going to modify that storeroom out in the servant's passage into two rooms, pleasant rooms, with all the comforts staff has."

"Maybe with television," Lucasi said. "The seniors are asking for it. It should be easy to do."

"Well, if *they* have television, *you* should have it," Cajeiri said.

"*You* should have it," Lucasi said.

He had not thought of that. It would never do in the sitting room. But it would be nice in the bedroom. He remembered the archives, from the ship. And horses and dinosaurs. They all could enjoy them. He could improve his ship-speak. That was the good part.

And his aishid was not unhappy with Rieni's unit, and Eisi and Liedi *would* have less to do if they did find a home for Boji. Four more people needed things—cleaning, packing, all sorts of things. He was worried about finding rooms for everybody. But if they could make the servants' passage into a comfortable place . . .

He had thought about growing up, and about his own household, and finding more room—someday. He had been sure when he had gotten back from the space station that the walls would close about him again and swallow him up—his tutor was a good tutor, and not unpleasant; but there would be dinners he had to attend and court sessions he had to attend, and parties he had to attend, and it would just all get back to routine the same as ever.

He had not expected a trip on his own to Tirnamardi. Nobody had expected Nomari showing up. He had *still* not gotten back to his lessons, but that was going to happen, he was well sure of it.

Except—now he had his associates living just across the strait, and he had letters to write and contact with them by phone—he had to work out how that would be; and, Father had promised, he could have his associates visit. Someday.

And meanwhile he had Uncle wanting to set up new stables and get Jeichido out of his herd before there was trouble with the old herd-leader; and then there was little sister, who was now heir to Great-uncle, and who would *need* a canny older brother to keep her safe *and* adventurous.

It was not just Eisi and Liedi who needed help. *He* did. Or he would. His life was expanding, as if the circle of everything he dealt with was just getting larger and larger and larger all in a handful of days, and he could not afford to make mistakes.

The way he had not been a fool when things at Tirnamardi had gotten dangerous, and he had sat back and not ventured to go outside into trouble—he could not afford to be a fool in the future. He had to have people around him who were not fools, and who, like Antaro and Jegari, would never hesitate to tell him the truth.

8

The market truck had gone out under guard, taking the crates to the train station, and before it had gotten back from that mission, the estate bus arrived from the same place. It had been black and red and shiny, and it came back now with a good deal of unpainted aluminum. Replaced windows and windshield still had their stickers and markings on them, and by the patchwork and replacements, it had been a shocking lot of gunfire. One was appalled—not at the sad condition of the bus—but at the seriousness of the assault on people of Tatiseigi's household.

"That woman," Ilisidi muttered. "And her associates."

Well, the tires were sound and the bus was promised to be running well enough. They boarded, with all their people, and Bren and Ilisidi rode together in a great deal of silence—not angry silence, but a thinking silence, and one certainly knew better than to intrude with observations when the dowager was thinking. They shared a cup of tea on the way—the bus had not lost all its amenities, even with bullet rips in some of the seat cushions.

"We missed an interesting time at Tirnamardi," was the dowager's eventual comment on the matter of the bus, to which Bren replied, "One is very glad to hear that the house is safe—and that nand' Tatiseigi himself is back in the Bujavid."

"One does not mourn that vicious woman," Ilisidi said, referring to Geidaro, in Ajuri. "We may mourn the information lost. She was likely to spill secrets to save herself. But they have opened up all the cellars of Ajiden to inspection, now. Fire failed and the secrets there will be interesting. Still, one does not believe we are done with that lot of scoundrels, and we are glad to know my great-grandson is out of Tirnamardi at the moment. We will very soon have to deal with Kadagidi. And Machigi has chosen this moment to light a fire in the Marid. He claims his reason is a tantrum by that child in Dojisigi. There will be much more to it. As there is much more to Machigi's plan than he has confided in us, one suspects."

"One hesitates to trust him," Bren said, "without knowing his reasons."

"Indeed not. Perhaps he thinks us too busy in the north and not paying him sufficient attention. But that would be a simple answer. The Marid is the Marid, and moves for its own reasons." She lapsed back into silence, frowning in thought, and not all of it, Bren was sure, focused on Machigi.

One did rather wonder how the conversation would go between Tatiseigi and Ilisidi once she was alone with him. Not hot, no. Temper was a weakness Ilisidi did not choose to demonstrate. But there would be discussion. Had there been an opportunity for Lord Tatiseigi to consult her, before Tatiseigi had done what he had done?

It was not Tatiseigi who had moved on this one. It was Damiri—wholly Damiri, by what Bren understood, and he did not think it was spur of the moment—not from the time she had conceived a second child.

Ilisidi had had Tatiseigi as her closest ally. The reliable. The dependable. The devoted.

Now here was an heir to Ajuri who might know Machigi personally. Here was an heir to Atageini clan intimately related to her great-grandson. Here was a move, a major move, by Tatiseigi—without even a phone call to Ilisidi.

But how could the man have refused what Damiri offered, under the circumstances?

And here was Machigi on his own doorstep wanting the dowager's help, in effect, to take over the entire Marid.

Did the whole thing somehow form a design of interconnecting threads?

The aishidi'tat will ultimately face the indignation of the west coast, with all its problems; Machigi may ally with Senjin and have Dojisigi literally cornered against the mountains.

A man with connections to Machigi has turned up to take Ajuri, on one side of Tatiseigi, and Kadagidi, on the other, is still to fill.

He had no idea in what quarter of that maze Ilisidi's thoughts were wandering, but it was a very silent bus ride.

Twice aiji-regent. The outsider who forced a close national union on the continent with most of the lords resisting, and handed it to her grandson.

Damiri has waited nine years to challenge her and make a move.

Tatiseigi has been maneuvered into a corner—but one he wanted desperately—and he accepted Damiri's daughter without consulting Ilisidi—or, possibly, without consulting Tabini himself.

What occupies Ilisidi's mind right now? The one—or the other?

It was always a mistake to try to figure atevi emotion, when it was this complicated. One knew where her heart and her expectations were anchored: her great-grandson, to whom she was entrusting her life's work, the aishidi'tat. And the one was in danger of being maneuvered by his mother, and the other was potentially under assault by an old enemy under the control of an undisciplined young tyrant in the Dojisigin.

What is she feeling?

One thing she will not do is melt.

She will not give up her grandson, her great-grandson, or

her allies. Most of all she will not give up her plans for the aishidi'tat.

How do I advise her? What do I say to her that will make sense?

In a word . . . nothing.

Let her think. This is no territory for a human.

The Red Train offered unblemished comfort, and they could sit and sip tea in red velvet luxury while things loaded. The bus went fairly smoothly back onto the flatcar that had brought it, to be dropped off for repair. And simultaneously, with local workers to help, crates went into the baggage car.

In short order, they were ready to move.

There was, besides the Red Car's usual amenities, the dowager's serving staff and a galley which gave forth all manner of light delicacies for a formal tea—no few of a sort poisonous to humans, but delicious spice to atevi tastes, clear as the arrangement of red flowers and black stones in the center that it was a meal mostly aimed at Ilisidi—her favorite things, set up by Bujavid staff. The paidhi-aiji who had arrived in the center of the controversy had an auspicious trio of white flowers and a pale branch in the mix, vastly overcome by red, and he did not need Jago's warning to avoid the sauces.

One was very glad to stay understated at the moment, while the dowager worked on improving her own mood.

"Well," was Ilisidi's comment, seeing the extravagant display. A somewhat mollified: *"Well."*

They settled on the comfortable bench seat, with small tables placed; staff, both bodyguards and attending servants, were likewise made comfortable for the trip.

Then the dowager said quite calmly, as if she had settled her mind and come to terms with the issue: "Clearly my grandson will need to focus on the changing situation in the north. Clearly then *we* may dispose the issues in the south."

She even smiled when she said it.

That, Bren thought, was potentially worrisome, but it was better than confrontation with Damiri. She was coming to a decision on Machigi, and on a quarter of the continent for which she had had plans and seen them frustrated for decades.

She had made some sort of decision.

"Trust your great-grandson, aiji-ma," he said, perhaps completely off-topic regarding the dowager's intended discussion, but direct to a major point. "One does not believe your teaching can produce anything in him but good sense, and I have no doubt he will gain his sister's man'chi. A human can hardly judge, but he will always be fortunate nine years older than she. He will advise her by principles *you* have taught him, aiji-ma. And if I understand anything at all, he will be extremely anxious now to hear your opinion of his reasoning."

"The aiji-consort lost *no* time. She has planned this from before that child was born."

"It may be. But was not Lord Tatiseigi's original plan decades ago to tie Ajuri to him, to stand off Kadagidi?"

"That woman has her own agenda."

"And cannot it be fulfilled, and still serve Lord Tatiseigi's interests? The aiji-consort's daughter will be important, certainly, but *your* grandson is aiji and your great-grandson will be, one day. He is the one who will deal with the future. And he is *far* more like his father."

"Inconveniently independent," Ilisidi muttered. But the expression was softer.

"And if his sister should likewise take after her father, aiji-ma, who will understand her more than her brother? And if she does take after her mother, do you think her brother cannot understand that, too?"

"My grandson to this day does not read that woman well."

"Perhaps, aiji-ma, Damiri-daja is changing. Does not time and experience have some effect? She has gotten past her feud with her uncle. That has changed."

"Ha! That has changed one way and the other for decades."

"Now, however, she has a daughter who is also *your* great-granddaughter."

There was a silence after that. "That should worry everyone," Ilisidi said, but seemed in slightly better humor. "Well, well, there are years to prove, are there not? How much will you tell my *grandson* of my interview with Machigi?"

God. What a question. Tabini needed to know all of it. "I am bound to tell him, aiji-ma."

"But you can cast it favorably or unfavorably, can you not?"

"I shall give both facts and opinion, aiji-ma, as I always do. I know only one thing for fact. You have *never* harmed the aishidi'tat. I am certain your grandson will ask what you intend to do with Machigi's idea. May one then ask—what *do* you intend?"

A slow, wicked, absolutely pleased smile spread on Ilisidi's face. Even the eyes participated, hooded and golden. "My favorite human. You are predictably unpredictable in your own actions. I also hold the opinion *you* would never harm the aishidi'tat."

"I would not, aiji-ma."

"Well," Ilisidi said, smiled, asked for more tea, and that was the end of discussion on that matter, all the way to Shejidan. Ilisidi remained quiet and thoughtful through a very, very long train ride.

One was glad to nap, finally, and not to anticipate what one was going to say to Tabini—but it assuredly had to be something.

Arrival in the Bujavid station was late. Ilisidi was stiff and out of sorts about it, which was actually a good sign—she was not actively planning anything except a late supper, and early bed.

Bren delayed on the train platform with a staff matter— deliberately delayed regarding the disposition of his personal wardrobe crate, a maneuver which let Ilisidi have the lift to herself and Cenedi and *her* bodyguard, leaving her staff behind to manage *her* baggage, and not dividing up the Guild presence.

One could feel a little sorry for Cenedi—Cenedi would get the benefit of the dowager's bluntly honest and probably peeved discussion tonight: that, one was certain would happen as soon as they were off the lift and safely enclosed again in their own apartment upstairs. Cenedi was the dowager's longest-present and closest confidant, her first advisor, having her ear before anyone, be it her grandson or the paidhi-aiji, and *Cenedi* would quietly talk her into a reasonable course and better frame of mind. Bren believed it, as he believed Cenedi would relay any alteration of her already-stated views over to Banichi, and Banichi would tell *him* how things were really going.

No, things were not always smooth with the dowager when she was crossed. He had his own introduction to her to teach him that. But he was, so far as she was concerned, one of hers, and that was that. She would reach a conclusion. With luck, she would tell him what she would do before she did it, and she would certainly want to know what he had said to Tabini and how Tabini viewed it.

Would she *ask* Tabini? Oh, that awarded far too many points to Tabini. That would not happen until she already knew the answer.

He was ever so glad to reach his own door, and to be welcomed in by staff—the same, he was sure, for all of them. Hands took their traveling coats, and there was the aroma of pizza in the air, a household tradition—despite their sojourn on Mospheira and a lengthy exposure to that cuisine. It was home. It was perfect. The bowl of correspondence on the foyer table had been reduced to three ribbon-tied bundles of cylinders, neatly arranged, examined as to urgency, and in a number far, far better than he had expected.

His valets, Koharu and Supani, had filled Narani and Jeladi's posts in his absence. Those four were all smiles and happy to have things back to normal. Bindanda was there, Cook, come out from his kitchen to see them arrive. The domestics were there, who saw to the details, who kept everyone's laundry and the kitchen linens and service pieces in good order. There was so much work in a household—he was only the public face of it; there was correspondence and accounting, purchasing and preparing and keeping records. His was not even an establishment that held regular dinners and large meetings, but he received reports, stacks and bundles of reports, which had to be sifted for significance. All the machinery of the paidhi's office closed about him with the comfort of home, familiar faces, absolute trust and safety.

And a quick scan proved the message-cylinders, thank God, were not worrisome.

He could go into his own sitting room, cast himself into his favorite chair and draw a truly easy breath for the first time since he'd come ashore. Banichi and the rest could go shed the armament, hang up their gear and truly rest, which they had not done since they had *left* this apartment. Narani would take up his post as major domo, but tonight was holiday, the buffet was being laid out in the dining room, the pizzas in the oven filled the place with the scent of baking bread, and all of them who had made the trip were to do nothing but let others serve.

The dowager was likely receiving the same sort of welcome. Lord Tatiseigi was, staff reported to him, in his residence down the hall; Damiri-daja, Cajeiri and the baby were safely home in Tabini's apartments next door; the claimant for Ajuri was lodged in diplomatic splendor downstairs, and the Bujavid had not broken out in armed conflict.

He had arrived prepared to be summoned over to Tabini's apartment to debrief tonight, but no summons came, for which he was deeply grateful. He had the supper Bindanda had laid out, and after that there was his own bed, exactly as he liked it, and Jago came to share it. The both of them were tired, but not that tired, and the fire, after so many days of caution, was in full force. The Bujavid was always cold—Shejidan had the winds off the mountain ridge; and there was a spot in the middle of an atevi-scale bed where shared warmth made a common refuge.

Home. Finally.

9

The summons from Tabini did come, for a meeting after breakfast, and breakfast was, after all the extravagance of supper, a small one—a little toast, an egg, a cup of tea—anticipating there would be tea before the meeting, as well.

And it was to be not the downstairs office, but the intimacy and informality of Tabini's sitting room, for which Bren was also grateful. It was just a walk next door, with only Tano and Algini in attendance, turn about in shifts, as Banichi and Jago enjoyed a leisurely morning and a late breakfast.

They knocked at the door, were admitted to the foyer.

And ambushed from the adjacent apartment—Cajeiri, in shirt sleeves and barefoot, no less, in the foyer.

"Nand' Bren!" An enthusiastic, child's deep bow. And a beaming face. "One is glad you are safe!"

"Was there a doubt?" Bren answered.

"Never!" the rascal said. "Not with your aishid!" As two of Cajeiri's own arrived from the apartment, clearly taken by surprise. "And my associates?"

"All very well," Bren said, "and settled in—you remember Kate-aiji. *She* is with them. And Sandra-daja, whom you have not met. But she is there, taking care of all of them."

"I so want a phone call!"

"Be patient, young gentleman. But I do have—" He reached inside his coat, and extracted a thick packet of densely-printed paper, folded in the island way.

"Letters!"

"They are letters from your associates, young sir. I was handed them before I left, and they are clearly printed. I have asked your father, so thank him for the permission. There is a slight difficulty—they are part in Ragi, part in ship-speak, all in human characters. But I think you have been able to work it out in the past."

"I can do it!" Cajeiri said, receiving them into his hands, and gave another bow. "Thank you, nand' Bren! Thank you!"

"Ask me if you have any questions. They wrote them before landing, so they have no information on their new lodgings, but I can say it is a handsome old building, historic and very comfortable. They will be learning to write in Ragi, so I dare say they will be more informative in their next letters, which will come now with the regular mail."

"Thank you, thank you!" Cajeiri fairly beamed. "Thank you ever so much. And one is very glad you are home!"

"That I am," Bren said, and meant it.

"Is everything all right with mani?"

"Your great-grandmother is naturally concerned about your welfare and Lord Tatiseigi's, and she has a great deal to think about, but she is indeed considering the changes, young gentleman. She is quite tired from the trip, so take that into account, but it would be good for you to talk to her."

A very sober face. "Yes," Cajeiri said. "She is not at all pleased, is she?"

"She is concerned for you and for your sister. It would be best for you to talk to her without too much information from me."

"One understands," Cajeiri said solemnly. "I shall."

Brave lad, Bren thought, but a boy who understood his great-grandmother. He would go. And he would find his own way to Ilisidi's good graces.

Himself, he received a nod from Tabini's Guild-senior. Tabini was waiting, and he had to go.

"I shall give your father my report," Bren said.

"Nand' Bren." Cajeiri gave a polite little bow, and stayed as Bren went down the hall to the meeting.

Barefoot and shirt sleeves was not the form in which to meet mani on any day. But, too, full court dress represented Father's heir, and all the changes; and Cajeiri had a sense that his country wardrobe, comfortable and junior-like, plain leather and a dark red shirt—was the best way to pay the needful visit.

Nothing puffed up and ceremonial. Mani might be all prickly and insist on cups and cups of tea, but he was going to come in quietly and just sit there and listen if he had to. He really, truly did not want to be caught between Mother and mani in a quarrel about Great-uncle.

Mani was up, and had just had breakfast. His seniormost Guild found that out from Nawari, messaging up and down the hall. Mani was willing to see him.

That had not been a given.

"One does not believe this is the best day to introduce everybody," Cajeiri said to Rieni, and Rieni wisely agreed—Great-grandmother's disposition was no secret at all, and that her mood was not going to be the best . . . they were all keenly aware that the absence of the bus had inconvenienced her significantly.

So their understanding was one problem solved. Veijico and Lucasi were happy to stay behind—going just down the hall in the Bujavid, on an informal visit, did not take an entire Guild unit. So it was only Antaro and Jegari, whom mani had known longest, and who also were capable of being very still and attracting no attention. Hunting skills were very useful when Great-grandmother was in a bad mood.

As for himself, he knew what he was walking into, and he was resolved to accept anything that came. He took his precious letters with him, because, well, if mani decided he could wait a while, he would have something to do; and if mani decided to bring down storm and thunder, they were a comfort just being there. His country coat had ample pockets, and he put them in one, and headed out of the foyer and down the hall, seeing nobody on duty outside, which meant it would be a very bad idea to knock *without* an invitation. He had Antaro do that, and it was a very quiet knock, three soft raps.

Nawari let them in, advised them mani was in her sitting room, and that was probably the best news he could ask for. Tea. There would certainly be tea and a moment to sit and take stock of mani's mood. He hoped for it, and just to let mani look at him and maybe find herself a little less upset.

He entered the sitting room: Antaro and Jegari quietly took stations in the usual places, with Cenedi in sole attendance on mani. Cajeiri took the appropriately placed chair and sat down very quietly, very properly.

Mani was reading letters. She did not look at him. She signaled a servant, who busied himself at the sideboard and offered tea—mani first, and then a cup for him.

Mani took a sip. He took a sip.

"Well," mani said, finally looking at him, head to toe. "Well. *You* are very informal today."

Mani was not. Mani was in court dress, black, with rubies at her collar.

"Yes, mani-ma," he said.

"Is there a reason?"

"I am home, mani-ma," he said.

Mani nodded. "One can appreciate that. Home. So." She set down her cup. He set down his. "So. I am told you have news."

"I have letters," he said. It was not the brightest thing he had ever said, there being so much else—but mani already knew those things, and was stalking certain other subjects. He put a hand on his pocket, embarrassed now that he had said it, but it *was* the only news that was a surprise and a diversion.

Mani did look a little surprised. Even a little amused, perhaps because she saw right through him. "Nand' Bren brought them?"

"He did. He is meeting with Father right now."

"So what do these letters say?"

"One has no idea, mani. I only just now got them. And they are written in human characters and part Ragi and part ship, and it will take me time to work them out. But I wanted to come see you."

Great-grandmother nodded slowly. "Well. We are glad to rate so highly with *someone* in the family."

"Everyone is afraid of you, mani."

He did not expect to say that particular thing. Mani could do that to people—make them make mistakes they were not even thinking of. And when mani was already angry it was not a good idea to put her off with compliments.

"Are you? Or am I to have the truth of things?"

"I hope to have done nothing to make you angry at me. Have I?"

Mani looked at him. Everybody truly was afraid of her. Even Father gave her room. But she looked at him a long moment in the way adult people looked at each other, and said, "No. You have not," in a gentle way that still did not make him anxious to ask her whether his mother or even Great-uncle Tatiseigi was the object of her mood.

He had come to blunt the anger. He wanted to talk past it. And he knew if she was not angry at him, and if nand' Bren had not been able to intervene, he was the one who could do it.

"It was very unexpected," he said, "everything that happened. And one is terribly sorry about the bus."

She waved a dismissal of the topic. "The bus is far from the center of the matter."

"I shall do everything," he said, "to be sure my sister is safe, and to be sure Uncle lives a long, long time. I have done everything I have done, remembering your advice, mani-ma."

"One does not doubt Lord Tatiseigi's management of a situation, but this sudden cousin has certainly bent events sideways. What is *your* opinion of him?"

That was deep into the pit—talking to him as if he did have an opinion that mattered. The law did not give him that, in public. But with mani—it did.

"Uncle started off not believing him, but Aunt Geidaro was really, really upset about him. She came to Tirnamardi and made a scene. I think that may have been when Uncle started taking Nomari-nadi seriously."

Mani lifted a brow ever so slightly, and the frown shattered. She began to be thoughtful, putting the scene together. "And then?"

"Great-aunt was really, truly upset. Uncle told her to leave. And Uncle had Nomari to supper and invited him to stay in the house and not in the tents."

"The others, as we understand. You are leaving out things."

"Others did come. Ajuri that were in hiding, like him."

"Hiding under false names."

"Some. Not all. The ones that Great-aunt was hunting. They support him."

"And how do you find this person?"

"His hands are callused. He has done hard work. But he lived on the estate when Mother was little. And she remembers meeting him when she was very small. She was climbing a statue."

"Climbing a statue."

"Which she should not have been doing. But he recalled it to her, and she says nobody else would know that. So she thinks he is the boy she met when she was small. And the Ajuri— both the ones who were living in Ajuri, and the ones who were hiding from Shishogi's people—they say he is who he says he is."

Mani nodded slowly. "And his character? Would we be impressed?"

"His manners are sometimes at fault. But he watches and he learns, and Uncle's house is more particular than Father's, and I think, more than Ajuri."

"We know *that*, to be sure. So what else did you learn about this Nomari?"

"He once ran the switching for the Red Train, in Shejidan. He was quite proud of that."

Both brows, this time. And a slight smile. "A switchman, then."

"I think he has done a lot of things. He moved about a lot . . . he said he always volunteered to be transferred, so he could learn new jobs."

"And move about the countryside."

"He did that."

"Clever fellow, this. Perhaps we shall talk to him before long. So many changes, so abruptly done. And your great-uncle choosing an heir. Are you pleased?"

With Great-grandmother in a chancy mood, it was like waiting for a trap to spring. This felt like one.

"I want my sister to be happy, most of all. And to be safe."

"Someday I shall have to consider a successor of my own," mani said.

It was a scary thought. "I want you to be there always," he said. "I want you *and* Great-uncle to be there always. I depend on you."

Mani smiled. "That is not in the nature of things, Great-grandson. But in the meanwhile I shall watch over you—and your sister. I shall not accept situations that endanger *you*, in particular, whatever the origin of them, and I shall certainly not be patient when I am surprised by decisions that affect your future."

"I think getting somebody new into Ajuri is a good thing, mani. I know I worried about it and Uncle did, too, and I did think about all the things you would say and the questions you would ask, and I did my best to ask them for you. And I would have objected if I had thought you would disapprove. I *would* have objected."

"Truly."

"I swear I would, mani. I would have ordered my guard to arrest him. And I would have called Father."

A second smile. "There is my great-grandson. And at a certain time, I have to stand by and watch you do what I have taught you to do. This was a rather tall cliff on which to try your wings. But we shall see, shall we not? Your associates have landed safely, meanwhile, despite a little set-to among humans, and one trusts they are now in good hands. We have to trust, having no choice in that matter, either. And you rushed to my door instead of reading their letters. Shall we be extraordinarily flattered?"

Great-grandmother could be upset by flattery. But she also liked being first in anything. "The letters are on paper, mani. They will be there. You are here now, and I have been worried you were angry."

"And people are afraid of me, are they?"

"People also want you on their side. Father does. I do." He took a chance. "*Mother* does. She truly does."

Mani gave an indelicate snort, but said nothing.

Cajeiri said, to divert the issue: "I know my sister will."

The silence went on. One did not flatter mani into agreement. Even Father would back off.

"You," mani said eventually, "are a budding scoundrel, Great-grandson. There will come a day when people will be afraid of *you*."

He had never thought that would be so. But mani was his pattern, always his pattern.

"You do need a bit more finesse, boy."

"No, mani."

"No?"

"I do not, because *I* am telling the truth."

"Ah, but telling the truth requires absolutely extreme finesse, because so many people do not want to hear it."

"The truth is, and everybody knows it, you are the best ally besides Father. And probably better than Father because *you* do not have to stay in Shejidan."

"Well, we are a far better ally, when we have *transport*."

Now mani was arguing about the bus. She was in a far better mood. "Sending the bus was Father's idea. And if we had not had it, we would have been in trouble."

"Ha."

"It was a very scary night. And I am afraid Antaro would have been killed if we had not had it."

"It was *stupid* of your great-uncle to sit in that house to be besieged, with his lawn full of strangers."

"But you would not vacate Malguri if it were like that. You would not leave your staff to defend the house."

"I would be exactly the same kind of fool as your great-uncle," mani said, "but I would hope not to have my great-grandson on the premises when I did it."

"I was very good, mani. I stayed where security told me to stay, I kept with my bodyguard and I did not go anywhere I should not. And I had a very senior bodyguard with me."

"And still have them? You accept this new aishid?"

"My aishid is glad to have them. And they are very good. They have a good sense of humor, too."

"That will often be helpful," mani said, and signaled a servant, a quick movement of the fingers that meant more tea, and cakes.

It was a good idea to have come here first, before anything but breakfast—a very good idea, Cajeiri decided. Mani did not like to be outmaneuvered, but she was feeling better about him, which was a good thing. And once she forgave him, Tatiseigi and Father would have no trouble being forgiven.

He was less sure about Mother. Mother and Great-grandmother could strike sparks just sitting at the same table.

But Great-grandmother was no longer frowning. He had done that much.

"One is glad to hear the Presidenta is doing well," Tabini said, in the course of things. "One is less glad to hear this *Heritage* party—" He used the Mospheiran word. "—has resurrected itself."

"They made a serious mistake when they brought violence near the children," Bren said. "The children were not welcome on Mospheira when we began. The danger now is too much attention and too many gifts, but these are sensible young people, who have seen terrible things as well as this outpouring of welcome. They have their way of striking a balance, and Kate-nandi and my former aide Sandra-nadi, one is certain, will keep them steady and sensible."

"My son will be asking when and where they will meet," Tabini said, "importunately so. And the meeting, be it understood, will not take place on Mospheira. Never on Mospheira. Things change, but they will not change that much."

"They will always be welcome at Najida. And very likely at Tirnamardi."

Tabini nodded. "Granted Lord Tatiseigi survives my grandmother's immediate displeasure."

"One does not believe it that extreme. There will surely be discussion. But if a human can judge, the dowager seems open to reason."

"Ha," Tabini said, with a shake of his head. "One debated whether to send you a warning by way of the navy, but we have a reasonable hesitation to expose family quarrels to bystanders, and secondly, your honest surprise would plead your innocence in the matter of my intentions. How angry is she—and did she summon Machigi, or do we have a *security* problem?"

"One cannot honestly say, aiji-ma. The indications were the latter, but one cannot exclude the first possibility."

"So in response to events ongoing—he wants a railroad. And my grandmother *is* aware that this new claimant to Ajuri has dealt with Machigi *and* Senjin. That Machigi should not be aware of his potential appointment—one hopes not, but he certainly was well-informed on my grandmother's whereabouts, and perhaps he knows why she diverted to the coast rather than taking up residence in the Bujavid *or* adding herself to the commotion in the midlands. She was perched there, understand, like

a wi'itikin on a cliff, waiting for your return, to secure *your* attention and be sure of your man'chi before she entered the matters here. And here sit I, amid all this, hoping to believe she did
not surreptitiously stir up Machigi—if *only* to come at the question of this candidate's connection with the Marid before she
arrived here."

When Tabini began to sort Ilisidi's motives—two masters of
misdirection—one began to feel the earth shift. Add Machigi to
the question, and there was complication upon complication.

"Your grandmother knows about this Nomari's connection
to Machigi," Bren said. "One waited for it to surface during
their meeting from one side or the other. Your grandmother did
create an opening for that matter, without mentioning Ajuri or
this man, but Lord Machigi failed to take it. He claimed his
motive in seeking to work out some bargain with Senjin on the
railroad was a quarrel arising between Bregani and Tiajo . . .
which may be the truth. He did show some awareness of problems in the north, but he never mentioned any direct connection of his own. Protecting an agent, your grandmother said,
aiji-ma, and she dismissed it with that. But one is certain she
still wants him to admit to her that his agent has become the
candidate for Ajuri."

"My esteemed grandmother's security remains silent on
the matter," Tabini said, "except to say she is aware, and wants
details. Your information, paidhi-ji, has been clear and
forthcoming—which we are sure she believes covers everything
necessary."

God, the communication on this floor of the Bujavid.

"Machigi claims, aiji-ma, that there is an opportunity to
lever Senjin away from the Dojisigin. The dowager offered him
the *semblance* of approval for his plan—the shipment of rails,
which one assumes must be picked up in Najida and carried
into the Taisigin Marid by truck. I informed him Najida would
not be happy with a new rail line direct from Tanaja. The Edi
would not be happy with any expansion of that station into a

major shipping point. And on the same matter, we know the opinion of any expansion of Najida Station to run a rail line down to Ashidama Bay—and the same would definitely apply to a line run from Machigi's capital to Najida. They oppose any rail extension or expansion as harming their business, and they view Machigi as an enemy. That would leave Machigi a possible agreement with the Maschi at Targai, but I do not think a railroad is actually what Lord Machigi wants at this juncture unless it links to Senjin's capital. I think it is *all* aimed at Senjin, and he and the Senjin Marid are either going to agree, or this project will not happen."

"Does it occur to you that this mysterious Ajuri claimant *has* been in Senjin and is intimately acquainted with all these issues with the rail system?" Tabini had a stare—a very affecting stare: pale eyes in a dark face that absolutely did not give away his secrets. Or his reactions.

"Aiji-ma, it does seem beyond coincidence that one has surfaced and the other is suddenly an issue."

"It will certainly be interesting to learn where this idea originated," Tabini said. The pale stare was hooded at the moment, thoughtful. "How did you read Machigi?"

"Ambitious, as always. Refusing to give your grandmother the personal honorific. Speaking as aiji of all the Marid, which is, one is certain, his view of himself. If Senjin joins him, Senjin will either have a short alliance with him or a long dependence on him. Machigi will not be second in that association, very certainly."

"Senjin has been dependent on some overlord in most of living memory," Tabini said. "Its last burst of independence was with the Farai in charge. Beyond that, in Cosadi's rule in Dojisigi, with all that line that troubled us in the north, they were always in second place. *We* have given the Dojisigi lord considerable line to run only because she is inconveniently distant from us, but if Senjin should try to take the Dojisigin down even with Machigi's blessing, he would face a long war in mountainous terrain. It would be simpler to make that obnoxious young woman irrelevant—and it would not be strange if the lord of Senjin would prefer a sane neighbor, *if* he can be persuaded that Machigi will make an alliance and not dislodge him from power. Especially if there was an agreement to be had that would give him the benefits of Machigi's trade agreement with my grandmother, granted that ever comes to pass. One day we shall have to deal with Machigi, but we are quietly giving Machigi something substantial to lose—in any future quarrel with us. My grandmother operates on very ancient principles. And I have suggested to the Guild that they preserve this troublesome southerner and let my grandmother build him up. I suppose I may add Bregani of Senjin to the list of people we hope stay alive, and back my grandmother's current notion. Her sea route is in the future. This could be rather more short term. And logistically useful."

"The route he proposes has previously been surveyed and lacks only a single extension of rail. And the aiji-dowager is prepared to ship him finished rail."

"Via Cobo district, the long way round," Tabini said. "An initial shipment through the heart of the aishidi'tat, should *anyone* miss the gesture." There was amusement in the tone. "My grandmother does *not* do things by half-measures. She has demanded the Red Train for an immediate trip to Hasjuran. While steel rail is being freighted through the midlands—*she* is moving in another direction. South."

Snow, ice, and the southern mountains. Hasjuran was the last depot before the winding descent to the Marid. He tried, in principle, to keep an atevi-like calm expression in briefings. But Lord Topari's little capital? Log walls and a sixty-day summer, and a lord who had only recently agreed that humans were tolerable?

"She wants you, *and* she wants this guest of Lord Tatiseigi's, my wife's somewhat remote cousin. Nomari. For his railroad experience. She says she intends to hold a consultation with Lord Topari."

God, the man was—

Rough, to say the least. Apt to say what he thought ahead of any second thought on the matter. Apt to call the paidhi-aiji an *excellent creature* while thanking him for favors, and that was the length and breadth of Topari's sense of diplomacy, while the aiji-dowager. . . .

So Ilisidi wanted *him.* And the Ajuri candidate. . . .

To discuss the state of the railroad? Not likely. Nomari was the issue under close scrutiny.

"She is quite serious," Tabini said. "She is deadly serious. She wants Nomari-nadi . . . one hopes not intending to serve him tea."

Ilisidi had poisoned *him* at first encounter. It was a very rough route to Ilisidi's circle of trusted persons. But if there was one individual in recent years positioned to threaten Ilisidi's most essential assets—her great-grandson, Tatiseigi and her long alliance with the Atageini—it was this sudden claimant. Would she try him?

He had no doubt. "Do you," he asked cautiously, "wish me to watch over him?"

"If you are present, my grandmother will more likely ask your estimation of the man. So shall I. He is potentially too close to the heart of my household."

"I am human, aiji-ma. I am not—"

"She will seek your estimation, I say, and she will balance it with hers. That combination has produced good advice in the past."

"Then I shall go, aiji-ma. I shall do my best."

"My son, needless to say, will *not* be aboard. Nor will my wife."

"Yes, aiji-ma."

"Did Machigi mention *anything* about coming to Shejidan?"

"No, aiji-ma." He was surprised. Very surprised. The man did not exit his territory, as a rule, even for a few hours. "He said his absence from Tanaja would invite problems. I would be surprised if he came."

"Prepare to be surprised. He did return to Tanaja, but he is now headed back to Najida. Reports are scant, but he *has* received a communication from my grandmother, and we believe he is taking the train there and coming here. My grandmother has ordered a private car—we are gratified to know, *not* the Red Train—to pick him up at Najida. She has not informed you."

"No, aiji-ma." That was to say, Cenedi had not informed Banichi, either. It was strictest security around *that* move. "He is coming *here,* then."

"Evidently. Perhaps for a face-to-face consultation. Or—she wishes to introduce Machigi to his former agent. Or—she is taking them *both* to Hasjuran."

He was appalled. "One—had no idea, aiji-ma."

"I daresay *we* would have had no idea—were we not keeping a close watch on all parties concerned—at least in places where we have assets. My grandmother is requesting a train, the Ajuri candidate, and the lord of Tanaja, and she wants *you* and your aishid to accompany her to meet Lord Topari in the least comfortable mountain fastness this side of Malguri. You are just come from a situation on the station, an attempted assassination and a lengthy mission on the island. Not to mention the stress of a welcome by my grandmother. We wish we could give you and your aishid an entire fortnight to sit at Najida and do nothing. But there is too much involved here."

"I shall go, aiji-ma. I would *get* no rest from wondering. I have to go."

Tabini nodded slowly. "I rely on you. Forgive Lord Topari. I ask that already. He means well."

"I shall be more concerned for Lord Topari dealing with your grandmother, aiji-ma."

"He will remind her of his ilk in Malguri. He should be safe—unless he attempts familiarity with her once back in

Shejidan. And he may need to learn to deal with her—if this venture goes one step further than Hasjuran."

"Senjin?" It was the logical step.

"If it does, I say. I know my grandmother, and of places where every attendee will be at disadvantage—except herself—she has chosen a place inconvenient for everybody, at an altitude and an environment where she is perfectly comfortable, and where strangers do not easily blend in. *You* are there for me, this time. That may prove a test of your diplomacy, but you will manage, as *my* agent."

"Yes, aiji-ma. I shall advise her of that. Early, lest there be any confusion."

"I am not superstitious," Tabini said. "But you will meet those who are. Remember it."

10

It was a good thing, Cajeiri thought, that he had gone to see mani. She *had* wanted the visit, but she would not have ordered it. He was not eager to report the visit to his parents, who might ask him to report on Great-grandmother's reaction, and reporting on Great-grandmother was never a good idea. He simply went back to his own suite and sat down at his desk, letting his staff do whatever needed doing.

For himself—the letters, the precious letters, were an unexpected gift, and he *hoped* Father and nand' Bren had had a good talk and that there was not going to be a family row.

It was not, now, his concern. His associates' letters *were* his concern, letters written on proper paper, with Lord Geigi's heraldry in the watermark—paper was difficult to come by on the station. It was usually a little gray, remade again and again, but paper like this was imported. Guests of the house would have been given it, to write letters to the Bujavid and such.

And to his associates, to write to him about their voyage down.

It was written in various sizes and various hands, the first very small and neat, Ragi characters interspersed with human ones. He knew the writing as he knew their individual voices.

We are very excited and a little scared. We know that nand' Bren's people are going to take care of us when we get down to the surface, and we hope nand' Bren will be there.

Lord Geigi is giving us a dinner before we go down. We will miss him and everybody. They have taken very good care of us.

That was from Artur, and as best Cajeiri could read it, filling in a good many words and guessing on others.

And from Gene, a little heavier hand, with Ragi words written as they sounded in human characters:

My mother is worried about the shuttle. But she is brave, and it is only one time that she has to do this. She says she wants to see the ocean. So do I. And I hope she really likes living on Mospheira. I know everybody is very excited about the food. A lot of people want to come down for that. Many people are signing up because of the food.

Food had been rationed for years and years for the Reunioners, rationed on the ship, rationed even after they had gotten to the station, and things had gotten even worse from there before they had begun getting better. Shuttles had already started carrying food up, and once they got more people down, everybody would be better off. He could not imagine being hungry most of his life, but that was the way Reunioners had lived, measuring everything, just glad to have something to put in their stomachs. He was not surprised people wanted to come down and never have rationing again.

And from Irene:

I am determined not to be sick going down this time. I will not be scared. I saw my mother yesterday, because I am leaving. She said she hoped I was sorry. I said I hoped she was sorry. She said there was no way back from the planet and I said I was happy with that. I said goodbye and I left.

I am still not sorry. I want to go down to the world and I want to see the sky. I wish you could come to Mospheira when we come down, but nand' Geigi said we shall be going to the mainland to see you. All of us will have tutors on Mospheira and we will live in Port Jackson. I will be writing more on the way down.

And again she wrote:

I talked to Bjorn before we left. He is unhappy we are going but he says good luck and he says he will see us someday.

I am not sick. I am not scared now. I want to be on Mospheira. I want to see you soon. Tell all your household thank you very much. I wish so much you could be there. We are very happy.

Irene was the one who had stopped them from having all kinds of troubles on the station and stopped people from being killed. She was extremely brave. Irene's mother was still under arrest, maybe not to be punished, nand' Bren had said to him, but she was never to have authority over Irene again unless Irene wanted it, and Irene was staying with Gene and Artur and their parents. It was probably a good thing Irene had gone to say goodbye to her mother; but he was very glad her mother would not be joining them at all soon.

It was very curious, the feeling he had about that. He and his associates had tried very hard to puzzle out what man'chi was compared to being *friends* in the human way, or having parents to look to, and they had concluded it was a lot like, but not entirely like. Irene did not even have all of that. Irene's mother had been through very bad things—so had all the Reunioners—but something important was broken in that relationship. Irene had a strong man'chi toward them: that strength of attachment that had fastened onto him and Gene and Artur had given her courage to do very brave things, so whatever was broken was not broken from her side. Maybe he should ask nand' Bren to explain it, but then, he feared he might not make it clear, and Bren might think he thought badly of Irene, or that Irene posed a problem, which he never wanted Bren to think.

So he held that question unasked.

He did have a good feeling about Gene's mother. Gene's mother was a small person and looked old and frail; but Gene's attachment to her was strong; and Irene came to her as if she and Gene were the adults, taking care of Gene's mother as much as Gene's mother tried to take care of them. Artur's parents took care of each other and of Artur, who was strongly tied to them in what seemed the most atevi-like way, respectful on all sides, once Artur's father had understood they would be free on Mospheira and that nobody would take Artur away. Things were rightside up in that household, though Artur's parents seemed not as brave as Artur was: they were always prone to worry things would go badly—which, if one had survived on Reunion, they had seen happen over and over.

But together—together, all of them were strong. And they were coming down to try to live where, Bren said, they would all be foreigners to start with. They would not understand Mospheirans, even if they were all human—and he supposed he did understand that: certainly there were atevi one could not understand.

And what *he* had, and his associates had, however hard it was to figure out, was an attachment they had formed together on a long voyage. Nand' Bren was one thing—nand' Bren had understood *him* first, and there was never any question of man'chi where nand' Bren was concerned, because he had grown up with nand' Bren and just—knew that, whatever else, nand' Bren would protect him. He had never known people his own age, so it was hard to judge, but he thought he could trust his associates from the ship, and having associates to whom everything in the world was new—was a happy association. There was so much to share.

They had landed. *They* were safe, thanks to nand' Bren and the Presidenta. And he and Uncle Tatiseigi were safe, and mani was somewhat happier.

What was more, *Mother* was happy, which was fairly well the first time she had ever seemed happy with him for days on end.

Father was happy.

Meanwhile he had a letter to write, and he had his tutor's mail on the hall table, asking when they might resume lessons, and he had to answer that, too.

Everything was splendid.

Until Rieni came in and said, quietly, "Nandi, are you aware the aiji-dowager has called for the Red Train, and that the paidhi-aiji *and* Nomari-nadi are to travel with her?"

"Where?" he asked, dismayed.

"We have asked," Rieni said. "We have not gotten an answer, except to say that it will go east."

Not to Najjida, then. "Is she going to Malguri?" She might want to question Nomari, and if that was the case, it was good for nand' Bren to be there. Mani could be more than frightening.

"That is the assumption."

"Is there any hope I might go, nadi?"

There was a slight hesitation. "Your father the aiji has ordered us to be sure you do not, aiji-meni. We are sorry."

He gazed up from his desk at Rieni—at a very hard Guild face, behind which, he well knew now, hid a habit of kindness and an occasional sense of humor—and he told himself no, Father had given him orders to get back to study, to prepare himself—not to run off with mani on another adventure. He had managed to get Mother's good will. It was not a time to go running off to Malguri to stay with mani.

"One understands," he said. "Father knows I have far too much to do here. For one thing, my associates on Mospheira might call, and I should be here if they do. But will you do one thing? Will you arrange it for me to go down to the train and be there when it goes?"

"Young gentleman."

"Rieni-nadi, I trust you. And you will trust me, will you not? I wish to speak to nand' Bren. I wish to introduce him to Nomari. I have been in the middle of things. I was in Tirnamardi and I did what I had to. I stayed safe. Now mani is upset and she is going off with my mother's cousin. I know nand' Bren will protect him. But I want her to remember that he is *my* cousin, too. Do you not think—I can go down and wish my great-grandmother and nand' Bren and my cousin well—without causing a problem? Can I not do that? And do you not trust me to tell you the truth?"

There was a lengthy silence. Rieni stared at him, he stared at Rieni, and eventually Rieni gave a little nod. "Yes, nandi."

There was one person Bren had to see before he left: Lord Tatiseigi—once upon a time far from his favorite social contact, but the old man had become a close ally in the passage of time, he was certainly distressed by Ilisidi's displeasure, and Tatiseigi had just had a hellish time in Tirnamardi. Courtesy to the old gentleman was a must.

Tatiseigi was, moreover, supporting Nomari's candidacy, and that involved questions needing answers.

Madam Saidin was on duty, serving tea in the sitting room—Tatiseigi's longterm major d' and a person to whom Bren himself owed considerable gratitude. Bren gave her a smile as she served, said, "Thank you, Saidin-daja,"—lady she was, a lady of some rank and distinction in the township, but choosing to manage Lord Tatiseigi's Bujavid residence, in what longterm relationship one declined to ask.

"Nand' paidhi," she said softly, and gave a gentle bow as Tatiseigi himself made a belated and informal entry to the sitting room. Saidin poured him a cup, too, and for most of that cup there was silence—longer than usual, with more worry than usual in the silence.

"So," said Tatiseigi, as host, finally setting his cup aside. "You are going with her. Advise her to take precautions, paidhi. This venture is reckless in the extreme, and I am distressed to be left behind, but I suppose I am not in her good graces at the moment."

"One does not believe that her distress is with you, nandi. Not truly."

"My niece's presence certainly is part of it," Tatiseigi said. "But I cannot wish that had not happened."

"Nor can I," Bren said, "as one best understands it. The aiji-dowager could not be at Tirnamardi as quickly, and as I understand the outcome, I am, forgive an outsider to the matter, very pleased at what resulted."

"An heir, a prospective reasonable neighbor, and a reconciliation between my niece and her son. I cannot regret it. I do regret the dowager's inconvenience, and yours, and the damage to the bus."

"I am particularly glad the bus could serve. Think nothing of it."

"We would have repaired it entirely, nandi, but clearly that would have taken far too much time—and I *was* truly concerned that the dowager had moved recklessly across country with things stirred up as they were, without adequate protection. The Guild is on the alert, but some problems may slip through the net, and the dowager *still* will not hear my objections."

"You have spoken with her."

Tatiseigi gave a brief sigh. *"That.* Briefly. Indeed, the aiji-dowager is understandably upset at being forestalled. But had she been at hand, as you say, none of the things that happened might have happened, and the Ajuri might have hesitated to approach the house."

"Are you confident in this Ajuri claimant, nandi?"

"Let us say that he is a far more pleasant neighbor than Geidaro. The question is whether the Guild can keep him alive long enough to serve any good purpose, and whether he has enough tempered strength to deal with the factions in that house. He is absolutely untutored in accounting, but he is well-read in law."

"If you are approving of him, nandi, your judgment will carry great weight."

Tatiseigi nodded. "One is not utterly certain, but I have hope for him. Ajuri cannot do worse than they have done if they selected a random criminal. It is time for better leadership—but since the climate there has favored scoundrels, it may be a time coming."

"Najida's small vote, nandi, will be yours."

"Keep him *alive*, paidhi."

"You know, then."

"That the dowager has invited him on this unlikely trip to the mountains? Protect *her*, paidhi. She does listen to your advice."

"I shall do my best, nandi."

"With Machigi. Her retired pirate."

"So you *do* know the whole business."

Tatiseigi's eyes acquired a sullen fire. "She is convinced she knows his motives. *You* negotiated her agreement with this young scoundrel. And now he wants a railroad. Tell me. Do *you* find him charming?"

Jealousy. Of a decidedly atevi flavor, but jealousy, nonetheless. An old man for a younger? Was there attraction—the dowager for a rakish young lord with an large overdose of ambition and very little restraint? Lord Tatiseigi's feelings were evident even to a human.

"Say, rather, compelling. I have my own apprehensions, which I do state—but Cenedi will be more forward in cautioning the dowager than *I* dare, nandi, and one is very certain Cenedi is not blindly trusting of anyone."

"True," the old man said with relief, as if he had indeed not thought of Cenedi in the matter. "There is a man of good sense."

"My notion is, nandi, that the dowager is too wise to trust a lord who has double-crossed every neighbor he does not rule. I think rather the trap she wishes to set is for Machigi *and* this candidate of yours, who *has* been in Tanaja, and in Koperna. It is not the way I would wish to go about the inquiry—and I hope your candidate justifies your good opinion."

Again Lord Tatiseigi nodded. "Paidhi, I am glad she is at least consulting you. Call me by phone at any hour, if I can be of any assistance."

Lord Tatiseigi did *not* favor telephones. God, no.

"One is honored, nandi, and one understands the depth of your concern. Would it give you peace of mind if I say I truly shall use that permission if I feel the dowager is at risk?"

"Do not hesitate, nand' paidhi. Do not hesitate at all."

11

The dowager's dislike of night train rides notwithstanding—they were about to take another.

"The dowager is already aboard," Banichi said as they prepared to leave the apartment for the train station downstairs. Banichi and his team carried full kit, rifles and sidearms, not to mention Guild baggage—the black bag Tano carried, that they never gave into outsider hands. Bren's own large cases had gone down before them. Narani and Jeladi were escorting those, to board the train only after they were satisfied of the security of the cases; and with the dowager's young men supervising the loading, that should be a fairly smooth and practiced operation. Koharu and Supani were handling details in the apartment foyer, helping Bren on with his traveling coat.

He was, yes, wearing the damned bulletproof vest, despite that he was to walk a guarded hall and ride the Bujavid's internal lift down and stand among enough Guild to stand off anyone of ill intent. He had argued, but not strenuously. He intended to shed it once aboard.

"So what is the schedule?" Bren asked, letting Koharu adjust his collar. "Will there be a brandy hour, or are the meetings for the morning?"

"We assume the morning," Banichi said. "Cenedi says the dowager has settled for the night, that there will be a cold supper waiting in each car, and that we are advised to be quiet in boarding. She does not wish to be disturbed."

There were worse scenarios, one of which was a tension-fraught elaborate dinner in cramped spaces followed by late-evening verbal fencing over too much brandy. Cold supper, meat, eggs, and pickle, atevi-style, was perfectly acceptable. "How *are* we set up?" Bren asked. "One assumes we are between the dowager and Machigi."

"The Red Car does not come hindmost in this train," Banichi said. "It has no passageway aft, but they have changed out one of the trucks, the wheel assembly . . . to enable a coupling. A common boxcar follows it. The dowager's car, second up from the Red Car, is a special sleeper, the one she used on transcontinental rail before she took to flying. There were always two such in years past, one waiting wherever she happened to be. She has afforded you her own alternate car on this occasion, armored and secure. There are three others of like construction, destined for Machigi and Nomari and one additional. One regrets, Bren-ji, there are no windows. None, on the entire train."

Of course. Security. Windows that looked ordinary from the outside, but from inside, no. Not a glimpse of the outside. He had never seen the land eastward of Shejidan, never seen the northern face of the mountains. "Safety," he said. "One can appreciate it. What is our schedule?"

"None," Banichi said. "Her passage door will be locked until breakfast, which will be in the Red Car," Banichi said. "We recommend your door be locked, too, until that hour."

"I can conceive no reason to be wandering about."

"You will sleep between two special cars," Algini said, "Cenedi's units are in the one nearest the dowager, then your car, and the operations car allotted to us and other Guild, a buffer between you and Lord Machigi. Machigi will share a car with his security, and Nomari will share the next car with his. There is the baggage car, and a third sleeper between them, and then an additional Guild car. Twelve cars in all, the engine making felicitous thirteen—including a galley—Bindanda will travel there, with the dowager's staff, and Narani and Jeladi will have the staff compartment in yours. General operations has the sixth car, Cenedi's operations the eighth. The dowager's car occupies auspicious ninth position, and yours, felicitous seventh. Machigi occupies relatively lucky fifth and Nomari, least in consideration, has risky fourth, with a baggage car between him in third place; then come the two cars we will send down to contact Lord Bregani, a sleeper car for him and his security and a Guild car to protect the train as a whole. It places Bregani at risky second position, but so he is, in all regards, and knows it. There is attention to such details, should any 'counter take note, and 'counters do abound in the mountain clans, professional and amateur. Lord Bregani can talk. Or he can refuse. The dowager is making the situation clear."

"We are also," Jago said, "equipped with mortars, should we need them."

Bren glanced at her, rather hoping she was joking—but her expression said she was not; and probably he should be glad they had the capability.

"We are informed," Tano said, having listened to something in his ear plug, "that Lord Machigi is currently boarding, with his aishid. He has come up from the regular train station."

"We had best go down, then," Bren said. Machigi might require some attention, some slight bit more courtesy than the dowager was likely prepared to give tonight. He perfectly well understood that Ilisidi needed to conserve her own energy. It was up to the paidhi-aiji to keep civility in the occasion—to offer Machigi a little brandy if needed to soothe travel-jangled nerves, and to be sure there were no unexpected events or delays. Narani, Jeladi, and Bindanda should not be the only recourse to handle problems down there.

Machigi had to have taken the ordinary train, though possibly a sleeper car and isolation, boarding, likely, at Najida for a lengthy trip. Then there would be a van ride up the hill from the public train station, surely a new experience for the lord of the Taisigin Marid. Machigi might easily have taken a plane at the airport halfway between Cobo and Najida and been here very shortly. But then—he might never have flown before, either. Likely he had not.

For that matter, he probably had never taken a train, either. It *all* might be new to Machigi, power and terror though he was in his own seaside world. Machigi indeed might be glad of a familiar face, even his, though one was sure Cenedi had someone assigned to ease difficulties and be sure Machigi and his Taisigi bodyguard were safe from public curiosity.

As for Nomari, there was certainly nothing about train transport they needed explain to him. And he would have come down from upstairs.

It was clearly time. The Red Train rolled when it wanted to, and everything else on the tracks had to give it priority—but the powers that commanded it did try to be considerate in the privilege. There was a good window of movement coming up, after certain regular trains had passed the junction, and the usual way of the Red Train was to slip into an opportune slot and not stall traffic any worse than need be. It was disruption enough that they would have delayed the habitual delivery runs up from the city to the Bujavid, to assure a secure boarding. There would be van-loads of vegetables stalled down in the markets.

"The paidhi is going out to the lifts," Antaro said.

So it was time, and Cajeiri let Eisi help him into his coat—court dress, to be absolutely proper in the very strong likelihood of meeting great-grandmother, and because he wanted not to be at fault in any particular.

His seniormost bodyguard was trying to monitor communications, but there was, they said, nothing from the train station, nothing flowing even on Guild channels. Onami was down there already, using his keys and passes to go where he needed to go—the only one of them, Rieni had said, that had never met Banichi or Algini. Onami was not using Guild communications, because Cenedi would likely track that.

The Transportation Guild office downstairs had ceased operations—or at least was not answering inquiries from upstairs.

"An uncommon shutdown," Rieni called it. "Uncommon precautions. They are clearing track eastward."

"Anticipation of trouble," Janachi remarked. "There is a rail check in progress."

"What is a rail check?" Cajeiri asked.

"Exactly that. There will be a train preceding the dowager's, checking all track, all bridges. And communication is silenced. Once we are inside the restriction we shall not be able to communicate outside the area while the information hold lasts."

"Is it ordinary?" He was used to his aishid being shut out of information. He had not expected the seniors to be shut out. "It cannot be."

"Given your great-aunt was murdered, nandi, given the controversial Ajuri heir is traveling with the dowager, presumably so that she can examine his claim and question him—and given that the Guild still has not laid hands on your great-aunt's killer—there is reason enough for these precautions for a train leaving the city. The Red Train will be in a security bubble as far as it goes, which we are given to understand is Malguri."

"*If* it goes east," Cajeiri said. There had been some speculation among them that it all might be a cover, and great-grandmother might be taking Nomari back to Najida.

"We shall not know until it reaches the city junction."

It was worrisome. Until he had heard they were taking along extra Guild units, it had seemed a trip mani chose to take, the way mani suddenly *chose* to do things for her own comfort, or for effect, or, he thought, to have days with Nomari where there was no escaping her questions.

But his seniormost aishid was thinking other things, now, like Aunt Geidaro's killer, and Shadow Guild, and attacks on the train.

"Let us go down," he said. He was all the more determined,

having heard from years back what great-grandmother had done when she had first met nand' Bren—and he could not doubt it had happened, even though it was not mani as *he* had known her. Father had crossed her considerably in appointing nand' Bren. Mani had been in a temper, and nand' Bren had suffered for it. It was the same now, with Mother supporting Nomari and Father siding with Mother.

In that light, he intended to visit the train even if mani had shut herself away. He intended to be clearly understood as concerned, and he intended all involved to relay to mani that he *was* aware and cared about the outcome, for himself, and likewise for Uncle and for his own sister, who might be Nomari's neighbor someday.

It *was* his concern and it *was* his business, and if he had not made that point clear enough to mani when he had gone to her apartment, he would do it now, so she had that to think about.

The lift door opened on the echoing gray vastness that was the Bujavid station—quieter than ordinary, to Bren's ears: no competing sound of engines this evening, no voices reflecting off the concrete ceilings, no rumble of iron-wheeled baggage trolleys, just the single steam-engine presence on track number one—that, his ears did detect—and their own footsteps as they exited the lift. Narani and Jeladi were there to meet them, proper and collected.

"The baggage is all aboard, nandi," Narani said. "We are ready. Bindanda is checking in with the galley staff—the dowager's people."

It was not the usual consist of the Red Train—which ordinarily ran with the Red Car and a single baggage car, perhaps two. This was a row of gray cars, sparsely windowed, and those all blank behind the glass, by what he knew, at least for the dowager's cars and the Guild cars. That was all one could see. There was not even a view of the Red Car from the vantage of the personnel lifts.

The Red Train's usual engine, ornate and steam-powered, was facing the downhill direction, ready to move. Twelve cars was an uncommon length even to be up here in the Bujavid station: and, typical of the Red Train boarding, there *was* no train on the other tracks. Black-uniformed Guild moved about the platform. That was ordinary, where the dowager was concerned. They would be the dowager's young men, likely, all of them Easterners, from Malguri.

Bren walked out with his own people as far as the end of the elevator block, and he could see the whole train laid out then, the Red Car *next* to hindmost, unprecedented, the whole train sleek and gray, and the beautiful old Red Car, ahead of a common well-used freight car.

"The sleeping berths," Jago said quietly, "all convert to seating, we are told. You will have a proper working area. And, excepting the dowager, we advise you invite guests *in*, Bren-ji, rather than go to other cars. You will have ample supplies for courtesies. We are assured of that."

"Yes," he said.

"All traffic is being held until we clear the junction," Algini said. "A train will precede us, to assure our safety. It has already left."

"Have we heard a particular threat?"

"No," Jago said. "But Topari will be getting a message within the hour that he will be visited, and by whom; and considering how very seriously Tiajo must take this move, if she finds out. And considering who is aboard, who also may not have been utterly discreet—security does worry us."

"Once we get there," Banichi said, "we are moving agents into the region. Lord Topari's bodyguard and that of every lord in Halrun is untrained and armed with less than Guild standard, besides lacking our communications. They are more apt to shoot us by mistake."

"One fervently hopes—" he began to say.

Just then, however, there was an arrival in the lift system some distance behind them, and Bren checked step and turned to see another Guild escort emerge with a young man in traveling dress, an average-looking young fellow, looking uncertain and worried, and certainly noticing them.

The place was under extreme lockdown, so it was equally certainly no random passenger.

"Would that be Nomari-nadi, nadiin-ji?"

Jago touched her earplug and asked a question. "Yes," she said with certainty.

"I should like to meet him," Bren said.

The message passed. The young man listened to something said by his bodyguard, smoothed his coat, and started toward them.

An anxious gesture. Not pretentious in the least. Bren was favorably impressed with that. He waited, a little breach of security—his bodyguard liked him to keep moving—but there was overpowering Guild presence all around him, and he had agreed to the damnable bulletproof vest.

The young man approached with a very quiet and worried demeanor, and the bow he gave was in deepest degree, no pretension of a rank he did not yet hold.

"Lord paidhi."

He was not hard to recognize.

"Nomari-nadi." Bren gave a slight bow and allowed a pleasant expression. "One has looked forward to meeting you."

"One is honored to meet you, nandi. One is extremely honored."

"One understands you have knowledge that may assist the dowager's decisions on this trip."

"I should never claim it, nand' paidhi. I shall be very—"

Nomari's gaze was suddenly fixed past his shoulder, in the direction of the engine, and since Banichi and the rest had not reacted, Bren's instant estimation was that, whatever Nomari had seen that gave him pause, it was not something that greatly alarmed his bodyguard. Exactly what—was almost worth a guess.

Bren gave it a casual glance, turning a little stiffly because of the vest.

And indeed, among the myriad sounds of a waiting train and arriving baggage—

Machigi stepped out the side exit of his assigned car, ahead of his non-regulation bodyguard.

Either Machigi had had an observer posted or the dowager had deliberately had the Guild make him aware. Certainly, Bren thought, given that he and Machigi had recently met, it was not likely that *he* was the object of Machigi's excursion.

Nomari had seen, too, and stood frozen in place.

"Ah," Bren said, instantly sorting whether he wanted to say to Nomari: *This is someone you know, is it not?*

Or, blithely innocent: *May I introduce you, nadi?*

He was quite sure at least that the dowager would want a meticulous account of both reactions.

"Lord Machigi," Nomari said in an undertone. "I worked for him, nandi, during the Troubles. One never expected *him* here."

Honesty raced forth before the possibility of exposure. But one could put a favorable light on the matter. He had reacted with the truth.

"Was it a good parting?" Bren asked.

Nomari said nothing. Machigi and his bodyguard were aggressively on the move, too close for any lengthy answer. Bren simply put on a warm but dignified smile, and walked forward while, likely, every Guild agent in the entire station went on alert.

"Lord Machigi." A proper bow.

"Nand' paidhi," Machigi said. An equally proper one, and a nod. "Good evening. And to your companion, who one understands has met with extraordinary good fortune. Nomari-nadi, good evening. One might ask why you might be part of this venture—but perhaps you have shared certain facts with the aiji-dowager."

"I have not met the aiji-dowager, nandi," Nomari said with a bow, "and I am not entirely sure why I am here."

"Well," Machigi said, "but you do have a certain perspective on the rail system. Have you mentioned it? Surely you have."

Nomari made a second, slighter bow. "To the extent the Guild asked, I answered, nandi, it is on record, and the Guild knows.—I have told them, nand' paidhi, that I am in Lord Machigi's debt. I did not conceal it. I hid when my family was killed. Through my mother's associates' influence I enrolled in the Transportation Guild. And when the Troubles started, I began to be a danger to my associates. I fled to the south, to Tanaja, finally. And I was arrested and questioned. Lord Machigi— to whom I am deeply indebted—heard my situation and asked me to work for him, which I was glad to do. I was in and out of Senjin and throughout the system, and I did provide Lord Machigi intelligence on Senjin, Dojisigi, and Maschi districts, and Najida, clear to the coast, all through the time of the Troubles. All that is true."

"And currently?" Bren asked.

"When Tabini-aiji came back to power, I went back to my guild—as many did. But, yes. I have given Lord Machigi information on shipments into Senjin and onward."

"To this day, we have an interest in shipments to and from Dojisigi, how not?" Machigi said. "You were useful. But now our one-time spy has found a far better situation, and we have no desire to let rumors of past associations hamper his rise. Be assured, nandi, he has never betrayed the aishidi'tat. It was never my impression that he *would*. All his information has been on the aiji's enemies as well as mine."

Machigi was unqualifiedly the most glib rascal on the continent, a lord with ambitions only limited by the ethnic divide, a substantial mountain range, and the storms of the Southern Ocean.

But likewise, Machigi's interests and the dowager's *and* those of the aishidi'tat did occasionally overlap. A stable midlands was one of those instances. The north forming a stable relationship with the Marid was another desirable outcome, so long as Machigi stayed his current course.

Bren nodded, projecting satisfaction. "I appreciate your candor, nandi, nadi, and, knowing the dowager, I would expect her to know rather more about all this than I do. May I offer you a brandy in my car? I am assured I have the means."

The lift car had stopped a floor above the train station, just stopped short of its destination. And that had never happened. "Have we been prevented?" Cajeiri asked as the car stayed quiet, and he saw Rieni consult that bracelet Guild wore. Every bracelet in that unit flashed a small red light. Antaro's and her unit, not at all.

"There is a problem, nandi," Rieni said. "We shall wait here. A general order stopped us. Onami is coming up."

"Are they safe?" he asked. "Is everyone all right?"

"I think it is a problem of permissions," Rieni said. "Wait, nandi."

Another car was moving, somewhere in the bank of lifts. Cajeiri waited. He had no choice. His younger aishid moved closer to him, Antaro and Jegari putting themselves between him and the door, Lucasi and Veijico close at his back. They were armed. They all were armed. The lower floors of the Bujavid were lonely places, dim places, some not even lighted until someone threw the switch or a presence threw one of the automatic ones. It was very spooky.

The moving car reached their level. Bracelets flashed once. Rieni opened the lift door and used a key to hold the car in place. Janachi and Haniri stepped out into the dim corridor, as quick footsteps came toward them. Cajeiri stayed still, seeing the seniors' attention generally focused to the right, though Janachi took a stance in the doorway, glancing leftward.

Professional. Businesslike. No hands were near weapons, which was reassurance of a kind.

Onami arrived and came into the car. Everybody folded inward, and Rieni shut the door.

Handsigns flashed, one of which indicated the overhead.

"Disengaged," Rieni said. "But keep it quiet."

"Machigi," Onami said, and gave a little nod to Cajeiri. "Lord *Machigi* is on the train. Did you know, nandi?"

"No," Cajeiri said shortly. "No, nadi, I did not."

"As best I understand, he came up by bus from the city with his own bodyguard and boarded by the dowager's permission, under observation of the dowager's guard. He is afforded one of seven sleeping cars."

"Seven!"

"Lord Machigi arrived in the city by train less than an hour ago, and the reason of the late departure may be that. More, the destination is not Malguri, but Hasjuran."

Hasjuran. Lord Topari, who was mostly just a joke.

The southern mountains. The border with the Marid.

"We are left to speculate whether your father knows," Rieni said, "or whether the paidhi himself had any advisement on the matter."

"One has no idea," Cajeiri said quietly, and silence followed, a lengthy silence, his bodyguards waiting for him to have an opinion, a plan, a direction to go from here. He had made promises. He could go down there. He could ask questions and perhaps mani would answer, or nand' Bren would, but nothing in progress seemed to be what he had thought it was.

And perhaps *Father* had no idea.

Great-grandmother had been disrespected in the situation at Tirnamardi. She had gone down to Najida rather than stay in the Bujavid. She had been at Najida to meet nand' Bren when he came back, but had she, in that delay, been sending messages to the Marid? It was easier from Najida.

And she was not inviting Uncle Tatiseigi to come along, but

she had nand' Bren with her. Nand' Bren would do *nothing* Father would not approve, he believed that. But nand' Bren could have been surprised and caught in a situation. He believed in that possibility as he believed that mani might be up to *something* Father might not approve.

He stood there, trying to gather up all the pieces while everybody stared at him—grown, gray-haired men and his young aishid alike, nobody telling him what to do, when he most in his life wished somebody *would* tell him what to do.

"One does *not* believe we should go down there," Antaro ventured quietly, and that, at least, seemed a helpful opinion. Antaro knew mani. Rieni did not, in any personal way.

And it was true. His elder aishid did *not* know. They were asking *him*. And listening to the juniors. And expecting him to honor his promises of sensible behavior.

"We *should* not," he said, with the terrible feeling that four people high up in the Guild, while they had no experience of mani, might be aware that, if mani was up to something, that *something* could rebound in dangerous ways. Things were out of joint. Something was underway Father might not know, and if he told Father—all sorts of things could go wrong in the house. He did not think Great-grandmother would hate him if he told—he could not imagine that. But he had seen Great-grandmother's anger bounce off one person and land on another. It was a fault, not a virtue: he knew that beyond any doubt. But everybody had faults. His own was going on such ventures without consulting, which had gotten him in all sorts of trouble in his nine years, so if anyone understood Great-grandmother, he did, in that respect.

But should he tell Father what she was doing? And should he tell Father now, so that Father could prevent the train leaving—and strand Machigi and embarrass Great-grandmother and have all sorts of consequences he could not predict from where he stood?

He could tell Father after the train had left, so Father could order it to stop in some place less connected to people who would gossip and make up their own conclusions . . . and maybe not connected to him . . .

But Father was smart enough to think of that on his own. Just—

If Mother heard about it, and *Mother* came into it—

Mother and Great-grandmother were always fighting each other. And Mother had just reconciled with Great-Uncle Tatiseigi, who was Great-grandmother's chiefest ally and closest associate. . . .

"I think," he said, "I think, nadiin, that we should go back upstairs, and I should talk with my father."

Rieni gave a little nod, and opened the door of the car. "Go back down," he said to Onami. "Keep us advised."

"Yes," Onami said, and left them. Rieni shut the door, then turned the key that brought the car back into service. Machinery thumped, and the car jolted and began to rise again.

He was not wrong, Cajeiri thought, to have come down for the reason he had. He was doing the right thing. He had promised not to join Great-grandmother. He had been sensible. He had known when to come back.

But—

He had never crossed Great-grandmother in his whole life. He had never given out information that involved nand' Bren's actions. He had never thought he would be put in the position of betraying nand' Bren.

He wished he had never had the idea to be here in the first place.

But given everything that could go wrong, he could not wish that, either.

12

Doubtless sharing a brandy with Machigi was an experience a fugitive railway worker and spy had not enjoyed previously. One had no idea to what degree Nomari had been educated to social graces before the calamity to his family had sent him into the countryside as a desperate young boy, but he did, Bren judged, have a good bearing, and managed a graceful acceptance of a very awkward situation.

Machigi seemed wryly amused in the situation, perhaps assessing whether they were bugged in this seating area. Indeed they were. Everything was bugged. Of *course* they were bugged, and there were three Guild stations, one belonging to the dowager, one belonging to the Shejidani Guild, not to mention his own, monitoring everything that moved on the train—so that everybody could trust everybody as much as they had to.

Bren himself held some trepidation of the early meeting tonight interfering with the dowager's plans for the morning, but an understanding with Machigi and a good start to the trip seemed a good idea, one of those opportunities that simply had to be taken as and when it came. There would be a record of the meeting, and the dowager would have it in due course, and would possibly get more forthright information than if she had been here. Machigi was the primary concern, the one that could truly pose a problem. It was up to the paidhi-aiji to ask the right questions and it was up to Guild presence to ensure they all were safe.

"We will be rolling at any moment, nandi," Narani leaned close to say, and that in fact began to happen as Narani poured the brandy, gently so, and with no disturbance of the process.

"May we have a peaceful trip," Bren said after the first sip and a lift of his glass. "The dowager will usually be up with the sun, and expect us all at breakfast, I warn you, at a very early hour. The Red Train is old, but it yields nothing to the new engines in speed, so we shall likely make Hasjuran in good time."

"We have yet to hear," Machigi said, "what the dowager intends in this visit. We hear hints that we will be talking to the lord of Hasjuran, a given, and to his association. We hear that we *may* be contacting the lord of Senjin . . . in which meeting not all of us may be comfortable."

Nomari looked at the table, then up, with no expression at all. Machigi had not been referring to himself, Bren interpreted it.

"You think Lord Bregani might recognize you, nadi?" Bren asked him.

"One has no idea," Nomari said. "We never met but once face to face. But if word of my association is spreading in the north, it will reach the south, and there may be questions raised."

"Ah, well," Machigi said, "as ultimately they will be. But let us both pretend your spying never happened, and if Bregani is wise, he will pretend the same."

"We shall try to keep that issue from notice," Bren said. "How *is* the route from Koperna up to Hasjuran, one wonders. Can it be done at all quickly?"

"By night generally," Nomari said, "and this is one of the problems in the system." He paused. "If you wish."

"If you would," Bren said. "Explain."

"By night is not wholly accurate," Nomari said, "but it is a single-track run between the two stations. So any trains running south, notably to Koperna, Targai, Najida, and the middle coast, are scheduled against the four so-called night freights coming *up* from Koperna and points west. The track is slow on the descent because speed is dangerous on the curves. The track is slow on the ascent because speed is impossible on the climb. There are three tunnels, and the track is, besides, aging. On the rare occasions when the Red Train runs that track, it disrupts regular freight schedules. There is no reason it cannot make the climb, as it usually carries only two or three cars, but it has never gone up that grade, to my knowledge."

"Which is to say a regular increase in traffic northward," Machigi said, "would be few cars, and would only run at night."

"It is a long detour to reach the transcontinental line from Koperna," Nomari said, "but it is necessary for most shipments. I am by no means qualified to judge, nandiin, but I would estimate that the greatest improvement in Koperna's connection to Hasjuran would be by dual-track where it can be done, but the tunnels pose a problem. It has been discussed, but always tabled because of expense and difficulty. The same with dual track in the south."

"Interesting," Machigi said.

They had only just reached the apartment, their own front door, when Rieni said, after a signal flash from his bracelet. "The hold has ended in the system. The train is underway."

Cajeiri's heart, already beating hard, beat harder. His stomach was upset. "Wait," he said, because Father's major d' and Father's doorman had let them into the apartment. "Let us go into my rooms for a moment," he said, and his aishid moved in that direction and let him in.

The door shut. Eisi was there, and Liedi. Across the room, Boji bounced to another perch and chittered at them.

"No," Cajeiri said, when Liedi moved to take his coat. "No, nadiin-ji. We have a problem."

"Nandi." His servants looked concerned, but helpless. His bodyguards stood there, knowing, but not knowing.

"How much time do I have?" he asked. "How much can you find out, and can I communicate with nand' Bren?"

"They will be within reach by Guild message, nandi," Rieni said. "But if they are in secrecy, it is possible there may be a careful routing of calls in and calls out. I would discourage any contact, aiji-meni. It becomes a risk of exposing their where-abouts and their purpose."

He looked at his younger aishid, the ones who knew Great-grandmother by experience—the ones who knew nand' Bren.

Nand' Bren would not countenance anything against Father. He was sure of it. If nand' Bren were not absolutely kidnapped and under restraint, *he* was Father's hand on the whole busi-ness. But—

But he had never seen Great-grandmother do such things as she was doing now. And he *believed* Father understood what she was doing, but there were times Father just stood back and let Great-grandmother alone for a time. And if Great-grandmother was *really* upset, it was hard to say what she might do. She had poisoned nand' Bren once. On purpose.

"I need to know what you know," he said to his bodyguards. "I need to know all that you know."

The train had reached that point in the Bujavid tunnel where the engine began its runout toward open track. They were on their way, to turn not toward the coast as advertised, but east-ward, once they passed the junction. And at a certain point, tomorrow, they would turn toward the south. The Transporta-tion Guild knew where its trains were, but the general public would not.

Brandy eased the sociality of the meeting. Machigi wanted the news from Tirnamardi, particularly on the aiji-consort's reconciliation with Lord Tatiseigi, and the appointment of her infant daughter Seimiro as Tatiseigi's heir-apparent—a sea change in the politics at the very heart of the aishidi'tat.

"One cannot think that Kadagidi will be far behind, in being restored to dignity," Machigi said, on the second glass of brandy. "The entity in the heart of the aishidi'tat that has so *often* sent a wave of assassination and unpleasantness southward. It would be far better if that happened *without* the child in Dojisigi still above ground."

The *child in Dojisigi* was no child—but a girl past eighteen, and already dyed with murders and plots to murder. There seemed no discernable strategy in her moves except to churn up everything in reach, foment trouble in every province within reach—and it was not, Bren thought, that it was *her* thought-out strategy. Tiajo, heir to Dojisigi, last heir standing after every other one had died violently and her father, Mujito, became ill— was supported by the remnant of the Shadow Guild, once clandestinely, now—not so secretly. Tiajo could flail about in tantrums that ended in someone's death, and terrorize her own region, and her own theory might be that terrorizing her people and her neighbors made her somehow safer from assassination, but the Shadow Guild used her operations as cover for their own far more purposeful moves.

"Is *Kadagidi's* restoration one inspiration for your railroad, nandi?" Bren asked.

"The argument could be made," Machigi said. "So might my inspiration be this fool on Jorida Isle. So might the enfranchisement of the Tribal Peoples, which, believe it or not, I favor and he will oppose. This is not a whim, paidhi. The political activity of the Tribal Peoples and the organization of the west coast, the triad of Najida, Kajiminda, and the Maschi—another non-Ragi clan—creates a new constellation in the heavens. We in the Marid are an ancient people who sit on the fringes of the aishidi'tat, neither truly participant, nor truly bystanders. For that to change, for the Marid to become fully participant, truly linking our fortunes to the aishidi'tat, as the aiji-dowager herself has done, is impossible without linkage of trade. The dowager has made an important step toward us. We have made another, toward her. But *if* we are to make a thorough link, if we are to involve ourselves directly, trade is essential *within* the Marid. If we can bring Senjin to sense, if he can seize the moment, we can make other steps. What is *your* latest, Nomari-nadi, on the brat in the Dojisigin?"

"I am not current, nandi. I fear I cannot be useful. I have been stationed in the capital the last season."

"The dowager will know," Bren said. "At breakfast, she may get around to it. Or she may not. She may wish simply to enjoy the train ride, and to hear *your* gossip, Lord Machigi."

"Does Tabini-aiji know what she intends?"

"Deal with the aiji-dowager. The aiji will track what happens. I could never say that stability in Tanaja or peace in the western Marid would go against his wishes."

"And stability in the Dojisigin Marid?"

"Stability under a *good* administration is always desirable. I cannot say that it seems likely there now."

Machigi gave one of his short, grim laughs. "That district has used the Koperna railhead, indirectly, shipping by sea to Lusi'ei, and trucking to and from the station in Koperna. The threat to *that* link, which we will pose, will disturb some moneyed interests both in Lusi'ei *and* in Amarja."

Lusi'ei was Senjin's one good harbor. Amarja was the Dojisigin capital. Tiajo's base, an inland city.

"For or against Tiajo, those interests?"

"Not desperate enough to oppose her right now."

"Where *is* her support, nandi?"

"Nomari-nadi?" Machigi said. "You *can* answer that question."

"Nandi," Nomari said. "Nand' paidhi. I had contacts in Lusi'ei. There is a network of sub-clans with industry reliant on foreign supply. The companies would fail were that shut off. They support the network because they rely on it, and her people run the network. That money reaches all the way into Koperna."

"Elaborate on this, nadi," Bren said, "if you would. We have leisure." The Red Train was gathering speed now, having passed the junction. It was headed for a connection with the dual-track transcontinental line. "I would suspect that your own situation in Ajuri set up the connections now keeping her in power."

"What I know from Lord Tatiseigi and from the aiji-consort— I do not know if I am free to speculate on that connection, nand' paidhi. May one at all mention the recent authority in Ajuri?"

"Geidaro, Shishogi, Komaji—Aseida, the Kadagidi,—whatever name you need. I was involved in it. Mention any name you need. And if Lord Machigi does not yet know, he should."

"Geidaro, in Ajuri, nandiin, was still supporting the actions in the Dojisigin Marid, and before her, Shishogi. Funds, goods, support, small items easily shipped, sold high especially in Separti."

Separti. Clear over on the west coast.

Now that, Bren thought, was a revelation. Separti township had no rail connection. The rail went from Koperna to Targai, inland, then via Najida, northward. Goods from the southern coastal townships, mostly foodstuffs and cloth, moved by sea, generally—and as he understood it, Marid ships, fishing and trade alike, did not put in at Separti: they sailed all the way to Cobo. "I am prepared to be extremely embarrassed if the connection for this illegal traffic is Najida."

"Cobo, nandi. The port at Caigi."

Where *Mospheiran* goods came in, the only allowable port for Mospheiran sea trade.

The port was, moreover, the principal port used by the traders of Ashidama Bay. It was due to expand its operations, as Tabini-aiji had agreed to allow freight landers from the space station to use the northern range. Atevi would then truck and ship goods over to Mospheira. A *lot* of trade was going in and out there, and it was about to add exotics and high tech from space.

"What sort of thing are they trading, nadi, that is *not* legal?"

"Tadja," was the answer—an intoxicant banned from regular trade, locally grown in the south. "And antiquities from the Southern Isle."

The Southern Isle. Ancient pottery. A single fragment of that rare blue glaze could go for an astonishing price. Significant items did turn up in the Marid, once colonies of the Southern Island, and reached the legitimate market in the north, destined for licensed collections or museums. What Nomari implied . . . was far from legitimate. The Marid was in a unique position to send illicit operations to those ancient sites, places forbidden and sacred, if that human word could translate the extreme emotional connection for those descended from the Southern Island—and most of the Marid could claim that.

If the Southern Isle was being systematically mined for antiquities and relics—it was a disgrace and a problem that some Marid folk would take very, very hard—while other Marid folk *were* the looters.

"Such are our secrets," Machigi commented. "My house holds two such treasures. They are currency of a sort we never spend. The Dojisigi have far more than their share, and we suspect that store is increasing."

One had to wonder how long that systematic looting had been going on . . . if it was, indeed, going on. Something had funded the coup that had ousted Tabini for over a year. Something still funded the Shadow Guild.

It was a serious risk to attempt the Southern Isle—treacherous currents, uncharted rocks, and storms raking that coast with very little warning, but collectors—illicit collectors—collectors who had no concern about the emotional connection of the descendants, one might even say the heirs of, those ancient artisans. . . . Such collectors might well push poor Marid fisherfolk into risking everything for a little prospecting in the ruins.

And if artifacts and relics had a ready market in Dojisigin— that trade became far, far more attractive a risk, possibly enough for Tiajo to bypass the fisherfolk altogether and send in her own people.

So Machigi had only two secret treasures, besides his beautiful porcelains. Did he hope to expand that nest egg? His expansionist notions did not come without cost.

It was *not* the dowager's plan to bring space age weather science and charting to Machigi for the purpose of making the Southern Isle more accessible.

"How great a problem is it now," Bren asked Machigi, "compared to fifty years ago?"

"Greater, as technology improves. Maps reach us. The eyes in space see detail not on our maps, and the information now available is a problem. There are some who talk about secret settlements on the Southern Island, illicit settlements dug in, and even if it is no more than speculation that they even exist, once the idea is there, and the technology permits—there will be those wanting to take that step. And once there is settlement on the Southern Island, even if there is a single well-known cluster of tents, it will upset the balance of power in the Marid, because that is the homeland and no one will accept any single clan assuming control of it. Change can come quickly down here—" Machigi checked himself, a man never before north of his homeland. "Change can come to the Marid, with a single gunshot . . . or a sudden shift in wealth. Or better ships. I am being quite frank with you, paidhi. Poverty and desperation characterize the Sungeni and the Dausigi coasts. No one would begrudge them the occasional 'discovery' of a family treasure; and there is, besides the looting, some market in forgeries and sometimes legitimate family heirlooms, sold in desperation. We in the Taisigin fare well enough, by the resources we have, including a large hunting reserve, and we do what we can to help our sister clans to the south, an obligation we accepted along with their man'chi. We provide food, help when a boat is lost . . . but they are a proud folk and independent, in their own way. I would *not* have the Sungeni and Dausigi suffer from Tiajo's displeasure with me."

Those small coastal clans eked out a living on the edge of the fierce Southern Ocean. They'd been the first to benefit from Machigi's plan to unify the Marid. If their small trade in artifacts and copies had been undermined by a larger operation out of the Dojisigi, or if Tiajo was using them, pressuring them for greater and greater risk . . . no, that would not be welcome news to Machigi.

"There are very, very old quarrels that did not die with the Great Wave, nand' paidhi. We are not Ragi. We have diverse aims, and we would not *want* the north except to assure it stayed out of our affairs. We have old animosities with the folk of the southwestern coast, Separti, Talidi, and Jorida, but the Maschi have been reasonable neighbors to us. Their old enemies the Farai and the Maladesi have taken up residence with Senjin, to Senjin's sometime regret—you know that those clans *are* west coast clans, not native to the Marid, once possessors of your own estate, nand' paidhi, before they fell out of favor with the Ragi clans and attached themselves to Senjin."

"I am aware."

"Senjin itself has been content to join with Dojisigi for the last number of decades, until Dojisigi was left with a fool in charge and northerners feeding her whatever her greed demands."

"By northerners in this instance, nandi, you mean the Shadow Guild."

"Exactly so. And now we have this fool child in the Dojisigin who is submitting to this splinter of a northern guild, and wasting her resources in its useless northern war, all to win what we in the Marid by no means want. You have asked me to join *my* bodyguard to the Guild in Shejidan—you understand, I think, my reluctance, under recent circumstances—and to accept other northern guilds, which have, in theory, certain usefulness to us. We do not, however, wish to become northerners, ourselves, or to be ruled by northern laws. But the north has changed. The dowager has broken the precedent at least of her own bodyguard submitting to Shejidani rules, and given that movement on the issue of central authority in the guilds, we are far more interested in association with the aishidi'tat. The Marid has been approached by the East, by the aiji-dowager, with a mutually beneficial proposal, and the aiji in Shejidan has allowed it to happen." Machigi lifted his brandy glass, a small salute. "This is progress. But while alliance with the aishidi'tat may be in the future, our immediate interest, to be blunt, nand' paidhi, is ending that Dojisigin trade with Jorida, cutting off the flow of finance to that brat in Amarja, and being rid of her enforcers, because while she sits in power, there is no peace."

Jorida, was it now? Currently Hurshina's little mercantile empire, a perpetual opponent to the Tribal Peoples, consisted of a pair of independent townships that had killed off their last two court appointed lords and provoked four wars with the Taisigin Marid and their associates. Tabini's grandfather had refused to appoint a new lord over the district, Hurshina's house being the only choice, and so old business simmered on.

Smuggling, Hurshina money, feeding the Shadow Guild?

"Have you mentioned the Dojisigi trade in artifacts to the aiji-dowager, nandi?" Certainly the dowager would hear it tomorrow morning, thanks to Guild monitoring. He was also far from sure he was not being led for Machigi's amusement—or Machigi's designs against the west coast—but an interest in eliminating Dojisigi as a threat fit neatly into more than one agenda.

"I have mentioned the smuggling before, in communications, yes," Machigi said. "The old connection was by transcontinental rail, and the offloading was, presumably, somewhere north, likely in Kadagidi territory. Now, with that boil lanced—will another have arisen on Jorida? And is there the Shadow Guild presence in a township not that far south of Najida and Kajiminda? I cannot say. But it is reasonable to suspect Jorida's trade office in Separti, which is large, and walled, might house more than clerks."

"And does the dowager know *that*, nandi?"

Machigi gave one of his more enigmatic smiles. "The dowager has yet to believe it, since I am not Hurshina's ally, nor ever will be. Whatever I say about the west coast is suspect. Suspect me as you will, but do us all a favor and also suspect Hurshina. An ally of the aiji-dowager, he is not. That much she does believe. I only suggest that he has interests in Dojisigi, not because he is generous, not even because he is a greedy, acquisitive vermin, but because he very much wants me dead. And that would greatly inconvenience her, and send the Marid up in flames." Machigi set down his glass. "Taking your warning that the dowager rises early, I shall leave you now to rest, nand' paidhi, trusting that the dowager *will* hear the reason I have for pursuing this business with Senjin at this precise moment, and that she will appreciate the true usefulness of a rail link that will absolutely outrage both Tiajo and Hurshina. Represent me well. You have done it in the past. I am sure she will see the purity of my motives. Doubt will be dangerous, where we are going."

Machigi rose, Nomari rose politely, and Bren did. There were bows all around, and Machigi swept up his bodyguard and withdrew into the vestibule and on toward his own car, as the train racketed along.

Nomari was left behind, facing a possible conversational ambush on his own way to his car, and possibly thinking that his own evening might only be beginning.

"Nandi," Nomari said uncomfortably.

"If you have apprehensions about the walk through his car to reach your own," Bren said, "consider that you are here by the dowager's invitation. If you have any concern about pressure from Lord Machigi, advise me or one of my aishid. That offer will stand throughout. As it does tonight."

"I did not expect him," Nomari said faintly. "I did not expect *this.*"

"Were you surprised by anything he said?"

"I was surprised by most everything he said. I fear I have just heard things that may threaten my life."

"Are you capable of discretion?"

A hesitation. "I have to be. I undertake to be, nand' paidhi. But I have yet to face the aiji-dowager's questions. Questions from the lords in general—I am told will be forthcoming. What shall I say?"

"Nothing of what Machigi just said. That is for the *dowager* to explain to her grandson, and it would not be wise to undertake its interpretation in any other quarter. Is there anything you *are* concealing from us still?"

A second pause, a sorting, perhaps, through memories and meetings. "Nothing I can think of, nand' paidhi, nothing of Lord Machigi's business he ever confided in me, nothing of the nature just now. *No one* has told me anything beyond the tadja business, which *is* known to the lord of Senjin. I have been to Separti once by truck, as a courier for Senjin, but observing the lay of the land and ships in harbor for Lord Machigi. That was during the Troubles. I have been to the other township for the same reasons, I have been to Caigi, I have been to Amarja, but not deeper into the Dojisigin. I have never been to Hasjuran. I have never been in Dausigi or the Isles. I do know about the smuggling in Separti: I know goods surface there. I know there is rebel Guild in Dojisigi and I know where, but that changes."

"Tell me this, of personal curiosity. Has *Najida* been used for smuggling? Or Kajiminda?"

"I know goods were traded out of Kajiminda. And up in Maschi clan, the old lord, not the new."

No difficulty knowing that was so: Geigi's nephew Baiji had been trading off some of Geigi's collection; and Bren had no trouble recalling the old lord of the Maschi, the man who had shot him, an experience which still gave him a twinge or two on cold mornings. The new lord in Targai was one of his most reliable supporters, and an honest man, who might be able to say something about his predecessor's business dealings.

"The new lord there must inconvenience the smugglers considerably."

"He has," Nomari said, "and he has a guard the aiji-dowager hand-picked. This I know."

"You likely have known far more than you may think you do. Appreciate its sensitivity and observe discretion with what you know, nadi. It may prove dangerous. One believes you have unburdened yourself to Lord Tatiseigi."

"And to the aiji-consort, nandi. I am in her debt and his."

"And to Machigi? Will you continue to inform him?"

Slight hesitation. "There is a debt. But for him—I worked for pay."

There *was* a difference, potentially.

"Nandi, in the north, I have done nothing of which I am ashamed. It was not Tabini-aiji I betrayed. It was not Lord Komaji I betrayed, either." That was the most recent lord of Ajuri, Cajeiri's grandfather. "My information, where I spied, where I divulged things I observed, involved specifically Lord Bregani and Lord Tiajo, and I hoped with everyone else for the return of the ship and the safety of Tabini-aiji, and if not that, then for someone to deal with the Troubles."

That had been the legitimate hope of a lot of people, in those days, and except for Lord Geigi's personal conviction that Tabini *was* alive, an aijinate might have been conducted from the space station, drastic as that would have been.

"You are not politically naive, nadi."

"No, nandi, at least where I have direct knowledge. My life has depended on listening carefully and on keeping more secrets than I sold."

"You left Lord Machigi—why?"

"When my guild recovered itself, nandi, when the aiji came back to power. Then I came back to the capital. But I did spy for Lord Machigi in those years. I reported what he asked, for pay. I left. There was no rancor in my leaving."

"Did you deal with him directly?"

"Only twice, nandi."

"Is there any reason you should be afraid of him?"

Nomari gave a short, startled laugh. "Most are. But he was

safety for me." The laughter turned to a somber look. "I am not hopeful if the aiji-dowager has some cause against me on that account."

"Her favor is worth winning." He said it in full knowledge that Ilisidi would hear it, and she did not like to be gossiped about. "And it is possible to win, but do not take it as granted that you have her favor now. You are here, I think, because a decision must be made regarding your candidacy, in which she has an interest; and because Machigi, with whom she has some agreement, is pressing an issue, and you have some knowledge of him as well as of the system at issue. Act for the interest you intend to serve hereafter. That is my unsolicited advice, nadi. Advise me if you find your position difficult, and I shall try to mediate. Above all, trust your bodyguard. They also have heard what was said here. They will advise you in your best interest."

"Nandi." Nomari gave a deep bow. "I appreciate all you say."

"Good rest to you," Bren said. He watched Nomari retreat in the direction Machigi had gone, and gather up the aishid that protected him, the four who would keep him safe during his transit through Machigi's car . . . but not safe from any conversation Nomari chose to involve himself in, if he decided to stop and pass a little time there.

They were up to speed now, thumping along eastward before their turn south.

Toward Hasjuran. Close to a pass overhanging the Marid.

Had Ilisidi summoned Machigi to that meeting in Najida?

Had that all been a show for his benefit?

Tabini did not exclude Ilisidi from events and go scot-free. Was that it?

But then—Ilisidi, in her own two terms as aiji-regent, had viewed the west coast as her particular concern, a time bomb she viewed as a greater threat to the aishidi'tat than the perpetually restive Marid *or* her grandson's fascination with human technology.

She had made an extravagant move on her own, bringing Machigi into a trade deal for which ships did not yet exist.

But had that trade package been a move on a chessboard toward something she wanted far more than a settlement with the Marid?

It was a question. It was very much a question.

13

Father *would* see him. Father was working in his office—he often worked in the evenings. Cajeiri came by himself, only a matter of walking down the hall, and much as his aishid might want to hear what happened—having the seniors there to overhear him when he was anxious and fearful of being stupid—was just too embarrassing. And he *could* not prefer his younger aishid over them, who had far more facts of the case. Father could call them if he wanted them.

But for himself, he just went down the hall in the formal dress he had chosen for his trip downstairs, knocked on the door, and identified himself.

"Come in," Father said, and he opened the door and slipped in, careful to close it.

"Father," he said, "Honored Father, one may have come on something not intended."

Father turned his chair from the desk to face him. "In what respect? And you are dressed very fine for an evening at home."

"Honored Father, I went down to the train station. I went only to say goodbye . . ." That was not exactly true. "I went down to talk to nand' Bren. I wanted to tell him to take care of Nomari, and to tell him what I know."

Father nodded. "That was enterprising."

That was another word for beyond his limits, Cajeiri thought.

"I stayed with my aishid, Father. All of them. I promised them that I would *not* do anything stupid, and they investigated the situation. Onami went down. Banichi would recognize any of the others. And he looked things over. He said that Great-grandmother had gone to bed aboard the train, but nand' Bren and my cousin were coming down about the same time. So I hoped to see both of them. And I was on my way down with the rest of my aishid. In proper dress."

"Indeed."

"And we stopped. The lift stopped. Onami signaled there was a problem, so we waited until Onami could come back up to us, and he said *Lord Machigi* was down there. Did you know that, Honored Father? By the time we could get back here, the train had already left, and there were *seven* sleeper cars. So I thought— one thought—I had better think and put things together. My aishid said there was no hurry then. That we could always stop the train. If we had to. Did you know, Honored Father?"

Father crossed one foot over another. "Actually, yes. I did know."

He had no idea what to say then. He sat for a breath or two, then began to feel uninvited in any business between Father and Great-grandmother. But he was worried about nand' Bren and Nomari.

"Your cousin worked for Lord Machigi," Father said, "and being that Lord Machigi has decided he wants a railroad very urgently, it seemed logical to include him."

"That is not the reason," Cajeiri said abruptly. It just burst out of him. And he immediately wished he had been quiet, but Father had gone whimsical and dismissive, and he thought he deserved at least not to have his concerns brushed off. As it was, he was left having said what he had said, and he had to hold on to it.

"Do you *know* the reason?" Father asked him, in that mode of teaching him something, making him follow the steps, bit by bit, and he was not sure he wanted to be led by the hand. Not in this.

"I do not, sir. Are you and Great-grandmother having a fight? Or is it Mother?"

Father looked at him a little askance. "What is *your* theory?"

"My theory is nowhere. You know the truth."

"I would find your theory instructive, son of mine. You have talked to your great-grandmother. You spent a fair amount of time with her, and she did not tell you what she was up to. You were sure she was up to something when she took possession of the candidate for Ajuri *and* the paidhi and ordered the Red Train—instead of flying. You must have thought something."

"On the train there are several days of being alone with him."

"With the Ajuri candidate. And nand' Bren. Where do you think they are going?"

"Malguri, one supposes."

"That would be the logical assumption . . . but all those sleeper cars . . ."

"Her guard. Her staff. Nand' Bren . . ."

"Still a great many, indeed."

"I did not go down there, Father. I did not see them. I came back up when I heard about Lord Machigi, to make certain you knew. What is she doing with Lord Machigi and my cousin?"

"Probably re-introducing them to each other and watching the reactions, would you think?"

"Maybe."

"But you stopped. You came back up. Would you have gone down had you known I knew?"

"Had I known what you know, I might have gone down. Or I might not have tried to go down at all, since nand' Bren probably knows what is going on."

"In any case, you are beyond stowing away on the train."

His early misdeeds perpetually came back on him and occasionally made him seem a fool. "I would have been fairly obvious, Honored Father, trying to stow away attended by eight bodyguards."

Father gave a gentle laugh. "One believes that."

"So what have you not told me? What *is* mani up to? What

has Lord Machigi got to do with it? Why is he here? And why are they going to *Hasjuran?*"

"Remember—Lord Machigi wants a railroad."

"The railroad already runs down from there."

"To?"

"Koperna, in Senjin. It turns west there. But—"

"But?"

"Are they going to assassinate Lord Bregani?"

Father looked a little surprised, and amused. "Not primarily, no. They would like to *persuade* Lord Bregani."

"I do not want mani and nand' Bren going down into Koperna!"

"One does not believe that is Grandmother's intention. Nor Lord Machigi's."

"They cannot send nand' Bren, either!"

"I would discourage that, yes."

"Well, she cannot do it!"

"Nor will she, I am quite convinced. I am impressed, however, that you came here to give me the news as you found it. Of available choices, including contacting your great-grandmother's aishid or nand' Bren's, you made the best one, to tell me. That is how power to make decisions has to flow, son of mine, and while there may be times you officially do not want to know, practically, you will need to know. Do you wish to know what your great-grandmother is really up to?"

"More than giving Lord Machigi a railroad. She did not need to go there to do that."

"Dealing with the lord of Senjin if she can."

"Bregani."

"That is correct. Dealing with him, and massively frustrating a girl who does not know as much as you do about running a province . . . or managing very dangerous people."

"Lord Tiajo."

"Tiajo, who did not respect her father, who refused to listen to councillors, who has let all sorts of problems through her gates, so to speak, and is tolerated by them simply because she is a fool. The very worst example of rule. She does not have the man'chi of her own people. Not even, one suspects, that of her own servants in her own house. She has a little nest of Shadow Guild. She relies on them, though no one is truly loyal to her. That is a very lonely situation to be in. But she does not seem to perceive that she is in it."

"I hear you, Honored Father. One hopes never to be that stupid."

"I am sure you are not. This is the situation. The head of the Shadow Guild as it currently exists is a woman named Suratho. Suratho aims at another Marid war in a year or so, which can do no good for the north. She is funding it by trade with the west coast, and the west coast is her most likely target when she attacks, *inviting* a war to reach the Marid across the Taisigi hunting range. We think Bregani of Senjin knows the state of affairs, and he is worried."

Now Father was telling him the truth, and telling him things that had to stay secret.

"My aishid did not come down the hall," he said, "and I am not carrying any communications, Father."

Father smiled and tapped a little black box on his desk. "I know you are not. Your aishid, senior and junior, are persons I would trust with state secrets or I would not trust them with my son; but they also would not send a listening device to my office. They will rely on you to tell them as much as they need to know, and I would advise you tell them frankly what the situation is, since they are in charge of protecting you. I would not have them surprised."

"Will you tell Great-uncle? And Mother?"

"I am *thinking* about telling them."

"I think you should. I think you can trust Mother. And Great-uncle."

"I have always trusted them, in the highest sense. I am glad you include your mother."

"Mother has trusted me, I think. I tried my hardest at Tirnamardi. I knew we were in trouble. And Mother was very brave, and very smart in everything she did. So was Great-uncle."

Father nodded thoughtfully. "So I have always perceived. So I perceive of you, son of mine. Go have a good night's sleep. Things are in hand, proceeding, we trust, as they need to be."

It was not wholly good news, if the Shadow Guild was trying to stir up the Marid.

But if this time they could get things settled down there and truly get rid of the Shadow Guild—that was good. That was very good.

"It went better than it might have," Bren said, as Jago slipped beneath the covers and the Red Train rumbled along eastbound.

"It was interesting," Jago said, turning to face him. It was a generous bunk, the master suite of the dowager's alternate sleeping car. There was, of all things, a crystal chandelier above them in the dark, set on dimmest light. Velvet coverlet. The slight aroma of pesticide, the car having been in storage.

"One believes Lord Machigi was intending to contact both of us tonight. But was it an accident we came down before Nomari?"

"Not an accident," Jago said. "Machigi was first. And he did not have an opportunity to speak to the dowager on any matter of business. She met him, yes. There was brandy, there was courtesy, there was a discussion of objectives in a very general way, but nothing specific. One suspects, once she retired for the evening, he was watching for your arrival, in hopes of just such a conversation—perhaps at her suggestion. And one believes she was very much in control of the timing—but there is no saying the aiji himself might have been aware you met. We do not control Cenedi's communications."

"One hopes not to have gone counter to the dowager's wishes."

"But, then, you are not here solely representing the dowager's wishes."

Are we monitored? He signed that, silently.

"Not at the moment. We control the switch in this car. As does the dowager in hers and in the Red Car."

"During our conversation with Machigi, surely—"

"All that was recorded. We deemed that of Guild interest, in your protection. Certainly the dowager will hear it."

"Correctly so. I am glad."

Jago propped herself on her elbow, looking at him, the usually sleek hair tumbled in recently braided waves about her face. "The Ajuri, even on first encounter, seems less a cipher than does the Marid lord after some experience of him. But perhaps the Ajuri is simply that much better."

"I would agree he seems to be dealing plainly in the truth," Bren said, "and in his position, suppositions left to run wild can harm him more than any admission of his old associations. If he reveals them all, then he has revealed them all and cannot be blackmailed. Or set at disadvantage by some sudden revelation."

"The only connections that truly cannot be read are those inside his mind," Jago said. "His true inclinations, his intentions, his ambitions and his hostilities. He cannot have forgiven Geidaro's house anything. And Geidaro's son Caradi is still alive."

"Future trouble. But Caradi is not the sharpest edge ever forged. Our young candidate for Ajuri will have far larger threats to deal with. Caradi—him, I do not know. I do *not* have a high opinion of his character."

"Nomari may give the impression of vulnerability," Jago said, "but one reflects that he has survived, working fairly well in the open. We do not know his attitude toward others in Ajuri, toward his neighbors, and toward the aijinate. It is a fairly large silence he has drawn about himself and his whereabouts and his activities, and *we* cannot penetrate it."

That was saying the Guild could not, so far as Jago was willing to say.

Still . . . "Lord Tatiseigi is no fool either," Bren said. "One trusts his judgment of character."

"Tatiseigi doubted you, once."

"He doubted me, but that was along with the rest of the continent. One does not hold that against him. Tatiseigi praises the young man. The aiji-consort confirms his identity."

"The aiji-consort . . ." Jago left that statement unadorned. Damiri had had the good sense to marry Tabini, but she had trusted untrustworthy people in her life. Often. And repeatedly.

But much of that had been as a child, well before she had found her footing.

"Cajeiri finds no fault in him," Bren said. "But again—his information is restricted."

"And immature. The heir's judgment is good, but he is still innocent of some motives adults have."

"I promise I shall not trust this person further than my aishid advises."

"To the relief of us all," Jago said. "As we shall rely on Cenedi and on the dowager for their observations."

"One sincerely hopes she does not test anyone as she did me."

"Tabini has loosed her upon him, upon Machigi *and* Topari," Jago said. "Not to mention the lord of Senjin. Her hand is usually sure. But—she is uncommonly tolerant of Machigi."

"If I were Machigi," Bren said, "I would worry about that."

"With cause," Jago said with a little laugh. "And with equal cause—her aishid worries on this point. I do not think she worries as much as they wish she would."

The dowager loved a challenge. Loved a test of boundaries. *Worked* by pushing a fragile alliance to the limit . . . in the theory it might prove the alliance or expose a problem.

He had been along for more than one of the dowager's experiments. Not mentioning the cup of tea.

Jago slipped a warm arm under him. They had shared a bed in some strange places, and under stranger circumstances, but on a train in such company, hurtling through the night—with so very much at stake—it lent a particular sense of risk.

"I have a question." He kept his voice very low.

"Ask."

"Topari is not the most discreet lord in the aishidi'tat."

He felt Jago laugh. "No." Jago said. "What is the question?"

"Was this venue particularly chosen for that virtue?"

Second laugh. "Yes, Bren-ji. You have learned her ways."

"She *wants* gossip to reach Tiajo. She *wants* to provoke an attack."

"News will reach Tiajo, first. And second—we might fairly easily have arranged this meeting in the Marid, in Lord Machigi's capital. Instead she chose the house of the most guileless, most ill-defended lord in the aishidi'tat."

"She is inviting trouble."

"She is setting a place for it at table and offering dessert. Tiajo will know she is challenged—but being a creature of passions, may not use her better sense. And since we are not dealing with the most discreet lord in the aishidi'tat, gossip will circulate through every pass and every campsite in the mountains, and Bregani will *know* Tiajo will know. He will have to realize it would be wise to move—one direction or the other. No one would recommend he trust Tiajo's good sense and self-restraint. His *sane* choice is obvious."

One had the map of it.

"Besides," Jago said, "Topari is *not* a man one would rely on as co-conspirator in any plot. His feckless honesty must reassure Bregani he is far safer establishing credentials with the dowager and letting her arrange a deal than sitting at home hoping Tiajo has forgotten her quarrel with him."

"Machigi's presence, however . . ."

"It is the same equation. The dowager would never allow a guest of hers to assassinate another invitee. That is unthinkable. Bregani has his safest course clear. Or will have, very shortly. He will never have a better offer."

"One only hopes," Bren said, "that Tiajo does not launch an all-out assault."

"Whatever Tiajo does, we shall deal with it," Jago said, winding his hair around her finger, tugging gently. "Meanwhile it is likely *you* will have to deal with Lord Topari."

14

Cajeiri had thought he might sleep better, having had Father's reassurance about mani and nand' Bren. That had not been the case. He kept thinking about danger and waking with nightmares. And well before his usual time, and still without much sleep, he became too restless, slid out of bed and moved about trying to dress quietly without disturbing his staff. He put on his dressing robe and slippers and went out to his small desk in the sitting room, his little office just seeming too lonely with the door shut. He settled quietly—almost; Boji began to move about his cage. Boji decided it was breakfast—but then, Boji was sure breakfast was coming the moment anyone stirred. Fortunately Eisi had set a bowl with two raw eggs on the table nearest.

"Here," Cajeiri said, and gave the rascal one, which would keep him quiet for a while.

He had far rather be on the train right now. He so wanted to know what mani was up to.

But that could not be. At the same time Father had agreed to have his human associates come down to live, Father had made him heir.

And with that—he found himself fairly well locked in and locked down. He *had* to be responsible. He had to prove he was responsible, so when he did ask for things—such as his associates visiting Najida—Father would be sure he was not sending a fool out to nand' Bren's estate.

Father had not sent a fool when he had sent nand' Bren with mani, either. He told himself they would both certainly manage without him. They had managed before he was born, had they not?

Lord Topari was a fool not worth worrying about, or at least acted like one. Machigi, on the other hand—

He could not help worrying.

But Nomari was no fool, either.

And if mani really was going after Tiajo, it was to everybody's good. Machigi was no ally of Tiajo's, that much was very certain. So if there was a cause that would get everybody together—Tiajo might be it.

It was just not his to do. Not his matter to solve. What he did have under his control—was a parid'ja that needed a home and a staff that had suddenly gotten older, and larger. And in an hour or so there would be more hammering and sawing in the servants' passage trying to make room, the consequence of all the changes in his life. Poor Boji hated it, and bounded around rattling his cage in complaint—

But there was no helping it. Even if the laundry was late and the servants' hall became a dusty mess, they had to do it.

He sat at his desk, looking through his notebooks and his studies, and his little stack of correspondence. And to console himself till breakfast, he took up a pen and began to write.

I was very glad to get your letters. I am back in the Bu-javid now.

He could not say what mani and nand' Bren were doing. That was deeply secret. He could not mention Nomari and the appointment, because that was probably secret until it happened or failed, which he truly hoped would turn out to favor Nomari.

He wrote: *I am trying to find a place for Boji.* That was safe to talk about. *He is getting too big for his cage, and it is unfair to ask Eisi and Liedi to go on riding in a baggage car.*

I am trying to get back to my studies. My tutor is going to

*come in, maybe tomorrow. I have been collecting questions
for him.*

*I did get to see Jeichido recently. She is beautiful. Uncle says
she needs her own herd. So I may have more than one mecheita
and you can ride.*

*I hope you are comfortable in your new apartments. I wish
I could be there. I once landed at that airport, when we first
came down. I heard what happened there and I am very sorry,
but one also hears that Mospheirans are sending you gifts and
they welcome you. I hope the Presidenta is doing well.*

*Nand' Bren tells me you are safe where you are. I hope you
will please mind your security and do not explore on your own.
Please keep yourselves safe and advise your parents the same.
There are very good people watching you and if you ever have a
misunderstanding about something, still trust them and do as
they ask. If you have any problems tell them to call nand' Bren.*

*And if you can get a camera, take pictures. I want to see
where you live and what sort of things you do. Tell me about
the people you see and tell me about your tutors: nand' Bren
says they speak Ragi, and you should speak Ragi too, every
chance you get.*

It was a stupid letter, full of holes and saying nothing useful.
He wadded it up and then, because he did not want even his
staff knowing how stupid it was, he smoothed it out, folded it
and tore it into tiny pieces.

*I want to travel again. I want to go to Najida and I want
them to come there, but Father is going to insist I do my lessons, and if what mani and nand' Bren are doing starts a war
with the Marid—*

He remembered all too vividly being in Najida when it came
under attack. When mortars had sounded across the hills. When
enemies had gotten inside.

He could not travel to Najida if the Marid situation went
wrong. His associates might come to the capital. He supposed
so. But—

Everything should be better, now that they were about to solve the problems in the Padi Valley.

But now they might be starting up again in the Marid.

He was not used to sitting still while mani and nand' Bren went off into trouble, that was one thing. He was not used to knowing that his associates were just a train ride and a boat trip away—and he could not even talk to them. He had to go about his lessons and his routines and just ignore the fact that they were that close.

But—he *had* the freedom now to travel. Or at least—he had enough bodyguards that his parents thought he was safe, even if that had been tested. He was home. He was safe. Everything had worked out.

And Father was pleased with him, at least, for telling him about Machigi; and Mother was pleased with him for—well, he was not sure, except that he had not been a fool at Tirnamardi. Maybe that was all it took, after all. He had just done what he needed to do—he had stayed put and looked to his guard to protect him, because there was nothing else he was supposed to do. Maybe it was just that easy.

Only nothing ever was. His household had changed and he had not chosen the changes. They were not bad men, Rieni and the new aishid. In fact—they had made his aishid happy. Only—

Eisi and Liedi, besides taking care of Boji, now had to do everything for eight Guild, not four, and Rieni and his unit wanted an office. And a television. Which probably, regarding the news, was a good thing for them to have. But Antaro's unit had no television—and was that fair?

He had no television. Mother had none. Father had one in his private rooms, but now it seemed a necessity his senior aishid wanted. He was not sure what considerations Father had promised the senior unit to get them to come into the household, but evidently they could get whatever they asked for, and a refrigerator in their office was another of those things.

It was not such a bad idea. It made it unnecessary for staff to run the long route to the kitchen at whatever hour. He had just never thought of needing such a thing—until, of course, he had his own apartment.

Which he could not have for years, being only fortunate nine.

But he had an aishid actually senior to Father's. So having to run to the kitchen for this and that was something juniors should do for them, but for his insistence that the *actual* senior unit in his ranking of things was Antaro's, which would never be understood among the general staff. It was all tangled up in an upside-down seniority, and in four extremely senior Guild who were used to comforts and conveniences.

At least Rieni was not asking Antaro's unit to run errands, or laying another task on Eisi and Liedi, who had already been inconvenienced and overworked and moved out of their original quarters to let his senior aishid be closest to his bedroom.

It was all very complicated. And they were going to start hammering and sawing in the servants' passage. And everything was going to spread out larger and larger.

Eisi and Liedi had stayed up late trying to organize what had gotten out of order in their traveling. And they had missed the laundry, for which Eisi had apologized, but it was not their fault. They were exhausted, doing every small thing for five people and answering the whims of a spoiled parid'ja.

He had been awake half the night thinking these thoughts. And not knowing what to do, but to go back to work on his lessons and stay where he was and not be involved if mani and nand' Bren got into trouble. He just was—

Not happy, that was what was truly keeping him awake. Not happy. In spite of so many things going uncommonly well, he was locked in like Boji in his cage. As many eggs as Boji wanted Boji could have. But—it was still a cage. When Boji had been small, it had been enough. It had been safety for a foolish young parid'ja. Now—it was just a cage.

Sorry, he thought, looking back at the little black face looking at him through bronze filigree, the metal imitating flowers and vines Boji had never seen. If I let you into a forest now you will just sit and wait for eggs to come and starve to death. I am sorry. I think I am doing much the same.

Waiting for eggs. Foolish of me. I cannot stay like this. I am outgrowing my own cage. But there is no place for me, yet, either.

15

"The dowager is not displeased," Banichi said in the morning, just that, which was a relief, after one had been put to improvising the night before, and without knowing whether the dowager's retirement to her own car had signaled disgust for the entire enterprise or a wish to have a fresh encounter this morning.

And this morning, she was extraordinarily—late. Which one could suspect was because she had been reviewing the interesting parts of last night's security recordings.

They were let through—there came word from Cenedi that the passageways of his car and the dowager's were both unlocked, at which point Bren, long since dressed for breakfast, ordered the passageway in his car unlocked, and the other two guests advised that they might come through. Nomari had waited to be advised; Machigi had met a locked passage door in Banichi's car; and now with everything open, everybody could go through the galley car's passage all the way to the Red Car.

Bren went first, quietly, thinking that the dowager might be *in* the Red Car, already at table, but no. He was the first to arrive, except two of Cenedi's young men and four of Ilisidi's servants. They had a round table set, a moveable affair from some source: it had displaced some of the usual seating, which had vanished as mysteriously as the table had apppeared—the first time in many journeys Bren had ever seen the car transformed.

The table was linen-draped, with a service set for five persons. One seat was likely for Cenedi, to bring the company to a fortunate number. The rest of the bodyguards would stand, waiting for their breakfast until afterward.

Machigi arrived, with half his bodyguard, most likely by instruction; Nomari came, with two of his.

"I would, nandiin," Bren said, "expect that this is the dowager's place, mine to her left, her Guild-senior to her right." It left Machigi and Nomari sitting side by side. "But wait."

He remained standing. They did. And in no long time at all, the dowager herself arrived with Cenedi, Nawari, and two more of her usual bodyguard, so there was an overwhelming force of Guild on her side—should it be needed, which one sincerely did not expect.

"Nandiin, nadi," she greeted them, and sat, as expected, in the nearest chair, arranging her napkin and smiling, while they took their seats. Back at the entry, servers from the galley brought tea and wafers to start.

Bindanda was, Bren was sure, assisting Ilisidi's chef, and Nawari and Jeladi were helping with service, possibly yet to appear, or not. Ilisidi's chef was in charge, and one only hoped she intended no tests of manners, loyalty, or tolerance for poisons.

She was still smiling, and specifically welcomed Nomari with, "We have a stranger to our table. The candidate for Ajuri. We trust our invitation has not inconvenienced you, nadi."

"One was surprised, aiji-ma, and honored to be included."

"Aiji-ma," she said quietly, looking quizzical. "Indeed."

The term of personal loyalty—which Machigi continually dodged. And she wickedly challenged it, for openers. Nomari looked far from oblivious, maybe not grasping the whole context involving Machigi, maybe taking it as a personal question, to which there was *no* useful answer, and wisely he did not try.

"Nand' dowager," Machigi said, smooth as silk.

"Well, well," Ilisidi said, and picked up her teacup, after

which they all could do the same. "A good morning to us all. You know where we are going. Do you, Nomari-nadi?"

"One is informed, yes, aiji-ma."

"Have you ever visited Hasjuran?"

"No, aiji-ma. This will be the first time."

A sip of tea. "Tell me," she said, "have *you* ever been in the mountains, Lord Machigi?"

"No, nand' dowager," was the answer.

"One hopes you brought a warm coat."

"A moderately warm one," Machigi said, "but I would expect there is indoor heating."

"Well, well, one hopes it will be adequate. And you, nadi?" This to Nomari.

"Aiji-ma, I shall manage."

"Pish. We have called you into this chilly event with absolutely inadequate wardrobe, and alas, little forewarning for your staff. On the train, we shall manage, and we may use it as a refuge: we have electric heat, assuming the local station has the means to deliver power. I shall have my staff scour the local market at least for a winter coat. There is no need to suffer."

God, she was playing the beneficent grandmother to the lot of them, himself possibly excluded. Something was on her mind.

Conversation ran on to the snow pack, the advent of winter in the highlands, and a query after the fishing in Sungeni this season, granted a severe and early storm front.

Breakfast ended, and as she took her cane from Cenedi's hand and rose from the table, she said, ever so primly, "I think we shall detach the first several cars and send the train down to Koperna with an invitation, once we arrive in Hasjuran. Should we say you are here, Lord Machigi? Is it something Lord Bregani's spies are adequate to learn in advance, or not?"

Machigi was not set off balance. "I could in no wise say, nand' dowager. Perhaps we should ask the candidate for Ajuri to venture a guess."

There was silence. Ilisidi turned a questioning look in Nomari's direction. "Should we, or should we not, nadi, assume that the lord of Koperna is that well-informed on our business?"

"Lord Bregani might be made aware the Red Train had arrived in Hasjuran, but one is not sure the news would come very quickly, aiji-ma."

"And will he tell Tiajo?"

"He might. But—if I were in his place, aiji-ma—"

"Go on."

"She still might assume he was not to be trusted. He could offend you and refuse to come and still not make her happy."

"Do amplify your thought, nadi."

"If he ignores the invitation, he offends you. If he comes— he can always claim he was just looking for information. But even so it might not move Tiajo."

Ilisidi arched a brow. "Indeed, nadi. And aside from your own choices, what do you think Lord Bregani is apt to do?"

"I think it would not go well, aiji-ma, whichever he chooses, but that is only my opinion."

"Your opinion was our request, nadi." And to Machigi: "And what do *you* think of his situation, nandi?"

"That would depend on Tiajo's mood of the hour," Machigi said. "He might run to her instead, but that would afford him no protection, and he has enemies in her court, as likely you know. Her advisers pull her one way and another, she trusts no one, and her extreme temper fits take lives she may later regret, but then—there is no way to mend an assassination."

"Indeed not." Ilisidi nodded thoughtfully. "How is Bregani? What of his stability?"

"Bregani is scared," Machigi said, "and though he has played the fool to survive, reports are—are they not, nadi?—that he is not a fool, though he is certainly not my ally. Will eliminating Tiajo make *him* a threat? One cannot entirely predict."

"Hasjuran," Ilisidi said, "seems the sort of place where spies may come and go. The question remains to whom they report. There are so many choices."

The hammering had started up again in the servants' passage, and there was music playing down the hall, his mother's defense of Seimei's naptime. Nothing in the house could be settled with that going on, and now a drill had added itself to the racket, which set Boji off. Peace and quiet had fled the house, Father was working down on the first floor, in his formal office, and Mother was considering moving herself and Seimei down the hall to guest with Uncle Tatiseigi. Cajeiri thought he might himself take refuge with nand' Bren's staff.

But that seemed a desertion, since his household was the source of it all. He felt responsible for the disturbance, and he felt that, whoever fled, he should be the last. He simply sat down at his desk and opened his book on laws and regulations and tried to remember where he had been when everything had gone wrong and he had left his regular lessons with his tutor. He had, besides, a list of things to ask, that he had written down from as diverse places as the space station and Uncle Tatiseigi's estate, things about history and things about the treaty that had atevi and humans sharing the station.

And things about Ajuri. A great deal about Ajuri, and the history of the Nichono line.

Someone came to the door, no secret, since they had no proper foyer, but it was fairly unusual. Perhaps, he thought, Mother really was leaving him in charge.

Back came Eisi from the door, bearing the message bowl, and a single cylinder, with Father's sigil on it.

He opened it. It was not from Father, but from Father's major domo, to him.

It said: *Considering the burden of expanded personnel in your residence, young gentleman, and a point of decision regarding the revision of the servants' passages, it would be appropriate for you to request an increase in domestic staff. Your esteemed father concurs. Be assured of my cooperation at all levels.*

It did not say, Consult your father.

It did not say, precisely, what to do or what sort of increase to ask for.

He sat at the writing desk he maintained in the sitting room. He could go to his small office—but it had no resources except the means to phone Father downstairs and ask, and what the major d' had sent him actually had the flavor of one of Father's messages: this is a test . . . *do something.*

He understood about household budget. Sometimes he was included in it. Sometimes, as when he had new wardrobe for an event, he heard about payment, but he had never in his life handled money, and he was not sure even Father had. Papers went back and forth and drew against the house account, which Father said he meant to keep within limits.

But he had no idea even how much it cost to have one servant, and he could not just send to the major d' and say, send me servants. He *supposed*, like Eisi and Liedi, they would just be reassigned to his household, but how many—he did not know.

The persons who really might know such things were the seniors, he thought; but the persons who should most have a word in the matter were Eisi and Liedi, who were the ones most affected. He thought about it. And he rang for them.

They came from the back of the suite, where everything was going on, and where both sets of his bodyguard were apparently involved with the hammering and sawing. They stood by his desk, two grown men, not nearly as old or as experienced as the seniors, but like his younger aishid, they had seen a great deal of the world, attending him.

"Nandi?" Eisi asked.

He certainly owed Eisi and Liedi better than they had yet had from him.

"I think," he said, and amended it, "I know you have a great deal more work to do since there are more of us. I have just had a letter from the major d'. He thinks you should have help. More staff. I am not sure how to go about this, but how much do you think you need?"

"We are managing, nandi," Eisi said. "We missed the laundry last night, but—"

"One is certain that is not your fault, nadi. I do not think this note is at all because of that."

"It is just all the confusion, nandi. Once Boji does go, there will be far, far less to do."

"And we have four more people, four more beds, that much more laundry of all sorts. We have the chance now to ask for help."

"Once the new rooms are ready, and things are back in order, we shall be absolutely on time, nandi. We are sorry."

They were very earnest faces, good faces, apologizing for a situation they were sure left them at fault. He could never even manage clean clothes or find half his belongings if it were not for Eisi and Liedi.

"Tell me the truth, nadiin-ji. *Are* you Guild?"

That drew a little laugh. "We are Servants' Guild," Liedi said, "nothing more."

"But," Eisi said, "we take instruction and we know some things your aishid has taught us."

No few of Father's and mani's servants were plainclothes Assassins' Guild. It was the case with nand' Bren's staff. And Uncle's. But Eisi and Liedi were not that, if they had admitted the truth. Father had plainclothes Guild minding the door, and in the kitchens. And maybe he should ask for that.

But he knew increasingly what he wanted, who he trusted, and how he wanted to arrange his household.

And since Father asked . . .

"I am going to give orders," he said to them, "and I cannot promise that my father will honor them, but I shall argue for them. First, Eisi-ji we do not have anything but a door and a message bowl, but you are *my* major d' from now on, and, Liedi-ji, you are the doorman. I shall have to confirm that with my father, but that is what I want. And there should be people to take your orders."

"Nandi," Eisi said. "We thank you for the honor. We shall perfectly understand if the decision comes down otherwise."

"I shall argue in that case," Cajeiri said, "and I shall do everything I can, and I shall hope to be heard. *You* tell me the staff we should reasonably have, what would be helpful to you, and how you would arrange things. What do we need? What would make my father say we have a well-run household?"

Eisi and Liedi looked at each other. Then Eisi said, "The laundry and the beds take time. The more people, the more laundry. Your wardrobe, all that sort of work, Liedi and I gladly manage—we *should* manage it, and do double duty as valets. We have the skills for fine fabrics. If we only had two young people to manage the servant's quarters, the light cleaning and regular laundry and beds, we should be well-set. Maintaining the rooms in order is not difficult."

"Can you find two people who would get along with us?"

"I think without any difficulty, nandi," Liedi said. "Any instruction they lack—we can give."

"And clearances. I trust these people would come from Father's staff."

"They would, nandi, yes. Nobody can come in here, but from there. And we shall ask the major d's help."

"Then I shall advise him, and you will requisition whatever we need. Requisition. That *is* the word."

"Indeed," Eisi said.

"I take it there are forms?"

"There are, nandi, there indeed are. What we need are personnel requests and supply requisitions. We shall file them if you will sign them."

He was increasingly sure of his moves. There were forms. That meant there were routes things had to follow. He had watched them all his life. "Fill them out as you can and bring them to me." A thought occurred to him. It landed with particular force in a spate of hammering from behind his bedroom. "If we have two more people, we are out of room again."

"That will be so, nandi. We shall have to ask for that, too."

"Forms," he said. It occurred to him that there might be a reason in Father suggesting he do something now, before the new construction was finished. There was an upstairs and a downstairs that was only accessible in the servant passages, and that extended this way and that, sharing walls with nand' Bren's servants if one went back far enough. He had no idea. The halls back there changed—they had changed when his sister was born and Mother took on staff, and now they would change again, very likely, and Mother and his baby sister might yet take refuge with Great-uncle until the hammering stopped. Great-uncle would not be unhappy to have them. But Mother was never happy to be disarranged.

"We shall advise the major d'," was Eisi's reply. "We shall make everything proper."

"I shall advise my mother," he said. "Eisi-ji, Liedi-ji, you have been extraordinarily patient with me, in everything. You will always be first, in my staff, whether or not we can carry this through right now."

"We are honored even by your thought, nandi," Eisi said. "We shall go find out what we can do."

"I shall give you a letter. I shall write it right now. And you will do whatever you need to do to be proper. If we need more room—one has no idea. There is the upstairs."

He dashed off the letter to Father's major d'. *Please be advised . . .* That was how staff letters always started. *. . . that I have made Eisi major domo and Liedi doorman to my small household according to your letter and they will receive the mail from you.* Not that there was very much or very often, but if there was, that was the proper function of their posts. *Please give them the right forms and tell them what they need to do to get two domestic staff. Also we need the forms for their rooms, and if it is at all possible, can there also be a domestic staff room with table, chairs, and a refrigerator? Thank you very much, nadi, for your advice and your assistance.*

He sealed it. He had, lately, his own smaller seal ring. He had a small roll of red ribbon that had come with the ring and the waxjack, and he did it properly, with the seal atop the ribbon, then solemnly handed it to Eisi.

"Nandi," Eisi said. And they left, happy, he thought. He hoped they were happy.

Things had changed—in just that little time. But they had started changing when Father had named him heir, the night Seimiro was born. They had changed again when Father assigned him the double bodyguard. They were eleven right now. They would be fortunate thirteen, perhaps by nightfall.

And Eisi and Liedi would, he thought, no longer have to ride in the baggage car feeding eggs to a spoiled parid'ja.

He cast a look toward the antique filigree cage, and Boji stared back, small, golden-eyed face between two black-furred fists clenching the stems of metal vines. Boji was uncommonly quiet, as if he was a little puzzled by Eisi and Liedi leaving so suddenly out the *front* door.

No more baggage cars. There would not likely be another such trip for Boji, ever again, unless it was to a new home.

There would not be another day on which he was at home only with his younger bodyguard.

Not be another day in which he could slip away and do something unreasonably stupid. Sad, even if the last had nearly ended in disaster.

Not be another day in which he could evade lessons and memorizations.

And when he was grown up and doing some of Father's work, there would be precious little excitement in a stack of forms and letters.

He so wished he were on the Red Train right now, and that he could postpone thinking about household problems, when deep down he was wondering and worrying what mani was doing.

Did Father think the same—that rather than being down in

his office talking to people with problems, he had rather be on that train himself?

He had never quite imagined Father that way. There was only once, well, twice, in all the varied upsets, when Father had not solved things from behind a desk.

He thought, Father had rather be doing something himself, had he not? Mani *used* to be aiji. But now she is free. Now she does as she pleases. And she *is* a help to Father. She does protect him.

But Father is probably worried too, right now. Things could go so wrong.

Father has to risk mani. There is no stopping her. But he has pinned me down, making me heir, and now that my sister is Uncle's, she will never be as free as I was. Poor Seimei.

I have to do what I have to do, that is the top and the bottom of it. And right now that is simply not to be a stupid child where my staff is concerned.

And to advise Mother there is apt to be more hammering.

Breakfast had been, for the dowager, very late, which argued she had had tea and cakes and done a little study, closeted with her aishid, reviewing security reports up and down the Red Train, not to mention intel that might have come in during the night.

Absolutely she wanted to prolong chitchat with the two people who were her current interest, there being nothing else to distract her, while the Red Train thumped along, prioritized on the track. They might pass other trains, and occasionally there was, unseen, a train going past them in the other direction on the dual track—freight and passenger trains alike. And if those trains were westbound, then those aboard might catch the sight of the Red Train out their windows and wonder at the rare sight. If eastbound, alas, they were seeing it in much more detail, while shunted onto a siding and delayed, as the Red Train rocketed past.

The Red Train did not move often. There was that saving virtue.

And when it did, it meant the business of the aishidi'tat was in progress, or headed that way, so wherever it went—people had reason to wonder.

The occupants of the Red Train were, however, blind and oblivious to it, except by the mild shock of air and the sound as someone passed—themselves having no way to view the scenery they were passing.

Certainly they were not blind to the world, however. They had a Guild operations center aboard, and information was accumulating as they went.

The train slowed markedly. Bren asked himself was that proper, but said nothing. The dowager gazed to her left, to Cenedi. None of the bodyguards, however, seemed perturbed, and not too strangely, neither did Nomari.

"Padisi Bridge," Nomari remarked. "It is a reduced speed crossing."

"Is it in decent repair?" Ilisidi asked.

"It is, aiji-ma, but old."

"There is nothing wrong with age," Ilisidi said shortly, and Nomari said nothing else. Then the dowager asked, more pleasantly, "Do you know *every* part of the system, nadi?"

"I have never been east of the Divide, aiji-ma," Nomari said. "Nor taken the southern spur."

"Well, well, the mountain route we understand is a long, cold trip, and without windows, exceedingly tiresome. Have you ever worked at the airport, nadi?"

"No, aiji-ma, for three years on the city system and then on the circular route."

"And then were absent a while," Ilisidi said.

A momentary silence, a consideration about the answer. "In those days, in the Troubles, aiji-ma, there were observers watching who came and went, and they stopped a man—a man I knew. Who knew me. I could not help him. There was nothing I could do."

"Where was this, and what was his name?"

"His name in those days was Asimi. His real name was Panveni. Not Ajuri. Madi clan. One of our allies. Once." Nomari's face showed disquiet. "There was nothing I could do."

Bet that Cenedi was taking notes.

"Where was this?"

"On the platform, at Koperna, aiji-ma. I felt then it was time to drop out of sight again. So I went south."

From Koperna, it was certainly a way to lose oneself, or to lose one's life—going straight down into the Taisigin Marid, out of Senjin.

"They were anxious times," Machigi said, hearing it all, "and our security knew fairly fast that he was *not* Taisigi. That was clear when he tried to barter a scarf for a bowl of soup—he had a small sum in Transportation coin, did you not, nadi? You knew better than to be caught that way. But the word for the scarf was the Dojisigi word, and the shopkeeper immediately called enforcement."

Nomari simply looked down, diffident in manner, usually that, when challenged.

"Look up," Ilisidi said sharply. "Nomari-nadi. Look us in the eye. We prefer that."

Nomari looked up, calmly, without anxiousness. He *owned* a good expressionless face when he chose to use it, better than a human paidhi often managed. The young man was polite, and probably had done a deal of spying for Machigi, playing a variety of roles.

"One gathers you immediately learned the Taisigi word," Ilisidi said.

"I shall never forget it, aiji-ma."

Aiji-ma, persistently, only to her, not to Machigi, in which one could be certain he *had* thought about the choice of terms.

Whether it represented a role he was playing now, or a sincere declaration of allegiance, his record left one unable to guess.

"Well, well," Ilisidi said easily, "Lord Machigi's service was certainly an intelligent choice in your circumstances. One rather suspects you have acquired a choice of accents over the years. You do not often sound midlands."

"I have generally tried not to, aiji-ma."

"And you have moved often?"

"I have generally tried to move, aiji-ma, whenever my guild had an opening to move."

"And you found other Ajuri as you moved. One understands you lost one protector early, but contacted another, being a mere boy. And kept moving. You became the needle catching all the scattered threads of Ajuri, stitching so long as they lasted, and apparently remembering in what fabric you had left them. *You* were the cause, when you were young, the lost heir of Nichono's line, the last alive—but you never stepped forward. Instead, you became the organizer, under quite a few names. You developed allies, you created associations, you brought people into contact, and you had as your own purpose—what? To take down Areito's line?"

"Areito's line includes the heir and the aiji-consort," Nomari said quickly, "and I never shall work against them. I owe the young aiji and the aiji-consort all I have and shall ever have. And I shall always be in Lord Tatiseigi's debt."

"A strong statement. Does it conflict with your association with Lord Machigi?"

"As I know Lord Machigi to be, it would not, aiji-ma." This without a glance in that direction. "I respect him greatly and I worked for pay, fairly given. But I remember the aiji-consort from when we were children, and I owe her and her son a moral debt. And a debt to Lord Tatiseigi."

It was unsteady ground. Perhaps Nomari was speaking in ignorance of the problems between Damiri and Ilisidi—but

Bren thought not: the rift was known in many quarters. The company at Tirnamardi and on the trip to Shejidan had been together for days—and if he had failed to understand there was something novel in Damiri's visit to Lord Tatiseigi, and that there was tension between her and her son—the Guild passed information, warnings, and cautions, social as well as operational, and when Nomari had acquired a Guild aishid, they would have told him.

So Nomari knew it was a troubled relationship. Nomari still steadfastly declared his debt to Damiri. And if Machigi did not pick up that little nuance he was uncharacteristically asleep.

"Well enough," Ilisidi said, "well enough. Connections will be as connections need to be. Our associate to the south has nothing to gain from involvement in the midlands, so we need not be concerned about a conflict of associations."

Pointed, that.

"I do not," Machigi said. "But a well-disposed acquaintance in the north is certainly no disadvantage."

God, rescue them from too fine a definition of a relationship not yet accepted by either side: Nomari was not yet confirmed as lord, but might more surely be if he gained the dowager's support, and the dowager was pushing to define the terms of her support, without which Ajuri relations with Tatiseigi—given Tatiseigi's strong connection to Ilisidi—would possibly blow up again.

It was a situation in which the paidhi-aiji was clearly challenged to say something, do something.

"Things are changing," Bren said quietly. "There are influences on Earth from two sources in the heavens, influences from Mospheira and from regions of the aishidi'tat the railroad is possibly about to reach. The dowager's great-grandson, young as he is, has the man'chi of the midlands excepting Kadagidi, which is yet to be filled. He has the man'chi of all the west coast except Ashidama Bay: he has connections well-placed on Mospheira, well-placed to advise him in whatever the future brings. You, nand' Machigi, aim at stabilization of the Marid and its connection to the East—and you certainly have Najida's good will in doing that. But the future of all the aishidi'tat is in jeopardy if the midlands cannot settle, and *you*, Nomari-nadi, are in a position to link Ajuri peacefully with Atageini and Taiben, to the good of everyone. You, Lord Machigi, have had reason to distrust Kadagidi's Dojisigi ambitions. Those are gone, and will *not* exist in any new lordship over that clan, and you have seen that the dowager keeps her word. So there is every potential for an agreement in this gathering which will bring not only a cessation of war, but a commonality of interests. Everyone prospers—yet holds on to what is essential to his region."

"The paidhi-aiji," Ilisidi said, "has pinned the issue to the table. I have been curious what connection you, Nomari-nadi, may still have with the south. Interference from the Dojisigi affecting the Kadagidi and the Ajuri has been a problem in the midlands for generations. Injudicious marriages for *trade* connections. The only trade they brought was offspring of Dojisigi origins and a host of relatives bent on using them. Marry as you will, gentlemen, but *gods!* beget with some discretion."

Machigi had frowned during much of that, but now he laughed. Nomari maintained a sober expression.

"I do not say I shall approve you to Ajuri, nadi," Ilisidi said with a wave of her hand, "but thus far we find no cause against you. Nandi, you will definitively release him?"

"I shall cut him free of all man'chi and obligation," Machigi said, and looked at Nomari. "You are not going to a safer place, nadi. If Ajuri becomes untenable—well, we southern folk are a welcoming lot."

Not a welcoming lot in the experience of the north, but had not Tanaja, capital of Machigi's Taisigin, welcomed all sorts of people not welcome elsewhere—especially if they did not agree with the Dojisigi? Notoriously so. One could only imagine the scoundrels at Machigi's beck and call through its various ports.

"Good," Ilsidi said. "Now go away. We have things to think on."

Machigi was not the sort to be dismissed with the wave of a hand, but he took it in good humor, nodded and gathered himself up. The paidhi-aiji and the candidate for Ajuri could hardly do otherwise.

"What was that?" Bren wondered to his bodyguard, when they were back in their own car. "Is Machigi questioning Nomari himself?"

"They have talked," Banichi said, "but always with Guild present, and with monitoring running."

The exchange regarding Ajuri and Nomari's man'chi had seemed dangerous and strangely aimed—Ilisidi and Machigi exchanging blunt statements that, at the end, only incidentally involved Nomari.

"Are *we* similarly monitored, nadiin-ji? One assumes we are."

"We control it. As Cenedi and Nawari control monitoring of the dowager's quarters. We will not turn it on unless there is some visitor in the premises."

At least *they* were still in the dowager's trust.

"Have we any direct contact with Tabini-aiji?"

"At the moment," Algini said, "he is as aware as he wishes to be. We *can* contact him, but have not."

Which was to say, Tabini wished not to touch this arrangement, thus retaining the option of rejecting the outcome. *That* was how Tabini and Ilisidi had operated in various enterprises. Tabini *still* had not officially recognized Ilisidi's trade agreement with Machigi. And need not, until Machigi himself had resolved what he wanted that relationship to be.

So the paidhi-aiji and his aishid were Tabini's eyes and ears on this train, no matter that they also served the dowager and took her orders—and he could at any point, he was relatively certain, call a halt and commandeer the Guild post on this train, either to protect the dowager or even, should he want to risk his usefulness to Tabini, to *stop* her from some action.

Could he countermand Cenedi and Cenedi's forces?

Technically, maybe. In actuality—he would have to gain Cenedi's consent. And that was *not* likely.

"In the interests of everyone's safety," he said, *"especially* hers, we should talk to Cenedi, constantly. I trust Cenedi. I trust the Guild." It was only lately that he could say that with some confidence. "And I trust those the Guild Council has assigned to Nomari. Beyond that—I do not trust the security of Hasjuran, no matter the good intentions of its lord, and I certainly do not trust the lord of Senjin to steer any straight course."

16

Eisi and Liedi were happy about the changes and about their appointments, Cajeiri saw that in their faces. They had put on their best suits to go out about their orders, and they had stayed gone a while.

When they came back, from the front door—Eisi entered first, bowed a little in Cajeiri's direction—they both did. Then Liedi opened the door again and let Eisi usher in two people, both young, male and female, both in staff dress, both looking worried.

Cajeiri stood up and received earnest and proper bows.

Boji bounded about in excitement, not much liking intruders, giving one ear-splitting alarm shriek.

"Aiji-meni," Eisi said, "these two have volunteered, and have the skills, should you approve them."

"Nadiin," Cajeiri said, himself trying not to look or act the fool. He gave a second little nod, and the pair bowed. "One hopes to have this arrangement approved. One hopes you yourselves approve."

The young woman bowed a third time. "Aiji-meni, we are very happy in the major domo's recommendation."

He was relatively sure he had seen them in the halls. There were half a hundred on staff, in this and that duty, counting Father's staff, and Mother's. He knew the names of all the heads of staff of this and that sort, and all their assistants—well, most of them that had any rank. And these two were known faces, to do, he was fairly certain, with cleaning and arranging in the private rooms, but they were not individuals he quite knew for certain.

"You are—?" he asked.

An energetic little bow. "Tariko, nandi."

"This is your brother?" Siblings often served together.

"Husband, nandi." That was to say, not a contract-match, then, but a marriage, like Father's with Mother. "Dimaji."

A bow from the young man.

"They only need one room," Liedi said.

"We do," Tariko said. "We can manage laundry, rooms, serving—we have done all those things."

"They have a security clearance for your father's presence," Eisi said, "and Dimaji can drive." That was not a skill everybody had. "Tariko is Benaji clan and Dimaji is Anari, both sub-clans to Dur. They have been on your father's staff this last year."

Dur was his very favorite, along with Taiben and Atageini. His first true ally besides Uncle had been Reijiri, the younger lord of Dur.

"Dur has helped us when we most needed it," he said. "Do you *know* Reijiri-nandi?"

"No," Dimaji said quietly. "We are from the villages. North of the Isle. We have seen him once. Only that."

"We are a little household," Cajeiri said, "and sometimes there is a lot of work. And then I have my tutor. And it is fairly boring and shut-in. But we do travel sometimes. We hope to."

"Yes, aiji-meni."

"They do understand, nandi," Eisi said. "We have told them—even the space station is not a foreign place to this household." Eisi said it with a note of pride. "And they say they will go wherever they need to."

"Is everything settled, then, nadiin?"

"The major domo has signed the transfers," Liedi said, and produced papers in a stiff folder. "And copies are in your father's office, along with the request for space, and the household budgets and accounts will be adjusted—unless you object, or your father the aiji does."

"I by no means object. And I shall send my father a note. He will answer by this evening."

"We shall put cots in the storeroom until we can arrange better," Eisi said, "and their baggage will come the back way. It is only one room," Eisi added, as a matter of particular pride in economy. "And the major d' approves."

"Well," he said, feeling as if things were suddenly in motion without him, "I hope everything works out." They were so sober, so anxious. "We laugh, in this household. I hope you do not mind a joke."

"No, aiji-meni." Nearly together.

One room, he thought. It really did disturb very little, and got them a great deal more help. And he thought—he hoped—the changes would make as nice a place as Father's and Mother's servants had. With television. He decided he would not put one in his bedroom. He was trying to impress his parents with his character and his studies—everything, so that he *could* take days away, and travel, and go out to Najida, or up to Tirnamardi, and have—well, guests. As often as he could. *His* recreation was going to be at Najida every chance he could make.

And a plan was taking shape. Not a stupid plan, the way he had slipped about to do things he should have thought better about. No. A plan that involved a senior bodyguard and the ability to say his lessons were perfect. He could do that. He could go to Father's office and ask to travel.

If only—

If only mani did not start a stupid war. If only the midlands could settle down and things could be safe.

If only. If only. If only.

He watched as Liedi took the pair back toward the servants' passages by way of his bedroom.

"We all could have died at Tirnamardi," he said quietly to Eisi. "Do they understand?"

"All your father's staff died in these rooms, nandi, before our time. No one escaped. *We* know. And we are determined that we will not have it happen again. Liedi and I are very careful, and we listen to your bodyguards. I hope they give a good report of us in that."

"Boji is going. To a happier life, I hope. I am very sorry about the baggage car."

"We had some good times, Liedi and I and Boji. A brandy flask and a store of boiled eggs."

He had had no idea. But it had been a cold ride. "I shall not object."

Eisi smiled. "After hours, nandi. And we shall miss the little creature—not to the point he should grow old in that cage, but say that he has enlivened our duty."

"One hopes so, nadi."

"Nandi." Eisi gave a little nod and left in the same direction as Liedi and the two domestics. Antaro had just come in, from the same route.

Liedi left, Antaro arrived, and Eisi left. His household moved like that. There was always someone within call.

"Have you met the two new people?" he asked Antaro. "Do you know them?"

"A cheerful pair," Antaro said. "We have seen them about. But we will make our own inquiry."

"Do," he said. "One hopes this is a good idea."

He went to his desk, uncapped the inkwell, took a small sheet of the better paper and wrote a note to Father.

We have received a letter from your staff encouraging—

He had to look up that spelling.

—us to bring in help for Eisi and Liedi. Eisi and Liedi have brought in two of your staff, Tariko and Dimaji, domestics, who will share one room, if you approve of them. I am assigning Eisi as my major domo and Liedi as doorman, even if we do not have an office for them, so they will make sure all the forms are filled out. Also I hope the hammering will finish

soon and I am glad if we can settle the hallway without too much more—

Another spelling check.

—construction, which I know disturbs everybody.

I am also sending to my tutor to start my lessons as soon as he can. I have already made a list of things I want to learn.

Please let my senior bodyguard have a refrigerator for our security station. They also need a television to keep track of the news. I think a samovar would be good, too, though no one has asked for that. Likewise may I have the same for staff, and set aside a room for them, with chairs! They have to go to the kitchens or go through my bedroom to get a pot of tea for themselves. I promise everything will be proper in that area, with Eisi in charge.

Thank you very much.

He sanded it, slipped it into one of his better cylinders and used his seal.

The fact that Father had not called him in today about the two new staff said to him that he might be having one of Father's lessons on management, and Father's lessons . . . some so simple, and generally unspoken . . . were more important than his tutor's, by far.

Rely on your aishid. He had heard that one from the day he had taken Antaro and Jegari. *Trust your aishid. Trust your staff.*

He would bet that *Father's* major d' had consulted Father on all of it. And that Father had already approved his senior Guild's request.

He would even bet Father was waiting for him to send a proper note to ask permission. He also bet that a message to Mother would not be unappreciated.

He sent Liedi with the message, to go downstairs. He had just sealed another note to go to Mother, when a message came back, the first to land in the enameled copper bowl Eisi had set by the door. Eisi brought it quite proudly, a letter in his father's red and black cylinder.

It said, simply, *Well and sensibly managed, son of mine, and felicitations on your sudden initiative. Your mother and I thought you and your staff would choose properly, and we are not disappointed. Your well-considered requests are approved.*

Well-considered. That was more than just *approved.*

He did not simply put the letter in the bin for Eisi to file. He slipped it into the left drawer, where he kept his personal things, his small treasures, not for staff to deal with.

They did not need to know anything but—*approved.* He kept the letter for himself, a treasure he might want to read again not so long from now, when he had to send Boji off, or if, his deepest concern, anything went wrong in Hasjuran.

He was *not* stupid. He was *not* a problem to his parents. He *deserved* to be with mani. It was just that—right now—he was obliged to be here to decide certain things that he had to decide.

He sat there a time, thinking, imagining mountains, still wishing he was there.

But knowing fairly surely why he could not be.

There was one window in Bren's car . . . one small, high window in the exterior door, at convenient height for atevi—not for a human, whose view out that window was a cloudy sky. It was an honor, this particular car. It was extravagantly comfortable, extravagant also in security provisions.

But the Red Train, having passed the junction at noon, had turned south now, and begun to climb. There was surely scenery to be had, and one very much wanted to see the mountains.

There was a portable step in the sleeping compartment, a simple matter to take it to the door, step up and stand on a level with the window.

It was a little foolish, perhaps. But it was a view of the southern mountains, closer than one ever had except in landing in Shejidan.

He loved mountains. The happiest days of his childhood had been on the slopes of Mt. Adam Thomas. Noburanjisu was the

Edi name, the atevi name, a mountain sacred to the Edi and the Gan folk, when Mospheira had been theirs.

He understood that sacredness. The peace it had. The strength. It cleansed the soul, that place. It took away the anger and the stress of a household with problems, and let him and Toby laugh and race and play boyish pranks in the snow. Their mother had a patience there, a freedom and tolerance for foolishness she had had nowhere else. Their mother laughed there.

And everything was clean.

He had no idea of the name of the mountain peak framed in the little window he had now. It was glacier-carved, a sharp fang of a mountain, its geologic history certainly written large in the diagonal band of gray rock—he'd sworn he would learn that sort of thing and he had never had time in Linguistic Studies to take that side course, never had the time to read aside from courses, never had found the impetus and the moment since . . . well, partly because mountains were no longer available to him on the continent. They were a distant, out-of-reach horizon.

But they were so close now. They were the destination.

He should find some geologist and ask about that dark band that serpentined along the foothills. That was simple enough. He should get a detailed map. Such things were easily within his reach. But—such projects just never managed to be critical at the moment.

Maybe they would be. He'd never have thought he'd need to understand the path of a starship, either.

How planets formed. He had picked that up in consequence of where life might be. Which was another thing he'd had to think about.

Gravity pulled planets into round shapes. Were mountains just too stubborn? Or what? He was remarkably ignorant in some areas.

He managed to miss, he thought, truly significant things in his life, just because they were not an emergency. Probably the children who'd landed here would be amazed at the things they knew that *he* had missed along the breakneck course he'd set . . .

Downhill skiing had been his temporary passion. He'd *almost* been good at it, had at least managed not to break anything fatal. He'd often thought since that it had been a good thing that he *had* gotten the appointment to the mainland, because without him there, Toby had given up the sport, before *he* broke something critical.

Sad, he'd thought, at the time. Toby had gotten mired in marriage and kids, given up skiing, and then, in a brother's lengthening absences, Toby's marital relationship had gone down in flames. Toby had answered all their mother's distress calls until she'd died, while *he* was off across space with no guarantee he'd ever come back—Tabini's government had fallen, disastrously so, and people had died, and the Mospheiran government had gone from unwelcome neighbor to the aishidi'tat—to its ally and rescuer.

And there had been Toby and his boat and his own ex-girlfriend Barb plying the waters back and forth, running risks, delivering goods and messages, and generally helping atevi resistence to the coup to stay alive. . . .

Toby's path from the mountain had been down to the sea, by a considerable detour through family breakup. Thank God Toby had stayed in one piece to be there, taking his absent brother's place, doing what he could—because his fool brother was off doing something else.

He had to face it. Much as he'd loved it, his own dealings with that mountain had not been wholly healthy. Healthy, hell—he'd had a crazy sort of death wish, challenging the mountain. It had been a dice roll, every descent, speed and risk wiping out the need to worry about anything or anyone. It had been his way of obliterating the Department, the University—the needs of his family—everything, for the few moments it took to do that one thing the fastest, the best that he could. It had been the most unfairly *oblivious* defiance of all the holds on him.

He'd blamed his father. He'd met him only once, and the conversation had been short. Good morning. Nice to see your face. Drop me a note if you feel like it. The man had never said why he left. He did business, one job and another, on the far side of the island. Never wrote. Neither had he. No profit in opening an old scar. Nothing meaningful there . . . probably never had been. That was the deep family secret, a relationship that had lasted into a second impending kid—and his father just wasn't interested anymore.

So he'd gotten back from deep space, two years gone, with answers to the world's problems, with the possibility of shaking the aishidi'tat back into order—and all he'd given his brother and Barb was a hello, I'm home and I've got to get to the mainland. Quietly. By smugglers' routes. No guarantee they'd ever meet again.

God, he sometimes thought there was more of his father in him than he liked. He'd leaned on Toby with far too little thank you. They did things like that to each other. He wished not. He'd not been available when Toby's marriage crashed. When he'd lost the house and kids. When their mother died.

This time—he'd rushed off onto Mospheira while Toby waited at sea, then a fast voyage back and not even a supper in peace.

He owed Toby so much. Likely he'd never get back to their mountain. Likely Toby wouldn't. And if they did, it wouldn't be the same.

It was always—thanks, brother. We'll get together next time. Thanks. Just—thanks.

Glad you have Barb. She's changed. She's a different person when she's with you. Hope to God your kids figure it out, and you get them back. They're growing up. They've got to figure it someday.

But then, when you work for the government, you don't get to tell the kids what you do, do you?

The mountain view shifted as the track bent to the right. There were other peaks, snow-capped, even now.

Wish you were here. Wish you could be here. Well, but probably not in this one, do I?

He'd slipped into Mosphei' in his thinking. Into Mospheiran thoughts, right along with the language. Relationships long past—except his connection to Toby. And Barb. He didn't want them to slip away.

Didn't want them on this train right now, for very damned sure.

A movement caught the tail of his eye, an approach drowned in the rattle and thump of the train. But then Jago was soft-footed in her arrivals and departures.

And she had only a mild amusement for him. He felt slightly foolish, standing where he was, so much smaller than atevi, and stepped down.

"There are mountains," he said, by way of excuse.

"The Daijin," Jago said. "We are following the Daijin River, which you cannot see from that window. We shall follow it for some distance before we reach the switchback."

Mt. Adam Thomas had streams that fed the Straussman River. Forever in his memory was the spot where one such came down off the heights in a waterfall. In spring, it thundered. He remembered that sound. He imagined it outside, past the noise of the train.

"One would like to see a map, Jago-ji. Might there be one?"

"Certainly," Jago said. "Are you worried, Bren-ji?"

"Lost, I think. This is new territory. One needs to become aware."

"Yes," Jago said, in that manner of an order taken, and with a short trip back in the car, brought a paper map which unfolded to offer details of the mountains, names, inhabited places, way-stations, hunting lodges, roads, even foot tracks.

It offered an entirely new perspective on the region, settlements and holdings scattered through the mountains, connections made by foot, apparently. Jago sat down on the bench seat by him and pointed out what she knew, which was a great deal more than he did.

"One hopes not to have to venture into such terrain," she said, pointing to the place where the tracks ran through a town. "But, yes. This is Hasjuran."

The scale was such on the inset that the buildings and streets were marked. Of streets, there were three. There was the mill, which produced cloth, the warehouse, several tanneries, a number of merchants. Numerous small buildings one took for houses. And the lord's residence, with its outliers, but it had its front on the first of the three streets. It was nestled, apparently, in fairly abrupt terrain, to look at the topographic lines.

"Not a large town. A very small one, by the look of it."

"There is, here," Jago said, indicating a long building on the second street, "a sort of hotel, which we shall not use. Traders come to the indoor bazaar, so there is considerable traffic in and out—for a place of this size. Market days are every thirteenth day, which is likely to be a large gathering—for a place of this size—if we are there that long."

"How much longer?" he asked. "And how long will we be?"

"We shall reach Hasjuran still in daylight tonight, though late. And one understands there *will* be an excursion from the train."

He was not entirely glad to hear that. "Is it safe?"

"Not as safe as the train," Jago said. "But that is the dowager's decision."

Cajeiri's tutor had thoughtfully, late in the day, sent along a set of history and geology and geography questions . . . which was a far earlier start to classwork than Cajeiri had hoped for, and none of them on the topics he had sent the man.

What was the principal export of the Kadagidi townships?

He quite frankly was not sure. And he was not sure, in the disappointment of his own questions being ignored, that he cared, but he was determined not to have it wrong. It might be textiles, if one considered the Atageini townships not that far removed, but he refused to put down a guess. He had been away. His tutor would expect him to fail, and would give him the lecture on observation and application. He had three books open on his desk, trying to find the answer, and was having no success.

All the while there was some confusion around the apartment, as Eisi and Liedi took the new people on a tour of all the drawers and all the cabinets in the sitting room. They were welcome, he heartily welcomed them, but right now he was in a mood.

Just go away, he wished them silently.

Or tell me what the Kadagidi townships make, so I can go to the next question.

Probably they had no idea. They were from Dur.

For Dur it was notably fresh fish, fish products, and fertilizer. And a small amount of flour. They imported *tin*, for something. He had no idea why they used tin. But he had memorized the fact.

Dur had always been more interesting. He wanted to visit there, and had never gotten the chance. But it was not Dur he was supposed to be thinking about today.

He had staff at his disposal, and it was not cheating. He *could* send Liedi to get an answer from the librarian downstairs.

But he needed to be sure that was the only question he was going to need answered.

And his questions to his tutor had been outright ignored. It was where they had left off, as if none of the things that had happened to him had happened. He had wanted to know the history of Dur with Ajuri, on that border. *That* was important right now. But his tutor had his own ideas of what he should know.

Possibly, he had asked questions his tutor simply did not know how to answer. *That* was discouraging, on its own.

Onami appeared in his doorway, fourth of his seniormost aishid, and came to him quietly as he sat at his desk looking up imports, exports, and dates.

"Nandi."

Cajeiri laid his pen down. "Nadi?"

"One may have a solution." Onami slipped a stack of three photographs onto his desk. They showed people in a park. And wrought iron fences, and tall trees beside an expanse of water. And flowers, and people walking about fenced and glassed-in areas. "This is Hanomiri Park, to the south of the city."

"One has heard of it."

"There are animal exhibits, and the whole is surrounded by a moat, which wends its way through the exhibits and *prevents* escape and mingling of incompatible animals. Visitors may walk through the safe exhibits with a guide. Otherwise they view through windows. There is a forest area, with trees of some age; a plains area; and a central area of stone spires, all artificial, but very well done. If a little run-down."

It was still interesting. "In the city?"

"Just outside. It suffered particularly in the Troubles, as many institutions did, and they are not what they once were, but they are looking to recover public attention, and they are interested. It was a whim of your great-great-grandfather, this place, but it has suffered from lack of maintenance—and attendance. I spoke to the director by phone yesterday. He took the train personally to come to the Bujavid bearing a case full of plans never realized. He is extremely interested in Boji, and would undertake to find him the company of several young parid'ji, and a new viewing-place for them—if you do take them as a solution. I have tried to find him a place without cages, where they will indulge him as much as possible. And this has ample room, in what used to be a reptile enclosure, with trees. And an artificial river shore. There is a windowed viewing area, but no bars, and people do not come within the exhibit. He would be free to climb the trees. To dig. To do entirely as he wishes."

"And eggs."

"There would not only be eggs, the director suggested the staff might bury them for the parid'jin to find along the sandy shore, in the natural way. They hope, quite plainly, nandi, that your gift would be public, and that your involvement might attract visitors. The director extends promises that Boji will have a brass name plate on the viewing window commemorating your gift, and that he and his companions will have the very best of care, all his life."

Could one find a better place for an egg-loving parid'ja? There would be people for him to watch. And he was a great showoff.

"If the place is well-visited," he said. "He would be lonely, otherwise."

"He would have the other parid'ji. *And* one cannot but imagine that every child in the city and towns round about would want to see him. It could bring great things for the park."

"It seems very good."

"It is the best all of us have been able to find. He is spoiled, he has no fear of people, he is a consummate thief, and as long as people hand him eggs, he will not starve, but he would be lost in a real forest. The wild ones will show him how to dig for eggs. And he will certainly have the best medical care and also the exercise he greatly needs."

"He is very good at escaping."

"But there can be modifications to keep him in, as he continues to grow. The walls can be made higher, the trees can be trimmed. And he will have plenty of entertainment there—the keepers, we are assured, until the crowds come."

"Will you go, then, and look at this place, and be sure of everything they promise?" He wanted to go himself—he ached to go. He had never seen an animal park. But he was not asking Father for more favors.

And now that he had arranged all this, and now that there

was a place, he was not sure he wanted to do it at all. But he had no choice, really. It was just—

He truly could not turn Boji loose in the woods.

"I do not want to send Boji to any place that cannot take good care of him. If he will not eat, if he is unhappy, I shall wish to take him back. Will they agree to that?"

"I am certain. Certainly if it does not work, we shall try again."

"Are they that run-down?"

"That is something I shall find out, nandi-meni. I shall have a clear understanding."

"Do you think I shall be able to visit him?"

"Certainly the park would be honored, nandi. One is relatively sure your father would agree, so long as you go before opening, or after hours, with all your bodyguard."

So as not to meet people. He understood. But it was a little reassurance. He wished he could see the place in operation.

"I might want to go more than once."

"One is certain the director and his staff would be delighted if you did. It is a little park, understand, fallen on very hard times. But they would like to build back. And Boji could indeed help them."

"If people came, you mean."

"Aiji-meni, if you wrote a few words explaining where he has been and what he has done, I think the park would be proud to engrave *that* on a plaque. You could make a difference for the little park."

"Have you ever seen it?"

"I used to go, as a child. It was wonderful, to a city boy. They had a river exhibit. And a plains exhibit. And a miniature train that went to them."

Onami had said from the first it ever was mentioned that he might know a place where Boji could go. It began to feel like a plot. But not the bad sort.

"Go look tomorrow. See what it would be like now. But I need to tell my father what we might be doing, first."

"Give me a note and I will take it down, aiji-meni."

"Jeri," he said. He could not have his elder aishid calling him nandi and aiji-meni in his own sitting room. "My aishid calls me Jeri. Say that to Rieni. To everybody."

"I shall tell him that."

Cajeiri nodded, shoved the homework aside, drew out a piece of good paper and uncapped the inkwell.

Honored Father, he wrote, *please hear Onami. He has found a place for Boji. The director hopes Boji may bring visitors, and there are trees to climb. The place is Honomiri Park. Onami says it is a little run-down, but Boji could help them get more visitors. And it would be a place I could visit, would it not? I would hope I could. Onami knows this place. He will go see it, and report tomorrow.*

He simply folded this one, and gave it to Onami, unsealed.

Onami left on that mission, and Cajeiri watched him leave.

And looked at Boji in his cage, the very pretty brass cage that had suggested something might go in it.

He could not describe on any plaque everywhere Boji had been, or tell all the things Boji had done.

What could he write?

I was lonely. Boji was my company. All my associates my own age were up in space and I had Boji.

That was fairly pitiful, was it not? His associates finally came down to the world and were still across the straits, unreachable. He did not know but one or two cousins his own age, and they lived across the continent. His household now had thirteen people, coming and going and opening doors, and the sawing continued in the back hall, to make more room, but there was nobody his own age, mani and nand' Bren were off across the country, and he suddenly did not know what he was going to do with a bare spot on that wall.

They could use another cabinet, but he had no idea what they would put in it.

There was no good keeping the cage. It was pretty, but that would be stupid.

He could have more chairs—but chairs were fairly useless. He never had company.

He left the desk and went over to Boji's cage. Boji usually set up a fuss to be fed—endlessly hungry, and he was increasingly inclined to nip fingers if one teased him. But on this occasion Boji looked at him very quietly, very solemnly, and small dark fingers adjusted their grip on the brass vines. The other hand extended fingers outside, touching his fingers, curling around them for a moment.

He had used to do that when he was smaller. He had used to do that after he had been scolded.

He had used to take Boji out of his cage and pet him, but Boji had figured how to slip his harness lately, and they had not figured how to prevent it. If the rascal could reach a buckle, he could undo it. Ties, he had figured out long ago. He could manage most latches. He had to warn the park about that.

Thieving, too. If it was small, if it could be lifted, it would be. If it could be lifted and hidden somewhere, even better. There was a teaspoon no one had yet found.

It was right. It was simply time, and it was right, and if it was not this place, it would need to be another.

17

The train moved much more slowly now, occasionally turning. And most often climbing, there was no question of it. There was little to see out the little window but gray rock and glaring white—hard to tell at times whether one was looking at a mountain or the overcast sky.

There was the regular, if slower, thump of the track under them and, amid so much ice and snow, ample warmth, a pot of tea, a quiet, private lunch, and the time-absorbing distraction of an unfamiliar map to learn, names and byways to memorize—in case.

There was in fact more than one map. Jago had a plan of the lord's residence, with its outlying buildings—storehouses, workshops, kitchens and such.

"Cenedi acquired these," Jago said. "And we are not spreading them about."

Given the company in which they traveled, that seemed a good decision.

Bren referenced one against the other, he memorized names, he followed their course on the map and took notes.

As the day passed, the air grew thinner, until he found himself uncharacteristically a little short of breath—Mospheiran-born at close to sea level, he never minded the elevation at Shejidan, which was about 1300 meters, and he had quickly adapted to the elevation of Mt. Adam Thomas on holidays. The dowager's own Malguri, where she annually spent time when she could, roughly quadrupled the elevation of the capital, and she had had no particular difficulty with the space station or the shuttle, but he *was* a little concerned for her, considering they were going to one of the higher elevations on the planet.

Hasjuran in winter also occasionally challenged its own temperature records, vying with Malguri for the coldest place regularly inhabited. And the dowager, they were informed, did not intend to sit on the train and invite visitors in.

Stay overnight under Topari's roof? He truly did not think so. But apparently some sort of dinner was planned, and he had packed for the worst—or Narani and Jeladi had. He had coats, not the latest style, since his last brush with winter weather had been some time back—but in Hasjuran, in Hasjuran's definition of cold, the latest and fussiest style was not that great a concern.

He enjoyed a late cup of tea with the dowager, who had apparently grown bored, a sociable, quiet cup of tea in the Red Car, and without significant information on any hand, the dowager talked about wildlife, and hunting, and a landscape they had no ability to see.

During that session they ceased steady climbing and gathered speed on long level track, which proved, if his tracking of their course was correct, that they had finally reached the high valley, with occasional climbs, that foretold arrival in Hasjuran. Indeed, Tano reported they were about two hours from the station, and presumably—a little more than two hours before dinner.

Late afternoon, Jago had predicted. At least it would still be daylight, though the lack of windows could hardly inform them.

"The word has passed, Bren-ji," Banichi said when he returned to his own car. "The aiji-dowager has officially informed Lord Topari of her visit—he was not informed until now."

"A considerable surprise to spring on him," Bren said. Topari was excitable to say the least, and granted his security was informal, the dowager had good reason not to have given him more warning.

Or told him she had invited herself and her entire entourage to dinner.

"Indeed," Banichi said, "and she has expressed the wish to dine under his roof, should he extend the invitation. He has replied that he is delighted and will welcome her."

"Has she happened to mention Lord Machigi?"

Banichi put on a wry expression. "One does not believe that that information was in the message. But Lord Topari has invited her and her party, and she has expressed interest in seeing his hall. We are informed this will not be an overnight visit. Your security is thankful for that. But there will be supper, and one is certain Topari will do his best, but do have care, Bren-ji. These people have never *seen* a human."

He thought of Malguri, and cups of tea, and resolved to eat and drink only what he could absolutely identify. He had very much hoped she would pursue her interviews inside the comfort and safety of the train—with Bindanda on guard in the galley.

But was he utterly surprised? It was Ilisidi's nature to place herself where she could directly view and assess, stake out a position and challenge another lord face to face. And if Hasjuran was rustic, well, her own Malguri was little changed from the feudal past—excepting its security systems. The plumbing and the lighting in Hasjuran would certainly not be of the current century. Fireplaces. Live fire for lighting.

And plenty of shadows, one could expect. A great many shadows and pillars and dark hallways where trouble might move.

If they were not closer than usual to a region that would wish to kill them all he might muster the fortitude to call it picaresque and enjoy the novelty—while being on his guard regarding the menu.

Since, however, they were within reach of Senjin and Tiajo's Dojisigin, and since they were about to stir that nest with a stick—

"Rani-ji," he said, finding Narani near the wardrobe storage steaming wrinkles from his winter coat, "—did you chance to pack the contents of my second dresser drawer?"

A discreet nod in the affirmative. He had not carried the gun to Mospheira. He certainly did not routinely carry it about the halls of the Bujavid, or Najida.

"Good," he said, and was comforted to know that would turn up in his outside coat pocket. Bodyguards, his and the dowager's, and the Guild unit protecting Nomari—had enough to do, and no telling what their situation might become, if there chanced to be any other guests.

Onami had talked to Father. Father had approved. It was nearly certain, then. And Cajeiri went down the hall, just with Antaro, informally, to knock and then wait outside while he met with Mother.

Beha, Seimei's nurse, answered the door, met him with a little bow.

Seimiro's crib was gone from the sitting room, with its tall, filmy curtains and its wonderful windows. It was all chairs and small tables again. The hammering and sawing had forced the move. He was sorry for that.

"Is my mother receiving?"

Beha widened the gap and let him in. He had come unattended—it was the inmost hallway, the most secure place in the Bujavid. Nothing moved here that the security station failed to note.

"Come in, aiji-meni. Wait a moment."

"Yes," he said, and Beha went back into the inner rooms.

Manners said he should simply wait where he stood, but the windows were a rare view of the outside—closed, now, when before they had admitted summer breezes and flared the curtains in a wonderful way. They were the greatest beauty of the whole residence, in his opinion, something he so wished he had.

Mother and Father both had windows, and Seimei had enjoyed them for a while.

But probably it was not only the noise. Perhaps they were beginning to think of fall, and cold air—morning chill off the southern mountains was fairly brisk. Mani, who owned another set of windows in *her* apartment, was very happy in a chill wind. But it was a bit much for his sister.

Or maybe being the heir to Atageini clan had changed *her* life, and deepened her security. He hoped it would not close too tightly about her.

There was still a view, however, of the fairground and some of the hotels, and the sitting room had gone back to being his mother's sitting room, for visitors. If Mother had visitors— which she never did, since Grandfather was dead and all her Ajuri household was lost.

Maybe, once Nomari held Ajuri, there would be visitors. He had not thought before how isolated Mother had been—until he had seen her at Tirnamardi, so definite and so assured, and dealing very well with Uncle . . . and then here, back in her apartment, seeing no one that was not one of Father's guests, and the only visitors all wanting to see the baby. Uncle had not come, and he had most interest. He had not invited Mother, either, or Mother had not accepted.

She just did not travel—except that one venture to Tirnamardi, when she most had to. She had been anxious to be back here, anxious to have everyone back under Guild protection.

Now Mother had pulled Seimei deeper into her apartments, no more visitors for Seimei, and still none for Mother.

Beha had not even offered tea while he waited.

That was—well, that was not *right*. That was not healthy. Yes, he was here on business, but Beha had no inkling of that. And yes, he was living under the same roof, but he was not dashing in and out again to deliver a message Antaro could have brought.

Mother arrived, wearing a plain green coat with a deal of lace—she always looked beautiful, always dressed for company, always that Cajeiri could remember.

"Son of mine," she said.

"Honored Mother," he said, and gave a little bow. "Might there be tea? Have you time?"

"Indeed," Mother said, and rang a bell. Beha entered, and at a signal, quietly set about the making of it. "It seems quieter in your area today."

"We are nearly settled, Honored Mother. There will be plastering and painting, and cabinets. So I understand. But it will be quieter. I am so sorry about the noise. But we are mostly down to noise on the lower floor, now. They are giving us a storage section. Just a small one."

"The new servants?"

"Seem very good. They are mostly learning right now. Eisi and Liedi are very particular."

"Eisi and Liedi are good people," Mother said. "They have taken very good care of you."

"Eisi is to be major domo in my household," he said, "and Liedi the doorman, has Father mentioned? Eisi says it is a good thing these new people are younger. So when Eisi and Liedi are old and retire, there will be a succession."

"You *are* looking ahead. And your new bodyguard, the cause of all the hammering and the dust . . . I understand they are setting up their own security station."

"We are doing very well, Honored Mother. Everybody is getting along. How is Seimei?"

"Sleeping more peacefully in the farthest room," Mother said, and Cajeiri felt a little warmth rise to his face.

"One is so sorry."

Mother shrugged. "Well, it cannot be helped, can it? As you say, it will pass and things will settle. I hear you are looking for a place for Boji."

Considering his mother had disapproved of Boji from the be-ginning, it was a moderate thing to say.

"Onami, fourth of the new guard . . . Onami knows a park that wants him. Where there are trees, and visitors will be be-hind a window, so he will be safe. Father approves the idea."

"It sounds like an excellent solution."

"And, Honored Mother, the park wants to advertise he was mine. And for me to write something for a plaque, to bring visitors."

"Are you sure the visitors will be protected? It would not be favorable publicity if he bit someone."

"One would not want that. One would not want Boji scared, either."

Mother smiled a little. "Honomiri Park, is it?"

"You know it."

"When I was very young. It is a very little park. Not as well-kept as one would wish. But, well, for your first public gesture to be a gift to a park—there is very little controversy about that."

"I just want Boji to be taken care of. To have as many eggs as he ever wants. And I do not think he could take care of him-self if I just turned him loose in the wild. He is not wild."

"No, he is not. But perhaps we should ask knowledgable people to take a look at the place and make suggestions, those egg-farms who keep the creatures, among the first, one would think, and perhaps biologists, and the park keepers. The enclo-sure should be proper."

"With trees. They say there are real trees."

"Exactly." Mother signaled more tea.

"With more of his kind, they are saying."

"A small colony. However shall they fence them in?"

"High walls. And there will be sand with eggs to dig. The director says they can bury them."

It was a happy conversation, none of it serious enough to put down the cups. It was the first absolutely trouble-free conversation on his business they had ever had, and Mother agreed if they could create excitement about the park, it might merit support from the city, as a public attraction. Other exhibits gained grants, and sponsorships from businesses who then put their names on plaques. And if *his* name was on the plaque—

"Can *I* sponsor him?" The thought came to him. "I do not know how one does that, but might I?"

"Talk to your father. If your name is going to be there, it cannot be shabby. One is quite sure the park knows that, and will use it. But again—it is not a bad thing, is it, not bad for Boji and not a bad way to become a presence in the city. Your grandfather in his early years made himself notorious with his private entertainments. A gift to this park, in your own name, is a wholesome, modest sort of thing. But talk to your father. Be sure this thing is done well, and responsibly."

"Honored Mother, I shall. I promise."

"He has been, over all, a good creature," Mother said, which was the nicest thing she had ever said about Boji. "And a good influence."

An influence, Cajeiri thought. He had had to look after a creature very talented at escapes and mischief—which had greatly limited his own. He had learned, on his own, the folly of going off against the rules. So he had never gotten to show it was not all Boji's influence. But it was at least partly Boji's influence. He had learned what it was to worry about a silly, escape-prone parid'ja.

So in just this summer, this wild and dangerous and now fading summer, he had found himself growing up, and he was not sure he wanted it. He was not through with being a child. He had not had enough of taking chances as he saw them. He would like to be completely irresponsible for just a little longer, but there was no choice about it. He owed so many people so much, he could not go on being Boji, and silly, and self-centered, could he?

18

Snow. That was the first impression as Bren, behind Banichi and Jago and ahead of Tano and Algini, stepped down from the Red Car.

Wind and thin, cold air.

A mountain face, layered with snow, casting premature dusk on the town. The eave of a wooden structure and the open deck of the platform.

He had loved skiing, in his youth. There had been a bus, and offloading all his gear from the underside had been exciting, a prospect of pure enjoyment. Now it was atevi faces meeting them in the steam of the train, atevi in furs and heavy coats, and he was not on a snowy outing with Toby . . . but with a comfortingly heavy complement of Assassins' Guild black.

Topari was there to meet them. Topari was in his own element, here, when all their meetings before had been in the halls of the Bujavid. One could read the man's extreme anxiousness— and very strangely, his undisguised relief to recognize a pale human face . . . a known quantity, to mediate between him and the towering prestige of the dowager as a guest. In all the uncertainty of the visit, it was a strange and mutual relief, despite past moments . . . despite Topari's uncertainty as to whether humans were, well . . . really *people*.

"Nand' paidhi!" Topari cried, breath frosting. "Welcome! Is she here?"

She. Of course, the dowager, who did not favor being shouted about across a train platform.

Bren gave a little bow, waited until Topari had reached conversational distance before answering, in a tone just above the chuff and hiss of the waiting engine. "Yes, nandi, the aiji-dowager is indeed here, and she will be pleased to see you. She will be along any moment now."

"This is a great honor!"

"Indeed it is, nandi. And there is a good prospect for you in this visit. She has chosen your town for a very important meeting, one in which you may well benefit, if you can please her and play the discreet host to very uncommon circumstances. Just let her unfold the details in her own way—in her *own way,* nandi, at all times, and at her own pace. That is very important."

The man, bundled in furs, was all but shivering in his uncertainty. "Shall I speak to her directly? Do you advise it?"

It was amazing: cornered in his own element, this was not the brash outsider Topari had been in the halls of the Bujavid. Here was reserve, and caution. Perhaps it had been nerves, in that environment.

But more people were crowding onto the platform, a disorder that threatened their orderly debarkation.

Bren cast a glance around about and spied one of Topari's guards, only two, inconspicuous in their fur-edged coats, carrying rifles, not that different in that respect from a number of other armed bystanders on the platform. In all this anonymity of dress, non-Guild guards and bulk of furs, he could read the anxiousness of his own aishid, while a number of other black-uniformed Guild were coming off the train, beginning to move the crowd back.

"Nand' Topari, you shall indeed be presented to her when she comes out, but let me urge you—the dowager's presence, even unannounced, presents a risk to everybody, given her enemies—please take advice from me, have your guard constantly about you during her visit, and let them discourage onlookers pressing too close to her. There is ice, she is elderly. She is a stickler for protocols, an absolute stickler and should not be touched, excepting her own bodyguard. She is Eastern, extreme in her observance of her customs, and this is a moment of greatest hazard and greatest opportunity for you. She has things ultimately she will say, but her custom is to go through the courtesies first, many of them, probably with no information forthcoming this evening."

He was gently moving the man back from Ilisidi's likely path, trying to manage the encounter.

"Paidhi, *what* things has she come to say?"

"One would never dare speak for the dowager," Bren said, no hesitation to turn *that* question. They were standing very close, breath frosting about them, and he said in a very low voice, "Nand' Topari, I do not see but two bodyguards that I recognize. Are things well here, in terms of security? Do not hesitate to tell me if they are not."

Eyes widened. "Yes, paidhi. Amdi and Reni are here. The other two are coming at any moment."

"Observe protocols. Keep your bodyguard very close and on alert until the dowager departs, and order them very strictly to tell one of *our* Guild if they spot anything in the least out of order, anything in the least suspicious. I tell you, nand' Topari, there is great gain you can make in the next few days, but security surrounding the dowager's presence and that of everyone with her is absolutely mandatory. Of course you have your habits and your customs, but you *must* guard yourself as well as her. Any persons with Marid associations are particularly to watch, any strangers here are to be watched, and her security must be made aware of them and their whereabouts at all times. I need not tell you the seriousness of any injury to her, or to any person under her escort. As well as yourself, nandi, so please take due precautions. I cannot overstress the immediacy of the threat her presence brings, or the importance it is about to accord your house and your town."

"I shall, paidhi, I shall protect her! My guard will be here!" Topari rushed aside to the guard he called Amdi and issued fervent orders close to the man's ear. Amdi spoke to his partner, then pushed an old-fashioned communications contact under his own collar and started, one presumed, ordering the other half of his team to get here at all speed and do their best.

"One believes the lord has just understood," Banichi said, close by Bren's right. "One hopes so."

"One almost dreads their assistance," Algini said. "Probably they are very *good* marksmen. The question of knowing when to shoot and what to shoot, however, is a matter of concern. They are not within our communications system."

"We should obtain a link at least to their senior," Banichi said. "Bren-ji, the dowager is awaiting some sort of organization in this meeting. One does not see it developing. Who *are* all these people?"

It was a question. Topari was giving orders himself, with Amdi and his partner right beside him, waving some people away, beckoning others, trying, one saw, to organize the platform and sort the mere onlookers from persons who might have some special function.

"Chaos," Jago said under her breath as they stood watching regular Guild establishing a clear perimeter for the dowager's exit, while two workers strewed gravel on the walk and steps and people beyond the platform shoveled to make a path, and someone—bizarre as it was—seemed to be selling food to the onlookers. A confused flurry of people was being moved off by Topari's guard, Topari himself shouting explanations, waving his mittened hands and trying to add courtesy to the orders.

"I think these are notables of the town and some sightseers curious about the train," Bren said. "They *are* moving off. But two of Topari's guard are still somewhere below the platform, if they are that close. Clearly this is not Shejidan's way of doing things."

"The people seem only enthusiastic," Tano said. "There seems no harm intended."

"We should keep close order," Banichi said. "And you will ease our minds, Bren-ji, if you wait right where we are."

"One agrees," Bren said. "I am reluctant to seem appalled and retreat back into the car. But they will surely settle this before the dowager trusts herself to this crowd."

"*You* are a sight most have never seen, nandi," Algini reminded him—which was true. Nobody in Hasjuran had ever seen a human. "The whole business offers sights never seen."

"Clearly, crowd control," Jago said dryly, "is a thing this capital has never seen."

Two tall men with rifles made their way up the wooden steps against the flow of persons being urged down them, a further moment of confusion.

"The bodyguards," Tano said. "There."

"Well, they are trying," Banichi said. And indeed there was beginning to be a sort of order, and a clear space, with *only* Lord Topari, several elderly folk of some presence, and Lord Topari's bodyguard finally distributed in something like order.

Algini said something into communications. Presumably someone had asked a question.

"The dowager will come out and meet Lord Topari before the others," Banichi said.

One was not surprised. The dowager was not going to escort Machigi or Nomari as if they held some equivalent rank to hers They were each on their own. And meanwhile the paidhi-aiji and about sixteen Guild of various units held a fairly clear space for her appearance.

"Nand' Topari," Bren said loudly. "Come stand close, if you will."

Topari came and the elderly dignitaries wandered uncertainly behind.

"They will be welcome," Bren said. "May one ask, are these members of your house?"

"My paternal uncle," Topari said, "my maternal aunt, my cousin, my wife, my third-eldest son."

There were bows, a fixed and anxious stare on the part of the uncle, as if the uncle expected the human to take flight or do something equally bizarre at any moment. The boy, about mid-teens, likewise stared. Bren put on a friendly but reserved expression, bowed liberally and remembered the names he was given—apparent that blood and kinship governed in Hasjuran, and he was not that surprised. It was true in various out-of-the-way holdings. Old-fashioned. Fairly stable, unless there was a falling-out in the family, and Lord Topari seemed protective and courteous to his household, a point in his favor.

Eyes darted to the train. And indeed the door opened, and more Guild came out, then Ilisidi herself, wrapped in black furs, her redoubtable black cane in hand—a diminutive woman, with her attendant security, eight in number, with Cenedi in charge. She walked forward, across gravel-flecked boards, the cane marking even steps and a deliberate course toward them.

Bren bowed. Topari bowed. Guild never did. And fur-trimmed hunter folk with old-style rifles faced black-clad Guild in a spreading wall of presence.

"Nand' dowager." Topari's voice seemed thin as the air. "We are greatly honored. Please join us. We have had only two hours' notice, but my staff and a number of households in the town have been cooking up a banquet as best they can. Please."

"Well," Ilisidi said, both hands on her cane, gazing about her. "A lovely view you have, nandi. And one of the few extant wooden great houses, we understand."

"We have, we have, aiji-ma. And yes, it is." Topari recovered wit enough to use the honorific of personal allegiance. "Please come view it. We can offer you seasonal game, and a great deal of it. We can offer you our warmest welcome."

"Excellent. We shall use our train for lodging, as it suits us, but we shall be glad of a tour. How do *you* rate your security here, for a walk to your door?"

"Everybody is honored. Everybody is absolutely honored. You are our guest—our welcome guest. We are your allies, your strong supporters."

"We are delighted." Ilisidi stayed standing as she was, but her bodyguard stirred, as more armed men came from the cars, some in Guild black, some in black with green. Machigi was arriving among them, conspicuous in a green coat, and with him, escorted by Shejidani Guild, Nomari, likely shivering in a fine but inadequate coat. *"My* guests," Ilisidi said. "Lord Machigi of Tanaja, in the Taisigin, and Nomari of the line of Nichono, candidate for Ajuri. We are here for a conference that may bring benefit to your district, nandi."

Bren had angled himself so as to see both the arrivals *and* Lord Topari with a shift of the eyes, and indeed, Topari had outright frozen where he stood, confronted with arguably the most dangerous man in the neighboring Marid, enemy to his nearest southern neighbors—and a northerner suddenly reported as a candidate to represent a key district in the heartland of the aishidi'tat.

Topari seemed not to breathe for a moment. And then recovered with an intake of air. "Indeed, aiji-ma." Possibly too much breath. He tried again. "Welcome."

That was the dowager in full flower, no question. One could not have warned the man. Topari was off-balance and wondering surely what the game was with Machigi and whether he was to be handed a war *and* the blame for it.

Just then the Red Train's engine puffed into activity, setting into leisurely and distracting motion. Two cars—only two cars, a baggage car and the spare sleeper—moved along with it, headed southward in a lingering cloud of steam, toward the steep descent to the Marid.

"We shall stay nights aboard the train," Ilisidi said sweetly, "but we shall be ever so glad of a good meal, and a chance to view the exquisite premises, nandi. What a beautiful snowfall! We so enjoy the mountains."

"Are they going to Shejidan, aiji-ma?" That was, likewise, Topari—the blunt question. Were the dowager's cars being left here indefinitely? Was the train, now lightly composed, going the long way round the entire rail system, when there *was* a perfectly good chance to turn around here at Hasjuran?

"No, no, nandi," Ilisidi said, "our conference has one more invitee. We are not granting him too much forewarning. In fact, we would appreciate Hasjuran's *not* gossiping about our being here, or at least, not intimating that the train will turn around in Koperna."

"Who is coming?" Topari asked and added a breathless: "Aiji-ma."

"Well, we do not *know* he is coming," Ilisidi said. "How are your relations with Bregani of Senjin?"

Another intake of breath, smaller, and a third. "Well enough, aiji-ma, that is, trains come and go, and we do trade with Senjin, both directions, and that is all. We have no occasion . . . that is, we have never met Lord Bregani. Or anybody of note, from Senjin. We have never exchanged messages, except—except the railroad office. If there is some problem we have exchanged notes."

"Well, well, we shall benefit by a brisk walk and a warm welcome to your extraordinary house. Show us this pretty scene, will you not?"

Cruel woman. She could be that—but never idly, never pointlessly—well, occasionally, yes, and recklessly so, Bren thought, when she was in a mood to test someone she expected to be a problem. He had had his own experience of that, but she had been at odds with Tabini on that occasion, and doubtless felt strongly, improperly challenged. The point was, still, in spite of it, he freely forgave her for it, and to this hour, he would throw himself between her and an attacker, to the absolute distress of his bodyguard. She meant well for Topari—*if* Topari was the ally he represented himself to be. One could feel sorry for the man—who probably could not truly advantage himself of her favor: he was too much a creature of impulse, and she was calculating to the extreme.

But he had come to believe there was nothing of ill intent in Topari, who truly had been oblivious to the fact *creature* was not the nicest way to refer to the human paidhi-aiji.

In very fact, seeing what Topari was, and where he was, and how very asea he was in the dowager's rising tide of plans and intentions—nor likely to gain enough wariness fast enough—he concluded he ought to look out for the man, and help him look out for his people's interests in what was about to land on his doorstep.

He walked behind the dowager now, a little ahead of Machigi and Nomari, both of whom, being warier and better-informed, had more direct worries about what the Red Train might bring back—or not—than about Lord Topari's actions.

Snow came thick, a veil across the public square. Piles of snow lined the area where shoveling had cleared a sort of public space, and defined a pathway leading toward the great house, but not a lonely great house with extensive grounds, as most were. A good many buildings of the same wooden style, with curving eaves, crowded close about it, some even seeming to share roofs, making sheltered walkways. Children and adults alike climbed up on the snow piles to watch their progress, and children, oblivious to the ceremony of the occasion, began to pelt other hills with snowballs and to run about in high spirits unchecked by their elders.

A few such darted across their path, and three danced about in high spirits. Lord Topari's guard waved them off. They ran away, shouting and throwing two snowballs, at which elders near one of the snow piles tried in vain to lay hands on them.

One began to see that this was not, in any regard, the formality of Shejidan, let alone the Bujavid—but it did not seem to disturb the dowager. Nomari seemed wary, but not upset at the children. And Machigi was, well, not Ragi, to say the least, and *he* was the one frowning. The crowd certainly made security harder, and it was fairly clear this place had never seen such a Guild presence. Guild surrounded them, a black lance driven into the white of Hasjuran, heavy with armament, troubling what in many ways seemed an innocent place, old-fashioned, lacking stone monuments, but having that massive wooden hall, centuries old. If there was threat here it veiled itself in the snowy air, and stayed out of their path for the moment.

They reached three sets of wooden steps, each with a railed terrace, and now Ilisidi took Cenedi's assistance on one side, but she made the stairs with the aid of her cane, and had to make the descent tonight as well, Bren thought, somewhat worried, but she would do what she would do.

And they were going to trust a strange house's cuisine.

But not quite. He was well sure that, while Narani and Jeladi and others were remaining aboard the train for security reasons, Bindanda was somewhere behind them, in Ragi black and red: a Guild uniform would not suit Bindanda's girth, though it indeed had, some decades ago. He traveled in plain clothes, he had not brought his chef's gear, nor would he be their principal cook on this venture, but he came equipped with a discerning nose and a knowledge of recipes and ingredients. He *would* manage to be in Topari's kitchen, lifting lids, asking questions, introducing himself to staff and answering their questions about the dowager's preferences, while watching—to be sure, also, that Hasjuran did not poison by accident the sole human Hasjuran had ever seen.

It was a mission of some professional delicacy—cooks being cooks—but Bindanda had his charming side, and knew how to use it.

Third terrace, and more stairs. It was not yet winter in the mountains, and it was possible that that snowy commons out there might become quite deep in snow in midwinter, making the entry the second terrace, even the third terrace, at worst case. There were, one understood, seasons where the trains simply did not run, and winter would settle here long before it arrived in Shejidan.

Two beautifully carved doors stood before them, a motif of mountains and clouds. These opened on a firelit corridor and walls half rough stone with wooden beams, reminiscent of Malguri, but larger. Ilisidi would surely be pleased with the sight, would take delight in the smell of wood smoke, and the harmonious wooden pillars.

"This is lovely, nandi," Ilisidi said. "We compliment you on this hall."

"Nand' dowager—aiji-ma—we are beyond honored." Poor Topari was having a little difficulty with his honorifics. He truly was trying to do the right thing.

They walked deeper into the hall, with a good many mounted heads and horns in evidence along the walls, and entered a grand wood-pillared hall, with a fireplace that could have roasted an entire beast, and a very large table laid with white cloth and set with metal and wood and pottery, all rustic, but very festive, a great three-sided arrangement of tables and linens. Iron chains held the live-fire lighting suspended in the center of the hall, well-anchored—Bren looked up at the anchor points, on a stout column, a single evergreen trunk, one of twelve holding up the roof-beams, noted the chain that let it down so that the oil lamps could be filled—effective oil lamps, with faceted glass chimneys that cast a jewel-case lighting about the hall.

It was, indeed, an architecture he had never seen, strong and rough, but harmony was in the design. Bundles of fragrant evergreen lay up and down the tables—a kabiu arrangement clearly not anticipating all the guests, but it was honest and local, and a few attendants were scurrying about adding proper elements of kabiu at the head table at a frantic pace, small and larger stones and here and there an additional sprig of berries.

One was not sure of the interpretation—the symbology varied regionally; but by the last-moment haste, one supposed it took into account the presence of Machigi and Nomari—a courteous gesture, considering the relations between the Taisigi and the north, and the fact Nomari as yet had no rank but guildsman.

There would be another scurry tomorrow, granted the Red Train's mission succeeded down in Senjin.

But *if* that mission failed, they would have to have another sort of discussion.

"The park will take Boji," Onami reported. It was past the time Father *usually* came upstairs after a day in the downstairs office, and there had been calls back and forth all day that Cajeiri understood to be involved with Boji—a very disturbing lot of calls, when one knew that Father had other things on his mind. The park director *wanted* Boji. That was in no doubt. But the park biologist had laid down changes that had to be made, and that were going to involve construction.

As if there was not already construction everywhere Cajeiri touched.

Perhaps we should postpone it, Cajeiri had sent down to Father, and Father had sent back, *Of items worrying me today, this is the smallest and most reasonable, and halfway pleasant to deal with, since it actually seems capable of resolution within this century and does not involve lives. It is a relief, between other actions on my desk. I shall have it before supper.*

"And Father is happy," Cajeiri asked Onami.

"As seems, there is a plan already drawn up for a general expansion and improvement," Onami said, "and it seems mostly a matter of making a current cost assessment and substituting modern materials. Which is to say—"

"I understand," Cajeiri said. He did. It was old, and the prices of things changed. And there were new materials from space. "They are going to do it."

"Your father is offering a loan, without interest, to be paid back after twenty years. And in your name, a gift, for the parid'ja enclosure."

"But Father is paying them to take him," he said to Onami. "I truly had not wanted that."

"He is not paying them to take him, aiji-meni, but paying them to keep him in. Your father's concern is Boji getting loose in the park and being far too ready to approach people. Your father will not have an event of good fortune turned into a bad one all because the enclosure was not able to contain a creature who has become skilled with latches and good at theft. The teaspoon . . ."

". . . Is still missing." That was only the most valuable thing that Boji had deposited somewhere.

"Whatever is shiny," Onami said.

"One understands," he said, envisioning Boji going right over roofs and up trees—to carry out one of his bounding thefts on a tourist. "I am glad, then." He added, envisioning the park of *his* imagination, a place borrowing some features from the space station. "I would like to go there when he is let go. I have never been to a place like that."

"I think your bodyguards would all support that idea," Onami said.

Onami left. He sat there thinking—maybe it was freedom for Boji.

And for him. He could travel now—given Father's permission. He could see Malguri. He could visit Najida, definitely. He could do that.

He looked across the room, at Boji, who looked back at him. Boji had been uncommonly quiet—as if he knew something was going on. Boji *could* read him at times.

It will be a good thing, he would tell Boji, if he could communicate that far. No more cage. No more leash.

You will have associates with you. Furry ones. You will have to dig your eggs, and they will not come boiled.

Perhaps I shall tell the keepers you like them that way, sometimes.

Screech.

It was dinnertime. That was one thing in the world Boji understood very clearly.

Drinks had preceded dinner, plain wine and ale, nothing that extraordinary, and while the crowd milled about and conversation grew loud and louder, Lord Topari on his own had found a well-padded wooden chair for the dowager, and several slightly less well-cushioned chairs for the rest of them.

Topari hovered constantly near, supervising, personally keeping a clear space around them, seeing to it that guests wishing to be presented to the dowager whisked near and away again in fair order.

There were merchants, tradesmen, craftsmen, and town dignitaries, and a small solemn band of townsfolk back at the edge of it all, which seemed to change from time to time, people in heavy furs, having come in from the cold, and then going back out into it. Topari advised them, too, there was another contingent coming in who would take some time getting here from the villages, but they were coming, and hoped to arrive before the dowager left.

The news of their arrival getting out to the villages might not please the Guild, but it was hard to prevent. Meanwhile Ilisidi seemed perfectly pleased, at her gracious best with the ones introduced and untroubled by the onlookers. Lord Machigi and Nomari had settled near the dowager, not courted, but definitely observed—anxiously.

A human sitting by them had to be one reason for the furtive stares. Bren left his chair, ostensibly to speak to his aishid, but also to catch a little detail in the conversations beyond. *He* naturally drew anxious stares, and some darker, worried looks— he could not blame them: between Machigi's presence and the unprecedented appearance of a human in Hasjuran, strangeness and threat had arrived in their midst on very short notice and with no explanation. They might not even be sure which of the two men *was* Machigi, but one was, and that was a southern neighbor with a reputation for retaliation.

And the aiji-dowager, twice aiji—was power of a kind that received visitors in Shejidan, never appearing in such places as Hasjuran. Yet here she sat, and Ilisidi, unlike Machigi, smiled at them. Those paying personal respects to Ilisidi arrived mostly shy and anxious, while Topari hovered at their shoulders, supplying names for the tongue-tied, trying to manage protocol, while Ilisidi herself radiated a grandmotherly serenity that dealt equally with the shy mill owner and the more assured head of the Merchants' Guild, and sent people away to join the dinner crowd in a kind of stunned relief.

It was over all a rustic and traditional community on display, a gathering which, Bren thought, explained a lot about Lord Topari—anxious to better his standing, but also anxious to better his people; ill at ease in the formality of the Bujavid, but among his own, protective, trying to make things work, and not sure anything was safe. Children, rarely seen at a Bujavid state dinner, cycled through with the fur-wrapped onlookers. A parid'ja, or something reasonably like it, scurried into the hall and dived under a table, to the consternation of serving staff, and then retreated to the exposed rafters. Topari waved off those trying to retrieve it and tried to resume his introduction of the local numerologist. The smell of wood smoke overpowered everything but the evergreen, not unpleasant at all, after the initial waft of melting snow on furs, which had been hastily carried off by servants. The room was beyond warm. Nomari in his light coat was surely faring much better than he had on the way from the train.

And all during the introduction and drinks, servants had begun carrying in perilously full and steaming soup tureens, noisily bringing in an extra table, arranging tableware and runner. Superintending all the fuss, the major d' kept running back and forth, occasionally carrying dishes himself.

Bindanda was somewhere behind all that confusion, Bren trusted, along with the dowager's own cook and her physician Siegi, doubtless interfering back there, lifting pot lids, sniffing sauces, asking locals to taste a dish, and generally giving the local staff fits of anxiety, making them aware what should *not* be served to the paidhi-aiji, and what the aiji-dowager preferred to be served.

It *was* a risk, accepting a dinner invitation, but with late notice to Topari, mischief had had very little time to plan or act.

A human was, however, in serious danger of innocent mistakes, and was wiser not to eat or drink anything he could not identify down to the spices. Bread was, Bindanda had generally informed him, the best recourse under chancy circumstances, and so long as he was resident on the train, he stood in no danger of starving.

Jeladi had reached him from Bindanda's side, however, as their host began to direct people to table. "Nandi, the seasonal game dish is simple, and is safe, likewise the yellow pickle and the winter root vegetable are safe. Do not add the red spice."

That was good news. The aroma of roast had been mingling with wood smoke and evergreen ever since they had come into the hall, and Bren was glad to be able to take that item onto his plate, along with the roasted winter tubers. It was a feast that made no apology for its rustic simplicity, and he found himself in a massive chair—his feet did not touch the floor—in an overheated hall, with a plate of far more abundance than he could eat and an assurance he would not die of it. It was not wine they poured, but ale, which he had never had in lowland dinners, a drink Jeladi poured for him; and a very good ale, at that.

The spectators continued to cycle through, with occasional wafts of an opened outside door. And the noise of conversation made it hard to hear anything distinctly. He had Nomari on his left, Topari on his right, the dowager and Machigi beyond them, in an order he was fairly sure the dowager had chosen, and there seemed no intention of speeches to get in the way of food and drink.

Only after they had been well-fed, Topari banged his knife against his metal charger to gain quiet in the hall, and proclaimed, "Welcome to the aiji-dowager and her guests!"

That was a fairly diplomatic way to navigate tricky protocols.

"She is our aiji-dowager, our firm ally, and forever welcome in Hasjuran!"

Cheers went up. Ilisidi acknowledged them with a nod and an uplifted hand. "We are extremely appreciative of the hospitality of Lord Topari and all of Hasjuran."

Another cheer.

A second uplifted hand. "I shall trust the paidhi-aiji to remark on our purpose here and to arrange certain meetings. You will have noted the departure of the Red Train this evening, on a mission we hope will open further dialogue. If it does, this meeting will go one way. If it does not, it will go another. In either event, we have confidence in the man'chi of Hasjuran. Nand' paidhi?"

God. The chair was a trap. He attempted to push it back and stand, respectfully, trying to gather his thoughts.

Banichi saved him, together with Jago, pulling the ironwood chair back a bit, so he could slip down and set his feet on the floor.

"One is honored," he began, the universal start to a polite request, which gave him two seconds to frame a reply, and to start with the obvious anomaly in their midst. "I thank the aiji-dowager, and Lord Topari. I thank Hasjuran for a warm and excellent welcome. I am personally grateful for your welcome

of the first of my kind to visit this highest point of the continent. In my capacity as an official of the court in Shejidan, in
service to the aiji-dowager, I thank you for your welcome for the
two guests of the aiji-dowager, who are here in support of her
efforts. Her mission here will, with you, await the return of the
train tomorrow, and hope that it brings an answer favorable to
you and to the aishidi'tat. May good fortune attend, may luck
be with us all, and let us thank the provider of this excellent
food and drink—Lord Topari."

Which obliged Lord Topari to take the floor himself, which
let the paidhi-aiji settle back into his chair without too obvious
a move to achieve a too-high seat, as his bodyguard eased the
chair back into place at the table.

"Honored guests," Lord Topari began, and began elaborating
on the scope of the honor Hasjuran was given, among them the
novelty of a human guest—fairly graciously done—and the
unprecedented visit of Lord Machigi, a new power in the southern Marid, as Topari described him, and a close ally of the
aiji-dowager . . .

Machigi could not be displeased by that. Topari was doing
rather well, in his own element, supported by his people.

Then Topari finished with the introduction of Nomari as
potentially the lord of Ajuri, and potentially an ally of the
dowager . . .

Well, that might be true, granted Nomari survived the honor.
Bren darted a glance at Ilisidi's reaction to that statement, but
Ilisidi had chosen that moment to take a sip of her cup, and remained unreadable. Nomari's glance in the same direction was
not quite expressionless. One might say—dismayed.

Topari went on to cite history going back to the first rail to
reach the mountains, and the building of the descending rail
to the Marid "despite assassinations."

There had been no few, and it was not a history useful to
raise now, since it was part of a general war with the Marid.

Intervene? He had no leverage on the damned chair, on the rough stone cobbles.

"Lord Topari," he said, and Banichi and Jago quickly assisted. He gained his feet. "Surely the part Hasjuran has had in the expansion of rail and communication will be a forecast of its future, as Hasjuran itself will come off well if things go smoothly. Thank you. Thank you. Thank you." He glanced about, trying to catch a signal from Ilisidi, and saw a clear cue in a slight nod. "Your hospitality is extraordinary, your table in no wise disappoints, and the dowager is pleased. But it has been a long journey, and the dowager will retire now to rest. We shall surely have some news tomorrow."

"Of course," Topari said. "Of course, nand' dowager."

Cenedi and Nawari moved Ilisidi's chair back, and Cenedi handed her her cane, with which she ably slipped down to her feet and lifted a hand glittering with rings. "We shall see to our own needs until the train returns, nandi, nandiin, nadiin, and then we shall see. Offer up favorable thoughts, and perhaps tomorrow we will have information. Favor and fortune on this house, and on the people of Hasjuran."

That pleased everybody.

"Coats!" Topari called out, and staff—one assumed they were staff—made shift to bring coats to their owners. Bodyguards took them, and deftly assured themselves they were proper, even while they assisted their principals to put them on.

And, without any fanfare or explanation, a heavy fur was found for Nomari, a little large, but very fine quality, and his bodyguard helped him with it, doubtless informing him whom to thank.

Bren fastened his own buttons, Jago standing very close. He had managed, quietly, to shift his small pistol to Jago in shedding his outdoor coat, and now, quietly, that weight slipped back into his right-hand pocket. They had an agreement about that gun. If trouble happened, the gun was *not* to assist his bodyguard. But there had been moments he had been glad to have it.

And he would be carrying it in every outing, with the same arrangement. Hasjuran, with rifles generally resting with the coats during dinner, rearmed itself, and the Guild, in heavy attendance, and waiting their own dinners back aboard the train, never *dis*armed, never sat, never left their individual charges.

Was Hasjuran made anxious by so much presence? It was the aiji-dowager. It was the touch of Shejidan and the Guild, it was—

Well, one hoped it spun out as pageantry and not as the threat it could become in an instant. Certainly the people seemed happy enough, buzzing in conversation, people still approaching the dowager to bow and offer felicitations, and as the doors opened to a waft of cold wind that fluttered the fire in the fireplace, everybody moved right along with the dowager's guard, apparently intent on escorting them all down the several flights of stairs and back to the train platform. Ilisidi could prevent that with a word, but Topari himself had donned his coat and his gloves and hurried to go with them—a slow matter, the dowager's negotiation of the several flights of stairs, but there were young folk out with brooms clearing the steps, adding sand, providing woven mats down certain places the dowager would walk and whisking them away to use again on lower levels.

In that fashion they reached the broad snowy courtyard under a dark and snowing sky. There were electric lights, fashioned to look like torches, and the picturesque buildings had their lights, as well as the train platform. As they came up onto the platform, the Red Car opened a door to welcome them, a rectangle of paler, foreign light.

They climbed aboard, the very last of the Guild filed in and closed the door. Ilisidi shed her cloak, bright-eyed and with snow still melting on her hair.

"Well!" she said, "we are none of us poisoned. Nand' paidhi, you will stay a moment; Lord Machigi and Nomari-nadi, we shall bid you good night, and we have ordered brandy for you in your separate cars, which may take the chill off."

That was a fairly quick dismissal. Something was up, Bren thought, something Cenedi might have passed to her.

The disinvited guests filed out, with their bodyguards. Bindanda and Jeladi went. Ilisidi, having handed Nawari her cane, sat at the end of a bench seat, taking her gloves off. One of her own servants put a brandy glass on the table beside her hand, and Ilisidi picked it up, murmuring, "One for the paidhi. Sit."

Bren took his own gloves off and, bulky coat and all, sat down on the end of the opposing bench. A brandy glass arrived in front of him.

"One is concerned, aiji-ma. Are you well? That was a long stairs."

"Pish. The air is thin and my cloak is unreasonably heavy. We are quite well." Ilisidi took a sip of the brandy and drew another deep breath. "Cold is not a difficulty. How are *you* faring, paidhi?"

"I feel the thin air, but the mountains are a pleasure. And it is an interesting place. Have you a concern, aiji-ma?"

"Topari, as ever, entertains us. And is innocent as a babe. But we are informed that these neighbors of his, the ones he says are coming in tomorrow, are delayed by the potential for avalanche, and one is tempted to assist one to happen, given the back country routes that may run down to the Marid. We are just as glad they have not arrived, and may not arrive."

"The same that came to Shejidan with him?"

"No. Those were present tonight, causing no difficulty. I have advised Lord Machigi of these less felicitous neighbors, and he understands. They are not smugglers, but they sit in dangerous proximity to routes such people use. We are informing Lord Topari that he will find a way to engage and divert these people if they do brave the avalanche to get here, or we shall, quietly, discreetly, comfortably, but definitively. We shall likewise, by tomorrow, either have Lord Bregani with us, or we shall have him sending to the Dojisigin to seek help of that young fool Tiajo. Were he to ask me, which perhaps he will, he will have a far longer life trusting Machigi—granted Machigi himself can be persuaded to forego revenge."

"His father's assassination . . ."

". . . May have launched from Senjin, but the organization and origin was Dojisigi. This entire maneuver is Machigi's notion, his idea that Senjin has come in play—" Ilisidi coughed and took a sip of brandy. "Dry air, paidhi."

"It affects me, too."

"Flatterer."

"I am pleased to be. I admire your fortitude, aiji-ma. I do extremely admire it. But please, be cautious of your health. Send me wherever I can be sent."

Ilisidi nodded. "We shall conduct business here, and possibly in your car. Our two guests are reported to have met cordially—Machigi has invited the prospective lord of Ajuri to his car, and they have had a quiet meeting, not at all productive of much information, however. Machigi is uncommonly cordial, Nomari anxious, but perhaps he is aware that he himself, if he survives this excursion, will become a power in his own right." A cough. A sip of brandy. "He seems a modest fellow, this Ajuri candidate. He has been so with his appointed staff and bodyguard. His staff has had to correct him. He has thanked them quite nicely. We assume he knows he is watched, likely that he is monitored. But all the same, modesty is a becoming trait, until it needs to become authority. Can he make that step, paidhi? And will he cast his own shadow?"

"I find common sense in him, thus far. Modesty, yes. Common sense, and a sensible awareness that his is a dangerous situation. He is aware of your dealings with Machigi. One believes he knows that Machigi's relationship to the aishidi'tat is uneasy; and one believes he knows that there is a delicate situation in his having gained Lord Tatiseigi's approval without gaining yours."

"To put it delicately." A sip. "Does he think my acceptance is guaranteed?"

"I think he believes it is *far* from guaranteed. I think he wishes to have it. I am not sure he understands the intricacies involved in his association with the aiji-consort in that regard."

Ilisidi gave a short, soundless laugh. "Say it. He is standing on a faultline, and the aiji-consort has made a very *wide* move to establish herself in Ajuri."

That was to say, Damiri's offering her daughter as Tatiseigi's heir.

"I think in all of that there are two people you may trust to guard your interests: Lord Tatiseigi *and* your great-grandson. And your *grandson* as well, I strongly believe, aiji-ma."

"And this pretender to Ajuri?"

"He would make a serious error to widen that gap on which he stands, aiji-ma. I have hesitated to advise him on the point, hoping he will acquire that understanding on his own. He knows that without your approval, his gaining the lordship is almost impossible. He surely knows that Ajuri is a difficult and dangerous lordship, in which he will have to change the course Ajuri has followed for decades, or become another murdered lord. He would surely wish your approval—and he may be increasingly aware that his two most essential associations are dangerously at variance with each other. *Machigi* is the least of his worries."

"His man'chi?"

"To your great-grandson, I think. To Lord Tatiseigi. To the aiji-consort. I do not think there is any attachment to Lord Machigi. He is not at ease in Machigi's presence."

"Nor in ours."

"Nor in mine, aiji-ma, though I think he wants advisement. I think he views my counsel as in his interest. I hope so."

"We would not oppose your advising him," Ilisidi said. "For my great-grandson's sake. And for the sake of some solution in Ajuri. Perhaps I shall have a conference tomorrow with Lord Machigi. Perhaps you may then find an opportunity to send this young man a note."

"Aiji-ma." Bren took a sip of brandy. "I shall simply say that you are his best ally, if he can achieve it, even above Tatiseigi."

19

Cajeiri was where he had rarely ventured in these days of good behavior, the servant corridors, and the construction zone. Time was, he had used the backstairs of mani's apartment on a regular basis, sometimes for mischief, but now that he *owned* a suite of rooms *and* their adjacent service passages, he had rarely even opened the access door to the world behind the doors—until now, that a day of hammering and a great deal of shifting heavy things about had produced some sort of—Eisi said—organization.

He wanted to see. He wanted a sense of where things were settling, and whether they were what he had promised, and most of all, he was curious where his people were situated.

His four younger bodyguards were undisturbed, in two rooms adjacent to his bedroom. But a step through the access brought the smell of fresh paint, and otherwise—no ladders, no canvas, no workmen such as had been there for days. The place was painted a cheerful pale green, and the hall that had used to go on and on—did not. To the right, past a new door, was a landing with stairs going down, which he had never suspected lay behind that wall.

His senior aishid gathered in the corridor, and his younger one followed him. Eisi and Liedi were there, to show him the new arrangements.

"They are not quite finished," Eisi said. "We have access to the downstairs throughway, as a route to the kitchens: and there is storage for supplies and seasonal wardrobe. Your father has granted you the space against future need, but there are no plans for any residence on that level. The carpenters have left, we have moved furnishings in from house storage, excepting what Guild may request, and an electrician will finish the work in the next few days."

It was all quite amazing, that they now had a door where there had been endless hallway, and that four little rooms had been combined into two, for the Guild station and a general sitting room for staff: and the sitting room had a recess with a refrigerator. It had, besides, a small television. The Guild station was similarly equipped.

Beds and chests had been moved in, and there were, besides the accommodation, three showers and a bath, with stacks of towels. Everyone was pleased with the bath, which had a steam closet.

And it was his, the whole arrangement, with room for everybody, and a security door, which, considering things that had happened in the Bujavid—was a reminder. The whole of the Bujavid was all an up and down maze, the family rooms, and the service areas, and the passages, with rooms and passages above and below the level where the lifts stopped, the level that had outside doors, while the service passages had exits only to the rooms and the kitchens and storage. Some of nand' Bren's servant passages intertwined with Father's on one level or another, nand' Bren's apartment lying next door, with arrangements spread out so that key people could be near their stations. The halls could be traded back and forth even with neighboring apartments, by knocking out walls or adding new ones, so it was all one well-guarded system . . . now. And there was history in them—assignations, assassinations, conspiracy, and secrecy.

Now there were cameras, and nobody moved unseen.

Security was always an issue. Storage was as great a one, and access. His staff had a sitting room of their own, and a security office that would communicate with Father's own—and the new security door meant control over staff that was *not* his coming and going—they simply could not, without a key. He owned two doors he could close and lock. And he never had, before.

Things were settling. The construction was nearly done. He was even looking forward to his tutor Dasi's lessons now that the hammering had ceased and everybody had a place to rest. He had seen and done things some of which he could not tell anybody outside. But he had questions, things to ask Dasi to teach him, things like how storms were made and how old the skeleton was in Great-uncle's basement, as well as how a computer worked and why the Southern Ocean had more storms than anywhere.

There would be the ordinary things, like math and geometry and economics, but he had his list of questions to divert Dasi onto more interesting tracks. And there was so much he wanted to know that just had no answers.

He could not talk at all about the kyo. He understood that. That was all secret, and what his father chose to let out was how it was going to be. But he had his little treasure, that Hakuut had given him, that he kept now in a locked drawer. He would like to know what that metal was and if it was metal at all. But it was a secret.

And he wanted to know more about parid'ji, and how they lived in the wild . . . and about the history of the park that might take Boji.

And about railroads. He had heard a lot from Nomari that he wanted to understand.

He was going to have to become like Father—Father rarely traveled anywhere except Taiben. But if there were new things to figure out, puzzles that had to be solved, things to learn—and *why* rules existed . . .

He might find ways to do things. Go places. Try things.

A door opened behind him. Hurried steps sounded in the new corridor, and he turned. Liedi arrived in some excitement.

"Young gentleman! There is a phone call!"

He had never gotten a phone call except from his mother and father. Great-grandmother? Mani did not use phones. Uncle barely did.

Mother would send a servant.

"Who is it, Liedi-ji?"

"The operator at Mogari-nai, nandi! I think it is the young people."

He could not run. His father's heir did not race to the phone. He followed Liedi back through the door to his proper apartment, to his writing desk, and the phone that rarely rang.

He was trembling with excitement when he picked up the phone. "Yes?" he said in Ragi. "This is Cajeiri."

"Jeri-ji, this is Gene! They have let us call! We are here! We are safe! We are in our quarters!"

"We all are!" That was Irene's voice in the background.

And Artur's: *"How are you? Did nand' Bren get back all right?"*

"Yes," Cajeiri said, catching his breath, "yes, he did, nadiin-ji! Are you in your new apartments? Are you in a good place?"

"A place like the Bujavid," Irene said, *"like nand' Tatiseigi's house, with security. And staff. And food! A lot of good food!"*

"We also have tutors," Artur said. *"They speak Ragi with us. They have machimi. They show us all sorts of things!"*

"And we have television," Gene said. *"With a lot of tapes about Mospheira."*

"How are your parents?"

"Well, very well. My mother is very happy. She wants to learn to cook."

"We all have Mospheiran clothes," Irene said. *"I have six shirts!"* She added, then: *"But no lace. I like my atevi shirts. And my boots. We brought all our clothes with us."*

"Have you seen much of the island?" Cajeiri asked.

"We cannot go outside yet," Artur said. *"But we can see trees from the window. Kate-nandi is in charge, and Sandra-daja—she has a man and two boys—they come and go, but*

there is a security station downstairs. Sandra-daja's sons ask us questions about the space station. We answer. Mospheira words are different. Some are."

"We want to come see you." That was Irene.

"I want you to come. You shall come. I promise it. But you have to be there. Nand' Bren wants you to learn about Mospheira. But please be careful! Please listen to security! I heard about the Presidenta. You have bodyguards with you."

"The man who shot the Presidenta is one man," Irene said. *"People send us presents, a lot of presents. We write cards for everybody that sends. My fingers hurt."*

"You are so happy there you will never want to come here," Cajeiri said, not that he really thought so, and he was very glad they were happy where they were, but he felt a little pang of worry about it.

"We shall come!" Gene said. *"If nand' Bren let us bring our parents, we would run to nand' Toby's boat and go today. We miss you. We miss Lord Tatiseigi and everybody."*

"I shall tell him. He will be pleased."

"How is the baby?"

"She is doing very well." He almost added she had become Uncle's heir, but it was probably something he should not say until he cleared it.

"And your father?"

"Everybody is fine." It was wonderful that everybody was fine, but people over there had wounded the Presidenta and *he* had just had to leave Tirnamardi for safety's sake because Aunt Geidaro had been murdered. There was so much not to tell them. It burned to be told. But—

"Nand' Bren said you visited Lord Tatiseigi," Irene said.

"By yourself," Gene added.

That was news. And it was a relief to know how much they did know.

"Well, not completely by myself. My aishid, of course. And Eisi and Liedi. And another aishid. My father sent them because, well, usually I have mani's aishid *and* nand' Bren's. And I visited my uncle all on my own, on the Red Train."

"Is your great-grandmother all right?"

"Oh, she is. She was in Malguri at the time."

"So did you have a good time?"

He hesitated just half a heartbeat too long on that, trying to think what he could say, what was allowable to say.

"So was it a good trip?" Gene repeated, who knew him best of anybody, and he could *not* start things off by lying to his associates.

"Well," he said. "I shall tell you all of it when you visit. You are going to visit. I am determined you shall visit."

"They promise us. We are not sure when. So is everybody really all right?"

"Mostly. Antaro broke her arm, but not a bad break, and she is mending."

"How?"

"It was a storm. The mecheiti got loose. But everything worked out, and the mecheiti are safe."

"Now you have to tell us," Gene said. And there was nothing for it. He had to admit there was a problem, or make up a string of half-truths. There was nobody at hand to say which, not even Jegari or Antaro at the moment.

His associates were under tightest security. Nand' Bren had said so. *Probably* somebody of his father's staff was listening— he hardly did anything unobserved, ever. So if it was wrong to do, somebody would come and tell him.

And nobody being there to see it, ignoring the desk chair, he slid down the wall and sat on the floor with his knees tucked up, as they had used to do in the tunnels of the starship. "It was Ajuri," he began the story, and started more questions.

They talked and talked, in Ragi, mixed with ship-speak, back and forth, finding words for what they had not seen to-gether, nobody intervening, nobody stopping them. He drew a fence around things he would not say—such as where mani and nand' Bren were right now.

But things that everybody in the aishidi'tat might hear on the news—he told them, which was about finding a cousin, and Aunt Geidaro being murdered, and Uncle declaring Seimei his heir.

So they knew. His closest associates knew what was going on in his life, and knew about him having more guards, and about him trying to send Boji to a park to live, and about the new people, and all. He felt if they knew, if he could have them understand, and follow his life, and if he could follow theirs, he was no longer like Boji, in a pretty, but too-small, cage.

"Please call me every time you can," he said, when someone in their residence called out to tell his associates they should end the call.

"*Call Heyden Court when you can,*" Gene said. "*They will tell us!*"

"Yes!" he said. Heyden Court. He got up and wrote it down as it sounded.

Heyden Court. A human name. A human place. He had the name. He meant to write.

Often.

. . . *in which approach,* Bren wrote to Nomari, in the sitting area of his own sleeping car, before retiring, *you can heal the breach on which you are standing, without reference to any relationships you may have in the south. The dowager's strong alliance with Lord Tatiseigi and the young gentleman's close association with Dur, Taiben and Lord Tatiseigi would secure Ajuri's perimeters and mend relationships fractured by recent actions.*

The dowager will likely not host breakfast or lunch tomorrow. Look to have meals with your aishid, at your request, and to spend a quiet day as you please. Your aishid can provide you reading material, or perhaps a game of chess, and generally keep you informed of any developments. We are all waiting for news at this point.

He wrote likewise to Machigi. *The dowager will not host breakfast or lunch tomorrow. She will be resting. Your aishid may contact the galley on your own schedule and they will be happy to comply. Please do not hesitate to message me should you have any need. I shall wake at the usual hour and spend my day reading. We shall be waiting for news, and I shall advise you at the earliest when we do hear from the train.*

Machigi could assume, if he wished, that the message passing through his corridor to Nomari was identical.

Perhaps Machigi and Nomari would breakfast together tomorrow morning. Perhaps they would not. They had had their conversation, a fairly brief one, in which he hoped Machigi had not plied Nomari with too much drink for discretion.

He dispatched the notes: Jago took them and returned in short order.

He was too wrought, himself, to go directly to bed despite the brandy. He stayed in the sitting area, and at Jago's return, Banichi came in, having finished *his* supper. Tano and Algini arrived, the same, and they sat and shared a rare glass of wine.

"Things are quiet in the town," Algini reported. "Lights are low on the town commons. The train station has had very little in the way of personnel moving about, nothing of concern."

"It went rather well," Bren said, "all things considered."

"We have assets outside," Banichi said. "You may sleep tonight, Bren-ji."

He heaved a sigh, wishing he were somewhere close to doing that. But his mind was turning over too many things, sifting memory of the dinner, remembering names, and faces, and the lay of the land outside. "What time tomorrow should we hear, one way or the other?"

"We are trying something new," Banichi said, "which may give us news. The team in charge of the train is communicating directly to the space station. And we will get the news relayed without use of the telephone—which is notoriously compromised—and the Messengers Guild. It should work. If that Guild protests—it was experimental."

The days when *everything* going to space and back passed through Mogari-nai were ending, then, challenging the close control of the Messengers' Guild—a guild nearly as old as the Assassins, and more concerned with maintaining of their privileges and prerogatives than they had been of keeping politics out of their operations. They had tolerated breaches of faith. They had excused partisan members. They had resisted reform. They had protested Lord Geigi's landers as violating *their* prerogatives, never mind they had been a communications link established to resist the coup.

And the Assassins had had to contemplate the problems of coordinating the drop of freight from space with local security, with the Messengers as intermediaries. The last thing they needed was local folk coming out to watch a pod coming down—an operation which historically had not been without disasters.

"So we are testing the satellite?" Bren asked.

"It seemed a good time to try the system. But yes, we are testing it."

"We are in an isolation which might see an attempt to cut us off entirely from communication," Algini said, "if things go badly. There are technicalities. But we are, thanks to the station, in a fairly infallible communication with Headquarters and, through them, with the Bujavid."

"We are," Banichi said, "testing the satellite *and* the relays."

So the landers—at least one or two of them—were powered up.

"We are going to hear from the Messengers," Bren said wryly, "I am fairly sure."

"One believes so," Algini said. "The Messengers may have difficulty penetrating the system. But that is their problem."

"Is monitoring off?" he asked.

"Yes," Banichi said.

"Does the dowager know all this?"

"Say that her grandson has not informed her of everything."

He almost wished he had not asked that question.

But was the dowager capable of recklessness when she was challenged?

Yes.

And was Tabini going to sit still while Ilisidi was engaged, as she was, with the source of war after war on the continent?

No.

If Machigi was not acting in good faith on this one, he thought, he might do something he had sworn he would never do, and personally File on the man.

But without Machigi as a distraction, at very least, they would still have to deal with Bregani, who had spent his whole lifetime working against the aishidi'dat.

Their ally was Machigi—whom nobody trusted. Whom no one *should* trust. A lifetime of dodging assassination from Dojisigi *or* Bregani or the lords of the West Coast had made him apt to turn any way he needed to turn to survive. The only thing that might keep him steady on was exactly what the dowager was doing, convincing him he might attain his ambitions and end up aiji over the whole Marid—not to the displeasure of three of the five clans—not that even the three southern clans trusted him that much, either.

If Machigi achieved power, he would almost certainly be challenged for it. Either Machigi would be able to keep them in line, or he would not—and Machigi as head of an association of all the districts might be the best answer for the Marid *and* for the aishidi'tat.

It was worth a deep breath and a thought that Ilisidi might indeed be doing exactly what needed to be done—fewest lives lost, greatest gain to be had; and the trap of offering too much for the Marid to lose—a region technologically behind the rest of the aishidi'tat, with increasing dependence on, as a very small item in the dowager's plans, space-based weather reports.

Ilisidi's East had something to win from the arrangement, too—a thinly populated region with iron and steel in abundance and a limited industry to deal with it.

That, and the dowager's personal determination to keep a foothold in the space age without losing her region's traditions and its independence.

That, the East had in common with the Marid . . . including its own deep-rooted contentions. And *without* the dowager, the same as the Marid without Machigi, things would slide back into chaos and local disagreements.

It was perhaps not the time to think of Filing on Machigi, whose ambitions toward the west coast had been a problem. Machigi did not abuse his people and he took care of his southern allies. There was that to recommend him. He had listened to a proposition for change. He was interested when a change seemed to benefit the Taisigin.

But, damn, the man worried him.

He'd never met the like on the Mospheiran side of the strait, but he had on the mainland . . . the first time he'd walked into Tabini's office . . . and found himself encouraged—*expected*, even—not only to speak, but to speak freely. That had been a critical time in his life. His apprehension of irreversible consequences in Mospheira's relations with atevi, the foreignness of all his emotional supports, and his doubts about the whole philosophy of the department that had sent him—all had had him living in fear that some single mistake could start a war. And his department back on Mospheira had tried its best to toss him out of office—

He'd survived that crisis because Tabini had outright insisted on having him back. But Tabini could still confound his expectations and set the ground quaking under him. So could the dowager.

So, also, did Machigi, on a continuing basis. And because

Machigi's aims were differently centered than Tabini's— Machigi being of a different culture, a different region, and a separate history, Machigi's intentions were a constant worry.

He was not sure he could maneuver the two forces into peaceful cooperation. He did not, in his less certain moments, even understand why Tabini and the dowager thought he could.

And then there were moments just as worrisome, when he began to think of *how* he could, and what that direction ought to be.

He might be dangerous. They might be mistaken to trust him.

He still—had to think of ways. *Feel* his way through. *Trust* his interpretations of motive, and come out with an answer.

Damned scary, was what it was. But the dowager, who *could* feel the push and pull of atevi emotion, *wanted* him involved.

Why kept him awake far too late.

20

Tano and Algini were still asleep, having been up half the night in conference with the other aishidi—excepting Machigi's. It was eggs and breakfast biscuit, nothing fancy, but after last night's excess of roast and pastry, modest fare was welcome. Bren had one, and a cup of black tea, and watched Banichi and Jago take care of the rest of the supply.

"There might be more biscuits," he said.

"Perhaps," Banichi said. "Do *you* want another?"

"Not I," Bren said. "I shall probably not want lunch. Was there any of the dinner sent back with us?"

"Guild respectfully declined the offer," Banichi said. "*We* are not being reckless, even if our principals are obliged to be. Cenedi was not pleased with the entire concept of the outing, let alone the dinner, but it was the dowager's insistence to arrive with a very short notice, defy the risk and satisfy social niceties, Lord Topari's anxiety being what it often is. Now he is pacified, it is the current plan that we shall sit on the train, amply supplied with food and drink, and conduct delicate negotiations *here*, such as we may arrange, without the need to run risks outside."

Lord Bregani had boarded the train down in Koperna. That information had come in the small hours of the night, by the alternate system, but other information was scant, save that the Red Train had completed a turnaround in Koperna last night and was on its way back up the grade, on the priority that let the

Red Train violate the normal Transportation Guild rules for anything coming *up* the grade.

But what Bregani's compliance in coming up here meant, whether it was to deliver an ultimatum or to get out of Tiajo's reach, was still a question. They at least had him—and *he* had the dowager's specific promise of safe conduct.

"Which will be honored," Banichi said, after rising to ask Narani for more biscuits, too much of concern to anyone not involved in operations, except to say they had set up several points of surveillance outside, and received information that the train that had preceded them to Hasjuran was also in Koperna, on a siding, and waited, presumably, where it *could* turn around. Traffic *would* be stalled there, pending turnaround, with delay on the entire rail system between Najida and Koperna, which was a smaller traffic than the northern lines, but not insignificant.

"We are expanding electronic surveillance outside," Jago said, as more biscuits arrived, "so we have eyes on the entire platform, and the tracks beside us. It is normally a trafficked area. We have posted signs and tape requesting a safe perimeter for the train from workers as well as onlookers, and thus far people—even the young ones, thanks to local Transportation workers—have been very cooperative. They have set up an alternate shipping office in the city administration building—people are becoming concerned about priority, granted the time we shall have the station shut down is uncertain. Topari himself is asking questions to which we have no answers."

"If you can take a quiet day to rest, nadiin-ji, do. Whatever the train brings us—is likely to mean long hours after it gets here."

"We are alternating shifts with Tano and Algini, and with Cenedi's team, taking rests, yes. Granted you yourself will be so sensible, Bren-ji."

"I shall. I promise."

They were not what one might call safe where they sat. Hasjuran was not what one might call a well-ordered clan, with its

several questionable subclans—still weather-delayed, one supposed, an absence not regretted. In Hasjuran, everyone knew
everyone and rumors were certainly flying—the Red Train and
its odd behavior possibly presaging things of advantage, but little as the remote rural places had to do with Shejidan ordinarily,
people had to be a little worried. If things unknown to them
were running well, could the dowager's visit improve on that?
And if they were not, were they about to find it out?

One could certainly understand the township in that regard.
Topari had to be in a dither, unable to answer questions, but
willing, he so wanted to make it clear. However things turned
out, Topari was obliged to be on the dowager's side, as the only
protection he was apt to find, being the border facing the uneasy
south. He was defended, but mostly by the sheer inconvenience
of the upward grade, and the avalanche danger on trails—simple
trails, nothing so dependable as roads—that connected the high
country villages. Some did lead down to—or up from—the
Marid. But winter was coming, when those routes were, one
understood, not reliable. Pack animals were how any quantity
of goods moved on the high trails. Self-sufficiency was more
than a virtue in such villages: it was a mode of survival.

And politics? One could not think the connection of villages
to the aishidi'tat was that strong, when survival was at stake,
and Lord Topari was not the most charismatic of lords—a decent lord, but that was probably true of a long succession of
lords in a province united only by a common threat of the elements and trails that might or might not allow a message to
reach their own lord. They were ethnically Sogi, not Ragi, nor
Maridi—not that tied to either: research indicated such.

Satellite access could indeed change the relationship. But it
had not, yet.

And here they sat, one Ragi-clan authority in a border clan
train depot, waiting for a contact with the Marid, with awareness of what was going on depending ultimately on a new
satellite—and Machigi's truthfulness.

———

A little note-taking. And a nap, making up for last night. There was nothing to see, nothing to do. No trains passed. The system was not allowing trains to pass them. Even footsteps were rare, slight vibration as one of his own aishid moved about, and twice, as someone came through the passageway of his car, probably one of Ilisidi's young men on an errand up to the Guild station.

Anxiety had moments of outright boredom—scarcity of information. And considering the scarcity—

"Ask Nomari-nadi to tea," Bren said to Jeladi. "Tell him—if convenient. There is no crisis."

One had little doubt it would be convenient. He summoned what he knew of the young man, the story as he had had it from Ilisidi, and what he knew from Tabini, and he was not surprised when, very quickly, Jeladi was back with the Ajuri candidate and two of his assigned bodyguard.

"Nandi," Nomari said. "You wished to see me."

"Politely so," Bren said. "Will you sit? I can offer tea."

"Yes," Nomari said, the unadorned *yes* of a young man accustomed to being under orders, and sat down opposite him at the table.

"Nothing formal," Bren said. "Ladi-ji, I believe we are affirmative on the tea.—I am curious," he began, directing Nomari to the seat opposite him at the little table, "though you say you are not familiar with Hasjuran, whether you have traveled through the area."

"Once, nandi, only passing through."

"So you *have* been to Hasjuran."

"I understood the intent of the question to be whether I knew Hasjuran, nandi, and I do not. I have never been off the train. We were workers in transit."

"A check of records did not turn up that transfer," Bren said.

"Not under my real name, nandi."

"Do you recall the name you used?"

"Padiro."

"A west coast name."

"Yes. I had his papers."

"One assumes the Padiro of wherever he was from—was deceased?"

"Yes, nandi."

"But why not tell *us* the fact?"

"Because—because it led to other connections, nandi, and I honestly do not remember all of them. I remember going down the grade. That is clear in my mind. But other parts of it, some of the first days in Koperna, are hazy."

"You were, then, traveling in other than luxury."

"It was not luxury, nandi, and I did not have a work pass, and two trying to make that trip—froze to death. Those names— also—I used."

It was certainly not a happy account. And tea arrived. "Nadi," Bren said, while Jeladi arranged and poured, "I have no wish to rouse such memories. Especially over tea. Please. Tell me happier things. You met the aiji's son at Tirnamardi, and he reports well of you."

"I am grateful for his good opinion, nandi. He is a remarkable young man. He truly is."

"I think so," Bren said, and drank a sip. "Quick. And fairly perceptive, for his age, and above it. That you have his good opinion and nand' Tatiseigi's informs me a great deal and makes the aiji-dowager curious."

"I should like her to know," Nomari said, "that I am grateful for her personal interest, and understand completely her reserve. And yours, nandi. The only proof I have of who I am is in my veins, and the Guild has asked me to provide that—they say there is a way to tell."

"There is. And they will. But I care less for that, frankly, nadi, than I do your intelligence, your good will, your honesty, and the fact that, as I hear, the element Shishogi drove out of Ajuri believes you. Are you *sure* of the people that support you?"

"Nandi, these people moved me about, enabled me to change identities, kept me ahead of the enforcers—they saved my life."

"As did Lord Machigi."

"He said we had a common problem."

"Did you tell him who you were?"

"No, nandi. I told him I was Ajuri, and that I had fled the clan. That was true of hundreds. I told him I was clever at going here and there. I told him things he wanted to know about Senjin. I kept him informed on cargoes. I did a few things—destructive in nature."

"Sabotage." It was an uncommon subject, over tea. But Nomari was, in recent life, not accustomed to social amenities.

"Yes, nandi."

"In his service."

"Yes, nandi."

"Well," Bren said, "and you are prepared, are you, to take up the lordship of Ajuri? Does it worry you, considering its history?"

"I am advised by the Guild, nandi, to govern from a distance until they can be sure of the house at Ajiden. And I have been advised by the aiji-consort and Lord Tatiseigi to listen to the Guild. I am not foolishly proud. I am, gods know, not proud, and not inclined to risk others' lives if I can make their job easier by using good sense."

"Your bodyguard will appreciate that, nadi. My own has told me bluntly that I can be a fool. I try not to be."

Nomari looked uncertain it was at all humor. At which Bren laughed softly. "I am not your enemy, nadi, nor inclined to be. I shall be asked my impression. It is not at all a bad one."

"I shall be grateful, nandi."

"Have you had lunch?"

"I have not, nandi."

"Then let us go beyond the tea. We have a store of breakfast biscuits. Filled biscuits. Will that please you? Or we can appeal to the galley."

"I would be perfectly content with a biscuit, nandi."

"Well, then," Bren said, and signaled Jeladi and Narani.

Tano and Algini were up and about, between his car and the next, and with Narani and Jeladi on duty, and two of Nomari's Guild-appointed bodyguard in the corridor outside, they were alone without *being* alone, in atevi convention. They shared the light lunch with lighter questions—such as the railroad yard down in Koperna, and what shipments normally went *up* the grade to Hasjuran.

"Primarily fish," was the answer, "and seaweed used for various purposes, salt, sometimes, a variety of materials. Speed is impossible coming up and a mortal danger coming down."

"Passengers?"

A frown. "During the Troubles, many."

"To or from?"

"Both. It was a quieter route and less exposed to trouble than the west coast."

The regular Guild had held out on the coast, and conducted operations against the upstart regime. It made sense that travelers loyal to the Shadow Guild would choose the route through Hasjuran, however uncomfortable that descent and climb must be.

"Were there particular contacts for the Shadow Guild *in* Hasjuran?" It was, given their location, a critical question, and one he was sure had been asked before they came here.

"I do not know, nandi. My operations were all in the western Marid."

Here they were, improperly discussing serious business over lunch. "Forgive me," Bren said, laying down his fork. "I have strayed into business, and Guild business at that."

Nomari likewise set down his fork and took a sip of tea. "I only wish I could answer your questions, nandi. I have no personal knowledge, but by all I knew, this was just a route and the trains scarcely stopped. That there were agents for the regime coming through here goes without saying. My own contacts, mostly Ajuri, knew other Ajuri; and Kadagidi who were indeed settled here. I knew several of them—but they are now dead."

"At your arranging?"

"I may have taken one life, nandi, but that was not by intent. Sabotage—that, yes, to that, I do confess. I *have* confessed it, to the Guild."

"An end of such topics, then. Tell me something lighter. How are you faring, since your nomination? Have you had to deal with legislators?"

"No." Nomari visibly relaxed. "Not yet. But I know I shall."

"Do you look to see your nomination go through?"

"One has no idea, nandi. I know that if it does not, Ajuri is likely to stay vacant, and I know the Guild is still searching the basement for records. And while they are there nothing untoward will happen. Or is likely to happen. I suppose if I am not approved, that they will stay there indefinitely, and put the clan under an ongoing inquiry, the same as Kadagidi."

"But you intend more for Ajuri."

"I would like to see people come home, nandi. I would like to have proper Guild there, digging into whatever they need to find, and names named and innocent names cleared on clan records, among them my own household. I would start there."

"And for the future?"

"Cooperation with Ajuri's neighbors. Excluding Kadagidi, until it rights itself. If it will."

"Have you a grudge against them?"

"I do not plan one. If they are agreeable with my neighbors, then I would take Lord Tatiseigi's advice—as their nearest neighbor."

"You lean on him."

"He has experience and I do not. I admire him. And I trust him."

"Your trust would not be misplaced," Bren said.

It was a satisfying meeting. It was far from certain that Nomari had the background to do all a clan lord might need to

do—he could say that of himself, in managing Najida and relations with the Edi folk—but no lord could manage without a
good staff and the willingness to listen to them. His own—was
protection, advice, and uncommon good sense: they kept the
books balanced, the supplies adequate, the staff fed, and helped
a human lord keep current with what he needed to know regarding Najida and its neighbors as well as the goings-on in the
Bujavid.

Nomari had been handed a first-rate bodyguard—reporting
to the Guild, no question; and avowed himself willing to take
advice. It was not a bad beginning . . . granted nothing turned
up from his past. And granted he could navigate Ajuri itself,
long under a malign influence, and stay alive without becoming
part of the problems. He did not envy the young man the learning of what there was to learn inside those walls.

"First impression of that young man," he said to Tano, who
came in when Nomari had left, "is favorable. The question remains whether he can govern a clan that has persistently killed
its lords."

"Not an enviable position," Tano said, then touched his ear,
listening to something. "Nandi," he said then. "The Red Train
has just come onto the plateau."

"Is there any word yet out of Koperna?"

"Not as yet," Tano said. "But we shall know something soon."

The Red Train had not been using either conventional communications or even Guild communications, considering the
nature of the enemy, and the doubtful character of the passenger. There were a hundred other questions pending: notably how
fast might Dojisigi learn that Bregani had left Koperna at the
dowager's request for a meeting; and how much they knew
about the dowager's presence here, not to mention the presence
of Lord Machigi.

They had, overall, moved fast in sending the train down to
Senjin immediately after their arrival, but the train was not
faster than a phone call down the tenuous physical line that

ran beside the tracks—and as for security, the Messengers' Guild itself—the antiquity of the Guild being evident in the name of the phone service—had been known for occasional corruption long before the problems in the Assassins' Guild had begun—long before there were phone lines, radio, *or* telegraph. *Nobody* trusted the phone system to stay out of an intrigue.

Had the dowager herself arranged a phone outage between Hasjuran and points south? Possibly. It would make sense, to forestall the passing of a warning, and an outage in this region would probably not be at all unusual. But there were other means of communication—and was there a phone link between the Senjin capital and the Dojisigin that the dowager could not reach? It would be remarkable only if there were not a multitude of them.

The question was, had Bregani boarded sensibly, quickly, quietly, as requested—and without phoning Tiajo? The Red Train was known to use the route over to Targai and Najida on its coastal run, so the simple fact of its arrival in Koperna would be news, but not a clear statement of its intent. But the Dojisigi would soon know something, no matter how discreet the boarding, and would certainly be interested when they learned the train had immediately turned around to go *back* up the grade.

So Bregani was aboard. That much they knew. The dowager would be informed as quickly as he had been that the train was on the plateau and would be gathering speed. And it was not for the paidhi-aiji to tell their security to pass word to Machigi and Nomari that they were about to deal with Lord Bregani.

Cup of tea? They were apt to be awash in tea as Bregani joined them, but it was an attractive idea, a calmative before what looked to be a long evening.

He called Narani and Jeladi, and passed them the news, and the request.

"See me," was Father's message, from his office.

Cajeiri wore his best day coat, ready to discuss the ongoing situation with Boji, if Father wanted his opinion—and very much hoping that solution was not going to come apart.

"One hears," Father said, "that there was a phone call."

Cajeiri's breath stopped a moment, as if he had missed a step on the stairs. "Yes, Honored Father."

Father seemed amused. "It was monitored, as one might expect. But security confessed itself a little at a loss."

Following the conversation, he realized. They mixed ship-speak and Ragi and now even a word or two in kyo.

"One did not intend it," he said, mind racing on strategy and whether he had gone into territory he should not. He had weakened. He had answered questions. He had said things—possibly—that he ought not.

"And how are they?"

"They are very glad and very grateful to be safe, Honored Father."

"And how are they situated?"

"In a very nice place. With security. Nand' Bren and Banichi-nadi laid it out. All of it."

"So we understand," Father said, seeming easy with it all, but that could be misleading.

"Did I do wrong?" Cajeiri asked. With Father, it was a good idea *not* to avoid a question. "I thought if they were calling, it was cleared."

"It was cleared," Father said, "and secured. But you should not assume."

"One regrets."

"Their calls are screened on both ends, as are yours. You did discuss matters of some sensitivity."

"Only what was on the news, Honored Father. One—"

That word again. *Assumed.*

"I used my judgment, Honored Father. It may have been in error."

"Well," Father said. "We do not always trust the news ser-vices to be completely discreet. They were uncommonly involved in the disturbance at Tirnamardi, and reported some things that could have cost lives. In point of fact, they may have cost your great-aunt her life—or at least some few days of it."

That was something he had not suspected.

"And let the Shadow Guild reach the records, Honored Father?"

Father looked at him, eyebrow lifted, mani's own look. "Cleverness, son of mine? Is that *your* thought?"

"It was what everybody was worried about. The Guild went right away to searching the records. I would, too. If I were in charge."

Father nodded slowly. "Then indeed I did not produce a fool. And how, with this same mature good sense, *do* you assess the arrangements in Port Jackson? Are your young associates content, are they safe, and were they adversely affected by the disturbance at their arrival?"

The shooting of the Presidenta.

"They are glad to be safe, they are glad to be here, and they are sorry about the attack on the Presidenta, but they are not worried. I talked with them a long time. I wanted to be sure they were safe and I wanted to know what they were really thinking. I wanted to be sure I understood."

"And you are satisfied."

"I am. I had to tell them *something*, Honored Father, about how I was, so they would tell me how *they* were. I was truly, truly careful. If I have let something escape I should not have, I am very sorry. But I thought I was doing a proper thing. And my associates are careful about what I say, and so is Kate-nandi and the other people nand' Bren put in charge."

Father gazed at him a moment, then nodded. "Well thought, then, son of mine. You took a chance. And you gained something. Do consider, however, that you may know enough to be dangerous and too little about the risks."

"Was this one of those sort, Honored Father?"

"By all you say, I do not think so. I know you will ask me

how soon they can visit. And I shall put that off a time, and I wonder how soon Tirnamardi will be a safe place for any of you; but—that may be worked out. Najida remains a possibility. But they need time to settle. They *are* human. You cannot make them otherwise. They are here, the paidhi informs us, first to learn about Mospheira, and form an attachment there They are the precursors of their settlement—they have that duty on their shoulders, to form a good opinion around them. But—" Father added, "it is not necessary for *all* of them to land before you may host these young people in some appropriate place. It is also politic for Mospheira to see their association on this side of the strait as good and powerful, and to view these young people as an asset they must treat with respect."

"They also know to keep my secrets," he said. "Aboard the ship, they did. And here, too, they will."

"Had you secrets, son of mine?"

"Where we went. What we talked about. They were stupid secrets. I was younger then."

"That you were. But now your secrets are heavier, and could create misunderstandings."

"One does understand," he said, and that was the truth. "I shall tell them to be careful."

"Do," Father said. "But tell them that the time will not be *too* long before we consider a visit, granted things stay quiet."

21

The train approached the station. Word was clear that Lord Bregani *was* aboard, and the dowager, from her car, sent word that there would be a formal dinner in the Red Car, once they had the whole train reassembled.

That meant the engine had to turn about and link them all up just as they had started out, with the engine facing the descent to Koperna. It was part of the promise—that Bregani had a safe conduct up here, and that after the conference they would again uncouple that section and the engine would make the run back down.

The operation took some maneuvering, which, without windows, they knew only as a great deal of puffing from the engine and, finally, a jolt as the forward section rejoined them.

There was quiet and stability, then. If it was to be a formal dinner, it would be formal dress, and no sparing the details—a diplomatic dinner, and afterward, probably into the depth of night, there might be serious talk. That meant a decent rest beforehand, no excess of drink during or after, even in the brandy service . . . and Bren was prepared for the negotiations. He knew the likely questions and he knew the things the dowager would want to achieve in any understanding with Senjin, the best outcome being acceptance of Machigi's proposal for a protected rail link through Senjin territory.

If that resulted, it was bound to upset Tiajo. The key questions were—whether Bregani preferred to be *bypassed* for what could become a lucrative matter, once the sea trade from the East did start; and if he did accept it, how far Tiajo's handlers would let her go in retaliation.

It was possible that Bregani had already discovered that Machigi was part of the equation, and that he was here because he intended to refuse and wanted that information to pass to Tiajo. Spying was the natural state of affairs in the Marid. And double-crosses were frequent. But—Bregani of all people should know that Tiajo was unpredictible, and that his life then hung on whether the Shadow Guild who really ran the province saw anything in the proposal useful to them—in, for instance, a way to cause problems, acquire information, and access targets.

There were moments, however, when Tiajo's tantrums flew wide and far.

Narani was helping Bren dress, with Jeladi's help. Definitely the bulletproof vest. He had no quarrel with that precaution tonight, and he tried not to think about Ilisidi's fragility. He stood still, thinking such thoughts as what he could do, what protection he could possibly offer, while Jeladi adjusted his queue and ribbon.

Tano came from the car forward, a Guild station, in some haste. Banichi and Jago had quietly moved in that direction, so it was no surprise that the other half of his aishid came back. But Tano's arrival, solo, was straight to him, with purpose.

"Nandi," Tano said. "We have a more complicated situation than anticipated. Bregani has brought his wife and daughter, and four security—his wife's *Farai* security."

That was not what they had planned.

That had a very different tone. Like—moving vulnerable relatives to safety.

"Worry is," Tano said, "that his absence, however brief, may invite trouble. Our understanding is that Bregani put his cousin in charge of the house at Koperna, and had his wife's family—a brother and contract wife and two children relocated to that facility under guard."

"We may have started something," Bren said. "The dowager is being informed?"

"At this moment," Tano said.

The Farai were a clan resident within Senjin, relegated to a mere sub-clan status, but never resigned to their lot, and always quick to seize any route to power. Bregani's wife was Farai, and in the absence of Bregani *and* his heir, that clan might well move in. That was the first worry.

But that left the Farai clan lord the unhappy prospect of explaining things to Tiajo, over in the Dojisigin, and that might dampen his enthusiasm.

"Information is incomplete," Tano said. "But Bregani has left orders sealing Senjin's border from all sides."

Against the Dojisigin *and* the Taisigin. Senjin was vulnerable to the Taisigin by land and sea, and to the Dojisigin primarily by sea, though they shared a broad and occasionally marshy plain and hunting range. Senjin had small villages up and down the coast, and the harbor at Lusi'ei all exposed to mischief arriving by ship.

The dowager had requested Bregani's quiet, even secret attendance for a conference. The man had instead evacuated his household and apparently appointed a successor.

"Is this cousin then holding place for him?" Bren asked. "Does he have actual authority in Bregani's absence?"

"There is no information, Bren-ji," Tano said. "Lord Bregani did not hesitate when the dowager's message reached him. That is what we hear. Why this is, or how the dowager's invitation intersected some local situation, we do not yet know."

"Consult with Cenedi. Do what you need to do, Tano-ji. Is Algini still in the command center?"

"Yes," Tano said. "With Banichi and Jago. Four non-Guild Farai bodyguards accompany this party, with weapons that the Guild aboard, due to protocol, have not examined thoroughly. Lord Bregani has agreed to keep all weapons out of the dowager's presence, but there is some discussion among us about sealing the passageway of the rearmost baggage car and forcing Lord Bregani's party to transit in the open to reach the dowager's area. We have also considered leaving that segment uncoupled, which also forces an exposed transit to an entry of our choosing. This is under discussion and awaiting the dowager's decision. We do not think she will agree."

"Go," Bren said. "Of all things, *I* am safe where this car sits. I shall message Machigi and Nomari as I receive information. See if we can assure this lord's good will while observing necessary precautions. Narani and Jeladi can be my couriers, *and* my protection, by turns."

"Yes," Tano said. And left, quickly. It was a rare moment when *all* his aishid was engaged apart from him, but he had no uneasiness about his own safety, sandwiched as he was between the dowager's domain and the car where, apparently, the urgent security conference was going on.

He sat down at the table—with due care for his formal coat. He immediately opened his writing kit, took out a note paper and his pen and buzzed Narani and Jeladi—no delay in response there. They waited while he wrote.

The first communication was to Machigi. *Lord Bregani has arrived along with his wife and daughter, plus four security, and those are of his wife's clan. In some urgency, if you know names and leanings of these individuals or other details which may be useful to know in negotiations, please commit them to writing and send them to me by return message. I shall relay them on to the dowager. We wish to limit movement in the corridors temporarily as a safety measure, but be assured your protection is high in priority. Please stay in the safety of your own car for now. If you have a message or query you would like to send to Lord Bregani, likewise provide that and I can relay it on.*

To Nomari, he wrote somewhat the same, and added: *Please stay close to your security. If in your acquaintance with Senjin you have either suspicion or reassurance regarding this move,* such information will be most welcome. What is your opinion of the security of Senjin, internal and external, granted the evacuation of these specific persons, and why would Lord Bregani make particular moves to protect the Farai?

He added a handwritten seal, there being no time to fire up the waxjack. *Mine, by my hand, Bren paidhi-aiji.*

Then he took out another note paper and wrote: *Lord Bregani, I am paidhi-aiji for the aiji-dowager, honored to serve as conduit for communications. Welcome. If there are concerns you would like me to relay to the dowager before our evening together, I shall do that gladly. If you have concerns you would like to urge other than verbally, please convey them to me. I am, nandi, your spokesman as well as the dowager's, in the ancient rules of my office, and you may rely on me to argue honestly on your behalf.*

He gave all three missives to Narani to carry. There was no need to send to Ilisidi. She owned the internal communications, she had Cenedi to inform her, and she would be dispensing information at her own discretion.

He had to sit and wait for answers to his notes, if answers could be had. He busied himself making a quick record of the messages he had just sent, to pass on to Ilisidi.

The first response was Nomari's. Jeladi brought it. *Nand' paidhi, if I can assist I will. I have no interpretation of events except that Lord Bregani is concerned for his household and wishes protection for them during his visit. That he should protect the Farai, in particular his wife's immediate family, is in character. He values his wife, she values her family, and a threat to her family would be strong leverage on his actions. He does not trust Lord Machigi, but he knows the danger of Tiajo's temper. He may believe that his own security, which is Talidi clan, is fatally compromised by the dowager's approach. Talidi and Dojisigi are related through Cosadi, who brought the Shadow Guild into the region, and who are thus also related to Lord Tiajo. Lord Bregani might fear a security breach, and he will reasonably fear that this invitation from the dowager will give Tiajo the pretext to move against him. In my opinion he fears very much that his family might be taken hostage either by parties wishing to force his action against Tiajo or by Dojisigi agents, and he believes Koperna has no protection for them. That he moved Farai security in numbers into his home along with her family might well be his preferred security arrangement.*

Both descendants of Cosadi, Bregani and Tiajo—both with close kin inside Talidi clan, the ruling clan in both provinces, and with kin on both sides of the provincial divide. It made a certain sense to rely on Farai, such as Farai could ever be relied upon. Farai was of longstanding reputation a blade that turned one way and the other, always for its own advantage. At worst, there was little to choose between Talidi and Farai . . . except to engage their self-interest, and hope that that self-interest included one's survival.

It was worth remembering, too, that there was a cultural divide between the Marid clans and the Ragi of the north, one that had to be worked with, understood, *used,* so far as he could, himself being human—if he could get a sense of it. The Maridi clans had a moral flexibility that made them volatile—and while volatility was not a good thing when it came to agreements, flexibility—even in honor—was not necessarily a fault. He had yet to understand them. That was the thing. The Ragi north could be inflexible. The Marid—not so much.

"Take these to Banichi and Cenedi," he said, handing Nomari's message back to Jeladi, as well as the precis of his own message. "Immediately."

One did *not* expect Senjin to discover the departure of their lord and half his household without some reaction. There would be a plethora of unanswerable questions—which in Koperna might already have sent factions scrambling for position.

The aishidi'tat itself moving to attack them—that had to rank lower on Senjin's list of worries—given the immediacy of threat from their own sister-state.

One tried to remember exactly what assets the aishidi'tat now had in the south that Tabini could bring in if their mission blew up, and it was, in terms of geography, not encouraging. Machigi could rouse the whole southern Marid to war if challenged. Tiajo would be a fool to challenge *him* at the moment.

But if Tiajo had a plan to take Senjin, among the first moves might be to cut the northern rail link—the fragile downward link between Hasjuran and Koperna, to the injury of their host . . . thus stranding the Red Train up here.

If conflict erupted, the aishidi'tat could quickly move forces eastward on the southern line via Najida. If Tiajo took Koperna, she could not *use* the rail center she would have captured.

But she could certainly create bloody mayhem in Senjin in the meantime.

The Farai, who thought they had a historic claim on Najida *and* his Bujavid apartment, had been a thorn in his side, personally, on more than one occasion, but they *were* the bulwark between Tiajo's Dojisigin and the rest of Senjin. The Farai lord might be an obnoxious, stubborn, and combative old man, but he did not deserve to be taken down by such a creature as Tiajo and her Shadow Guild supporters. And the aishidi'tat simply could not afford to have Tiajo break out of her box and start invading her neighbors to the south. Tabini would not tolerate it.

But it had been on the list of possibilities when Ilisidi had listened to Machigi's rail proposal.

Narani arrived with Machigi's answer, written in a difficult and angular hand. *Lord Bregani is not a timid man. He is either following Tiajo's orders, or he is convinced he has absolutely no choice but ally with me. Certainly he seems not to count on keeping Tiajo's agents out of Senjin. Whether they are already there in numbers, ready to move—is another matter.*

Machigi had urged them to call Senjin to conference. So how did they find out the set of hooks hidden in that proposition?

Which is it, nandi? he asked Machigi in absentia. You know the man. What do *you* think is the case here?

On the other hand . . . did Machigi *really* know him? They'd never, to Bren's knowledge, met face to face.

He jotted down a note of his own. *I am extremely uneasy in this evening, aiji-ma, and I am reluctant to see even one of Bregani's security enter your presence. As for Machigi himself, who says Bregani may be following Tiajo's orders, or fleeing her reaction, I now ask with what understanding has he advised this meeting?*

A two-step maneuver? He could readily believe that Machigi had not told them everything he knew; but he could not believe that Machigi wanted harm to Ilisidi or to the agreement he had with her, not from the goodness of his heart, but for the profit he stood to lose.

No. Whatever Machigi aimed at, there had to be some benefit to Machigi's interests.

Machigi had gone to unprecedented lengths to secure the dowager's help, coming out of Taisigin for the first time in his life to meet with her at Najida, and now sitting in the thin air of Hasjuran, an environment almost as alien as space itself, for a sea-dweller.

The choice of Hasjuran was one item not likely Machigi's. This operation equally well could have been run out of Targai, in Maschi clan territory, parallel with Koperna and safely in much lower, more open terrain, where they still had the advantage of access by Machigi's forces and with a neutral clan as host. No, this frosty venue was surely Ilisidi's choice. Hasjuran was a hilltop fortress by comparison, with a staggeringly high and snowy bulwark and a very difficult climb from the Marid side.

Ilisidi had invited Machigi to commit himself farther north than he had ever been and at greater altitude than he had ever been. If one of their party was suffering from the altitude here, it was surely Machigi—and that would apply to any other maritime lord or armed unit entering the mix. If Tiajo wanted to attack here, the altitude was not convenient for her people, nor was the cold, for which her forces were not likely equipped.

The Red Train having reassembled facing Senjin, that meant they could honor Ilisidi's promise to Bregani, to send him back down that steep descent—but one hoped the dowager did not decide to *take* Bregani back down to his capital. She was capable of that kind of recklessness. Experience had proven that.

Banichi came back, and joined him in the sitting area.

"Is monitoring off?" Bren asked.

"Yes," Banichi said.

"Then what is our situation?" he asked.

"Fluid," Banichi said.

"Does Tabini-aiji know what is happening here, Nichi-ji?"

That—was a perilous question. Banichi's man'chi was to him, but it was also, by previous service, to Tabini-aiji, as Algini's was—one tended to presume—to the central Guild.

"He is generally aware," Banichi said.

"Are you satisfied? Are you comfortable with what is happening here?"

No hesitation. "Yes. So far."

That was reassuring. "It was at no time theorized that Bregani would bring his wife and daughter, or commit his safety to Farai."

"It was a little surprise," Banichi said, "a contingency thought of."

"The dowager knew he might do this."

"Under conditions of threat, yes. If Talidi clan became untrustworthy."

"And has it become untrustworthy?"

"Indications are, yes."

"*Machigi* has forced this."

"Possibly," Banichi said. "Machigi is certainly no ally of the Talidi."

"You—have such a connection, Nichi-ji. Do you not? I say nothing to—"

Banichi lifted a hand from the table, forestalling apology.

"Maternally Talidi. But there is no man'chi. I am Guild, from birth. The connection is meaningless."

"I have *no* doubt of you. None. Ever. But their connections . . ."

"Talidi is not strictly Maridi," Banichi said, "and I tell you that not from within myself: I am as foreign to the Marid as Tabini-aiji himself. And that is the way of Talidi. They shed pieces here and there, from far back. They began as a west coast clan, and now the west has no common tradition with the branch here. They began on the west coast. Some settled as far north as Dur, but hold man'chi to Ajuri. In the middle coast, they married into the Maladesi, *and* the Farai."

"But the Maladesi are gone."

"The Maladesi, now extinct, are Senjin. The Talidi *and* the Farai are neither one Maridi in origin. The Maladesi *were* Maridi, who attempted to colonize the west coast—ancient history. The surviving clans, Talidi and Farai, are west coast clans in origin, who became tributary to the Maladesi—or at least, so did the part of Talidi that did *not* settle at Dur."

"One's head could spin."

"The Maladesi are all gone. Talidi is in three parts, the Senjin Talidi ruling the district. The Farai are now extinct except in Senjin, and both Senjin Talidi and Farai now claim to be Southern Isle in origin—which is completely false."

"I remember about the Farai. I have never put it together."

"The Maladesi were the link, the only claim Talidi and Farai have on Southern Isle heritage—and that is largely folklore. The modern clans are whatever they locally need to be. My own attachment of record is to the Talidi branch near Dur—should you wonder. Senjin is, in terms of antiquity of both its extant clans, a tree of shallow roots, not quite fitting into the Marid, but not separate from it, either. It gets along with the Maschi holdings at Targai. The Taisigin is another story. *Machigi* is a very different story."

"Is he—?"

"—Southern Isle, as he claims? He has no way to prove it. The Sungeni and the Dausigi find it convenient to believe it at the moment. The Senjin just want him to not to invade them; and the Dojisigi clearly deny *Machigi* and do not challenge whatever the Senjin want to say they are, so long as they ally with Dojisigi. Tiajo *claims* Maladesi heritage. So does Bregani— both reckon their descent from Cosadi, who was Dojisigi *and* Maladesi. But one would advise against opening that topic tonight."

"Fervently. I need advice in this tangle. I thought I knew, but clearly there are connections both real and imaginary that could affect this."

"Say that this meeting is either nothing or a great deal. Your own reasoning comes without clan attachments, in a situation with far too *many* clan attachments, and that is actually an advantage. They cannot anticipate your reactions; and sometimes your advice comes from directions one would have sworn were a blank wall. That, I can say. Bregani has brought a clan other than his own. He is very possibly in difficulty. Machigi may be right about the timing of this. Whether Machigi's intentions toward him are benign is another matter. But Tiajo is our mutual problem, and the Shadow Guild is guiding her outbursts."

"One aches to know what link Cosadi had with Shishogi. They were contemporaries. Is it all one thing, this whole Marid problem? Sometimes I suspect it is."

"Certainly the Shadow Guild knew where they could be safest," Banichi said. "But it is almost certainly *two* things, Bren-ji. No matter what way the wind blows in the north, the Marid is always the Marid."

"And Machigi's visit to Najida? His extraordinarily well-timed visit to Najida? Whose idea was that, Nichi-ji? Have you any better idea? Are we operating in the dowager's plan— or his?"

"We cannot dig that deep into Cenedi's silences, but Machigi has developed lines of communication with the dowager regarding the state of affairs in the south. That she desires stability in the south before she dies is *no* secret. If her information from whatever source saw either opportunity or worsening crisis . . . she might well have informed Machigi she was in Najida, with the implication that, if he wanted to talk, that was his time to do it—and if he would ever move, now would be the moment."

"While Nomari turns up in the north, claiming Ajuri. With a connection to Machigi. At this particular moment."

"The dowager truly is not pleased with his move to take Ajuri. And she surely questions that connection. Legislative pressure was mounting for Tabini-aiji to fill that seat. Nomari had to act then or see some appointment made and his own cause lost. But is it possible that Machigi delivered the news about Ajuri and *set* the man in motion? One can believe he might. One can equally believe in a connection in the *other* direction—that the exposure of Shadow Guild records in Ajuri might stir the Shadow Guild to make desperate moves in the Marid. Seizing Senjin would be one of them. Machigi, whatever else he is, is *not* a fool. That, I do trust."

Bren heaved a sigh, reassured and disquieted at once. "One assumes Tabini-aiji is following this."

"At a certain point the yarn is beyond tangled. It is tied in knots. The dowager's men *are* the aiji's guard. Secure communication is as easy as a walk down the hall. I know the aiji is involved—but at what point in this sequence, we are not sure. It is worth noting, however, he has chosen to let you represent *the aiji-dowager* in this, not the aishidi'tat."

Meaning that should things go wrong, there was still a level of government that could step in to right the ship. It was not the first time they had been sent out on such terms. Deniability, definitely. In case it all blew up.

"As for the candidate for Ajuri," Banichi said, "we now have a much freer flow of information on him, independent in source. He has called himself Heteni, among other names, served

Machigi not as an active agent, but an observer, and passed variously for Maschi, Separi, Furi, *and* Kadagidi."

"Has he admitted to all this?"

"Yes, even the Kadagidi identity, when asked, though he says it was an identity he claimed only in Senjin. He has given an account of his time and assignments according to his memory, and we have matched it to his assignments by Transportation. He was assumed dead during the Troubles, when he used multiple identities, and some of the identities he assumed were of members of his guild he knew to be deceased, particularly the Kadagidi, Heteni, who is, indeed, still deceased."

The dead had risen since the Troubles, in some instances. Heteni, apparently, had not.

"Nomari-nadi volunteered as much, wisely enough, since it was likely to be found out, given our access to Machigi. But— one cannot fault him for surviving, and he is not proven to have supported the Kadagidi in any way. He swore he had no dealings with the Dojisigi, nor wished to have. We are still making inquiries, but to be fair, no lord of the aishidi'tat has ever answered as many questions in advance of his confirmation."

"One is somewhat hopeful he may come through," Bren said. "He has impressed the young gentleman and the aiji-consort. And Lord Tatiseigi. I may say—I have dealt with far less agreeable lords through the years."

"Cenedi himself is not unfavorable to him. But we all remain cautious. Do not meet him alone, Bren-ji."

"I do *nothing* alone on this outing, Nichi-ji. I do not say I am alarmed, but I am spending my idle time constructing dire scenarios. I do not have enough facts to distract me. When am I to meet the lord of Senjin, and do I interview him in advance of the dowager?"

"It is my understanding there will be a social hour," Banichi said.

"A social hour." The before-dinner ritual, for a state occasion. The dowager would, in effect, throw a small party before dinner, in which they would all be constrained to smile and behave. "Is the lady invited? Or the daughter?"

"They may be," Banichi said. "They may *specifically* be invited."

To a social hour with Machigi—with the dowager. One felt a twinge of pity for the accompanying family.

But it *was* why they had come.

22

Dinner with Father and Mother meant one's almost-best, the very best being reserved for public occasions. It also meant a nice dinner brought in for staff, which was a happy occasion. Cajeiri had tried to excuse his younger aishid from duty—it was *only* to the dining room, in the heart of the household, and with absolutely reliable people about, but his staff was determined, having just been given recognition, to dress him properly and attend him properly. Eisi and Liedi still served as his valets, but they were wearing their new coats, with cuff and collar lace, and feeling very proud, looking forward to presiding at their own table, set up with proper tableware and all, back in the new staff room.

Antaro and Jegari, Veijico and Lucasi would stand attendance with him, and they went out the door together, going down the main inner hall to the dining room just as Mother with her escort exited her own suite at the end of the hall.

Cajeiri waited, feeling uncommonly well put together and comfortable in his new arrangement, comfortable with Mother, finally. And being so, he waited for her, gave a little bow as they met.

"Honored Mother."

"Son of mine. You are looking very handsome this evening."

"I am very happy with the new staff. They are very good, and Eisi and Liedi are happy with the arrangement."

"Are you making progress on finding Boji a place? I heard your father saying he might fund an improvement in the park you mentioned."

"So he cannot get loose and bite anyone.—He is the gentlest fellow," he added quickly, because Mother had always worried about his sister's safety. "But if he was scared."

"Well, one could not blame him for that," Mother said. "I wish the little creature well. And a long life. Have you heard anything from Malguri?"

He was startled, surprised, dismayed all in one stroke, and it showed, he knew it did. He saw his mother's face change—to perplexity, then—something else.

Mother had approved of him at Tirnamardi. Mother had been kind to him since then. Mother had been sympathetic about Boji.

And suddenly—the wall was back. Everything was back.

"Not Malguri," he said, desperately.

"Where, then?"

"Hasjuran, Honored Mother. One thought—one thought you knew."

"Why should I know?" Mother was angry, extremely angry. "Why Hasjuran, in all reason?"

"Mother. Honored Mother. I found out. It was a secret. We should not talk here."

Mother's face had gone hard. But she nodded agreement, and motioned toward the dining room, and motioned him ahead of her.

That was how things were, now. He was not used to secrets in this new arrangement. He wanted to be polite, he wanted to make amends, and when they were inside, and the door was shut, with just two each of their bodyguards in the room, he turned and gave a deep, apologetic bow.

"It was a mistake, Honored Mother. I found out by accident and told Father, and Father told me—told me he knew, and to keep quiet, so I supposed you knew."

Mother looked a little less angry. He kept going.

"Nand' Bren is with them. He can talk to Great-grandmother."

"That, we were assured was the case. But what are they doing in Hasjuran?"

"Honored Mother, you know—we know—that Cousin did take refuge in the Taisigin Marid during the Troubles."

"Given."

"Lord Machigi came to see mani and nand' Bren, and he is with them. Mani wants to compare what they say. She wants to know what they did, and whether they still talk to each other."

"In *Hasjuran?*" Mother asked. "They are holding a delicate conference with Lord *Topari?*"

"Not with him." Father's voice sounded from the open sitting room doorway, and Father walked in without his bodyguard. "Not with him, Miri-ji. It has been a deep secret, one of my grandmother's notions, and one of the most dangerous—a matter of timing, and a need to seize a moment quietly, if it can be done. Cajeiri was not to know, but he sent his senior bodyguard down ahead of his visit to the station, to be sure of things, and seeing what he saw, had the sense to draw back and report to me when he found things not as he expected. Nomari-nadi is in a sense undergoing a critical examination, but so is Lord Machigi, who is asking Grandmother to link him to Senjin by rail."

"Gods less favorable." Mother did not, as a rule, swear. "To do *what?*"

"They are calling the lord of Senjin up to Hasjuran to discuss his situation. Senjin, we are told, has come under increased pressure from the Dojisigi because of Grandmother's agreement with Machigi—because of the prospect of ship-building that will make the southern Marid a threat to them. They imagine weapons. They imagine all manner of things. And Machigi imagines, probably, gaining exactly what his agreement with Grandmother forbids him to have—the west coast. That will *not* happen. But in the meanwhile, Senjin is, according to Machigi, in disfavor with Tiajo on several accounts. Lord Bregani has reason to fear a move to assassinate him and replace him, and he might welcome a contact offering him participation in Machigi's deal with Grandmother."

"Is that the offer?"

"That will be the offer. His capital will have a rail link to Machigi's capital, and together, including Machigi's dominance in the south, they will give Tiajo something very specific to worry about."

"And if he refuses?"

"Well, in that case, he probably will be assassinated—eventually. But not by us. Tiajo is only a figurehead, of use only for an appearance of legitimacy. The forces behind Tiajo will move. Senjin will be annexed. War will break out. We had rather not have that. And your cousin Nomari, as well as having sheltered in Lord Machigi's court, *spied* for him in Senjin. He is a check on the truth, on both sides. Grandmother is presiding over what we hope will be face to face negotiations, and *if* we can secure the cooperation of the lord of Senjin, and his economic linkage to Machigi, we can both keep Machigi busy, and gain information about the Dojisigin Marid we can very well use. The Shadow Guild will have one less dark corner to hide in."

"And they are quite likely to figure this out, are they not?"

"Indeed they are. Which is why the Red Train is defended as it is, and parked where access is not easy. It is prepared for defense. Now you know all of it. I am curious how you did find out, past all our precautions."

"Our son's face. When I said *Malguri*."

"Face," Cajeiri said ruefully. "I was—I was not—I was surprised, Honored Father. I was not on my guard."

"And why *should* you be, if I did not warn you specifically, which I did not?"

"You did not, on the other hand, tell *me*," Mother said.

"I did not want to worry you," Father said. "In fact I wanted the best chance to be sure of your cousin in my own mind as well as Grandmother's—if I am trusting him in a close relationship to our most precious assets. Ajuri is not an easy creature to ride, and I need assurances I am not trusting a scoundrel or giving an inexperienced young man a post he cannot long survive. Neither is my wish."

"He *is* my cousin."

"And therefore family, and therefore obliged to deal with Grandmother, *and* with the associates he may have made during his exile. If he can manage all three and come out in good favor, he may indeed be what Ajuri needs."

"Nand' Bren will look out for him," Cajeiri said, hoping to calm the argument. "He will, and his guard will, and nand' Bren can talk anyone into anything."

"One day I shall ask him to reason with your great-grandmother," Mother said, frowning. "But then, that may be an impossibility."

"She favors you, Honored Mother. She truly does. She says—" Actually what mani had said was that Mother had reined in Father's temper, but that was hardly what to say at the moment. "—You are a good influence. And she only wishes you to be good to Uncle Tatiseigi, which you are, and you have done, and I am glad."

"*You* have been learning from nand' Bren," Father said dryly. "But come, I think your mother forgives us both, and she has far more to forgive in my case."

"If *your* grandmother is going to start a war," Mother said, "bear in mind I want my cousin back undamaged."

"I shall do my best," Father said. "Come to table. Son of ours, do not worry. Everybody is safe and warm and well-protected in Hasjuran at this hour, and probably enjoying a good dinner. I have argued with Grandmother, but she views the Marid situation as hers; and she has advisors she *will* listen to, so we simply wait and watch."

The passage doors were unlocked. The dinner was set up.

The question was in what mood Bregani had boarded, and what mood he was in right now.

The man had to travel the whole length of the train to reach the Red Car, and the dowager, having rested in seclusion all day, had invited everyone aboard to drinks and dinner. She had invited Machigi and Nomari to come to the Red Car at a certain time—and only them at first.

Receive Lord Bregani and establish an acquaintance sufficient to introduce him, had been Ilisidi's note to Bren. *We hope he will be receptive and not too distressed to find his neighbor and our Ajuri guest present. We trust your management of the situation.*

Of course. Management of the situation. God help him.

Bren waited to intercept Bregani. And it was an occasion, at very least, for one's best coat and social graces.

And the pistol. In case.

Jago reported as, separately, with two each of their bodyguards, Machigi and Nomari went down the passage to the Red Car, presumably to have pleasant converse with the dowager.

"Lord Bregani is on his way," Jago reported, word coming through the Guild. "Murai-daja his wife, Husai their daughter. The girl is sixteen."

A child, then, still. Old enough to be sensible, not old enough for alcohol or political conversation. One was glad to be advised of the age.

And it made the meeting actually easier that there were, so to speak, true non-combatants in the group.

He waited. Banichi and Jago were by the door, Tano and Algini moved into position on the other side of his own car's sitting area. Banichi and Jago walked out to block the corridor. Bren exited, and met the Senjin party, who were likewise escorted by two of their Farai bodyguard, typical enough—two with the lord, two left behind to secure the lord's quarters. The two Farai were in civilian dress, not conspicuously armed. Banichi and Jago were not. Tano and Algini—were.

Bregani and his wife and daughter stopped still—and one had to recall that they had never seen a human before. Bren took that into account, and gave a little bow.

"Nandiin. Welcome. I am Bren-paidhi, in service to the aiji-dowager on this venture, and I am willing to represent your interests as well, if you will do me that honor."

"Nand' paidhi." Lord Bregani and his family returned the bow. The daughter, poor kid, looked scared.

"Please be assured," Bren said, "that the dowager is by no means ill-disposed to you. I should advise you, too, that Lord Machigi is present this evening, also expressing good will toward you and hopes for better relations. Lord Machigi has presented the dowager a proposal which does involve Senjin—to your advantage as well as his, in the dowager's opinion. In any event, you are under the aiji-dowager's personal protection inside and outside her premises. Should you wish to return to Senjin at any time, that wish will be honored, and you and your family will be sent back in the same way you left, but in the dowager's name, please delay that until the end of this evening."

Bregani's face had gone from neutral to cold during that explanation—an understandable reaction to Machigi's name.

"We *are* in danger," Bregani said. "And Lord Machigi is *not* our ally."

"I believe, nandi, that you have a great deal to gain in what the dowager will propose—if you and Lord Machigi can possibly settle issues—and we will try to broker such an agreement. Recent events have not been kind to Senjin, and the dowager understands you have had a limited choice of allies. The dowager will offer a route to verifiable peace in all directions, with economic advantage, if you will only hear her out."

A little expression was back.

"I have no choice," Bregani said. "From last night, when I received that message, I have had no choice."

"The dowager is not willing to see you fall from power. Your continuance in Senjin is critical to her plans, and she has tried to make this contact as quick and quiet as possible, in hopes of preventing attention from Dojisigi. Beyond that, Tiajo's power is not what it was, nor will it be again, especially if you and Lord Machigi can find common interest tonight. The aishidi'tat is rapidly settling its own problems and looking southward, not for conquest, but for useful alliance. The dowager's second guest may or may not be known to you—but he is himself likely to have the lordship of Ajuri before the year is out, and he does know you, not to your discredit, either. He is the aiji-consort's cousin, Nomari by name. He was also Lord Machigi's agent during the Troubles. You may possibly have known him as Het-eni. He has given a good report of you. Through it, you are assumed, on Lord Machigi's word, to be a potential ally."

Expressions did subtly chase one another across Bregani's face, not, one was certain, escaping Bregani's control. The man was capable of a stone face under stress: he had shown that. But now Bregani let reactions show, ever so slightly—an indication he was at least opening the door to conversation. Or that he was considerably at a loss what to do. The lady and the daughter were not reassured.

"I have said enough," Bren said. "The dowager will discuss these matters in detail after dinner, and the engine remains poised to take you back to Koperna at any moment—should you wish. In the interim—enjoy the dinner and do not worry for your safety. *All* the dowager's guests are under her protection."

The Red Car had been reconfigured for the occasion—*completely* reconfigured, down to the removal of ordinary seats and tables and the installation of a formally set dinner table in the middle. A few bench seats had been reoriented on their stanchions with gaps to allow standing room for Guild—exclusively the dowager's bodyguard—and passing room for servants—exclusively the dowager's servants, this evening. Only the red velvet bench seats at the rear remained fixed in their usual place, apt for a conference.

How staff had managed to relocate the seats elsewhere without disturbing the occupied cars was a wonder. It must surely have been done outside on the platform, Bren thought, maybe porting them up the length of the train to one of the baggage cars. However they had done it, staff had transformed the space: linen cloths, brocade runners, crystal candelabras, the candles only now being lit, crystal goblets and bottles of white wine and red. There were seven places at table, and three additional chairs facing the rear bench for a conversational seating.

Ilisidi sat on that bench, centermost of the room, with Cenedi standing on her left and Machigi and Nomari standing on her right, turned to face their arrival.

Bregani and his family stopped cold. Their bodyguard had been diverted—with Banichi and Jago—to the galley; and they had not taken alarm at that situation. But confronting Machigi, even prepared for the meeting—

Ilisidi, with a thump of her cane on the floor, and Cenedi's offered hand, stiffly rose to meet them, uncommon courtesy. "Nand' Bregani. Nandiin." Which encompassed wife, daughter, and paidhi-aiji. "Come. There is brandy, and there is juice. We shall sit, it being so small a gathering. Come. Let us become acquainted."

Bregani escorted his family resolutely forward. Machigi put on a fairly pleasant face, Nomari bowed, and Ilisidi settled back to her seat, enabling everyone else to sit.

"You will understand we are crowded for space," Ilisidi said, "and my staff alone will serve tonight. You are *my* guests, and we assure you, at any time you wish, you may begin your return journey, but you have surprised us, nand' Bregani, with your family. Will you do the courtesies of introduction, nand' paidhi?"

"Aiji-ma, nandiin," Bren said, "one presents Lord Bregani, with his married wife Murai-daja and daughter Husai-daja, of that marriage.—Nandiin, one presents Nomari-nadi, currently under consideration for the Ajuri lordship . . ."

It was incumbent on Bregani, the wife and the daughter all to smile, nod politely, and ignore prior acquaintance, if any, with the spy who had lived in Senjin and delivered rail schedules and cargo lists to their enemy. "One is pleased to make your acquaintance," Murai said; and from Husai, a movement of the lips and a gaze fixed, absolutely fixed on Nomari, who looked up into that stare. And likewise froze a moment, stock still.

Prior meeting? Bren wondered. Acquaintance? God, what kind of subtext was that?

"One is likewise pleased," Nomari managed to say.

Then: "Lord Bregani, one presents Lord Machigi of Tanaja," Bren said, and damn him, Machigi flashed the broadest smile he had ever seen on the man—a challenging smile that bent the scar, on a face that could look absolutely grim.

From the wife and daughter there were polite, worried nods, and from Bregani, perforce, a stiff: "A meeting unlooked for, nand' Machigi."

"Honored, sir." Machigi made an extravagant bow. "Honored, ladies."

"Nandi." From Bregani.

"Well, well," Ilisidi said. "And let us not be too formal. Husai-daja, we daresay you might appreciate a watered wine. A fruit ice, perhaps."

"The ice, please." It was a shy, soft voice, without the requisite honorific.

"Nand' dowager," Bregani said quickly. "An ice for her. Wine will be welcome for us."

"An ice, and the wine," Ilisidi said, and servants went into action. "Nand' Machigi, Nomari-nadi, wine for you, also, one would imagine."

Staff moved quickly to provide drinks. The social occasion

lurched into tense motion, everyone seated, momentarily distracted by the arrival of refreshment, eyeing one another warily. Husai looked frightened, but managed to answer a courtesy from Nomari. Bregani and his wife sat darting looks at Machigi, who said nothing.

"Come, come." Ilisidi said, lifting a glass of red wine. "Be at ease. We are all safe here. And we shall not draw this out extremely late tonight. Were you able to rest at all on the trip, nand' Bregani?"

"Very little, nand' dowager. Very little since your message last night."

"Well, well, we hope that we can make tonight much easier. And for your peace of mind, we do have a report from Senjin—you surely are not shocked to know we have observers—that Senjin has been quiet today. There are two Dojisigi ships in port, one Sungeni, simply off-loading. The trains, however, are not running at the moment, which is a topic of conversation. There is considerable talk of the Red Train's visit—which is speculated to be a courier run, and the question of your whereabouts today has arisen, but in the context of a meeting with a courier from the north. And it is not remarkable that traffic on a line stops when the Red Train moves." Another sip, a conspiratorial: "We understand you have set a cousin in charge during your absence. We trust this was your action."

"I have, nand' dowager, empowered a cousin to issue orders and make decisions, and I have put him under a reliable guard."

"Well, well, we shall hope he will welcome you back soon. But do not worry excessively. Not a teacup will be disturbed in Koperna during your visit here, or the culprits will meet my *extreme* displeasure."

"Nand' dowager," Bregani said, frowning. "I shall hope not to delay too long."

"And we are delighted you came. Be assured the aishidi'tat will not invite a lord to negotiate while enemies wreak havoc on his land. You will return at your pleasure, and find, as we say, not a teacup out of place. Be assured *I* am not of a mind to seize territory in the Marid. Lord Machigi would be extremely upset if that were the case."

"I can also assure my neighbor," Machigi said, "that I have no intention of occupying Senjin. That leaves, of serious worries, only your allies in the Dojisigin."

"Nandi," Bregani said, acknowledging the remark, but nothing more.

"And Murai-daja," Ilisidi said, "you are most welcome this evening. We should not be surprised at your arrival. We hear you are a wise and able aid to your husband—and have been these eighteen years."

"We are a firm marriage, nand' dowager," Murai said quietly. "Not a contract."

"And a well-chosen partner, as we hear, contributing strength and stability to the district. Together, too, you have given the world a very accomplished daughter. Lady Husai, we hear *you* are quite the artist."

"One would not dare claim it, nand' dowager." It was a faint little voice. "But thank you."

"Pish, girl. Practice. Practice. Then claim everything you can. And become what you will.—A fine family. And we have heard little untoward about you, Lord Bregani, even from your adversary to the south."

"One is astonished to hear it, nand' dowager."

"Well, well, you have favorably impressed us. We shall not begin our business before dinner, but over brandy, afterward."

Small talk. And little disposition to talk much at all. Ilisidi took up the matter of weather in Hasjuran, and the trip from the capital, and weather in Malguri, from which she had come. She segued to the disturbance in the midlands, and her great-grandson's visit to Tirnamardi—"Joined by the aiji-consort," Ilisidi said. "Which, however, stranded us in the capital for want of transport—so, seeing things there were dealt with, we took the opportunity to meet the paidhi-aiji, returning from his own trip. The paidhi has just concluded an event of considerable consequence among the Mospheirans. Which you may relate, nand' paidhi."

So *he* had to carry the burden. "One was delivering a treaty to Mospheira," he said, "a treaty made in the heavens, with our foreign visitors, which we are glad to say has settled various issues. The kyo have left us in peace—their departure was noted when I was on the island."

Husai looked up, and at him, as if a question fairly burned to be asked.

"Husai-daja?" he asked.

"They are *real*, the kyo?"

"Indeed they are," he said. "They look quite unlike humans or atevi. They are broad of body and large, and their language is full of sounds we simply cannot make. But they are also very smart, and together we did manage a sensible agreement. I must add that the aiji-dowager played a great part in those negotiations from the very beginning. So we have concluded a peace with strangers who do not in the least look like us. And if we can achieve agreement with people so different, we can surely do the same with people like ourselves, dare we hope for it? We can have a much better future if we do."

"And we believe dinner is in the immediate future," Ilisidi said. "We are ready, are we not, Meri-ji?"

A servant moved in with a tray to receive the glasses. Ilisidi set hers on it, and Bren followed suit, with Machigi and Nomari. So did Bregani and Murai. Husai added her glass of fruit ice still half full . . . nerves, Bren thought, poor girl. Bregani and Murai had downed theirs to the last, politely so, a matter of diplomatic courtesy, defying any expectation of ill effects.

"Come," Ilisidi said, planting her cane and holding out her hand for Cenedi's assistance. She rose. "We have a light midlands meal before us, nothing elaborate. We cannot stand on much ceremony of state in this little car, but let us continue a pleasant conversation over our chef's good efforts."

Ilisidi led the way to table, Bren and Machigi followed, with Bregani and Murai, while Nomari and Husai, least in rank, brought up the rear. And by the time they were at their places, the young lady had Nomari to assist her with her chair, usually a servant's action. It was an attention which Husai received a little nervously, but as Nomari sat down across from her and engaged her in conversation, she answered, and looked more confident.

One was not certain how far one might wish *that* to go, but right now, under present circumstances, it was a welcome counter to Machigi's presence on Nomari's other side. Bregani and his wife were opposite Machigi and Cenedi, who was on the dowager's left, the dowager held one end of the table, with Cenedi on her left to make the fortunate number, and leaving Bren the seat at Ilisidi's right, facing Cenedi, and next to Bregani. The table was laid with a wintry centerpiece of bare wood and seven stones pleasingly arranged. White candles, newly lit, shed a warmer glow as the ordinary lights dimmed.

The dining car began to send forth dishes, then, fragrant with spices and sending steam up into the candlelight.

"So," Ilisidi began, cheerfully, over a serving of soup, "we were provided one dinner with Lord Topari, in the great house— quite a distinctive architecture. A treasure. Have you been in Hasjuran before, nand' Bregani?"

"I have never left Senjin until now, nand' dowager."

"Nor you, Murai-daja?"

"No, nand' dowager," Murai said. "We have not."

"Well, well, perhaps the future holds many new experiences for all of us. Curiously, we have had a limited view of the town with the snowfall—but trees are still in full leaf in the midlands and on the coast. Summer persists for us—and a mild summer at that. Has it been so in the Marid?"

"Mild, yes, nand' dowager."

This all interspersed with service. And after a pause for sampling and generally complimenting the offerings:

"Nand' paidhi. You elected to cross the strait both ways by boat. But not your own boat."

Clearly Ilisidi was handing him the dinner topic. One was obliged to take the hint and make of it something constructive. "No. My brother and his lady carried me over and back. Calm seas in both directions. Shall I mention the nature of my other business, aiji-ma?"

"Indeed you may."

Talk, the order was, clearly. Distract us. Entertain us. Fill the silence. Put the guests at ease. Ilisidi was meanwhile thinking, estimating, watching interactions and reactions during this and that topic.

Regarding Mospheira, there was no scarcity of recent material, the landing of the young gentleman's guests, the preparation of the facilities, the difference in customs, the virtues of street food, the existence of the university and the several presidential residences—then the curious trio of tutors he'd found for the children, the landing of the shuttle, the arrival of the children—

"There were pictures of the children." Husai, who had been following it all quite closely, ventured hesitantly. "On the news. They seemed . . . very small."

"We *are a* small people," Bren said. Sixteen-year-old Husai was taller than he was. "But yes, they are small, even for us. They suffered in their earliest years. Want of food. Want of most everything."

"Is the space station *like* that?"

A good question from an unlikely source. He knew that *some* in the Marid's more remote areas denied there *was* a functioning station, and said it was all a plot by Tabini-aiji. Some who believed the station was functional, and even that the starship had come home, called it a threat to atevi tradition and civilization. They trusted Tabini-aiji's ownership of half of it no more than they trusted the human half, expecting it to work, as usual, to the Marid's disadvantage as, in their view, everything did. It was *Machigi* who had been offered the Marid's first chance to tap into the benefits of the space station, namely the weather observation, the technical advances, and space-directed navigation. Machigi certainly believed in it and had a fairly realistic idea of its capabilities. It was a question what the Senjin leadership believed.

But it was the sixteen-year-old who asked the salient question.

"Not this station," Bren said, "but the other one—far, far away, now abandoned—suffered damage and a great many died. All its surviving people have come here, five thousand of them—which is five thousand too many for our own station to support, so food has still been short, and continues to be, even though the aiji is sending up supplies. So the five thousand will land—but they will not live on the mainland. They are entirely Mospheira's problem."

"What of other strangers in the heavens?" Bregani found a question. "How do we keep them out?"

"The ones who visited us are gone," Bren said, "and understand, we do not share the same sun. Travel between suns takes years." Husai's lips parted as if she would immediately ask a question, but she ducked her head and declined to interrupt.

"There are many, many suns," Bren said, guessing what would have aroused a question. "The stars visible in the heavens are suns, each of them, with worlds around them—but they are impossibly distant, so far separated that our best telescopes can scarcely see them. Over such distances, travel takes years. And the kyo are not the least interested in our affairs so long as we leave them alone. That is what they want. The five thousand sat too close to them. They wanted these people to go, and the kyo are satisfied that they will live here and not there."

"Indeed," Bregani said. "You do not foresee war."

"I do not. Isolation is the subject of the treaty. We know now we have well-disposed neighbors in one direction who just do not want visitors. And that is good news."

"Very good news," Ilisidi said. "But as for us—do try the red sauce. There is so much we can share and trade—since we *do* share the same sun. Tastes may vary, but then, I would not care for bland porridge for every meal."

Bregani returned his attention to his plate, reaching for the recommended sauce, and adding a small dot of it to his plate. "Yet," Bregani said, frowning at a sample of it, "there is risk. Tastes differ. I find it—a little hot."

"That it is," Ilisidi said. "But it is a favorite of mine."

"We have imported a few northern spices," Machigi said, "not to mention a handful of guilds—once the northern guilds agreed to allow service to one's own clan."

"But upholding standards," Ilisidi said, "so the locals are fully the equal of the central Guild. More than equal in some instances. Cenedi could say so."

"Knowing one's own district," Cenedi said, "is an advantage. Now that the Assassins and Transportation have made certain adjustments in administration, we have found advantages. And now that we have shown the way, other guilds are feeling challenged to do so."

"With certain benefits," Ilisidi said. "We readily share information which used to stall quite long in certain offices before getting to the capital. Things do change. Attitudes change. Nand' Bren can tell you the *Hasjurani* have finally entered the larger world and entertained a human in their great and ancient hall. Who knows but what, in the future, some young Hasjurani will venture to space and open a trade office? Who knows but what a Taisigi might someday be part of the weather office up there. But first," Ilisidi waved a hand, "and much nearer to realization, I have an ocean port under construction. And people looking forward to Marid trade."

For the dowager's strict rule, that was perilously close to a business discussion at dinner, which did *not* happen.

"So are we looking forward to it, nand' dowager," Machigi said.

"Ah," the dowager said, "but *dessert*. Dessert first, before we concentrate on business. I have such a weakness for dessert."

Ilisidi *had* no weaknesses, Bren thought. And it was not an accident, that shift away from the imperial we, that warm and casual slip from court manners, while she offered hints, danced them forth and back again and watched reactions. No business at the dinner table, indeed. They delayed for dessert, and Ilisidi was watching every reaction.

The regular plates departed. A light and frothy confection arrived, one Bren knew and trusted. He took a couple of spoonfuls, and more, as Ilisidi delayed the pace, letting the subjects think and worry—he knew the tactic. Likely so did Bregani, at least, likely his wife.

The hour was getting on. It would be well dark outside, but there were no windows to say so. The candles had burned to half, themselves as good as any timepiece. Dessert arrived, a small, light one, consumed and gone.

Then Ilisidi said, "Shall we get to business? Murai-daja, you and your daughter will have an escort to the comfort of your own car. Do not hesitate to ask staff for anything for your comfort. Lord Bregani, a short consultation."

Murai was not happy with that dismissal. A frown, a glance toward her daughter, who otherwise was to be sent off alone—

"Go," Bregani said. "Rai-ji, go, and do not worry. I shall not be long."

Servants were quietly collecting the table settings, which went quickly out of the area. Murai accompanied her daughter and likely collected at least one of the pair of bodyguards waiting in the galley car.

"You are safe, nandi," Bren said quietly to Bregani, who gazed after them. "So will they be, I say so in absolute confidence. I am equally *your* representative."

Bregani shot him a look that said he had no great confidence at the moment, but they moved back to the seating arrangement at the rear, two fewer, now, with Ilisidi, Machigi, Nomari, Bregani, and himself: five, that chancy combination of dangerous two and felicitous three—a number balanced between risk and felicity.

And the paidhi *was* poised to represent Bregani. Ilisidi had *not* briefed him—probably, he thought, because Ilisidi had briefed no one except, one hoped, her grandson, and *wanted* the paidhi to take the position she left him and read reactions as they happened.

Might she *possibly* have briefed Machigi? He thought not. She was doing what Machigi had asked her to do, so Machigi was free to assume he knew *all* she was doing.

Machigi, Bren thought, was unlikely to believe it—being no fool.

As for Nomari—he remained a question.

He took his seat this time between the dowager and Machigi, and with Nomari on Machigi's other side—Bregani had the freestanding chair opposite, and took that seat as servants provided brandy.

Nobody spoke. Nobody should speak until the host spoke.

"Well," Ilisidi said, setting down her glass after a single sip. "Lord Bregani, let us begin with a few statements of principle. Our intention at this moment, is *not* to have a war in the western Marid, and *not* to see you deposed."

"That has never," Bregani said stolidly, "depended on Shejidani influences."

Defiance. But also the truth, and one with which Machigi himself might agree.

"Indeed," Ilisidi said. "But then, you have a railroad which *is* our interest, a fairly important asset in the region. You also have a neighbor who is our ally—and who would not take it at all well should the Dojisigi lord replace you. Bluntly put, nandi, what *is* your opinion of the lord of the Dojisigi?"

A deep breath. "That I have been in a desperate position from the moment the Red Train delivered an invitation to come here. I *have* come here at great risk. The only greater risk would have been to stay in Koperna and let her interpret the situation."

"We are told you did not bring your own guard. That you slipped away with four men related to your wife but not yourself."

"They are my wife's cousins. Her aishid, Farai clan. As she is."

"You trust your wife," Ilisidi said.

"As no other, nand' dowager. I do trust her. And trust the cousin I put in charge. I rely on them."

"You are Talidi."

"Yes."

"Son of Cosadi. Lord Tiajo is your cousin."

"My cousin once removed. Yes."

"And, again, your opinion of her, nandi?" Back to the question. Inevitably. "Do you trust *her*?"

A pause. "Say that I can predict her moves, and that you have placed me in a position, nand' dowager, but I think you know that."

"I think you have *been* in a position since you became lord of Senjin. I think you are at a crossroads, in more ways than one, and we have something to offer. But the proposal is Lord Machigi's. Will you hear him?"

Bregani's answer did not come quickly. And he did not look at Machigi. "I will hear him."

"Lord Machigi," Ilisidi said. "Will you speak with your neighbor?"

"I will," Machigi said, and still to Ilisidi: "I have no quarrel with Senjin. Lord Bregani knows I am at least one reason that the bandit-backed regime in the Dojisigin has not breakfasted on the Farai and moved on to Koperna." And to Bregani: "And *you* are, likewise, nandi, the strong roof over the Taisigin, which I do not fail to appreciate. We rely on each other even while calling ourselves adversaries. We have maintained that situation as the best maneuver we can manage to keep Dojisigin from venturing more than it does."

"An interesting interpretation, Lord Machigi."

"You know that should I attack you, I would be starting a general war. You equally know that I have never done so, and I do not intend it now. My interests, nandi, lie in an economically stable, politically strong Taisigin. I once saw the west coast as my means to that end, and in that, we might have been rivals, but the dowager extended an alternative offer which is achievable with far less trouble."

"Sailing to the east."

"Which I believe can be done, and done steadily. But even if you doubt it, were we linked in trade, were Senjin and the Taisigin *both* treaty-bound to the dowager in a trade agreement, the Dojisigin would instantly have *us* to fear, not the other way around: you would be allied with the Taisigin, with the Sungeni *and* the Dausigin. And not least—with Malguri, which would assure your safety."

"A trade agreement."

Machigi nodded. Quick. Sharp.

"Here is my essential proposal, nandi. A rail link between Koperna and Tanaja, which would bring you direct benefit from our trade with the East, when it comes—a geographical advantage to us both. Even if the Dojisigin were well-disposed, it is *Senjin* that lies in a direct line between the Taisigin and the provinces of the aishidi'tat, and were that rail line attacked, it involves the interests of the aishidi'tat, and would bring down the very thing Tiajo's supporters would wish to postpone forever. It is simple common sense. We can forego building warehouses you already have, a savings of materials for us and a profit to you. We can open a direct land trade that will profit both districts *and* make it clear to the Dojisigin that their profit does not lie in annoying the rest of the Marid, who would be united in one vast association *against* them. When trade with the east does becomes a reality, we shall both benefit. If it never does, you will still benefit."

There was quiet for a moment. A muscle worked in Bregani's jaw. He took several long breaths. "Tiajo *has* assets that have too much to lose. Were we to make such an agreement, they would immediately move against Senjin, and then the Taisigin would *have* no roof, sir, because we are not able to withstand incursion by sea and land."

"And should they make such a move, they will find themselves with far more than Senjin to deal with."

"And I should trust you . . . why?"

"If for no other reason, trust I will enjoy increased revenue with far less effort, while inconveniencing a regime I detest. I have never sought to harm your interests. Bear in mind, though I had agents in your district during the Troubles, I *never* ordered sabotage, nor have I ever ordered action against Senjin. I used my agents in Koperna to spy on the sea traffic out of Dojisigi. Admittedly I arranged some actions that may have irritated Jorida and inconvenienced the Dojisigin, but I did not attack *you*."

Nomari listened, wisely simply listened, uncomfortable as his position in the situation might be, having been one of those agents.

"You *deny* attacks against our shipping," Bregani said.

"I absolutely deny them. It would be impolitic to cast any blame on the newly enfranchised Edi, but they were angry at everybody during the Troubles. And there were resistance forces operating on the west coast. I assure you, nand' Bregani, we had no interest in bringing down Senjin."

"And what now? No matter the picture you paint, if I enter into this agreement, *we* become the buffer between you and the Dojisigin, nandi, and it will not be fighting in the field, but assassins sent against me and my family, my councillors and my clan."

"I have brought two documents," Ilisidi said, assuming

control. "One of which, if it passes your council, will give you seats in the tashrid and the hasdrawad—as the Taisigin has contemplated signing, but not yet agreed. Their choice has been a trade representative in Shejidan, which you may also choose, certainly. The other document, which we can sign this evening, should you agree, and which is no way contingent upon the first, is a statement of association around the railroad. An association needs a declared point of common interest, and in the railroad, we have it, and *because* I have certain status firmly within the aishidi'tat, *the association* thus created can claim Guild protection of its personnel and assets. You will sign in protection of the rail within your province, Machigi will sign in interest of obtaining the benefit of an extension of rail to his capital, and I shall sign as a shipper depending on that rail. I am fairly certain that we can also obtain the seal of Hasjuran and possibly its neighbors, Lord Topari being quite anxious to secure profit for his district. Lord Bren can sign for Najida, also affected by any damage to the railroad, and he can sign by proxy for Lord Geigi, his neighbor, also affected. I can guarantee the signatures of Taiben and Atageini, also served by rail, and my grandson can sign for the interests of the spaceport, and all points remote from the rail, but served by it. Nomari-nadi can at least offer good will and intent to sign if he is confirmed as lord of Ajuri; not to mention my own associations in the East, who will all be affected by this agreement. All these interests would act to protect the rail without your signature, but with your signature our response would require no debate at all— were that asset in any wise threatened."

Ilisidi's document was both simple, with ample precedent, and scarily potent. It was the railroad—crossing many clans in its initial operation up north, around which the aishidi'tat had been created. The Guilds. The aijinate. The whole centuries-old questions of Marid independence and relations with the aishidi'tat, the issue of the tribal peoples' lands and lately their admission to the aishidi'tat. That common dependence had *founded* the aishidi'tat and established the first aiji in Shejidan. Now—Ilisidi made strong reference to that origin, not, surely, lost on a lord of the Marid.

"We are not Ragi. We are *not* part of the north."

"Our own East understands that. Note that my own region operates fairly well as it pleases, including the independent trade agreement we are inviting you to join, and that trade association has negotiated recognition of local guild centers. Lord Machigi found it an important issue. And that concession is written into the agreement."

Bregani sat thinking for a moment, thinking and frowning. "If I sign—what is the schedule for this?"

"Surveying to progress from both Koperna and Tanaja within the next fortnight. Track will ship, foundation will be laid . . . it all can progress as fast as workers can lay roadbed and track, and from two directions, since I am sure Lord Machigi will work from his end. We would wish Hasjuran likewise to sign, and also his neighbors, making this a regional association."

"Presided over by—?"

"Me," Ilisidi said firmly, "since I have no territorial issues. And I *have* interests involved."

"And the budget for this project?"

"Ten percent of profit until repayment of my loan is complete: warehousing and operational charges to be in line with the rest of the railroad. The same terms are in Lord Machigi's agreement. You already have Transportation Guild within your borders who can handle the surveying, construction, and operation. Might we suggest, considering the threat from the Dojisigin, that you add the Assassins to that list. Tonight. That agreement can be relayed to Guild Headquarters in Shejidan tonight, and once it is received, you *will* be under their protection."

There was a moment of silence.

"You say you cannot trust your own bodyguard," Ilisidi, "and we would strongly suggest that you not return to Koperna without the Assassins' agreement in place—for your safety, nandi.

They will be under your orders. They will not take actions you disapprove."

Silence still. Bregani took a sizeable drink of brandy, and Bren watched his face. Bregani and his wife had held on to the notion of returning tonight, but the man had not trusted his own body-guard enough to commit his safety to them in this venture. He might have told himself he could answer the dowager's sum-mons, hear what she had to say, and still go back to business as usual, such as it was, still holding off both Machigi *and* Tiajo— but he had come here with his wife's bodyguard, all cousins to her, and not, perhaps, the people Tiajo's backers had set in place to keep him in line. He was *already* committed, perhaps with a ready set of excuses such as—needing his bodyguard to protect the residence, and going to Hasjuran to find out what the dowa-ger was up to—but fairly clearly he had come up here because he feared something was going on with the dowager's agreements regarding his neighbor to the south that might put him in a hard place, something he might argue with, but he had also had an apprehension that his Dojisigi allies might threaten his family. He had *not* planned on meeting Machigi, *not* planned on being offered an alliance with him, and *not* planned on opening his province to the Shejidani Guild tonight . . . a decision that could, to say the least, unsettle members of his own clan who had made their own deals with the Dojisigi, complete with trade connections and business offices.

But if he returned without signing, he would be on his own with Tiajo, who might or might not get rumors of what had gone on up here. He had had peace with the Dojisigin because he was useful and his whole regime was useful, a bridge to sup-ply that otherwise had to come all the way from Cobo by sea. The Dojisigi had found it a great convenience to have a *some-what* law-abiding member of the Transportation Guild system, gateway for the Marid as a whole. And now—

"I have no choice," Bregani said.

He was atevi. He *was* in a leader's position. He held responsibilities for lives, not only his wife's and his daughter's, but the
lives of Senjin folk even down to the untrustable bodyguards,
who might be advised, if they were advised at all, to head for
Dojisigin territory, and still might die if Tiajo took the overnight defection of Senjin personally. Bregani's burden reached
all the way to the shopkeepers and the fisherfolk of the townships, and to his own local branch of Talidi clan and its several
subclans, some areas which had had a long, long feud with
Machigi's Taisigin over land and fishing rights.

Everything came down to—I have no choice—and a human
could only imagine the inner turmoil. It was something the
man had to decide in his own way. Bregani was, one sensed, a
man who felt his responsibilities keenly. A good leader.

"There is no choice," Bregani repeated. "There was none, the
moment I received your invitation to take the train. I will go
back to Koperna. I will not abandon my office. I will not step
aside. But I shall not change my position on issues between
Senjin and the Taisigin."

"Sign," Machigi said, "and I will accept your position on the
several matters. Including Osego Bay."

One had no idea where that stood. But it surprised Bregani.

"We advise you," Ilisidi said, "accept the Assassins, tonight.
They are in position to act, *if* Tiajo should move in your absence, and I promise you, I shall not delay your return, but I
wish to see that protection in place. I spoke of stalled traffic.
There was, in fact a train that preceded us, that sits at this hour
in Koperna, ostensibly awaiting repair. It will sit there until you
return, *assuring* that the Dojisigin make no moves against you.
I would not call you here to conference and leave your city and
people to the displeasure of that child in Dojisigin. But if you
sign with the Guild tonight, and authorize them to deploy in
Koperna, they will do so, and extend operations to the port at
Lusi'ei."

There was a lengthy period of silence.

"And if I do not?" Bregani said.

"They will leave your city as you return. There is nothing the matter with that train."

Bregani stared at the dowager, at Machigi, at Bren, last. "You have the means to know the situation in Senjin."

"Peaceful, at this hour," the dowager said.

"My staff is not infallible. I cannot say there is not gossip flying wherever it can. I have been obliged to accept spies in my household. *Her* spies. And I cannot rely on my own bodyguard."

"Are you sure of all of the ones with you?"

"The youngest of my wife's guard," Bregani said, "I do not trust to be discreet. But I do not think he is disloyal."

"If you ask the Guild in," Ilisidi said, "you may ask the Guild to investigate and sort that matter out. At your discretion, and by your own judgment, nandi. Should you wish to sign the agreement, an order from the Guild Council can temporarily assign two units now with me to your personal protection, to cooperate with the units waiting in Koperna. Should you wish to authorize any specific actions in Senjin, to prevent harm to persons and property, those actions can happen. Understand that due process would follow any arrest."

"I would wish it to. Let me read the document," Bregani said. "In its entirety. I will not sign what I have not read."

"Of course," Ilisidi said, and signaled Nawari, who pulled a leather document case from a built-in cabinet. The document inside was a single page with two seals and the ribbons of Malguri and those of the Taisigin Marid. Nawari laid that on the table in front of Bregani, who flattened it on the table, took out a reading-glass, and began to go over it, taking occasional sips of brandy.

"I shall sign it," he said finally. "It is simple. It is straightforward, and I find no objection. And I shall sign with the Guild, for our defense."

Bren softly let go a breath. It was not settled. It was only the beginning of problems. But it ensured Guild in position to deal with those problems.

"The Guild will provide its own document," Ilisidi said. "Cenedi?"

"In short order," Cenedi said, and withdrew to speak to someone remote.

Meanwhile, from storage near the side door, a waxjack was brought and lit, ribbons chosen from the same cabinet: the dowager had come prepared—the whole business had been set up from the outset, one copy for filing in Shejidan, one for Ilisidi, one for Machigi, one for Bregani.

Bregani's ring seal went into red wax, fixing the ribbons; so did Bren's, with a white ribbon, as witness to each, as paidhi-aiji.

"We shall file this," Ilisidi said, "and you shall take your copy, for your own archive. Along with the Guild agreement, if you wish to sign it."

"Bring it," Bregani said, and in very little time, Cenedi was able to hand the requisite documents to him.

Signature required another arrangement of red and blue ribbon, and this time, Cenedi's seal as witness, and a black ribbon. This original also stayed, to be filed at Guild Headquarters, and Bregani took the copy.

"Nawari," Cenedi said, "pass the order. Deploy."

"Yes," Nawari said, and went as far as the passage door to send that message on.

There was a prolonged quiet then, as servants extinguished the candle and returned the document kit to its storage beside the rear bench. Bregani finished his brandy in silence, with the two documents on the table before him, while Nawari, having sent his message, stood talking quietly to someone through communications. The stalled train would send small groups out into the dark to deal with any surveillance, establish their perimeter—Bren envisioned that much, typical of such operations. Protection came first, protection of certain premises, certain individuals.

Then—whatever was necessary, as limited in noise as possible.

"So we are associates," Ilisidi said, "and you are at peace with Malguri, with the Taisigin, the Sungenin, and the Dausigin, with Najida, Taiben, and Atageini, and by tomorrow, at peace with Lord Topari and his association in Hasjuran, small though it be, but holding a very important pass which is in our mutual interest and under our mutual protection. You will not regret this document, nandi. If you wish to communicate with your household in Koperna, that can be arranged shortly. I would expect that to come within the hour. Should you wish to leave tonight, that can be arranged."

"Our advice," Cenedi said quietly, "is to wait for morning, nandi. Guild operations are now in progress, and will continue through the night. For the safety of your people, nandi, we do not want to engage in a firefight."

Bregani frowned. Said, after a moment's hesitation. "I am concerned for my cousin."

"Plain-clothes Guild will approach him and deliver a report, if you wish to send it. Are you sure of him, nandi?"

"He is in Lusi'ei, in the broadcast center, which is his post. I can provide a code which will indicate the message is from me, that I am well, and beyond that . . . protect him. Advise him. He has codes of his own which can move people who I am relatively sure can be trusted."

Cenedi nodded solemnly. "We can work with this, and the sooner the better for everyone. Aiji-ma?"

"Go," Ilisidi said.

Things began to move. And would move rapidly.

Bren watched the departure and let go a pent breath, while Nawari moved closer to the dowager.

"A man who has kept his independence from both the fool

girl *and* the Shadow Guild for years," Ilisidi said. "Not a fool, himself. Do you think he will keep his agreement? Shishogi did give him several of his finest, who will have to be removed tonight down in Koperna, first of all operations. But that man may know quite clearly who they are."

"Not a fool, indeed," Machigi said. "I have preferred him as a neighbor, in spite of his inconveniences. And I kept the harbor controversy alive only to keep Dojisigi spies at a distance, and give my own agents access."

Nomari, spy, provider of Machigi's information, sipped his brandy very, very slowly, meanwhile, and avoided looking at Machigi or the dowager at the moment.

Bren took another brandy himself, still with a charge of adrenaline, and wondering whether they would see war broken out by morning—or a long slip toward it, after a seamless, silent takeover of the Dojisigi lord's only remaining ally.

23

It was night. The whole household was quiet, only the few nightlights aglow so that staff abroad by night would not misstep. Boji was quiet, which said that nobody was moving in the outer room.

But Cajeiri was awake, and Jegari was. They settled on the immense bed to talk as they sometimes would, and within very little time Lucasi, and Antaro and Veijico all came quietly from their rooms and joined in, the way they had done all their lives together. They sat in near total darkness. They sat in nightrobes, in the chill, and tucked folds of the coverlets over bare feet. They had done it when it had been just himself and Antaro and Jegari. They had done it when Lucasi and Veijico added themselves to the household.

They had begun to be a little old for such conferences, Cajeiri thought, recalling himself and his human associates sitting as children in the icy dark of the ship's service passages, learning to talk to each other, sharing food, sharing stories, sharing what they had. But he still felt comfort in talking like this in the dark, less stupid, perhaps, in an association they still kept apart and private, insulated from his senior aishid and their different, grown-up ways.

"We have not found out a thing," was the general report on mani, which argued, with important people going away so quietly, that whatever was going on in the world did not involve just questions about Nomari.

"One worries," Cajeiri said, "about him. About everybody."

"He lived down in the Marid," Cajeiri said, "he stayed alive, because he was *not* up here where they were hunting people. The Transportation Guild let a lot of people move around when moving around was not that safe. And Onami says, and I think this is probably the truth, that the rebels had to keep the trains running or see business stop, and they had to have the people who could run the trains and keep everything going. So they could not threaten the Transportation Guild. It was the Assassins and some of the Merchants and Treasurers who were mostly the targets. So Nomari had that advantage if he just kept quiet and tried not to attract attention. That is what I understand. The people hunting exiles from Ajuri had far more interest in the north than the south."

"The south," Antaro said, "with Lord Machigi resisting the Shadow Guild, does not seem a terribly troublesome association for your cousin to have even today—if it is in the past."

"I do not think it is entirely in the past. Machigi might want it to go on. I am a little worried that mani might want it to go on, for her own reasons. I do not trust Machigi. But maybe she does not trust him, either."

"That is possible."

"I would not want him to be involved with the Taisigin," Cajeiri said. "Nomari is *our* cousin and needs to be up here, putting *his* clan to rights, not in the South doing who knows what. *We* say the Marid is part of the aishidi'tat, but the Marid clans are always quarreling with each other, and they hold no seats in the tashrid or the hasdrawad. They pick and choose which guilds they let in. And I looked up Bregani. *He* is related to Tiajo. He actually could have a claim on Dojisigi, while he is holding Senjin."

"It might be better," Lucasi said, "if he did step in."

"If," Veijico said, "they can get rid of the Shadow Guild."

"I, for one," Antaro said, "want to be sure they *do* get rid of the Shadow Guild—before he steps in . . . if that is his ambition.

Tiajo is a fool, and they use *her*. But handing some remnant of them to a lord who may have some cleverness, who may find a way to use *them*, who is not firmly in the aishidi'tat, and who has an uneasy relationship with Machigi—could be trouble."

It was something to think about, Cajeiri thought: and then thought: "If Machigi and Bregani start trading, and Machigi has the port dealing with mani, then the Dojisigi port is not going to be as important and neither is Lusi'ei in Bregani's territory. That could be a problem."

"That is so," Jegari said. "They have fishing. They have local trade. But the loss of shipping . . . that will be a problem for everybody."

"The north trading down there," Lucasi said, "can moderate that."

"There is also the thing Machigi has always wanted," Antaro said. "The west coast. I would not be surprised to see that matter boil up again—if he has Bregani as an ally."

"He will lose mani's support, if he tries that," Cajeiri said. "I do not trust him, but I also do not think he would be that stupid."

"And Dojisigi will keep them busy for a while," Jegari said.

"Dojisigi is apt to explode," Antaro said, "and explode within days, if this goes through."

"If Bregani meets with mani and goes home," Cajeiri said, "he will die, whether or not he signs that agreement. So what are they going to do?"

Veijico said, "Maybe they will bring him all the way back to Shejidan."

"If they do," Lucasi said, "the Dojisigi will lose no time moving on Senjin. And it would be very easy to disrupt the rail that comes down from Hasjuran, and stop the whole system, at least as far as any shipments to the Marid. Surely your great-grandmother will not risk going down there."

"Winter is coming," Lucasi said, "when that whole route is

a little chancy. Sometimes it closes. And there is always the coastal route. Shejidan can reach them that way."

"Right now the Hasjuran route is likely closed for security reasons," Antaro said. "I would be surprised if Transportation is letting anything move past the Red Train."

True, Cajeiri thought. And: "Maybe closing that rail is exactly what my great-grandmother has in mind."

"Surely your great-grandmother would not go down into Senjin herself."

"Cenedi would not let her," Cajeiri said, and hoped it was the truth. "No. She will not. She will listen to him."

"And having Machigi aboard . . ." Veijico said. "That will not make Lord Bregani feel easier."

"It shows he listens to her," Jegari said. "It shows Machigi is really part of whatever she is offering."

"If one can trust Lord Machigi that far," Antaro said.

"The paidhi-aiji *can* talk to him," Jegari said. "He arranged the agreement with Machigi in the first place."

"Bregani would never have seen a human," Veijico said. "That has to make him a little worried."

"And why would she take nand' Bren with her," Lucasi asked, "if she expected a fight?"

Mani thought nothing of putting herself into the middle of dangerous action, if it suited her purposes. She would hardly think twice about anyone else. He knew that.

"Nand' Bren carries a gun," Cajeiri said. "Did you know that?"

"We were told so," Lucasi said. "But has he ever used it?"

"His aishid would never let him have it if they had not taught him how."

"I think he would use it," Antaro said, "if he had to. But he has Banichi. And Banichi would not *let* it be necessary."

"Neither would Jago," Jegari said, with a little amusement. And soberly: "It will not come to that, Jeri-ji. Cenedi will pull them all back to Shejidan, if anything develops."

Not, Cajeiri thought, if mani ordered otherwise, and said, another concern: "If they can turn around."

"They can," Veijico said firmly. "Trains can, there. Sometimes they must . . . in the winter, when the track to Senjin has a problem."

"Then I hope they have already turned the train around," Cajeiri said, staring into the darkness. "I wish they were on their way back right now."

Bren stirred, found the lights in the car had brightened, and rolled over, propping his head with a pillow and gathering his thoughts back.

Jago had not joined him. There had been a general Guild conference including Bregani, Murai, Machigi's bodyguard and Murai's, running late into the night, and he had not heard the issue of it, except that Bregani and his family were receiving current reports from the units down in Koperna, and the cousin had been contacted, finally, once the Guild force reached the harbor at Lusi'ei.

They had gone further than that, setting up in several places of vantage, including the old rail spur into Dojisigin. The rail itself had long since become impassible, but it marked a land route, and a means by which foot traffic could slip through. Despite the fact the Dojisigin had inserted themselves into the heart of aishidi'tat politics, had marriage ties to the Kadagidi and were involved in Murini's short-lived regime, the Dojisigi heartland had never accepted rail past a single town on its fringe. The railroad, historically, was the origin and backbone of the aishidi'tat, and the Dojisigi wanted none of it. They saw it as a threat, a way for a northern force to travel all the way to its heart. That spur, built during a brief coziness between the Dojisigin and Kadagidi, had gotten no further than the border, and stopped, as the coziness fell afoul of Dojisigi suspicion, and a Kadagidi marriage ended.

The Dojisigin had always thought of itself as a sea power. And it *was* that, in the Marid. Goods and people moved by ship from the Dojisigi port into Lusi'ei . . . and into Sungeni and Dausigi. In some decades, they had traded with the Taisigin, but no longer. Dojisigi ships still traded clear to the strait of Mospheira, up the coast to Cobo, but goods also moved by rail, generally, going by truck from the port in Lusi-ei, through Koperna, and onto the rails there. And all that was, by the stamp of a seal ring, in danger.

Koperna might not expect a stalled train sitting on a siding to change their future, but tonight, that was happening, step by step, certain targets neutralized, various offices secured, communications appropriated, and equipment offloaded while the advance teams moved on various assignments.

Bregani's cousin had gotten the message, and there had been arrangements for direct communication, calling on Talidi and Farai clan officials and all subclan authorities to cooperate with northern Guild, and to smooth out any points of difficulty. The Transportation Guild was being notified to relay any calls to the Residency to Bregani himself, aboard the Red Train, and that he would be available to answer questions and direct operations.

They had not yet involved the Messengers Guild, but it was fairly sure that someone somewhere would have made a regular phone call asking questions, and once that happened—Dojisigi would have gotten the word.

Nothing had happened yet. Likely it would, soon, but if Tiajo had found out—her handlers were not letting her make a move. The Shadow Guild had thinking to do.

Bregani's message meanwhile had gone out, and Bregani had been receiving answers and inquiries through Transportation channels before Bren had gone to bed last night. The Shejidani Guild in Koperna had reported some small disturbance in the streets, but it had quickly dispersed. Senjin province had experienced Shadow Guild enforcement, sad to say, and that fear had actually proved useful. Ordinary people were keeping behind locked doors, and making no conspicuous moves, at the last reports he had gotten.

Confusion was inevitable if the two forces did begin to engage, but it would be stealthy, and technical. Guild might be Guild, to the average citizen: they wore the same uniforms, they looked alike, but the two forces both had means to identify their own, and they would not willingly commit unless there was some clear gain to be had.

Bregani himself had entered into direct communication with his cousin well past midnight, and Guild had widened its perimeter steadily. Bregani had been giving specific instructions to certain officials, and Murai had done the same with her own clan, particularly in Lusi'ei, while Husai sat in the corner, trying not to sleep, but giving way to it from time to time, curled around a wad of someone's coat.

That had been the scene in the Guild car, but a little after midnight, Bren had concluded someone should have his wits about him tomorrow—in the ongoing operation down in Senjin, he was no more useful than Husai, desperately as he wanted to understand what was going on. But his questions could only distract, not inform, and he had left the scene. The dowager had long since gone to bed, and he had courted a few hours of fitful sleep, replaying the evening, replaying what they knew of events southward, none of which gave him answers about the dowager's intentions.

The clock said an hour before dawn when he gave up, sat up, raked a hand through his tangled hair and headed for the accommodation. Cold water aboard was almost as cold as the winter outside, tanks and lines evidently protected from freezing, but only just. He splashed it into his face, shocking his system to wakefulness, and threw on a dressing gown.

No one was up. It was a prickly, exhausted morning, with no sunlight, no window except the very little one he had used before, and it—he had indeed tried it—offered no view but a snowy roof edge. There was no clue it *was* morning except the clock on the wall, which one only trusted was accurate.

He could make his own tea, he thought, without disturbing Narani and Jeladi, who had refused to go to bed until he did. He managed to heat water, made the tea strong and added sugar, not always his habit, but it was a sort of breakfast, until he could get a better one. Too much stirring about and opening cabinets would certainly wake his staff. So he stood there, sipping hot, sweet tea, and wondering when or whether his aishid had ever gotten to bed.

The dowager, he was sure, had slept. She had done her thinking, laid her plans, gotten an agreement out of Machigi, and, for all he knew, set it all up starting with that unprecedented excursion to Najida, starting a chain of events that would worry the Dojisigi and present Senjin both a lure and a threat to their economy.

Thank God he had gotten no invitation this morning to one of her crack of dawn breakfasts. She had some compassion.

"Nandi?" Jeladi appeared behind him, in the mirror.

He turned ruefully, cup in hand. "Ladi-ji. One tried to be quiet."

"I was awake."

"Is there any news?"

"Things stand much the same as last night, nandi, by what I know."

"The engine has not gone back down."

"No, nandi. Lord Bregani and his family are sleeping, now. There was a minor action in Lusi'ei as a Dojisigi ship tried to leave port. It was boarded and the crew is detained. There was a sniping incident in the rail yard, but that was handled to our advantage."

"Good." He thought he would have waked if the forward cars had uncoupled, but he had been over-tired. He still was. Not having done anything but trade one seat for another yesterday, he still felt exhausted, and not just from the thin air and the chill.

That Bregani was still with them, and that nothing had gone wrong in the last number of hours, however, was good news.

"I shall have breakfast, Ladi-ji. A cold roll will do very nicely, if we can manage it without noise. Dinner last night is not setting all that well. And if Narani is sleeping, let him. I can dress myself."

"Nandi." Jeladi went to handle breakfast. Bren found the day's clothes hanging on the closet door—Narani had arranged that. He dressed, braided his own hair into a ribbonless queue, sat down at the little table grouping, and when the breakfast roll arrived with hot tea, he washed down large bites of the roll and took a few scant notes on the sequence of events Jeladi had reported, in the running account he had kept, times approximate, but at least fairly so.

Then he put his head back against the seat and rested his eyes a moment.

He opened his eyes at Narani's quiet arrival, rubbed his face and realized it had been an hour, the remaining tea was cold, and he still had not shaved.

"One regrets to disturb you," Narani said. "Will you want something else?"

"No," he said. "I am fine, Rani-ji. How do we fare?"

"So far, quiet prevails here and in Senjin. The dowager has asked Lord Topari to share tea in the Red Car, and there will be papers to sign."

"I need a headache powder," Bren said. "Do we believe this is, again, the association document to be signed?"

"We do think so," Narani said.

"I put my pistol in the top drawer last night. If we are to have strangers aboard, I shall have it."

"I shall bring it *and* the headache remedy. Green tea, black, or spiced?"

"Black. With sugar," he said, and read what he had written before he had fallen asleep in mid-sentence. He had no idea how he had intended to finish that line.

He rewrote it—with a verb this time—and sorted papers in the briefcase until he had located a map of Senjin. He sat trying to fix in his head the relative position of the rail yard, the lord's residence, the media station, the road that led to Lusi'ei, places where action had taken place. The maps were detailed, but there was no overview.

He hoped, fervently hoped, that they would not be going down there on this trip. He was not strongly in favor of risking even the engine in sending Bregani home to deal with the crisis, leaving them stranded here for who knew how long, if the train or track were to be compromised.

But the dowager had promised it, and by all rights, Bregani needed to go back, even to a situation of great risk. That risk was part of being who he was.

And it was not as if the Shadow Guild was going to invade Senjin. That might well have happened during the Troubles; but the Shadow Guild was few in number, no longer masquerading as other than they were, and most of all, no longer able to issue orders to honest Guild. The more of that breed the true Guild *could* draw out of the landlocked Dojisigi mountains and into confrontation, the better.

But as Bregani had said yesterday evening, the Shadow Guild's moves would be stealth. Assassination and sabotage. And it was fairly doubtful they would send their major assets into Senjin now. Once they realized Shejidani Guild was present in force, they might actually try to withdraw whatever they did have in Senjin, to keep from losing them. And just as energetically, the Guild operating now in Senjin would want to prevent that.

"Bren-ji." Jago arrived quietly beside his sitting area and slipped into a seat, forearms on knees. "We have just received a signal from Homura, through the Guild network."

That was a surprise.

Homura and Momichi, the team who had theoretically doubled on the Shadow Guild and settled their man'chi on *him*—before disappearing again into the south to try to find their missing partners.

"In Senjin?" he asked, and Jago indicated the negative.

"They are here," Jago said. "Or at least one is, using short-range to signal us. They do not have our current codes, but the sender is using what we arranged when they departed our company, a signal unique to them. They request a meeting, with some urgency, responding to *our* attempt to contact them when we left Najida."

"They cannot have come up from Senjin last night."

"Nothing has come up the grade, and we have watchers on that route."

Half-frozen watchers, if that was the case.

"There are," Jago added, "other routes, the ways the local folk use, and likely have used to enter the town. We have them mapped. But it is not easy for outsiders to find a welcome in those remote villages. No. The likeliest answer is that they have been here. There *are* outsiders coming and going in Hasjuran. When they came north to move against Lord Tatiseigi, Hasjuran could have been the route they used, and they well may have contacts here."

"Not necessarily ones we would approve."

"Or innocent ones. Trade connections who had no idea of their original business in the north."

"They *could* have phoned." It was a poor joke. But it was also true.

"Easily. Now they turn up here, *after* an action in Senjin is in progress. Either they have important news, or they are simply reporting in because they do not want to be found to have ignored our summons, or, the third possibility, they are in trouble. If they do have news of Dojisigi moves at this point, we would be remiss to ignore them. Of Guild available, they know us and they know a few of the dowager's aishid by sight. We are the logical ones to go out and make contact."

"I am anxious about this."

"So are we. Tano and Algini are electing to arrange a meeting near the train."

It was in principle less risk than *all* of them had run, going out to Topari's dinner in the great hall—except that time had elapsed and events down in Senjin had changed things. There *were* watchers set up outside the train, and on it. Tano and Algini would not be without backup, but it was a worry.

"Tell them—" Be careful? They always were. "Tell them I value them extremely. Err on the side of self-protection. We have yet to see this pair proved."

"Yes," Jago said, and quickly rose and left.

That she had come to him without Banichi indicated the excursion might be already beyond planning. He worried.

If he had been slow starting the day, he was awake now. Putting Tano and Algini at risk—he would rather be out there himself; but that was exactly the sort of thing his aishid was there to prevent.

He was the one who had told them to contact this chancy team, before any of this had ever come up. He had done it to query them on *Machigi's* intentions, following the meeting at Najida. That was now fairly passe, unless they knew something he truly needed to know.

The simple fact they were up here—by what Jago said, they had to have arrived *before* the Red Train had come here, since the downward route had been under observation. It was remotely possible they had ridden the *exterior* of the Red Train on the climb up, but that would have been bitterly, bitterly cold.

It might indicate someone down in the Marid had had advance information that the Red Train was on the move, and that he was aboard—if it was indeed his summons that had drawn them. That the dowager was aboard was information the message to Bregani had revealed, but—if they were privy to that, then they were in receipt of a message they never should have accessed, and that was another problem.

What was going on, what that contact meant, would *not* be going on outside Cenedi's knowledge, but to be absolutely certain the dowager knew, he dashed off a note to Ilisidi and handed it to Narani with neither seal nor cylinder.

Aiji-ma. At least one of the Assassins we encountered at Tirnamardi has signaled us from within the town. I believe this is in response to a message I sent them from Najida, intending to discover any recent developments in the Marid. Tano and Algini are going out to meet this contact. Evidently my presence here is known to the sender, whether one or both of these individuals, or someone they have improperly entrusted with their contact code. I am proceeding in the assumption Cenedi is aware and monitoring my team.

Narani left with the message.

Beyond that, it was a matter of waiting.

A longer wait than expected, a worrisome long wait, but nothing signaled trouble, either.

Then there was some agitation that traveled through the train, a distant opening and closing of passage doors.

It was not a time, Bren thought, to go out into the corridor and find out.

Then he heard movement in his own section of the corridor, that stopped. He looked toward the door, stood up, hand in his pocket, finger on the trigger, in case.

Jeladi moved from elsewhere toward the door and queried some presence outside. There was an exchange of some kind, a familiar male voice—Nawari, he thought—and the click of the door catch—Jago must have locked it, Bren thought, when she left, and Jeladi unlocked it.

Nawari came in. Ilisidi's bodyguard.

"Nand' paidhi," Nawari said. "Your assistance, if you will."

"Yes," he said, and stood up with no idea what was toward. "Is the dowager well?"

"She is well, nandi. It is a difficulty with nand' Bregani's party."

It was only Narani and Jeladi in attendance in the car. Banichi and Jago were likely up in the Guild operations car, in communication with Tano and Algini, who were, he presumed, out making contact with their supposed informant. He ought not, strictly, to leave the secure space without them, but Ilisidi's bodyguard judged he was needed and he had no hesitation in complying with the request.

"Lock after I leave," he told Narani, and went out into the corridor with only Nawari.

"Come," Nawari said. And, as they walked: "Your aishid's contact identifies an untrustworthy person in Lord Bregani's bodyguard. Tano and Algini are on their way back, signaling a compromised condition, and Banichi's attention is for them at the moment. We hope you can finesse this and extract the lord and his family without alarming the target."

"I am willing to try," he said, as they negotiated the passage door to the Guild car.

Jago met them in the next corridor.

"You are wearing the vest, nandi."

"Yes," he said. "Jago-ji, are Tano and Algini all right?"

"Yes," Jago said. "Coming back as quickly as they can: I am stationed here. Go, Bren-ji! And be careful!"

Jago, dismissing him into another aishid's care—the matter was indeed urgent. He kept pace with Nawari, walking as fast as his shorter strides could manage, lungs burning in the thin air.

"Do they need help out there?" Bren asked.

"They say no. They are satisfied. They are coming in."

They passed through the Guild car and reached the next passage door, Machigi's, and hurried through that passage. Machigi's own compartment opened behind them, but nobody asked and they spared no time to answer. Machigi's aishid would surely *not* encourage their principal to go out to ask questions.

The next passage door led to Nomari's car, and Nomari's guard came out to intercept them, Shejidani Guild, Guild-trained.

"Hold this area," Nawari ordered them. "Keep your principal inside. Wait for orders."

No question of Nawari's authority. No objections. They reached the next passage, the baggage car, sparsely packed with wardrobe crates, the galley supplies, medical supplies, water, and black boxes with the Guild seal on them. Two Guild guards held that chilly area, in heavy coats, and were on their feet instantly to meet them.

"Guard the forward door," was all Nawari said.

Conference, that would be the story, Bren thought, trying to figure how to extract the whole family.

He wanted to talk with the whole family regarding—what? Briefing them on events down in Senjin? The aishid might take an interest. Consulting them on a point of law? It hardly took the daughter to answer that.

An invitation to tea. Brainless. But socially likely . . .

They reached the passage door into Bregani's car and burst through. Cenedi was in that corridor with four of Ilisidi's young men, at the farthest remove from the compartment door on the left. Bren walked more slowly, evening out his breathing, not to give any impression of haste approaching that door.

Everything calm. No indication of haste. Ask Bregani outside, get Bregani to summon his family for a social occasion—and Nawari and Cenedi would—

Explosion compressed the air, and Bren staggered against the wall, in sudden utter darkness. He pushed back for balance and felt a steadying hand on his shoulder. The emergency lights were coming up slowly, faint yellow illumination, and a red-lit Please Remain Calm.

There was no immediate sense whether the train was breached at any point. *Tano. Algini.* That was his heart-stopping thought. A breach near the dowager was his second. Or a problem centered *here*.

The compartment door pressed against him, opening. Bregani's bodyguard were behind the push, the last thing they wanted. He heard women's voices inside, and Bregani's. Bregani was coming out of his compartment, next worst scenario.

Guild rule: a threat *inside* the perimeter came before anything.

"Nand' Bregani!" he said, catching Bregani's arm. It was sure that atevi could see him better than he could see them. Bregani's eyes caught the indirect light and shone gold, affecting his ability to see expression. "Nandi! Are you all right?" His own lightless eyes would be as disquieting to them as theirs to him. "Are you hurt?"

"No," Bregani said. Murai and Husai pressed outward, joining him, and Bregani threw an arm around them, exposing his back to his own guard. "What hit? Are we attacked?"

"Come with me," Bren said. "Murai-daja, Husai-daja, please come! This way! Quickly!"

The bodyguards moved to be first, as they should, but Cenedi and his men moved instantly to prevent that—a fast move and two were against the wall. Bregani threw himself, his wife, and daughter, against the near wall, shielding his family with his body. There were shouts, and a shot went off in the confined space.

It was not even thought. Bren snatched his gun from his pocket, flung himself clear, took aim at struggling dark bodies of Bregani's guard on the floor in front of him and yelled: "Hold! Hold! Do not get up! Do not get up, nadiin! Lord Bregani, order your guards! Please! This is a mistake! *Stop them!*"

Bregani was still shielding his family. "Stop!" he shouted out. "Everyone stop!"

There was quiet, except the moaning. The wonder was that struggle did stop, and the two on the floor stayed on the floor, and those standing stayed standing.

Bren stood with the pistol in both hands, aimed generally at any hint of a firearm or a motion that might indicate one. In the tangle on the floor, the injured man tried to get up and the other prevented him.

"Stay down!" That was Cenedi's voice, and Bren, eyes straining in the dim light, just held his position. "Tell them, nand' paidhi!"

Bren did not move a muscle, nor stop watching for sudden movements, including the resolving tangle on the floor. "Nand' Bregani," he said, "one means no harm whatsoever to you, your family, or your bodyguard. We have suffered some sort of accident or attack, one is unsure which, and those guarding the aiji-dowager *cannot—cannot* accept drawn weapons from any persons but her defenders on this train. Something has exploded. We do not know whether it was an attack on the train, or whether it was an accident outside, but we do not blame you. The dowager's guard will be far easier once your bodyguard stands down."

There was a thump, an attempt by somebody in the baggage car to get through the passage door at their backs, which did not help the situation.

"What is being done with *Machigi's* guard?" Bregani asked.

"From here, one cannot be sure, nandi, but I swear to you, no one bearing weapons will be welcomed by the dowager's bodyguard. Nomari's guard is under the dowager's command, as am I. Only your guard and Machigi's are under other authority, and I ask you again, nandi, as courteously as I can—and so that we can fairly ask the same of Lord Machigi—please order your guard to stand down. There is a man injured, and this is delaying his medical attention. Please. We may have enemies inside the train, and if this is the case, we need to find out as quickly as possible."

"Stand down," Bregani said. "All of you. Stand down."

There was slow compliance—but Bren did not move. The deep shadow indicated it was a man in Bregani's guard who was on the floor, likewise the man tending him. One of Cenedi's men relieved the kneeling man of a handgun, and another knelt down and applied pressure to the injured man's wound. Beyond those movements, everybody stood frozen, Bregani's two remaining body guards stood with weapons lowered. Weapons in the hands of Cenedi's men were not.

"Nandiin," Cenedi said, "we are receiving communication."

No one moved, then, for several moments while Cenedi asked coded questions and received answers.

"The train was not damaged," Cenedi said then. "The explosion involved the small transformer from which we were receiving power for lights, equipment, and heat. We are now on battery and emergency generators. There is also a loss of railway signaling and other functions in the area. Nand' paidhi, your team has reboarded, and is debriefing."

Thank God, Bren thought, and still held his pistol leveled at Bregani's three standing bodyguards.

"We do not believe this was an accident," Cenedi said. "We are in the process of making an end-to-end check of the entire train, outside and in. Lord Bregani, we have medical attention for your man in the Guild station forward. We ask you go with the paidhi-aiji and his bodyguard all the way to rear of the train, where you will be joined by the aiji-dowager and others. Lord Machigi and the Ajuri candidate are being given the same instruction, and are requested to move on toward the Red Car. Nand' paidhi?"

There was no move on Bregani's part to comply. Bren put the safety on his pistol, returned it to his pocket, and motioned toward the passage door. "Nandiin. Please. I shall go with you. Your man will be cared for, and the dowager's surgeon is aboard, if needed. We all need to cooperate with the Guild, for the dowager's protection and ours."

Bregani moved slowly, uncertainly, slipped an arm about his daughter, and drew her close. Murai-daja turned, and Bren moved, aware one of Cenedi's men was moving behind them, not sure who it was until Nawari stalled them all at the door, to radio the baggage car guards and ascertain that car was safe for them to enter.

Nawari opened the passage door then, and led them through into the faintly-lit baggage car and its hulking crates. The Guild on guard there walked them through to the next passage door.

Nomari's corridor was equally dim and apparently deserted.

So, too, was Machigi's, to Bregani's audible relief. The train was generally silent as they went, everyone evacuated ahead of them.

Then a distant sound.

"The engine is firing up," Nawari said. "We shall soon have power again."

One had not asked *where* electrical power was coming from. But the promise was comforting. And the passage into the next car presented both Jago, and Tano.

"Are you all right?" Bren asked.

"My ears," Tano said, and the dim light showed Tano's entire left side pale with dust.

"Come," Nawari said. "Tano. Jago. Come. The dowager is waiting."

Next was Bren's own corridor, then Cenedi's command center, and after that, the dowager's car, where two of the dowager's guard met them.

"Nand' paidhi," one said. "The dowager wishes to see you, inside, immediately, with your guard. Lord Bregani, please come with us to the Red Car. We are under heavy monitoring, and you and your family are under our protection."

"I have a man down," Lord Bregani said. "I want to know what is happening."

"We are aware, nandi. Please come with us. We are equipped to get answers as soon as we know anything."

It was not a happy Lord Bregani. Murai was less so, and the daughter, poor girl, was visibly upset.

But there was nothing for it. The door of the dowager's compartment stood open, a little brighter than the corridor—and Bren entered, with Jago and Tano. One of the dowager's young men appeared, a shadow against the light, and indicated to the right. A short distance on, in an area with several flashlights in use, the dowager sat in her own circle of light, an area of padded couches and cushions.

"Waste nothing on ceremony," she said. "Sit, paidhi. You also, nadiin."

Jago made a sign, and Tano protested. "I am all over dust, aiji-ma."

And blood. Bren saw that in the ambient lighting.

"Sit," the dowager said, ending the argument. They sat down, Bren directly facing the dowager, Tano and Jago nearby.

"Aiji-ma."

"One believes we are to have light very soon. And information. Tano-nadi. Report."

Jago again signed to him.

"Forgive me, aiji-ma," Tano said. "My ears are still ringing. We went out to contact Homura, one of the pair we met at Tirnamardi on the occasion of the children's visit. We had invited a contact at Najida. It came. Here."

"How?" Ilisidi said.

Jago translated.

"We—my teammate and I—went out to contact him. We were suspicious—that he was here. My teammate and I know him by sight, and the code given was one we arranged. So we went out and met him in the plaza. He reported to us that his partner is in Senjin at the moment. And that Bregani's wife's aishid is compromised. One man, named Tenjin. Homura said that there have been Shadow Guild here in Hasjuran, but that he eliminated two last night. He said he will not come aboard. He wishes to maintain his cover and to maintain his relationship with nand' Bren. He said—more—"

"Go on."

"Aiji-ma, he said that the Shadow Guild has changed. It will not take the field. It has chosen soft targets, as it did with Homura and his team. They have kidnapped those who can compel others to do simple things for the Shadow Guild; or greater ones. Tenjin's mother, his wife, and his son have been kidnapped. He is compromised, whether for small things like passing information, or a major one: assassination of key targets. The usual method is either a specific direction at a target— or a signal to act. One believes," Tano added ruefully, "that we may have been spotted exiting the train and stopping on the plaza, near a workman—and that someone sent Tenjin-nadi a signal to act, for maximum damage. Nand' Bren *was*, we think, the target, rather than his own lord."

Sobering thought, definitely. Reasonable. Cold and logical.

"This Tenjin," Ilisidi said.

"The whole aishid is in custody, aiji-ma," Bren said. "One man is wounded fairly seriously, and he was the only one who fired. It might have been a ricochet."

"Self-harm, possibly," Jago said. "An attempt *not* to carry out his orders."

"Will he die?" Ilisidi asked.

"A Guild medic is likely attending him in the car next to Lord Bregani's," Bren said.

"Nand' Siegi will go," Ilisidi said, with a wave of her hand at the servant standing in the shadows. "Now."

Nand' Siegi was the dowager's personal physician, a surgeon, as well, and he was good.

Very good.

And the order would be passed.

"This is what we feared," Ilisidi said. "They did not succeed with Homura and Momichi. But their tactic has potential to get them information and open doors. To ask someone to murder—such agents are a problem. The Guild will have to take this into account in checking security. Tano-nadi. How did Algini fare?"

Again, a translation.

"Stitches, aiji-ma. Superficial. The deafness is, we think, temporary."

"Go see to your own welfare. My own young men will attend the paidhi."

A flurry of hand-signs, and Tano looked at Bren for confirmation—evidence in itself of a little shock. Or regret.

"Yes." Bren nodded, adding his own signs. "Go. See to Algini."

"Nandi. Aiji-ma." That, too, was in the wrong order. Tano was doing his best. Almost Bren ordered Jago to go with him, but Ilisidi gave her own order, and one of her young men moved to handle that matter.

"A fine young man," Ilisidi said.

"He is," Bren said. "He is very fine. Thank you, aiji-ma."

"Well, well, we may assume we have more exposure here than we wish, and we may be glad that these Dojisigi agents, however recruited, chose only to observe us in our one excursion to Topari's house. We may also suspect that fear held them from acting until they were ordered to do so. We walked out and back safely once. But Homura himself must also stand a little scrutiny. He has broken free of their orders once. Still, the partners may still be alive, still in Shadow Guild hands, and we only hope his teammate is safe down in Senjin. Who knows what pressure may be on him?"

"It is worrisome, aiji-ma. But they showed themselves men of character at Tirnamardi."

"Not of character enough, perhaps, to have trusted us soon enough. They found their conscience late. One has to ask, however, whether a fruitless search for their partners has worn on them, and what their state of mind is now."

"One wishes to help them. This tactic they are using cannot be our future, aiji-ma."

"We are determined it will not be," Ilisidi said. "We *resolve* it will not. Mercy for the hands they use, but none for them. None. And no excuse for criminals that twist every rule of decency and upend civilization itself, paidhi. No pity."

It was no exaggeration, he thought. Everything they valued was under assault by a group cynical, desperate, and defying all that was civilized. It might be a small number of individuals, but it had the potential to tear at the social fabric of the aishidi'tat.

It would *not* become acceptable. He made himself that promise.

"Go," Ilisidi said. "Explain to Lord Bregani and the others. Do your job, paidhi-ji."

She was not accustomed to use that intimate address, as if he were of *her* household. It warmed a cold moment. "Aiji-ma," he said, and quietly got up, with Jago, and went out to do exactly that.

Just as he reached the corridor, the lights came on, powered this time by internal means, he thought, as they had been relying on a transformer near them.

It seemed a good omen.

A rap had come at Cajeiri's door, and instead of going himself, Cajeiri had let Eisi and Liedi answer it.

Which had not been an answer to his request to Bujavid storage for another bookcase, as he had expected, but mail.

That was unusual. Liedi closed the door, and Eisi brought the cylindrical and large brown packet to Cajeiri, at his desk. It bore the stamp of the Bujavid's direct courier, not just the mail room downstairs; and a second stamp that was Father's; and it had come to him.

The packet contained a protective wrapper that looked old,

Your receipt

Items that you checked out

Title: But where do I put the couch?
ID: 31240006247709
Due: Wednesday, March 04, 2020
Messages:
Item checkout ok.

Title: Resurgence : a Foreigner novel
ID: 31240006315852
Due: Wednesday, March 04, 2020
Messages:
Item checkout ok.

Total items: 2
Account balance: $0.00
2/19/2020 6:07 PM
Checked out: 11
Overdue: 0
Hold requests: 0
Ready for pickup: 0
Messages:
Patron status is ok.

Thank you for visiting the Winnetka-Northfield
Public Library!

wrinkled and scarred paper itself with several seals, saying Ha-nomiri Park.

It was the animal park. And it contained, amid blueprints, a note from Father.

What do you think? The park had this drawn up twenty-six years ago, but it is still their ambition, and it could be done from these plans.

Blueprints. Real blueprints. He had never handled any such serious thing. He looked it over, saw a modern erasable line that added the note: this is the area, and a second sheet that gave plans for huge windows. Little faceless people gave the scale.

It looked not quite tall enough, if those were people. He thought about it, and with some trepidation added another erasable note saying, *Boji can climb anything. Do not have a place for him to jump to from any tree. He can jump 20 dei sideways and nothing is too tall for him.*

Boji hopped to a branch in his cage, then to the rattling side filigree.

He would miss that sound. Even the screeches. A tapestry would be nice on that wall. But then it would be like every other sitting room.

Boji rattled the cage loudly—really loudly.

And looked toward the door.

Something was going on. A considerable to-and-fro out in the corridor, now he thought to listen, and when Antaro and the rest of his junior aishid came in from the depths of his apartment, looking very serious, he was certain of it.

"The seniors said stay with you, Jeri-ji," Antaro said. "They have gone to the security station."

"Is Father all right?"

"He is safe. The household is safe, or we would be receiving all manner of alarms," Jegari said. "But there is a great deal of movement within the Guild, here and elsewhere."

"We are trying to find out," Lucasi said, "but our codes do not bring us anything."

"Well, whatever is going on," Cajeiri said, "we must be ready." He was in his shirt sleeves, but Eisi and Liedi were in the doorway. "My coat, nadiin-ji!"

They moved, not asking which one. Boji was continuing to set up a fuss, but not so loud a one.

"The seniors are reporting in," Antaro said. "There has been an incident involving the Red Train. Information has reached your father's office."

"I shall go," he said, and hurried out into the hall, which did not *look* greatly disturbed, but as he headed for Father's office, he heard someone knock at the front door of the apartment, and a second later, heard it opened.

He stopped, turned back toward the hall to see, and it was Uncle Tatiseigi, and *his* aishid.

"Great-uncle!" he said. "Is mani all right?"

"There was an incident, aiji-meni," Uncle said, out of breath. "We heard from your great-grandmother's staff, but we have no specifics. No specifics. I am here to ask your father . . ."

"Come," he said. "Come." He led Uncle straight past Guild who were uncommonly numerous in the hall, and to his father's office door, which was also, uncommonly, open. Mother was coming, likewise, from the other end of the hall.

He did not wait. He dodged an outbound pair of Guild and brought Uncle into the office.

Father was on the phone, saying something about a suppression force in Senjin, and about Hasjuran, and the train.

And Shadow Guild.

Mother and Uncle stood quietly against the wall, and he joined them, while Guild consulted and left. Father knew they were there, clearly, but he continued to talk on the phone, receiving calls and making them.

Are they all right? he wanted to ask. So, he was sure, did Mother and Uncle, but they said nothing, and so he just watched

Father. And the Guild. His own aishid, outranked, was out in the hall, probably getting more information than he was, where he stood.

"There was an attack," Father said finally, turning to them. "It did not breach the train, and the only personnel who were outside are accounted for and safe. A device was detonated behind a transformer that was providing electrical power, and there was a fire, quickly suppressed. Two personnel were slightly injured, and suffered effects of the blast—neither seriously, and they have continued on duty. The Red Train is now supplying its own power, and can do so indefinitely. Lord Topari is extremely sorry, and has expressed that repeatedly, to any who will listen, but we doubt he is in any sense at fault. My grandmother is inconvenienced, which is to say—she will not let this pass, but she does not at present see a need to distract herself from operations in Senjin. Which are now underway. The lord of Senjin has signed into the railway association, and effectively will be doing business with Grandmother, and with Machigi of the Taisigin. That will annoy the Dojisigi considerably."

"But they are all right," Cajeiri said.

"They are all right," Father said. "Your great-grandmother can be fairly persuasive, when she is sure she is right, and when has she ever been caught being otherwise? Lord Tatiseigi." A nod. "Be assured she is comfortably in charge. And, Miri-ma." It was his private name for Mother. "Perhaps while the damage reports come in and we begin to figure compensation for Lord Topari's train station, we might settle ourselves to a little mid-afternoon brandy with our neighbor. Early, but it has already been such a day. Will you do us the honor, nand' Tatiseigi? And we shall hear any subsequent reports that come in, from Senjin or from Hasjuran. I am sure there will be details."

Tea. And quiet, in blessed light, a light that hid nothing and offered no illusions.

Bren set down his cup—he was in the curious place of host

for two lords and an almost-lord, and he was the possessor of information that greatly concerned their situation.

"Nandiin," he said, "we are under assault, for no greater ill than attempting to agree among ourselves, and please accept my apology for the roughness outside your quarters. Troubling news has reached us, which we are still assessing. One regrets to say, Murai-daja, that one of your trusted guards, Tenjin, has been compromised by the Shadow Guild."

"No," Murai said. *"No,* nand' paidhi. He never would."

"We do not blame him, Murai-daja. We are informed that the Shadow Guild has kidnapped his mother, his wife, and his son, they have threatened their lives, and they are, unfortunately, ruthless enough to carry out the threat. The aiji-dowager has great sympathy for his situation, as do I, and we are not releasing any information that might indicate what happened aboard this train, or that this man is in custody. For what they may know, he is still in play."

The lady was upset, clearly, likewise her daughter and lord Bregani.

"We do not believe," Bren continued, "that the others of your bodyguard had any knowledge of this—not even his partner. The dowager regards the unit as compromised, but innocent, and intends to assist this young man as best she can at this remove. We believe that the explosion was intended to signal an action on his part, whether against me, or you, Lord Machigi or the dowager herself—a crude and unspecific signal, but our enemies would be pleased by any harm they could work—for publicity, if no greater advantage. It entirely failed, but the Shadow Guild cannot know it yet. I also have every hope the agent who triggered the explosion will be found—alive, we sincerely hope. The dowager's men are looking further into it. We are safe here. The dowager will not be threatened with impunity. The incident has thus far served us, and exposed a problem—fortunately before anyone could be harmed, nand' Bregani, and before Tenjin-nadi had to commit such a breach of trust. He has to be desperately afraid for his own family, and it is up to us to protect them by keeping this incident quiet. We are now looking for any means to find his family, and free them. It is a very terrible situation, nandiin. Anyone who has *any* exposure to such tactics is wise to take precautions. Most of all, we do not want the kidnappers holding his family to realize he has lost his value."

"Nandi."

A very quiet voice, from the corner of the bench seat.

"Nadi?" Bren asked.

"In Lusi'ei and several other places," Nomari said, "I know people. People who can find people, and some who might know places."

Heads had turned. Even Machigi's, when it was likely Machigi had used such resources in the past.

"Granted," Nomari said, "that they have not run when the Guild began to move. Some have immoveable assets. Understand, I would not betray these people, nand' Bregani. They have done you no harm. And they might be supportive of a lord who ended Dojisigi threats and interference. I think they would be very grateful for a lord who did that."

There was a moment of profound silence.

"Inform us," Bregani said. "I shall be grateful for their assistance."

"Not all," Nomari said, "have a clean legal record. Not all are Senjin by birth, but few would be safe outside your territory."

"Doubtless," Machigi said, "some may be mine."

"I say it with the paidhi-aiji to witness," Bregani said. "I have signed the documents. I have joined the aiji-dowager's association. I ally myself with my neighbor to the south, and I will support the northern Guild in what action it takes to secure Senjin against Dojisigi retaliation. Tiajo is a blight on the Marid, and the organization that supports her is a far greater one. I say *that*, too, with the paidhi-aiji to witness. Nothing is safe from now on. She may do anything. Let me see Tenjin. Let me promise him we are doing all we can to find his family. And let it be true."

"I will support it," Machigi said. "With all my resources."

"Nandiin," Bren said, "Nomari-nadi, I shall inform the dowager." Given that monitoring was probably operating again, along with the lighting in the windowless cars—it was very likely the dowager already knew.

It might be a watershed on the way to peace. It might be the brink of disaster. At the moment, there was no way to know. But it signaled the union of the entire Marid, save one region of it, large and powerful as that portion might be.

It signaled linkage of the south to the rail system.

It signaled the likely approval of a new lord in Ajuri, one related to Tabini's heir *and* Atageini, so the old axis of the Dojisigin Marid with the Kadagidi in the north would find no resurgence, *if* Tabini did not sever that troublesome clan into its constituent parts.

It signaled—no one knew what, if Machigi's Taisigi replaced Dojisigi as a sea power, but with connections eastward instead of west.

"Brandy," he said. It was something, that the paidhi-aiji dispensed the dowager's brandy in charge of a meeting in the Red Car, but it seemed apt, at the moment. Lord Bregani had his man to see to, he had Tano and Algini on his mind, and Homura somewhere out there in the snowy township, with an agent on the loose who had triggered an assassination attempt in the Shadow Guild's new style.

There were things to do.

But right now, given that the lights were back on and two old rivals had found common ground, they could make a good beginning.